THE LOST KINGDOMS OF KARIBU

D1509062

KAREN PRINCE

Published by Karen Prince
Paperback ISBN: 978-1491255094
eBook ASIN: B009H28446
Cover Design: Karen Prince
Copyright © cover images iStockPhoto.com
Copyright © 2012 Karen Prince.

This book is a work of fiction. All of the names, characters and
incidents that bear any resemblance to actual people, paces or events are
entirely coincidental.

For Christopher, Lloyd, Michael, Robbie and Pamela. You guys are the best and I thank you for your patience and encouragement without which there would have been no book.

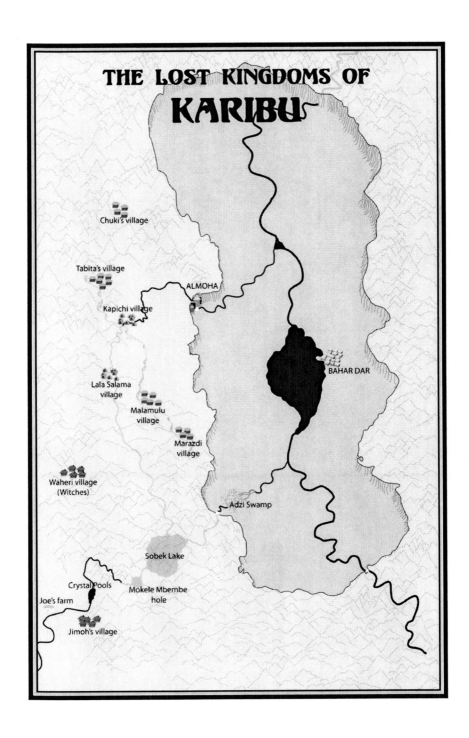

THE LOST KINGDOMS OF
KARIBU

Chuki's village

Tabita's village

ALMOHA

Kapichi village

BAHAR DAR

Lala Salama
village

Malamulu
village

Marazdi
village

Waheri village
(Witches)

Adzi Swamp

Sobek Lake

Crystal Pools

Mokele Mbembe
hole

Joe's farm

Jimoh's village

Visit www.karen-prince.com for downloadable map

CHAPTER 1

A DILEMMA

The high priest, Drogba, sat beside his meditation cave halfway up the mountain gazing disconsolately at his people as they went about their business in the valley far below. He had not jumped for a long time. Such a long time, in fact, that his body — which had not been that young when he got it — had reached an advanced stage of decrepitude. He wondered what would happen if he were still in it when it expired. Would he be reincarnated like everybody else, and not remember his past lives? Or would he finally be gone? Judging by the dreadful wheezing noise coming from his chest, he suspected that if he procrastinated . . . er . . . meditated any longer he was about to find out.

Now he faced a terrible choice. It was not that he liked what he could do, but strong magic pulled him; he was going to have to jump somebody soon.

The trouble was, he'd allowed himself to become too attached to his people over the last seventy-odd years. Once he'd got to know them it was hard to sacrifice a nice harmless person to provide him with a new body, even if it was for the greater good. He'd vacillated over Anuk occasionally. Now there was a man who was not exactly harmless, or particularly amicable, but Anuk had not looked after his body and it was almost as elderly as Drogba's. Drogba was looking forward to something more robust; something that could travel a long distance. He had to weigh his options carefully before he made his choice, which was why he was up in the mountains, in this cave, carefully observing the villagers when providence provided a body.

His eyes darted towards a furtive movement at the edge of the forest where a dark shadow glided towards him on silent feet. "Who is th–" he started to say, then stopped, his eyes widening. It was not quite the body he had in mind but he supposed he would get used to it; he always had. Clutching his robe around himself Drogba rose rather unsteadily to his feet, and stepped forwards, a dangerous chuckle escaping from his weak old throat that would have frozen the marrow in your bones if you had been close enough to hear. *Ha! I haven't quite lost my touch then,* he thought, vaguely surprised. He hadn't tried that in a long time. Then, before he could have second thoughts about the whole thing, he pounced.

CHAPTER 2
A WILY WITCH

The old witch poked a finger in her ear and wiggled it up and down, then cocked her head to one side to listen properly. She hadn't been aware of the cicadas singing till they stopped. The sudden silence in the forest raised the little grey hairs on the backs of her arms. She wasn't afraid, exactly. Gogo Maya was never afraid of anything, and she wasn't going to start now. Still, something felt oddly unsettling.

Hunkering back on her haunches, she ran a sharp black eye over the ancient forest. She could have sworn she had glimpsed a movement out the corner of her eye, almost as if something was creeping up on her. Then she smiled and shook her head. It couldn't be. Predators living in the forest had the sense to hunt in the rift valley below the escarpment, rather than eat anyone who had access to the magic in the water up here on the plateau. The more magic a creature ingested the more bitter they tasted, and if one magic creature ate another, the consequences could be most disturbing. Gogo Maya snorted. It would be pretty disturbing if anyone ate *her;* over the years she had ingested a lot of magic.

It was unlikely that anyone would have ventured up from the

valley either. The disgraceful Almohad saw to that by spreading spine-chilling rumours about dark happenings in the forest to keep the valley tribes away from the magic. If anyone was heroic enough to come looking for it, the Almohad promptly captured them, fulfilling some of those dark prophecies. She didn't suppose the Almohad themselves would bother her. Everyone knew witches made terrible slaves, and they wouldn't kill her because the Almohad had that silly superstition that witches could suck up their souls and take them with to the afterlife.

She let her breath out softly, and bent down once more to dig, but spun around moments later to confront the sound of a soft plop. The branches on the one side of a giant red mango tree on the edge of the clearing snapped up, then gently settled into place again, leaving an enormous mango on the ground.

In the uneasy silence that followed, she wondered if she should abandon her foraging and go back to her village, but she had come a long way, and if she hurried, she had just enough time to dig one last mbogo root out of the ground before the storm broke. Gripping her nose firmly between thumb and forefinger to block the pungent smell, Gogo Maya brushed a misshapen bloom aside and steeled herself to dig up a root from underneath. The roots were diabolically vile, but she needed them to enhance her magic. A cloud of mosquitoes took to the air, disturbed by the movement.

"Drat!" she muttered, letting go of her nose to swat at them, then gasped as she was almost fumigated by the dirty-sock smell.

Someone definitely sniggered.

She whirled around to face him, shaking her trowel at him, but as fearsome as her grimace was, it did not frighten him into revealing himself. Sighing heavily, she stood up, hefted her root basket onto her hip, picked her way out of the mbogo patch, and strode down the trail with as much haughtiness as she could muster. She would not give him the satisfaction of seeing her look over her shoulder.

4

A WILY WITCH

After a few steps she turned suddenly, her hands on her hips, elbows poking out defiantly, and glared down the path. Still, she couldn't see anyone. What she should have done in the first place, she supposed, was lie down under a nice safe bush and search for his mind pattern. A quick glance at the thunderheads rolling in above told her she was already too late, so she turned back and walked on.

Gradually, a low hair-raising chant drifted towards her, turning into a war cry, and she spun around to confront . . .

Nothing.

Only, this nothing had left a wide path of flattened undergrowth in its wake. Gogo Maya lobbed her digging trowel in its general direction, hiked up handfuls of her voluminous black skirt, and in a frightful din of jangly bangles and ankle bracelets, took flight down the path, her long grey dreadlocks streaming out behind her.

With a grunt she heaved herself up onto the trunk of a huge tree that lay fallen across the track and sat straddling it, scrambling to untangle her skirt that had snagged amongst the branches. She thought momentarily of untying the garment and abandoning it, but the loss would be too great. Her life was in the pockets of that skirt.

In the hope that her leopard familiar, Salih, was at least within hearing, she placed two shaky fingers into either side of her mouth, rolled her tongue back and blew, but her mouth was too dry to produce a whistle.

"Salih!" she yelled as a last resort.

A phosphorescent flash lit up the forest, followed almost immediately by a clap of thunder. Gogo Maya blinked and peered through the afterimage to see a scar of flattened grass snaking towards her. It came to rest before the fallen tree trunk and hesitated.

Grabbing a handful of her skirt, she ripped it off the snags and scrambled down the far side of the tree trunk, painfully scraping her bottom. She landed with a grunt, ducked under a bough and continued her headlong charge into the forest. She flinched as a trail of little treasures scattered out of her torn pockets behind her. There was no use worrying about it now, she thought, as long as she hadn't dropped her amulet. It would be an unmitigated disaster if that fell onto the wrong hands.

Rummaging amongst the throwing bones, skinning knives and lucky charms in her pockets for the amulet as she ran, she tried to remember when last she had seen it. It had been so long since she'd used it. She doubled over to relieve the stitch in her side, just as large drops of rain began to patter down, and within seconds she could barely see an arm's length in front of her face.

"Ugh!" She tried to push her dreadlocks away from her face and wipe the water out of her eyes with her skirt, while looking around for a shelter. The undergrowth would have to do, she decided, and scrambled under a shrub, hugging her knees to her chest to make herself small. Screwing her eyes shut, she tried to empty her mind before reaching out to find the mental pattern of the beast, but for the longest moment she could only think about thinking about nothing.

Now was not the time to panic, she told herself grimly, and taking a hold of herself, calmed her mind. Within moments Gogo Maya's eyes flew open at the bewildering muddle of tiny, sharp thoughts, and then they were upon her.

"Me first. Me first. Out my way!" lisped one.

"Charge!" yelled another.

"No biting, remember, we only got to catch her."

There were so many of them. They came hurtling through the air, landing all over her in a blur of sharp elbows and knees. Nothing like what she had imagined. Not a big beast at all. Silhouetted against the rain, she thought she caught glimpses of the knee-high, hairy Tokoloshe that lived in the forest. They certainly lisped like them. Only, when one of them revealed himself fully for a moment, he didn't look entirely Tokoloshe. He

6

was a translucent amber color. The long thick hair on his back bounced up and down as he moved, almost as if it was made of soft rubber.

There was nothing soft about the one she managed to get a grip on. She hurled him into the undergrowth where he bounced up again and came running back to join in the attack.

"I got her! I got her," he shouted, even as she pulled her slippery wet arm out of his grip.

"Get your elbows out of my face," wailed another one.

"Somebody bit me."

"*Gerroff* my hand."

A length of vine bounced up and down a foot above the ground, making its way towards Gogo Maya. She could almost make out the shapes of the shimmering wet little creatures carrying it.

"What do you think you're doing, chasing a nice old lady like this?" she spluttered, aiming a vicious kick along the length of the vine, hoping to strike down a few of them. It was like kicking a large warthog. Pain shot up her leg, reverberating through her body. One of them rammed a peeled mango into her mouth while it was open, stifling her shriek and nearly choking her. Before her hands could fly up to her mouth, some of the others got a firm grip on them, and tied them up behind her back with the vine. Gogo Maya struggled to sit up, fighting for breath as the heavy rain trickled up her nose. She coughed weakly, spluttered, and then glared at her attackers; her jaw, if it had not been jammed open, would have been set defiantly.

"Okay, lady, you going to walk with us a bit, or we going to tie up your feet and drag you?" lisped the little leader. She could see him quite clearly now. He stood bristling before her, completely visible but translucent – a couple of shades darker than honey. He was surrounded by about fifty of his band in various stages of transition back to visibility.

"Hi huk hy Heet!" Gogo Maya grumbled sarcastically around

the mango pip.

He drew himself up to his full eighteen inches and grinned in a nasty way, revealing long, sharp, pointy teeth. "Okay," he nodded.

"Nnng," Gogo Maya fumed.

He cocked his head to one side, and raised a bouncy, hairy eyebrow. "Drag then," he said, turning on his heel and striding back into the jungle the way they had come.

After a clumsy attempt at pulling her by her slippery, wet limbs, the gang swivelled her around, and grabbing handfuls of her hair, dragged her kicking and spluttering after him.

Gogo Maya was usually prepared to put up with quite a lot of pain – provided it was not happening to her. Lying on her side, amongst the wet leaf mould on the jungle floor, in considerable pain, she pretended to be asleep. It was not that easy. Covered in bites and bruises, she felt as if she had been hauled backwards up a waterfall, and her hair felt as if it had been pulled out by the roots. It very nearly had. She had found her amulet at last; only, she was lying on it, so it dug painfully into her left buttock.

The feather-light tickling sensation on her face turned out to be ants swarming over the mango pip still jammed in her mouth. Her jaw hurt. *Gah*! She thought. It was going to be almost impossible to incant a decent spell with a pip in her mouth. It took all her willpower to repress a spasm of revulsion, but it would not be wise to let her captors know she was awake till she knew what they intended to do with her.

Keeping her body perfectly still, she reached out to touch the minds nearby. Her first impression was of a very high-pitched buzz. That would be the ants, she thought, not stopping to delve any deeper – she would not be able to understand them anyway.

The second wave of thoughts she infiltrated came from the trees overhead and were just . . . well . . . nasty.

They could be Tokoloshe, she thought. Apart from that rubbery disappearing nonsense and their excessive violence of the night before, their hyperactive behavior was in keeping with the little rapscallions, but she wondered why she could not smell them. Tokoloshe usually trailed a strong odor of catnip behind them. They rubbed it on their hairy bodies to lure cats in the hope of capturing them for ransom. She should know – she'd supplied them with the ghastly herb herself once or twice when it had been useful to be able to smell them coming. Still, it hardly seemed right that *she* should be subjected to the indignity of being captured by them. Surely they knew how dangerous she was, and who on earth did they think would pay a ransom for her?

Deciding the game, whatever it was, had gone on long enough, Gogo Maya was about to lift her head to glower at them when she realised they had all frozen in terror.

"Very good work," murmured a cold, smooth voice in the clearing behind her.

Gogo Maya resisted the urge to crane her neck to see who it was. Instead, she sent telepathic tendrils out in search of his mind, but there was absolutely nothing where his thoughts should have been. She was wondering, grumpily, what the point was in having a skill that didn't work when she most needed it, when she realised it was working on the Tokoloshe. Sort of. A ripple of emotion passed through them. Not thoughts exactly, just a vague knowing, on the edges of her search for the mind of the voice, that he was gesturing towards something on the ground. Something he was subtly offering but they seemed afraid to take because even a Tokoloshe knows bait when he sees it.

"Oh, don't be a bunch of big babies," the voice snapped. "I am not going to hurt you."

If he had to keep behind her instead of revealing himself, Gogo Maya fumed, would it be too much to hope that one of the Tokoloshe would have the sense to think about his face so that she could read who he was?

But the Tokoloshe were totally focused on the thing on the ground, which looked, in their minds, something like a sticky glob of toffee. One or two of the little creatures crept tentatively out of the trees, followed by a few more, and a few more, until the forest exploded into activity as they boiled into the clearing and fell upon it.

"Reward!" whooped one.

"Oom noom noom noom," murmured another.

"Mine."

"No mine."

Gogo Maya noticed one or two of the little creatures held back, not entirely unaffected by the sinister undertones of that voice. Even she had almost felt a chill up her spine upon hearing the voice.

"Foolish! Must fight urge," one thought.

Another kept clearing his throat behind her. "Dangerous!" he said eventually.

While they were distracted, Gogo Maya tried to eject the mango pip by wiggling her tongue vigorously back and forth, but it was no use. Her eyes glinted, though, when her searching fingers fell on the icy cold surface of the small eerie opal of her amulet. Pausing only for a moment to absorb the magical shadowy darkness of it, she felt along the length of the leather thong to see if her precious amber was still attached to the other end. It was. It gave off a low vibration as she took the warm stone between her hands. The healing power of it crept slowly through her body and the numbness in her hands began to recede.

Peeping through slit eyes, Gogo Maya watched the little creatures settle down on a small mound in front of where she lay. They chewed on globs of the glutinous substance, and it seemed, the more they chewed, the more transparent they became, until she was able to look right through some of their little faces. It was quite unnerving the way she could watch the toffee shift from cheek to cheek. She wondered what sort of powerful new magic was in the innocent looking treat. It was definitely not forest magic.

"Morathi," drawled the stranger's cool voice.

"Yeeees," Morathi breathed nervously.

Gogo Maya knew that name. That bloody lunatic, Morathi, from Kapichi village. They *were* Tokoloshe, she realised, even if they did not look much like it at the moment. What sort of trouble had he got his clan into now?

"Morathi," the voice said. "You will find out how much the witch knows, and you will find out if she can hear my thoughts. Then you will get rid of her."

Gogo Maya's eyes flew open in astonishment. What did he mean, "*get rid of her*"? Did he mean for them to kill her?

Bristling with indignation, Gogo Maya tried to sit up and protest, but she might as well have saved her breath. No one could understand a word of what she was saying around the mango pip, and the air of relief emanating from the Tokoloshe told her the owner of the voice had disappeared back into the forest.

Morathi rounded on his men. Some looked keen to carry out the voice's orders but most shuffled about, looking embarrassed.

"You, you and you, drag the old crone over here, and you, go and fetch my bow," he ordered.

"I don't want to," whined an almost visible Tokoloshe.

"Yeah, fetch your own bow," another said, folding his arms across his bare chest and frowning.

"Look, you fools!" Morathi was now puffing himself up to his full height. "We made a deal. He gives us the *nzuri thana* and we do what he says."

"You mean like slaves?" an invisible Tokoloshe said, from beside Gogo Maya's ear.

"No, more like someone who has accepted something from someone, and now owes that someone something in return," Morathi said to a spot somewhere to the left of where the invisible Tokoloshe stood.

The rest of the Tokoloshe whispered anxiously amongst themselves.

"Please," a stumpy old Tokoloshe took the toffee out of his mouth and went to hand the sticky mess back to Morathi. "We thought we were just stealing it."

"Um," a small voice beside Gogo Maya said. "It seems altogether less risky if we just sort of . . . go home." Already, quite a few of them were edging their way in the direction of the woods.

Well, that served him right, Gogo Maya snorted to herself in approval. Usually the Tokoloshe did not have the sense they were born with, but one or two at least were showing an instinct for self-preservation.

However sinister their *nzuri thana* supplier was, Gogo Maya had not survived in this jungle for over fifty years without a trick or two up her own sleeve. She tightened her fist around her amulet. If push came to shove, she could use the power of the opal to make herself disappear and reappear someplace else, and the Tokoloshe would be left holding some small forest creature. Although she shuddered to think of the terrible ramifications if that particular trick went wrong again. Last time . . . Oh she did not even want to think about last time.

A loud snarl reverberated around the clearing and Gogo Maya watched as her leopard, Salih, backed jerkily into the clearing. Invisible Tokoloshe were apparently dragging him by the tail. This was going to get interesting. Salih could kill a Tokoloshe with a swipe of his paw, and if he did not think that would do, he had a plethora of mind tricks he could apply if he wanted to.

"What are they?" Salih said between gritted teeth while unseen little fingers tied him up against Gogo Maya. "I channelled a mildly repellant flow through them, but it had no effect. I couldn't quite get a fix on what they were. I didn't want to harm anyone unnecessarily if it turned out to be a game, because I think they are related to the Tokoloshe."

"They *are* Tokoloshe." Gagged by the mango in her mouth, Gogo Maya projected the words directly into Salih's mind. "Someone has given them something to enhance their powers, but as invincible as it's made them, they are as stupid as ever."

Salih snorted. "It *was* a bit stupid to tie us up together."

Ooh, thought Gogo Maya. If Salih was glad they were tied together, perhaps this was going to be one of those rare occasions when he was going to use his own magic. Better yet, if he was going to channel his magic through her, he would leave residues of his own powerful magic in her, vastly magnifying her own resources.

Salih gave her a stern look.

"No, then?" she said.

"You know I only do that as a last resort," he said. "Do you have the opal?"

"But what about the last time we used the opal?" she tried, but Gogo Maya was not that surprised; Salih was notoriously stingy with his magic.

"Are you sure we want to take the risk?" It was not just that she had hoped to use Salih's magic, but the opal was a bit hit and miss. If they did a switch using it, there was no telling where they might end up. Worse, they had no idea what or who might replace them.

"If we switch with another witch from the village," she said, "there is that small matter of who we 'borrowed' the magic from in the first place to make the amulet. There will be some awkward explaining to do. Besides, that would put someone else in danger with these Tokoloshe."

"I don't want to hurt them." The leopard sounded apologetic.

"The trouble with you, Salih, is that you are too much of a softy," Gogo Maya projected at him. "True, there are certain to be casualties among the Tokoloshe if you use your magic, especially in their present condition, but it would serve them right. They *had* been planning to kill me."

"It's not really their fault," Salih said. "You know how gullible they are. Also, we need them to have their wits about them so that we can sneak back afterwards and find out who's been manipulating them."

"Well, if you insist." Gogo Maya shrugged. "Hold on tight then." Keeping a firm grip on the opal of the amulet, she shut her eyes, and mentally and physically jumped into the abyss.

CHAPTER 3
A PICKY BOY

The heat did not let up in Harare, Zimbabwe, even with both bedroom windows open. Ethan Flynn pushed his hair out of his eyes and snapped his laptop shut with a sigh – the battery had run out. It was just about impossible to get anything done on it in this backwoods place because electricity supply was so erratic. The power was down now, and he'd heard it might be days before it was restored. He flung himself down the passage in the direction of the verandah where his dad and stepmother were having their evening cocktails. He supposed he would have to speak to them eventually; it might as well be now.

Sophie shot him a belligerent look from her deck chair as he came out onto the verandah. He guessed she couldn't help herself. She was dressed in a pair of short shorts, and a halter-top without a bra. The bitter lines of her face were smoothed by pulling her wispy blond hair up tightly behind her head in a high ponytail. Daintily extracting a slice of lemon from her gin and tonic with long, blood-red fingernails, she popped it into her mouth, then grimaced; possibly from the sourness of the lemon, but more likely at the sight of Ethan. With deliberate effort, she adjusted her features into some semblance of a welcoming smile.

"Ah, here he is now," she said. "Ethan, I was just telling your father that Uncle Alan is popping into town tomorrow to collect the kids from boarding school and has offered to take you on safari with him."

"But I only just got here," Ethan said, a bit taken aback. He poured himself a glass of orange squash from the drinks trolley. He hoped the water had been filtered properly. Sophie glared at him with that exaggeratedly expectant expression that she used to remind him of his manners.

"Oh, I forgot," he added. "Sophie, please may I have a drink."

Ethan glanced at his dad, who gave no indication whether or not he thought it was unreasonable for a fifteen-year-old to have to ask for a soft drink in what was technically his own home. Regarding Ethan placidly from behind steepled fingers, he said, "Something has come up. I have to fly to Malawi for a couple of weeks."

"I don't mind staying with Sophie then." Ethan knew it was going to be a nightmare staying alone with Sophie, but his skin crawled at the thought of being subjected to the questionable hygiene of a farm.

His dad ran a hand distractedly through his thinning brown hair and allowed it to flop back over his forehead. He took a sip of his whisky, swooshed it around his mouth, and swallowed. "Well, that's just the thing . . . Sophie has to come with."

Ethan opened his mouth, about to point out that there was no reason for a housewife to have to travel with her husband on business, but thought better of it. Sophie had reminded them often enough before that it was not her responsibility to look after Ethan. He wondered why Sophie and his dad had campaigned so heavily to have him visit them in the first place. Sophie had been even more insistent than his dad.

"It's Neil's turn," she'd spat down the phone at Ethan's mother. "It's his turn and he is entitled to have Ethan for at least

16

four weeks."

So Ethan had come. They must have known they would have to go to Malawi.

"Well, I would like to fly back to mom and Eric then," he said now.

Sophie's mouth tightened. "Don't be stupid," she said, as if Ethan wore upon her patience. "We can't send you home yet. You only just got here. Besides, your mother needs the break."

Ethan was flabbergasted. He would put up with a lot of things from Sophie if that was what his dad wanted, but she was not going to use his mother as an excuse. "No, actually, she doesn't need the break! She didn't want me to come, if you remember."

Sophie whipped her head back to glare at Ethan, her wispy ponytail swinging round and hitting her in the face. "Are you calling me a liar?" she hissed through her tightly pursed lips. "Spoiled little rich brat. You never do anything you don't want to." She slammed her drink down on the coffee table, then rose from her chair and stomped off into the house.

Ethan bit the inside of his lip. He glared at his father, waiting for an apology, or even some show of support, an explanation even, but the man could barely contain his irritation.

"Now look what you've done," he grumbled instead, through clenched teeth. For a moment or two Ethan watched the tendons pulsating in his father's neck, but his father's eyes stayed firmly fixed on the progress of the gardener who manhandled an ancient lawnmower back and forth across the yard in the semidarkness. It vaguely annoyed Ethan that there was enough fuel for the mower but not for the back-up generator that supplied the electricity for his computer, which he needed to complete his homework assignments for the holidays.

At last, his father sighed as if he had come to a decision. "I'm going to the gym," he said, shoving himself to his feet and stalking around the side of the house to his car.

SWITCH!

It actually came as a relief to Ethan when Uncle Alan collected him the next morning.

"Welcome to Zimbabwe!" his uncle declared, waving an arm expansively to indicate the whole country, as if he owned it. He was a beefy blonde man with a booming laugh and kindly eyes that slanted downwards at the corners like Ethan's mom's. He wore the same faded, ranger-style, olive green fatigues and shirt that he always wore, even on his visits to Ethan's family in Cape Town.

"What kind of a school are you going to now, boy, that lets you grow your hair so long?" Ethan ducked his blonde head out of Alan's reach before his uncle managed to tousle it. Ethan didn't like to be touched. Alan grinned sheepishly and withdrew his hand, patting the dog instead. The dog's tongue lolled out of the side of its mouth, dribbling disgustingly. Watching a glob of dribble fall and hit the driveway right next to Alan's foot, Ethan just stopped himself from gagging. It was a good thing his uncle had shaken hands with him before he touched the dog and not the other way around, he thought.

Alan looked Ethan over with an appraising eye. "Dad gone to work already?"

Ethan shrugged. "Not so much. He went to the gym again before I got up this morning. Sophie is sulking because I implied she was lying."

Alan didn't have to ask. It seemed even he was familiar with Sophie's outbursts. He hefted Ethan's rucksack onto the back of his beat-up Land Cruiser pickup, his rough, weathered features relaxing into a cheerful smile. "She is kind of hateful, isn't she?" he laughed. "Come along, Ethan, cheer up. You're going to have a fantastic holiday. I want to pop into the Farmers' Co-op to collect a few things for the guys from Tjalotjo village while I'm in town, and then we'll fetch your cousins. Joe has a friend coming to stay. A real character. Hop in, I'll tell you all about him on the way." He hooted and waved a friendly farewell to Sophie, who had twitched the curtain aside to glare out at the truck as it disappeared down the drive.

"She feeds her spite by brooding about the money," Alan explained later in the coffee shop at the Farmers' Co-op. "You see, she thought it belonged to your dad. It was a bitter blow when your mom took it all with her." He flashed Ethan a mischievous grin and heaped more cream on his apple pie. "Of course, when your mom and Eric sold his computer program for so much money, it was an even worse slap in the face for Sophie. She can't get her head around the idea that if it belongs to your step-dad, your mom doesn't have to pay any of it out to your dad."

After coffee Ethan helped his uncle load the back of the pickup with supplies for his farm and Tjalotjo village. They left three neat little nests amongst some grain bags up near the cab for the boys to sit in during the trip.

"Now about the boy, Tariro," Alan said, wrestling a tin of sheep dip into an impossibly small space. "He's a difficult customer. The oldest of four sons, you see, and used to bossing his brothers around. But that is not the worst of it." He leaned across the bed of the vehicle and regarded Ethan intently, as if contemplating whether or not to divulge a secret. "He's a good kid, but his dad is a very dangerous man – something in the government to do with land acquisitions. He could take away my hunting concession, and my farm, if he wanted to."

"Surely they would never get away with it," Ethan said. He'd heard this happened a lot in Zimbabwe, and he knew they *would* get away with it, but still, it didn't seem fair. "And why is Joe hanging around with a kid like that anyway?"

"Easy, I didn't say the dad will take my farm – just that he can." Alan placed a hand firmly on Ethan's arm. "According to the school, Joe saved the boy's life. Joe won't talk about it but they're as thick as thieves now." He moved to the other side of the truck where he made a slipknot at the end of a long rope, hooked it onto the side of the truck and threw it over the bed in Ethan's direction.

"Besides, I don't know. The more I get to know the boy, the more I like him." Uncle Alan smiled. "Who knows, if you try, you might find you have something in common. Either way, we have already committed to having him for the holidays so you'll have to make an effort to get on with him."

Ethan fed the rope under a hook on his side of the truck and passed it back over the bed to his uncle. He wasn't sure he wanted to find something in common with this boy. The more Ethan thought about it, the less he liked having someone so volatile around his family. The government this boy's father belonged to had seized most of the white-owned farm land in Zimbabwe and now they seemed to be seizing farms willy-nilly, according to which political party the rest of the people belonged to. Usually with the help of thugs with machetes.

"I'll do my best," he said somewhat hesitantly.

"Now what's all this about you not wanting to go on safari?" Alan said in the Land Cruiser on the way to the girls' school.

Ethan shook his head and smiled at his uncle. "There is just no way that I can ever get you guys to understand," he sighed. "Tramping around the bush after wildlife holds as little interest for me as learning to play games on the computer holds for you."

Alan retracted his neck into his shoulders like a tortoise. "Computers!" he laughed. "We don't need the belligerent blighters. They make no sense at all. In any case, we don't have power out at the farm most of the time. We only run the generator in an emergency. Have to save the fuel for the vehicles. But I get your point, my boy." He flashed Ethan a roguish smile and wiggled his eyebrows up and down. "If you want, you can stay at home with your Aunty Cheryl and the girls."

"That'll be the day," Ethan said. "The last time you left me alone with those two, they cut my hair while I was sleeping. Don't get me wrong, Alan, I love Amy and Jessie dearly, but they're a menace."

Ten-year-old Jessie shrieked across the schoolyard at the unexpected sight of Ethan. She raced towards him like a leaping impala, two flaxen plaits flying out behind her as she wove precariously in and out among the cars of the other parents collecting their children. She was followed closely by her sister. At twelve, Amy was a little more circumspect, but not much. She dropped her school bag on the road and launched herself at Ethan.

Since Jessie was already hanging on to his back, Amy's hug brought a squirming Ethan down on the filthy grass verge. He hoped no one had spat there. The three of them wrestled under the indulgent eye of Uncle Alan till Jessie manoeuvred herself on to Ethan's chest, pinning his arms above his head.

"Okay, I yield, you little animals," Ethan laughed. The more he showed his discomfort at being on the ground, the longer Amy and Jessie would keep him there.

The meeting with Tariro did not go nearly as well. Ethan's cousin, Joe, peeled away from a group of boys in formal uniform lounging beside their school trunks, and came over to the truck. The same age as Ethan, he was about six inches taller, well muscled, with short-cropped, coarse blonde hair and sparkling green eyes. His olive skin, darkly tanned in contrast to his crisp white uniform shirt, was only slightly marred by the beginnings of acne.

"Hi, Ethan," he said in a robust voice to match his father's, dropping his school sports bag between them and flashing Ethan a delighted smile. He did not extend a hand in greeting. He understood Ethan's aversion to being touched. An equally powerful looking boy of about the same height, also in uniform, trailed behind him. The boy was so dark Ethan wondered if that was what a black kid looked like with a suntan. He had almost shoulder-length dreadlocks twisted out of his own hair that looked like the tassels on the ends of a blanket, and not even a hint of a pimple.

"This is Tariro," Joe introduced his friend. "He's coming out to the farm with us."

"I know. Your dad's already briefed me," Ethan said, extending his hand awkwardly to Tariro, but the boy did not take it, preferring to keep his right hand clutched around his rugby ball. Ethan's scalp prickled with embarrassment as he dropped his own hand limply at his side. He wondered if Joe had told Tariro he didn't like being touched, and then remembered that Joe hadn't known he was coming.

"I'm also coming out to the farm," Ethan stumbled on in the face of the other boy's rudeness. Tariro didn't say anything.

Ethan glanced at Joe, who hardly seemed to notice. Joe threw his bag on to the back of the truck and scrambled up after it, settling himself comfortably in one of the nests. Tariro climbed up and settled into Ethan's nest, wiggling his backside up against the pillow Amy had given Ethan till he was comfortable.

"Um, I was sitting there," Ethan said.

"You'll have to sit in the middle, Ethan. Joe and I want to throw the ball to each other." Tariro's comment, when it came, was surprisingly soft-spoken, but his tone suggested it wouldn't be a very good idea to argue. Setting his mouth into a stubborn line, Ethan flopped down into the middle nest.

"I'm not your younger brother to boss around," he grumbled as the truck pulled out of the schoolyard. The boy raised one eyebrow in a mild challenge, but then turned away.

Ethan took out his cell phone to play a game on it, but it was no use. Every time Tariro and Joe threw the rugby ball to each other, it whizzed past his face, threatening to knock the phone out of his hand. He put it away with a sigh, and pretended to go to sleep. It was going to be a long four hours to the farm.

"We've got beef, dairy, sheep, goats, chickens, geese, pigs and we grow maize. And the ladies do it all!" Amy boasted to Ethan.

A PICKY BOY

The girls had dragged Ethan out of bed just before the sun rose the next morning to witness this phenomenon. A buxom woman sat on a small three-legged stool in the dim recesses of the diary. The light of a small kerosene lamp flickered across her broad shining face as her head leaned on the flank of a black and white cow. She squirted milk out of its udders into a bucket between her feet, using her bare hands.

Ethan mentally crossed milk off the things he would be drinking at the farm. He knew milk did not just arrive by some miracle in a bottle in the supermarket, but he had imagined, fondly, that it was extracted hygienically and mechanically. The cow did not seem to mind though. She stood there, unfettered, gazing at Ethan, her jaws moving rhythmically.

"So what do the men do?" he wondered out loud, stepping between the cow-pats, carefully avoiding touching anything.

"Oh, they track stuff," Amy said. "Even though it's only photographic safaris, they still have to get the clients quite close up for the best shots. Sometimes they patrol for rhino poachers but they haven't seen any around for years." She patted the cow on her forehead. The cow chose a mouthful of alfalfa from the trough and chewed absently.

"Come on, Ethan, the sun is coming up. Let's go and watch Jessie and the others feed their goats," Amy said, suddenly bored with the unresponsive cow. She dragged Ethan by the hand over to the goat enclosure. Jessie and a group of little girls sat cross-legged, in a circle on the floor, under a vast thatched shelter. Each one held a kid who they were feeding baby formula using baby bottles.

"Jessie is not allowed to own a goat because she is not here to look after it when she's away at boarding school," Amy explained, "but the other children each get one to look after. If they do it responsibly, they are allowed to have another. Some of the bigger girls have three or four."

"Are these the farm labourers' children?" Ethan said. He was sure his mom would have something to say to her brother about child labour.

"No, it's sort of a farmers' club. Most of them come from Tjalotjo, the village across the river." She leaned her elbows on the rickety pole-and-grass fence and sighed happily. "There's nothing quite like a whiff of manure to remind you that you're really home for the holidays."

Ethan noticed the entire floor of the enclosure the girls were happily sitting in was made up of dried goat dung. Aunt Cheryl didn't seem to mind the dirt either.

"Morning, Ethan," she waved from where she was mucking out a nearby pigsty. The horizontal bars running across the front of the sty ended about two feet off the ground, allowing a litter of piglets to escape and snuffle with happy grunts all over the yard, while their enormous mother busied herself with the running water hose and the slop bucket from inside her enclosure.

"Think quick!" Tariro yelled from behind Ethan. The dreaded rugby ball sailed past Ethan's head and landed in amongst the little girls, scattering goat droppings and giggling girls everywhere.

"What the hell?" Ethan said angrily, but Amy stepped back with an amused smile.

Tariro flashed a smug grin at her. "It was your catch, Ethan, you'll have to go in and fetch the ball."

The boy had homed in on his germ phobia like a heat-seeking missile, Ethan thought with sullen resentment. He backed away from the fence, stretched deliberately and then strolled with elaborate nonchalance towards the kitchen. "Get your own ball," he said over his shoulder. "I'm going in for a shower." Once he had rounded the corner, he turned back to watch how Tariro would react.

Amy punched Tariro hard in the arm. "Leave him alone, you great lout," she laughed. "Ethan just hates getting dirty – he's super sweet when you get to know him."

"Amy, do you have any idea how hard it was to get my dad to

agree to let me come out to the farm these holidays?" Tariro said. "I was really looking forward to having Joe to myself. We were going to do all sorts of crazy stuff with the local kids. For once I wouldn't have to be looking over my shoulder for my dad's minders because the kids here don't know who I am. Bloody Ethan is going to spoil all that. I mean, look at him! Even his pyjamas are flashy, and God knows what would happen if he actually got himself dirty. As rich and as picky as he is, I bet he hasn't done a day's work in his life."

"Well, neither have you." She gave him a friendly shove.

"Then watch me feed those goats." Tariro vaulted effortlessly over the gate and pushed his way into the circle of girls who, Ethan was surprised to note, immediately made room for him despite his fancy board-shorts and designer shirt, which were every bit as flashy as anything Ethan wore. Ethan shook his head as he watched Tariro help himself to a little girl's bottle, grab a kid confidently by the hind leg, pull it onto his lap and settle to feeding it as if he had been doing it all his life. Ethan had to hand it to the boy. He could certainly be charming when he wanted to be.

Ethan had a cold shower but at least he felt clean. He hadn't realised that he would have had to light a fire under the boiler before he could have hot water. He was just in time to help Joe with breakfast.

"Tariro is so mean," he grumbled at Joe, snatching the pan off the heat of the cast-iron stove before his pancake burned. "I don't understand why you have to be friends with him."

"I like him," Joe said. "If you went to boarding school you would understand. He looks after me and I look after him." He ducked under Ethan's outstretched arm with a hot pan and plopped a misshapen, thick pancake down on the serving plate, on top of Ethan's wafer-thin one. "Here you don't have to be so fussy," he added. "No one really cares how perfect the pancakes are. Put enough honey on them and everyone will just wolf them down."

Ethan jumped back in case he got burned by the pan Joe was waving about. "Couldn't you find someone a little more pleasant to hang out with at boarding school?"

"No," Joe said. "We're in the same rugby team and cricket team. He's actually a really nice guy, usually. He's just a bit pissed off because he wasn't expecting you to come along."

The rest of the family ambled into the kitchen, cutting off the private conversation – first Alan, then the girls with Tariro, and lastly, Cheryl, fresh from the shower. She still bore the faint whiff of pigsty.

Tariro sat down and helped himself to a stack of pancakes. He squeezed plenty of honey on top of them. Joe had been right; he didn't seem to care if they were fat or thin. He rolled up three or four together and took a huge bite. Ethan wrinkled his nose as he watched Tariro wipe honey off his chin with his fingers and lick them. He couldn't help wondering if Tariro had washed all the goat cooties off his hands.

"The girls at the goat pen tell me Jimoh is camping down by Crystal Pools for the week," Tariro said, wiping his hand on his shirt. "Is there any chance we could go and camp with them?" He looked imploringly at Alan. "The last time I was here Jimoh promised to take me hunting tribal style."

Alan looked quite sorry. Ethan wasn't sure if he had been looking forward to taking the boys on safari, or if he was anxious for Ethan's sake. "That would depend . . . Ethan, are you up for it? It will be pretty rough and ready. Either way, I have to take the good equipment with me. I have clients from a German wildlife magazine coming in tomorrow."

Ethan was furious. He turned towards the stove to give himself time to think. Lifting the fire pit cover, he fed a split log into the fire, and then took his time replacing the cover. There was an art to doing it without burning your fingers. What could he say? He was sure Tariro had put him on the spot deliberately. If he insisted on the safari with the deluxe camping equipment he would validate Tariro's opinion of him as a spoiled rich brat. If he went hunting, tribal style, whatever that entailed, he would be removing himself from Alan's protection, which was exactly what he feared Tariro wanted. Instinct told him to go with his uncle and to hell with what Tariro thought. Now, to add to his dilemma, he desperately needed a puff from his asthma pump, but he knew everyone would misinterpret this as an excuse to duck out of the trip and spoil their fun, just to get his own way.

"No, that's okay," he heard himself say to Alan. "I'm sure I can manage tribal style. With a bit of luck we won't shoot anything," he added under his breath. He slumped down at the table and helped himself to the top pancake. It was one of the thick ones. He lightly dusted it with cinnamon sugar, meticulously squirted a quarter of a lemon over it and rolled it up, all the while breathing carefully and deeply so as not to cave in to the asthma attack. He was right. The pancake didn't taste anything like a nice thin one.

"That's my boy!" Alan said.

"Wait till you meet Jimoh," Joe said, his green eyes glinting now that his fun was secured. "He is by far the greatest tracker in the district. He can shoot a rabbit on the run from twenty paces with a sling shot."

"What about lions at night?" Ethan said, hoping to scare them into having second thoughts.

"Don't be silly, my boy," Cheryl reassured him. "Lions won't come anywhere near a fire. All the local kids camp at those pools. No one's been attacked by wild animals for years." She looked up suddenly from her pancake. "You have been taking a malaria prophylactic, haven't you?"

"No." Ethan bit his lip. He hadn't expected to come to the bush at all, let alone camp at a river. Besides, whilst the prophylactic might stop him getting malaria, it was sure to clash with his asthma medication.

CHAPTER 4
THE CRYSTAL POOLS

The greatest tracker in the district was a bit of a shock. Ethan had expected someone bigger – a grown-up perhaps. When they got to the pools, a thin, barefoot boy came bouncing up the path to meet them. He adjusted his faded red shirt, which had lost all its buttons, spat on the palm of his hand, wiped it off on a pair of ancient khaki shorts, and stuck it out towards Ethan. Ethan hesitated for barely five seconds before he heard Tariro's sharp intake of breath. Was the boy taking it as a racial slight? He could not believe Tariro's audacity after deliberately failing to shake his hand the first time they'd met, and Tariro knew the spit would pose a problem for Ethan. Jimoh just stood there, grinning cheerfully from underneath his filthy felt hat, till Ethan shook his hand. He looked about twelve years old.

A string of hunters trailed along behind him, smelling strongly of sweat and wood smoke. They varied in weight and height, but all except one of them had extremely short-cropped, curly hair and beetle brown eyes. The odd one out wore his hair long. It stuck out all over the place in a cross between an Afro and random starbursts. Ethan guessed the khaki shorts that they all wore had once been part of their school uniform, grown too ragged to wear to school. Each boy's pockets were weighed down with pebbles. Two guys had on belts made out of rope, and another had a pair of suspenders, but the rest just kept hiking their pants up whenever the pebbles pulled them down too low. Besides Jimoh, only two of them wore shirts.

The two biggest – the one with the starburst afro, and one with a small scar above his eyebrow – carried lethal-looking machetes hanging from the ropes tied around their waists. Everyone, including Jimoh, wore slingshots around their necks as if they were jewels. The beautifully carved Y-shaped frames dangled from rubber strips, cut from the inner tube of a car tyre. The leather projectile-grips nestled comfortably behind their necks.

Ethan stood back as the group greeted one another like long-lost friends with hugs and complicated tribal handshakes. They spoke in a local dialect that he couldn't understand; even Tariro and Joe. Ethan strained to catch the slightest similarity to the Xhosa he learned at school, but couldn't pick up a word. Cape Town was two-and-a-half-thousand kilometers away, he reminded himself; there was too much distance between the two tribes to share a common tongue.

"This is my cousin, Ethan," Joe introduced him eventually, in English, and then surprised Ethan by knowing and rattling off each kid's name. They lined up and, one by one, shook hands with him. Ethan's face set into an expression of frantic geniality as each one spat on the palm of his hand and then took the time to guide Ethan's hand through the complicated tribal handshake. His composure only faltered slightly when one of them sniffed, and wiped the back of his hand across his nose before shaking.

Crystal pools were well named. The pool itself, roughly half the size of a football field, was as deep and clear as any swimming pool. It was separated from the dense jungle on the west side by a narrow sandy beach. Tall, jagged cliffs towered over the water on the village side.

Ethan cleaned his hands with waterless hand sanitiser from his backpack while the gang chose a place for their camp. A couple of boys wedged a long tent pole between two enormous msasa trees, and then threw the largest, and less tatty, of the tarpaulins over it. Using old ropes, they stretched the ends of the tarpaulin up into the nearby trees to make a shelter. Joe and the one with the afro rolled out the second tarpaulin as a groundsheet below. Jimoh and another boy attached a row of eight mosquito nets to the central tent pole and knotted them up out of the way. Ethan quietly chose one of the middle nets – just in case lions came in the night – and stashed his sleeping bag and rucksack below it. It seemed the whole gang would be spending the night.

They hunted upstream. Ethan crept slowly along the riverbank. Each step had to be carefully considered and inspected for spiders or scorpions, before he could put his foot down. He was startled once or twice by imaginary snakes. He didn't know how the other hunters did it. They seemed to be capable of the utmost stealth, without ever looking at their feet. He wondered if they had any idea, without the aid of documentaries on television, of what could be lurking in the undergrowth. Or perhaps it just took more than a bit of venom to scare them.

"Ethan, hurry up," Tariro hissed through clenched teeth. Of course, Tariro hiked up front, next to Jimoh. He carried the only gun, a .22 rifle, broken across the crook of his arm.

"I don't see why he has to have the first shot," Ethan grumbled to no one in particular. He would be horrified if they expected him to shoot something himself, but why should Tariro assume that he was entitled to go first? "Anyway, I'm not sure I want to trust my safety to Tariro's hunting expertise."

"Don't be mean, Ethan. All the other kids can protect you with their slingshots." Joe had dropped back in the ranks to keep pace with Ethan. Probably to keep the peace, Ethan realised a bit guiltily. He noticed the hunters held their slingshots in one hand, a pebble at the ready in their other, in case they stumbled across something to shoot.

"What if we see a lion?" he said, to highlight just how much danger they may be in.

"Well, the lion you see is better than the one you don't," a boy on the other side of his cousin said enigmatically. Ethan couldn't quite read the boy's face. Was he teasing?

Eventually Joe punched Ethan good-naturedly on the arm. "It's for sure, the one you don't see is busy sneaking up on you." He and the other kid laughed.

Joe's skin had turned a dark caramel color, but Ethan's fair skin went red with sunburn. He tried to avoid the merciless sunlight by ducking into the shade of every tree they passed, furtively scanning the overhead branches in case of leopards. He started to get quite drowsy too, lulled by the song of the cicadas. He was just wishing they could take a rest, well removed from the dust and dirt, preferably right by the river, so they could enjoy whatever breeze blew off it, when Jimoh signalled the hunters to crouch down. They squatted, perfectly still, while Jimoh and Tariro snuck belly down through a gap in the bushes. Ethan did not even try to see the animal as Tariro quietly loaded the rifle, cocked it, took careful aim and discharged it.

Before the echo of the gun report had died down, Jimoh and another boy were on their feet, missiles flying off the front of their slingshots. The two machete bearers leaped up and disappeared through the undergrowth. In a short while they returned, dragging a small antelope by its hind legs. Its throat had been slit. The scent of the blood that gathered in a dark pool beneath it made Ethan feel light headed. He sat down heavily on the ground and put his head between his legs. He took a little puff from his asthma pump.

"I think I have sunstroke," he croaked hopefully, but he knew he wasn't fooling anybody. It did not particularly matter –

everybody was busy focusing on the dead duiker.

The hunters strung the duiker up from a tree by its hind legs, its head dangling down. Ethan buried his head in the crook of his arm, but could not help taking a small peek at the creature. One glassy eye stared back at him accusingly, wide open with fright. Joe and Jimoh slit open its belly and allowed the entrails to land in a sloppy heap on the ground amongst their feet. They started to skin it expertly, stepping over the muddy entrails as if they were not revolting at all. They worked swiftly and efficiently, moving around each other like chefs in a busy kitchen. Ethan could see they had done this as a team before.

The animal had a gunshot wound on its rump and two shallower pebble wounds on its head, he noticed. The wretched thing probably died only after the machete guys slit its throat.

"Not bad for a first try," Tariro said, squatting down in the dirt beside Ethan, obviously delighted with his handiwork.

"I don't know what you are so pleased about." Ethan couldn't help himself. "All you did is wound the poor thing. You shot it in the bum."

"That's rich coming from you," Tariro said, furious. "The village has to eat and at least I tried. You couldn't even shoot a stationary target if you tried."

"Could too," Ethan said and, to the great amusement of all the assembled hunters, he stalked twenty paces down river and deposited the box of matches in the fork of a tree. He stomped back again, took the gun out of Tariro's surprised hands, cocked it, aimed, and blew the matches away. "*Call of Duty*," he said with relish.

"It's a computer game," Joe explained to the surprised hunters.

"Now you have gone and scattered the matches for our fire, Ethan," Tariro said.

Ethan felt better about the killing once they returned to the camp. Word had spread, and the campsite was crowded with children from the nearby kraal who could hardly contain their excitement for the protein feast. Once the duiker looked more like regular butchery meat, Ethan did not feel too sick to the stomach at the sight of it. Not to be outdone by the great hunter, Tariro, he volunteered to help Jimoh set up a spit braai.

The two machete bearers, Tafadzwa and Tendayi, each sharpened the end of a forked branch and drove them into the ground on either side of a shallow fire pit a short distance from their shelter. Jimoh struggled to sharpen a long thin branch with a small pocketknife. Ethan pulled out one of his Swiss Army knives and handed it to Jimoh shyly. He didn't want Jimoh to think he was being flashy, but he was very proud of that knife. It was the largest model with thirty-three tools and a bone shaft.

"Beautiful," breathed Jimoh, hefting the multi-bladed knife in his hand. "Too special for using."

"No, no, Jimoh. My step-dad gave it to me. He really wanted me to use it." Ethan swallowed a slight tingle in the back of his throat. He was kind of missing his mom and step-dad.

"You try then," Jimoh said, offering him the branch.

Ethan started to whittle but was soon interrupted by Jimoh, who seemed irresistibly drawn to the knife. He kept stopping Ethan to admire various blades and attachments and to ask what they were for. Soon, Joe and a couple of the other hunters joined in and Ethan found himself whittling with a machete while they admired and tested his knife.

Once Ethan had got the branch down to a fine point, Jimoh drove it right through the duiker, in through its neck and out through its backside. He stored it carefully in the fork of a tree for later when the fire was ready.

"We don't want hyenas coming for it," he said, causing Ethan to whip around and scan the surrounding area, and the rest of the boys to give way to hysterical laughter. Jimoh flicked away a fly with his hat and flopped down on the ground beside Joe when he was done.

SWITCH!

Tafadswa handed Ethan's knife back to him and said something in Shona, which clearly annoyed Tariro and made the other kids laugh again.

"It was funny what you did for Msalad," interpreted the one called Tendayi, the one with the wild hair. Ethan had been surprised earlier to find the boy spoke almost perfect English.

"What's Msalad?" Ethan said.

Tendayi grinned and glanced at Tariro. "It's what we like to call a black guy who is trying to be posh. They don't eat '*sadza ne muriwo*', the traditional food anymore, only salad. So we call them 'Msalad'."

Ethan didn't find it that funny, but he laughed anyway because Tariro had been especially amused at his fear of hyenas a moment before.

Tariro didn't seem that upset though. "And yet you speak such fluent English yourself, Tendayi," he said with a sardonic smile.

"Where did you learn to speak so fluently?" Ethan asked.

"I speak fluent Shona and Ndabele too, Ethan. You don't have to go to private school to get an excellent education. I go to boarding school in Domasi Town because I want to be a TV Presenter. The rest of these kids go to Tjalotjo School at the kraal. That's a village, in case you didn't know."

"That doesn't make them uneducated though," Tariro sprang to their defense, even though they had teased him. "It's just that they take their lessons in Shona."

"They are going to need English if they want to move to the city, or go on the Internet or anything," Ethan said.

"As crazy as this may seem to you, tech boy, they don't want to go live in the city or spend their time surfing the internet," Joe said. "They have everything they could possibly want right here. They are perfectly happy, hunting and farming with their families. That's exactly what I am planning to do."

That's if your best friend here's father doesn't pull a political

34

move and take away your farm, Ethan thought. And in any case he didn't believe the other kids were so indifferent to technology. They had liked the Swiss Army knife well enough, and a couple of them had eyed his laptop enviously, but he was not prepared to argue the point.

"If Tendayi and Joe are off at different boarding schools, how did you guys become such good friends?" he said, changing the subject.

"Jimoh and I are cousins," Tendayi said. "I come and stay with him every holiday to get back to my roots, but the thing with Joe and Jimoh started with their dads. Jimoh can tell you his story. It will do him good to practise his English."

"My dad, he runs farm with pigs and goats and some tobacco and things other side of river," Jimoh started, glancing from his cousin to Joe, to see if he was doing okay. "He friend with Joe dad from when they are children. Sometimes he help Joe dad with safari and camp when he need cash money for school fees, and Joe dad help with tractor and dipping cows for ticks and things. They do this for many years. Joe and me friends from baby." He put an arm around Joe's neck, pulled his head down into an arm lock and ruffled Joe's hair with his knuckles.

Tariro seemed to grow bored with the conversation and wondered downstream with a small entourage to supervise some local children in their game. Ethan watched his progress as he went, noticing for the first time that the river seemed to run towards the mountains instead of away.

"The river, he make a big tear in the mountain," Jimoh explained when Ethan asked about it. "Cannot see from here, but . . ." he looked at Joe for the words.

"A gorge," Joe said. "You can't see it properly because it turns the corner."

"Does anyone live there?" Ethan asked.

"No. There is a set of dangerous rapids blocking access from this side," Tendayi said. "In the past people have settled there, but never successfully. Some people used to live on a small beach down there for a time but the river is too turbulent to navigate. Every time they wanted to go somewhere, they would have to climb all the way up the escarpment. Some of them got fed up and left, and some died of malaria, living so close to the water."

"So where does it end up?" Ethan said.

"Don't know," Jimoh said. "Grandfather he say river run under mountain in big tunnel or something. We not allowed to go there."

By mid-afternoon the heat was stifling. Ethan propped himself up against the trunk of a shady mopane tree beside Jimoh, and dozed on and off.

Most of the other kids splashed about in the pool. Some of them built themselves a makeshift raft out of bamboo, and took it in turns to go for a sail into the deeper water. A couple of them perched precariously on top while the rest hung on to the sides and paddled it haphazardly to and fro.

Ethan watched Joe, Tariro and a group of the older kids snake their way along a crooked narrow path that twisted its way up the opposite cliffs to a ledge about fifteen meters above the water. From there, they launched themselves off with squeals of fear and delight and plummeted into the cold green water below. Some of them took a disturbingly long time to resurface, making Ethan vaguely anxious. He glanced over at Jimoh, who followed his gaze, but he looked completely unconcerned.

A group of little girls downstream waded in only up to their knees. Surrounded by battered enamel tubs full of washing, they beat lengths of coloured fabric against the rocks. Although they seemed happy enough, calling their songs back and forth in time to their pounding, Ethan hoped they were playing house and that this was not the actual family wash. They looked as if they were only about five years old. One little girl balanced a water bottle on her head while delicately picking her way across the rocks at the top of the rapids, which marked the end of the pool.

"Yoh, Ethan!" Joe yelled from the ledge. He and Tariro were nearing the front of the queue to take a jump. Ethan held back a small stab of envy. Even from this distance the two boys stood out in sharp contrast to himself and the local boys. It wasn't just their designer board-shorts and their athletic bodies. They both looked as though they owned the place, like heroes or movie stars.

Ethan wondered if it would be awkward to broach the subject of Joe and Tariro with Jimoh. He was curious to find out why Jimoh showed no animosity towards this golden boy who swanned about on Jimoh's territory, rounding up his gang to get up to all sorts of heroics with Jimoh's own best friend. He could see Jimoh was not intimidated by the boy, so why was he content to take a back seat?

"Um . . . Jimoh," he said. "What is the story with Tariro and Joe?"

Jimoh looked very uncomfortable. "You mean life saving thing?" he said.

That was not what Ethan had meant, but if Jimoh knew anything about it, here was a great opportunity to find out more. "Er . . . yes," he said.

Jimoh shook his head sadly and looked down at his feet. He seemed to be struggling to find the words. "White boys attack Tariro at school," he said quietly.

"What, you mean like bullying?" Ethan said. He'd imagined Joe had saved Tariro from choking or drowning or something. He couldn't imagine Tariro giving in to bullies to the point of taking his own life or anything, but you never knew.

"No, with knife," Jimoh said. He raised hurt eyes to meet Ethan's and held his gaze for a long time. "To kill," he added softly.

"Jimoh! You mean kids from Joe's actual school?" Ethan felt a horrible cold feeling in the pit of his stomach.

"No," said Jimoh, "Big boys from outside school. Joe injure

them very bad with cricket bat, but he is only one. Others run away when they see this thing. They afraid of knives."

"Well that explains a lot!" Ethan breathed out.

"Tariro very special for Joe. Risk own life to protect him," said Jimoh. He watched the two boys seriously from under the rim of his felt hat for a moment and then jumped up, grabbing Ethan's hand to drag him to the top of the cliff. "Come, Ethan. We jump,"

"No, thank you!" Ethan said, suppressing a shudder as he pulled away.

"Ah, don't be scared Ethan. Is not that high," Jimoh cajoled.

"It's not the height of the cliff that bothers me, it's the risk of crocodiles, not to mention this pool must be riddled with bilharzia."

"Ah, no Ethan," Jimoh told him, pointing downstream. "Those crocs, they won't bite, and we don't pee in this pool."

"You mean there really are crocodiles nearby? Shouldn't we get everyone out of the water?" Ethan was almost as shocked to have his crocodile suspicions confirmed as he was to discover that the kid knew that bilharzia was spread by urine.

"I tell you what," Jimoh said, over his shoulder, "you let me play with laptop thing tonight and I tell you secret about crocs." He sauntered off cheerfully in the direction of the path leading up to the jumping ledge, not seeming to care that part of his bum was showing through the seat of his raggedy shorts.

Ethan turned his attention back to Joe and Tariro. They were about to launch themselves off the ledge together when Ethan was overcome with a horrible feeling. He wondered if he was in the grip of a seizure or something because the air around him seemed to warp in slow motion and then ripple outwards from the pool in concentric circles, followed moments later by a sonic boom. He clutched his head between his hands, covering his ears, and screwed his eyes shut. When he opened them again he was just in time to see Tariro and Joe fall towards the water in slow motion. It looked as if Joe was being attacked by a leopard. And for some reason he had turned into an old black woman.

What the hell was in that inhaler? Ethan thought.

CHAPTER 5
A DROWNING WITCH

The leopard peeled away from Joe just before they hit the water. It dog-paddled, weaving its way between the scattering, screaming swimmers, and slunk out onto the beach where it stood for a moment, dripping. After gingerly lifting and shaking the water from one paw after another, it tested the air with its whiskers, and then sauntered over to a shady tree. Instead of slinking into the bush as Ethan had hoped, it leapt up, and draped itself over a low branch, from which it regarded him as if nothing unusual had happened.

Ethan shook his head. What was he seeing? He wasn't sure he should take his eyes off the leopard – it could pounce at any moment – but he had to see if Joe was safe. He saw Tariro drag a body out of the water onto the riverbank. What should have been Joe looked like an old woman with long dreadlocks that flopped around her like white kelp.

"Joe!" Ethan yelled, his stomach lurching. He ran towards the body, which lay limply on its side. "What happened to Joe?" He shook Tariro by the shoulders. Tariro flopped on the riverbank, panting from the effort of dragging the heavy body out of the water, in no shape to reply.

"Quickly! Help me roll him, uh . . . her on her back," Ethan said to two other boys. They helped him flop her over and then backed off to squat in the sand from where they watched Ethan expectantly, as if he were the expert in these things. As Ethan turned again to the woman, he shouted over his shoulder, "Someone, look for Joe. Now!"

He nearly retched when he went to clear the old woman's airway so that he could do mouth-to-mouth resuscitation. A soggy mango pip was lodged in her mouth and she was all scratched up and, well . . . old.

Ethan wormed his fingers in behind the mucilaginous mango, hauled it out of her mouth, and plopped it on the ground beside him with a shiver of revulsion. Trying to ignore a slimy strand of water hyacinth woven through her hair, he tilted her head back.

He had never actually done CPR before, but he hoped it would work the same way it always did on the Discovery channel. Taking a deep breath, he held her nose closed with his thumb and index finger, shuddered, put his lips to hers, and blew hard. He came up for air, spat and wiped his mouth, inhaled, and repeated the action. Halfway through, he remembered that there should be some pushing down on her chest, and counting one, one-thousand, so he tried doing that. His mind raced. Had he gone insane? Where had this woman come from? Where was Joe? Was it something the leopard had done? *The leopard!*

"Watch the little kids with that leopard around!" he warned between chest compressions.

He was relieved to notice that some of the bigger boys had already begun to encircle the animal. They advanced upon it, crouching low, slingshots at the ready, leaving a gap for the animal to escape into the bushes. The leopard seemed to be puzzled by the proceedings, his gaze moving from hunter to hunter with an appraising eye, but he made no move to escape.

"Weird," Ethan muttered, turning back to the old woman.

SWITCH!

"Don't blow so hard." Tariro rose up beside him. "What the hell do you think happened?" he said. "Where the hell is Joe?"

"Jimoh and his boys are looking for him in the pool," one of the boys told Tariro.

"No, I think this is Joe," Ethan gasped between breaths. He was shocked at his own words, but had spoken on instinct. It was all so unlikely, but the more time he had to process what had happened, the more he believed it. He had seen it with his own eyes – Joe had changed into this old woman as he jumped off the ledge.

Tariro threw him a dubious look.

"Tariro, as weird as this sounds, that is what I saw. That leopard attacked him and he changed." Ethan pointed in the direction of the leopard, who lounged over the branch, smoothing and grooming its fur. "There is definitely something not right with that leopard," he added, taking a breath and blowing once more into the woman's mouth.

Tariro peered at it. "Just looks like a leopard to me."

"It has an expression on its face," panted Ethan, "and it definitely attacked her. Look at her, she's covered in scratches." The old woman's injuries, although not that serious, included several bites. Ethan wished she would wake up and tell him what had happened.

Tariro frowned at him for a moment. "Yes, I can see she was attacked, but that does not make her Joe."

Without warning, the woman shot out a stream of vomit, sending bits of mango, brackish water and other vile things flying up at Ethan.

"Eugh!" He backed away, bringing his hand up to cover his mouth as a wave of nausea washed over him. He spun away and heaved his breakfast onto the ground, glancing at Tariro as he came up for air.

Just for a moment, Tariro had the ill grace to look pleased before he leaned over the woman, rolled her on to her side and shook her gently. "Where's Joe?" he asked in English, then again in a tongue-clicking language Ethan did not recognise. Then he asked her in the singsong-sounding Shona.

She just lay there coughing, but at least she was alive.

On the off chance that Joe was not somehow entwined with the old woman, Ethan decided to leave her with Tariro and search downstream to see if he had washed up near the rapids. He pulled his T-shirt over his head as he went, and tried to wipe as much of the vomit off himself as he could, almost vomiting again when he smelled it. A quick scan of the area showed Jimoh and the hunters, still diving under the water in the middle of the pool, but then Ethan froze. He rubbed his eyes.

The small girl from the rapids meandered towards him in no particular hurry, stalked by two enormous crocodiles. Ethan could hardly bear to look. She would surely die. They were almost on top of her.

"Go and help her!" he yelled at a boy who was closer to her than he was.

"Those crocs, they for that girl," the boy said casually, not rushing towards her.

Ethan could not believe it. Had the sonic boom somehow unbalanced everybody? *Stupid backwoods kids.* He would have to rescue her himself.

He sprinted towards her, streaking right past the treed leopard, withdrawing his knife as he went. He wished he had a machete but the machete guys were in the pool. Instead, he waved his T-shirt ineffectually at the crocodiles.

"Shoo!" he shouted, sweeping the surprised girl up onto his back and making a dash for it, expecting to be pounced on at any moment. One birthday, to encourage him to find something in common with his cousins, his mom had bought him a bush survival manual. In it, he'd read that crocodiles move unbelievably quickly, even on land. If he had known he would actually need the information he'd have paid more attention.

When he turned around to look, the crocodiles had flopped down onto the mud. They lay there eyeing him lazily, as if he had imagined the whole thing. No one else had made any move to help him in his daring rescue either. Some of the village kids shook their heads, astonished. Ethan started to feel as if he were in some sort of parallel world, where nothing made sense. He staggered over to the group surrounding the old woman and put the child down where she elbowed her way into the circle of spectators waiting for the old woman to revive.

Some of the kids leaped up suddenly, squealing and scrambling to their feet to scatter into the nearby bushes. Ethan looked up to see the leopard prowling towards him, its powerful muscles rippling under the sheen of its newly groomed coat. He thought he saw Tariro shift into position behind the old woman. Was he shielding himself, Ethan wondered, or was he just propping her up?

Ethan found himself getting angrier and angrier. Nobody else seemed to want to help. It was too late to run; the leopard was within springing distance. Heart racing, he groped on the ground beside him for his abandoned T-shirt, which he slowly wound around his left wrist, his knife already in his right hand. He crouched down into the fighting stance he had learned in Taekwando. Not that his patchy training in the martial art would be much help against a wild animal, but as long as there was any risk that the old woman could be his cousin Joe, he was not going to give up without a fight.

"You are a brave boy." The leopard's communication filled Ethan's head. "Now stand aside. I must see to the witch."

Ethan's legs went numb with fear. He whipped his head around to see if anyone else had heard the leopard speak. Not that it spoke, exactly. It emitted more of a faint spike of adrenalin that passed through his brain, with an icy edge to it, and then he knew what it meant. Everyone else looked blank.

Struggling to stand his ground, he said, "No! Back off!" and then for good measure, "Bad kitty! Sit!"

The leopard sat, as told, regarding him thoughtfully.

"I will not harm you," it said. "I need to help the witch. I will need you to do something for me."

"How do I know you are not lying?" Ethan said. *Have I gone completely mad? I am talking to an animal.*

Tariro's head turned from side to side, his eyes darting from friend to friend, as if hoping one of them held the answer to Ethan's strange behavior.

"Yussy!" Ethan said. "Am I the only one who can hear the leopard?"

"You must find the amulet," the leopard said, ignoring everyone's confusion. "I fear she has dropped it in the water."

"Are you out of your mind? I'm not going near that water." Ethan's eyes darted from Jimoh's group, who had climbed out of the water, and were resting on the other side of the pool, to the spot where the crocodiles had been. One was basking in the sun, but sure enough, the other was missing. *Most probably in this very pool*, he thought.

The leopard stood up and moved closer towards him in a menacing way. Its face, as it stared at Ethan, had a very un-leopard-like expression on it. Its jaw jutted out, and a single muscle twitched below its eye.

Ethan backed off. He was shaking but he knew he needed to sound as strong as he could. He knew if animals sense fear, they pounce. "Where's my cousin? Where's Joe?" He was trying to buy time till he could think what to do. It sounded absurd as he said it. Even if the cat really was talking to him, how would it know where Joe was?

"You cannot reach this Joe for now," it said, starting to show impatience. "Only the witch can find him, but she will need the amulet to recover. The amulet is in the water."

SWITCH!

They both looked towards the witch who slumped against Tariro, breathing erratically. Ethan wondered if he could get Tariro to go back into the pool and fetch this amulet, whatever it was. Aside from the crocodile, he was worried about the teaming throngs of parasites that lurk there. He shuddered, imagining microscopic creatures worming their way into every nook and cranny of his body.

"Why can't he do it?" Ethan said, pointing at Tariro, who was after all just as close, and had already exposed himself to the parasite-infested water by jumping off the ledge.

"He does not believe," the leopard said. "And look at him, he looks as if he has seen a demon."

Ethan looked hopefully in the direction of Jimoh.

"You are the one who kissed the witch. Only you can do this thing," the leopard said, following Ethan's train of thought. He didn't know if it could tell from the expression on his face or if it was actually reading his mind. It sat down and lifted a paw, inspected its claws pointedly, and glowered at him.

"It's too deep . . . I can't swim," Ethan tried.

"Then you will drown trying," the cat said, retracting its claws and stepping closer in a fluid move, "because the witch can wait no longer."

Time stood still for Ethan as the leopard's bright yellow eyes narrowed at him threateningly, less than a foot away from his face, betraying the internal battle raging within it. It was odd how Ethan was so easily preoccupied by it. It smelled mildly rank, like a wet puppy. Pure white whiskers grew out of either side of its face in sharp contrast to its perfectly symmetrical black rosette markings. Its dark golden fur looked so soft, Ethan had to control an impulse to reach out and touch the animal. Then he recoiled in confusion as a muscle tensed and relaxed across its powerful jaw. It did not blink. *Sjoe!* What was he thinking? He had never voluntarily touched an animal in his life before. An impatient talking leopard was not the place to start.

"Okay, what does this amulet look like?" He let out a long shuddering breath.

"It will shine," the cat said smoothly, all business now that it had won the stand off. "Do not touch the stones. Lift it only by the cord that connects them."

Ethan turned towards the water and forced himself to walk slowly to the edge. Whether his pounding heart drew the crocodile towards him, or the beast smelled his fear and came for him, one way or another he was convinced it was going to get him. Trying not to splash, he waded cautiously into the water, but it wasn't any use. His muscles twitched spasmodically, as if they had a life of their own.

Once the rippling water reached up to his shoulders he held his breath and dipped his face into it. His eyes shot open spontaneously. *I'll probably go blind,* he almost sobbed. At least the pool was crystal clear. He could see right to the other side where Jimoh's group sat dangling their feet in the water. Revolving slowly to get his bearings he looked out for the crocodile. He thought he could see it about thirty meters downstream with its back to him, so he swam cautiously towards the spot where the old witch had entered the water, and floated on the surface for a moment with his face submerged, scanning for the amulet.

He would have been able to see the amulet quite clearly even if it did not give off that eerie glow. It was in amongst the pebbles about six meters below him. An orangey stone lay on one end of a string connecting it to a strange dark stone on the other end. Its dim light pulsated so slowly that it looked as if time had slowed down. He was about to dive down towards it when a movement on the edge of his field of vision caused Ethan to whip around.

His scream turned into a gurgle as something huge and gnarly clamped down on his foot and spun him round and round, dragging him towards the bottom of the pool. Trying to curl up into a tight ball and go with the spin before the crocodile ripped his leg off, he opened his eyes but he couldn't see anything with the water bubbling around him. He doubled over and groped between his legs for an eyeball to poke his finger into. Feeling his way down the creature's nose, Ethan frantically moved his fingers backward towards the eyes and was about to dig his thumbs hard in to each squishy eyeball when his shoulder crashed painfully into the bottom of the pool and the crocodile let go abruptly, scattering sand and pebbles.

Ethan shook his head in slow motion as he righted himself. Perhaps he was just dizzy, but he could have sworn the amulet drifted purposefully towards him. Trying to ignore his burning lungs, he reached out and snatched it up, taking no care at all to avoid touching the stones. Energy rushed up Ethan's arm as he gripped it, sending waves of prickly heat reverberating through his body. About to push off from the bottom of the pool, he looked up towards the surface, and froze. The shadow of the crocodile circled slowly above him, choosing its moment . . .

It would be seconds before he ran out of breath. His chest was burning, a deafening drumming in his ears. If only he could make it to where he could see Jimoh's feet dangling in the water. They would help him out of the water, only, his arms and legs wouldn't move. He didn't seem to have the strength to propel himself towards them. He felt a massive surge of water pushing him along as he passed out.

CHAPTER 6
A PECULIAR FOREST

Joe woke up disoriented. His mind hovered for a few moments on the edge of reality. He was not sure if he had drowned or hit his head on the bottom of the pool. Strangely, he didn't even feel wet. He wondered if that was because he had been lying here long enough to dry out.

The forest canopy above his head wafted in and out of focus; the gigantic trees, nothing like the ones at Crystal Pools, were such an impossibly dark shade of green they were almost black. He blinked a couple of times, thinking there must be something wrong with his eyesight, but stopped, because that made him dizzy. He guessed Tariro had gone for help but he wondered where everyone else had got to. Someone was beating a drum. Just what he needed. His head wanted to explode.

Trying to roll over, he felt dread rising as he discovered that he could not move his arms or legs. He must have broken his neck! When he opened his mouth to howl in anguish, all that came out was a weak cough.

Turning his head to the side slowly and painfully, but with the relief of realising his neck wasn't broken after all, he squinted in the direction of the noise to see who was beating the drums, and swore he could see not just one, but a whole troop of Tokoloshes.

Am I hallucinating? He had heard the fairy stories about the hairy little men that lived in crevices and under riverbanks. They were supposed to be visible only to children. *And I'm not a child,* he thought.

One or two of the little creatures yelped as he moved, and bolted in fright towards the edges of the clearing, their scrappy animal-pelt skirts flapping around their knees. A few braver ones crept forward to take a look at him or touch him before running away again in a sort of delighted panic. Closing his eyes wearily, he wondered if the reason he couldn't move his arms and legs was because they had tied him up, and then he passed out again.

The second time Joe awoke, he was startled to find a Tokoloshe face swimming in front of his eyes. Yes, it was definitely a Tokoloshe. The little man perching on his chest gripped Joe's cheeks in both his hands and stared intently with his little jet black eyes into Joe's eyes. The long, spiky hairs growing out of his ears twitched while he and Joe considered each other. Joe noticed that, close up, the Tokoloshe had longish, bristly, clay red-coloured hair all over his body, but he looked closer to a gnome than any sort of an ape. He shifted a primitive-looking bow from one shoulder to another and reached down to a second Tokoloshe for a gourd, which he pressed to Joe's lips.

"Drink," he commanded. Joe had taken a swallow even before he got over his astonishment that he had understood the fellow. The soothing liquid slid down his throat more like cool oil than water. It had no taste but it gave off a smell of pears.

"Where am I?" he croaked, more to himself than to the creature. "How come I can't feel my legs?" The Tokoloshe turned and signalled to someone over his shoulder. Joe shrieked in agony, sitting up abruptly, clutching at his shin, and almost toppling the Tokoloshe from his chest. One of them had stabbed him in the leg with a spear or something.

A PECULIAR FOREST

The Tokoloshe – now dangling from Joe's neck – jumped down and squinted up at him looking a little embarrassed. "'Sokay now," he lisped.

The sudden movement was too much for Joe. He felt dizzy, and terribly sleepy. He lay back on the ground. At least he could feel his legs again, however weakly. His eyes grew heavy and he felt himself drifting back into unconsciousness.

The Tokoloshe shook Joe's cheeks uneasily. "Stay awake!" he cried. "We need to move you to a safer place."

Joe fought hard to keep his eyes open. What did the Tokoloshe mean? And were the Tokoloshes themselves safe to be with? He drifted back to sleep.

It was late afternoon by the time Joe woke again. There was no sign of the Tokoloshe. Instead, a huge tiger lounged on its back amongst the dappled shadows of the forest, a stone's throw away. Its giant paws dangled limp-wristed in the air like a playful puppy. Its mouth was closed and it blew through its nostrils, alternately producing a breathy snort and a thunderous purr that rumbled up through its chest and resounded through the jungle.

Joe groaned softly. This must be what the Tokoloshe meant about getting him to a safe place. There was no way he was going to survive this . . . Or would he? Surely if the tiger were going to eat him, it would have done so while he was unconscious, unless it liked to play with its food. Joe did not know all that much about tigers. What the hell had happened? Perhaps he was already dead, and it would just go away. Yes . . . Yes, he was probably dead. Being dead was the only way he could make any sense of the situation.

The tiger pounced so suddenly and so smoothly he could hardly follow its movement. One moment it had been scratching idly at its light furry underbelly and the next it had closed the distance between them and was all reddish orange fur and dark vertical stripes, one huge padded paw resting gently on Joe's chest. A small shift in the cat's weight would crush him, he realised.

"I know you are awake," it said, gently nudging him on the shoulder, its face an inch from his. Joe recoiled, shaking. Was he in a dream? He thought those trees were too dark. Was he in India? How the hell had that happened? He watched the muscles in the tiger's face tense and relax while it scrutinised him close up. The tip of its tongue, the texture of sandpaper, licked his face, leaving a light graze.

"Mmm . . ." it murmured enigmatically. Joe shot it a terrified look, but it merely sat back and watched him.

"I am Hajiri," it purred eventually. "I'm glad you came. I was looking for someone to light me a fire. You wouldn't mind, would you?"

It had spoken to him! He hadn't seen its lips move, yet he had heard it quite clearly.

"Where are those Tokoloshe?" Joe asked. He struggled to sit up, surreptitiously edging away from the tiger. He'd felt a lot safer with the Tokoloshe, and not only because they had given him water, although that may have been a trick. He'd heard they were tricky, and he *had* felt extremely sleepy afterwards.

"Oh, the Tokoloshe?" Hajiri purred, waving a paw in the general direction of the forest. "I chased them away. Pesky creatures. All one wants at the end of a long day is a nice fire and good company, not that lot of vandals with their noisy drums."

"Where am I?" Joe ventured, once he had got over the idea that there really were Tokoloshe, and he was actually talking to a tiger.

"Not from here then?" Hajiri said, flopping down and stretching out to his full three meters on the ground.

"I don't know? Is this India?" Obviously tigers came from India, he thought, and it had an Indian accent, but India was impossibly far away, unless he really was dreaming or had been unconscious for weeks. "I'm from Tjalotjo in Zimbabwe." He wondered if he would die in an instant, or if the tiger would take its time killing him and eating him. He knew there was no point in running. He felt too disorientated and, besides, running would probably make things worse.

"Tjalotjo," Hajiri drawled. "Never heard of it. I have heard of India though. My ancestors came from there.

"Er, where are we? And how did I get here? And how come you can talk?" Joe said shakily.

"Dear boy, I have always been able to talk. As to how you got here – I have no idea. I got separated from my party during the hunt this morning. Got bored and wandered off, if you must know. They will have gone back home without me, selfish lot." Joe's eyes widened as Hajiri unsheathed a four-inch claw but the tiger only scratched his chest with it in an unthreatening way.

"Now where was I?" Hajiri went on conversationally. "Oh yes, I was just casting about for someone to help me with my fire and there you were. Lying there all floppy." He looked as if he was trying to fix his face into a sympathetic expression but fell short of the mark.

"Do you suppose I wished you here?" the tiger said, livening up. "Such a strange kind of magic pervading this kingdom. Most unsettling. Can't get used to it myself, heaven knows I have tried. Just when you get used to one preposterous thing, another pops up. I blame the witches. In fact, you being here probably has something to do with the witches. Wouldn't question it too much – a waste of time, my boy." He shivered ever so slightly. "But I ramble," he said, turning to Joe. "You are in Karibu, and I am glad of the company. Perhaps you will be kind enough to light my fire. Then you can tell me all about . . . Tjalotjo, was it?"

CHAPTER 7
BEGRUDGING HELP

Gogo Maya slumped in the shade of a tree, alternately checking her pulse and anxiously watching the pool. It was taking an awfully long time to recover from the switching without the healing power of her amulet. Salih had finally persuaded the pale, weedy boy with the curly blond hair to go into the pool after it, but he was taking far too long to surface. It probably would have gone better for him if he had taken off his trousers and boots before going in. She hoped the silly boy had not gone and drowned himself, because she really needed that amulet, and soon.

"The handsome black kid would have been a better choice," she grumbled to Salih, flexing her jaw muscles. They were still sore from the wedged mango pip. "I suppose he was too busy trying to revive me."

Salih stood up and stretched, arching his back, then glanced towards the pool. "No, the smaller one was the only one I could read," he said. "And, as unlikely as it seems, it was the smaller one who took charge and revived you. He seems to have some magic of his own."

Gogo Maya shot him a skeptical look.

BEGRUDGING HELP

Her head snapped around as the surface of the water exploded at last, and a large crocodile launched itself out of the pool, dragging the hapless hero onto the muddy riverbank by the foot. Her amulet sailed through the air, almost landing back in the water. She watched Salih take a furtive look around to check if anyone else had noticed it in the confusion. He then sidled up to it, lifting it carefully by the leather thong that joined the two stones, and brought it over to her. She snatched it up eagerly and clutched it in both hands.

The expected fuzzy feelings of wellness did not channel up through her body. Uncurling her fingers, she inspected the amulet with a disgruntled grimace. It lay there on her palm, dead.

"He must have touched the amber!" she huffed. "The energy is completely spent. It will be hours before I have the strength to switch back to Karibu, even supposing I can make a bloody switch." She fixed the boy with a sour look as his handsome friend rushed to help him. "I don't know why he bothers," she grumbled. "The drenched brat will be perfectly fine after draining my amulet."

"You're going to have to engage with these people," Salih said in his stern voice. She hoped she was not going to have to remind him who was in charge. "Take some responsibility, even," Salih went on. "They are obviously distraught at the loss of the boy, Joe."

"No. He will settle down fine in Karibu once he gets over the shock," she assured him. "Lucky to be there, if you ask me." This was a nice place he came from, she mused, having a look around, but nothing near as beautiful and exciting as Karibu. There was plenty to entertain a boy there.

Salih gave her that look.

"Oh, stop worrying," she snapped at him. "Morathi will probably ransom the boy to us once we get back. If he really hates it at Waheri village, we could always get Tacari to take him through the tear." Gogo Maya was well aware that the exit through Tacari's tear was on the other side of the world, but she had heard that people in the outside world were capable of travelling great distances in a relatively short space of time. His people would have him home in no time at all.

"We can't take him to Waheri without explaining to Tacari how we got him there in the first place," Salih said.

Salih had a point, she groaned. Tacari was going to be furious. Not only at the risk to Karibu, if she and Salih were discovered on the outside of the hidden Kingdoms, but if he found out she and Salih had borrowed some of his own magic to construct the switching opal in the first place, he would be apoplectic.

"And we don't know that the boy is with Morathi," Salih said. "Even if he is, who knows what those Tokoloshes will do in their present state? They'll probably pass him on to whoever is supplying the *nzuri thana* that makes them so crazy. We have to make a plan to extract the boy from Karibu as quickly as possible, before anyone else finds out."

Absentmindedly selecting a fallen berry from the ground beneath her shady tree, Gogo Maya peeled away a section of the tough reddish brown skin and tasted the yellow brown pulp. It had an orangey flavor, almost exactly like the mahobohobo at her village, only smaller. She spat the familiar torpedo-shaped pip out into her hand and inspected it closely.

"Look at this fruit, Salih. It's almost exactly the same as the ones at home," she said. "We can't be that far from Karibu. Perhaps we can get the one who drained the amulet to go to Karibu and fetch the other one."

"He won't be able to find Karibu from here."

"He would if he knew what he was looking for," she said, and then adopted a slightly wheedling tone, adding, "and if he had someone to guide him."

Salih ignored her clumsy attempt to manipulate him. He gave her, and the pip, a noncommittal glance, and then settled down on his haunches to watch the drama with the half-drowned boy unfold.

The drenched one rolled over and retched into the sand, then shot up and scrambled away from his friend, whipping his head around in fright.

"Where is the crocodile?" he croaked, patting himself on the chest and wheezing. He pulled a piece of water hyacinth out of his hair, stared at it in disbelief, and retched again.

"You look like a drowned rat," his friend grinned. Oddly, he seemed quite smug about that.

"Thank you. I hardly hurt at all," the drenched boy huffed. Then he peered at his leg as if he'd lost something. "It must have grabbed me through my pants."

Gogo Maya leaned back against the tree trunk, crossed her arms over her chest and grinned. She was prepared to enjoy the boy's discomfort. Things would have gone much more smoothly if he had done what he'd been told instead of draining her amulet. She could have healed both of them if she'd had control of it, and she would still have had enough power left in the opal to switch home.

"What the hell did you think you were doing stalking into the water all creepy like that, Ethan?" the handsome one shouted at the drenched one. "You were down there so long I thought you had drowned." He stabbed an angry finger in the direction of the rapids. "You were lucky that croc pulled you out."

Where the boy pointed, Gogo Maya saw a small girl squatting on her haunches between two enormous crocodiles, patting them on their snouts and talking to them in soothing, clicking tones.

"Well, that's disturbing!" she said to Salih. "Is she a witch? Do I need to explore the minds of those crocodiles? Because I don't think I have the energy."

"No need," Salih said. "I can pick up on their thoughts."

Gogo Maya watched with interest as the leopard cocked his ears and twitched his whiskers, all the while gazing steadily at the crocodiles. Although she felt the little cold prickles of his awareness spread out to include the crocodiles, Gogo Maya was worried to discover that she could not quite understand what the crocodiles said to Salih. Perhaps the switch had made her a little weaker than she'd expected.

Salih gave her a quizzical look when she failed to respond to the crocodiles' information, then shrugged and told her what they'd said. "The little girl has a particular fondness for the crocodiles, but they are not her familiar. More . . . friends. Friends of the whole community, I understand. They have lived here for some time. They feel most anxious about the drowned boy."

Back in her youth, Gogo Maya had lived in the crocodile-infested Louisiana swamps. As an expert on these matters she felt compelled to argue. "I'm pretty sure you can't tame a crocodile," she said. "They don't have the memory for it. Just when you think you've made friends, they forget who you are, and bite you." On the other hand, she couldn't help wondering if the crocodile had been trying to help the boy. She prodded Salih on the shoulder. "Delve a little deeper," she said. "See if they are strange . . . or different. I have a feeling we were drawn to this place by something, and it sure as hell wasn't that boy, even if he does have a bit of magic of his own."

The drenched boy, Ethan, the other one had called him, obviously didn't see the crocodiles as suitable companions either. "Get her away from those crocodiles!" he croaked, trying to rise up and go towards them, but another boy planted a hand on his chest to stop him, speaking rapidly to the handsome one in a language Gogo Maya did not recognise.

"No, apparently they won't hurt her, they're some kind of a pet," the handsome one told his friend with a dismissive shrug. "So, why did you go into the water like that? We were worried about you. You could see Jimoh's guys already dredged the pool."

Muttering something unintelligible about having pit bulls as pets, the boy, Ethan, said, "The leopard made me." He sounded unconvincing, even to Gogo Maya, who knew it was true. "I was supposed to fetch the witch's amulet. Well, the leopard says she's a witch . . . Anyway, the amulet's a sort of jewel. I should have it here somewhere," he added, patting his pockets.

"Just because she's old doesn't make her a witch . . ." began the handsome one. "What do you mean, the leopard made you?"

"What a nice boy," Gogo Maya chuckled, with a touch of approval.

The boy, Ethan, pointed a finger at his temple. "It told me, right into my head," he practically wailed. "It threatened me." They both looked over at Gogo Maya and Salih. The leopard lounged beside her, preening and fluffing up the white tip of his tail, looking as harmless as a domestic cat.

The handsome one laughed. "Don't be lame, Ethan, you are making this up. It was just protecting the woman. It must be her pet."

"Familiar," corrected Salih mischievously, getting a smothered laugh from Gogo Maya.

The boy snapped his head around and glared at Salih with open animosity. "You see?"

"What?" said the handsome one.

A group of scruffy, barefoot boys picked their way past, careful to avoid going too close to Salih, and joined the two others. They were led by a scrawny youngster in a red shirt and a filthy hat pulled low over his eyes.

"Ah, you are feeling better, Ethan." He placed a hand on the forehead of the drenched one and held it there, even when the boy recoiled. "I will send some of my men to fetch my dad."

"Will your dad fetch my uncle?"

Before she could stop herself, Gogo Maya leaped up, almost choking on a pip, and cried, "No! No! Don't fetch him! He will not believe! Things will get too complicated! I will get trapped here!"

She clapped a hand over her mouth. *Drat*, she thought, she was going to have to help now. Past experience had led Gogo

Maya to be wary of grown-ups. They usually came armed with the authorities and awkward questions, and she felt in no shape to take them on, weakened as she was.

"We have to fetch men to help us find Joe," a boy explained to her. He spoke kindly enough, but Gogo Maya was not about to trust him just because he was smaller than her. He had a vicious-looking machete dangling from a rope around his waist. It had dried blood on it.

"I will help you find the boy, Joe," she said quickly. "I know where he is. Well, nearly."

The boy gave her a puzzled frown. "How do you know?"

"I just know in my bones," she said, as evasively as she dared.

"You mean in your *bones* bones or *throw* bones?" The boy, Ethan, was a bit too quick off the mark for Gogo Maya, and not the most polite. He shot his friend a self-satisfied look, then said, "See, I told you she was a witch."

Gogo Maya glowered at him. She did not hold with rudeness, even if he *had* blown some sort of life magic into her. Any point in pretending to be a kindly old woman had disappeared with the mention of grown-ups. "Well, you're perfectly right, young man. I am in fact a witch," she told him. "Now don't get all huffy, we've had a sort of . . . accident. I have exchanged places with your friend."

Ethan's eyes darted from the red-shirt boy to the boy with the wild hair to see if they had heard her, then fixed on Gogo Maya with an incredulous stare. "How?"

"I switched, using the amulet."

"What do you mean, *switched*?" Now he looked close to tears.

Having expected him to be smug once she admitted she was a witch, Gogo Maya felt a vague stirring of guilt that he looked so unhappy. "Well, it is difficult to explain," she said in a more conciliatory tone. "I hold the amulet and hope to be someplace else and the opal moves me. Of course, wherever I land, the thing occupying that space will be where I was before I switch places."

BEGRUDGING HELP

She still did not hold out much hope that he would believe her.

Surprisingly, he did. He straightened his shoulders, narrowed his eyes and went straight for the weakness in her story. "And it didn't occur to you that whoever you changed places with might not be happy with that?"

"Usually when I switch, Ethan, I am replaced by a rock or an animal or something," she offered by way of an excuse, "and I never move far, but this time I seem to have been drawn by this place. Perhaps by those crocodiles." She glared at the crocodiles. It wouldn't do any harm to her cause to deflect some of the blame.

Ethan raised an eyebrow doubtfully and glanced over at the crocodiles, but shook his head. "Well, where were you then? Before you . . . switched."

"In the magic Kingdoms of Karibu, where I come from."

Pandemonium broke out. The boy with the machete had been interpreting for the other kids. Some of them fell about laughing at Ethan's gullibility, but some argued vehemently that it was perfectly possible to have a magic kingdom. The handsome boy, who had been lounging up against a log with a half-bored, half-distracted expression, stood up and glared at Ethan.

"Okay, the joke's over, Ethan," he said. "You are scaring the little kids." He cupped his hands to his mouth and yelled out, "Joe! You can come out now!"

The others stared at him, taken aback, but a couple of them looked around as if the boy, Joe, might come walking out from behind a bush.

Gogo Maya exchanged glances with Salih. Handsome was an odd boy. Perhaps Salih was a better judge of character than she'd thought.

"And where is Karibu, exactly?" demanded Ethan, after the boy, Joe, had failed to materialise and the handsome one had stormed off in a huff.

"Somewhere beyond those mountains." Gogo Maya gave an expansive wave because she was not exactly sure.

SWITCH!

Ethan pushed out his lower lip. "How will Joe get back?"

She hadn't thought she would have to come up with a solution quite so soon. "I will try and get him back by reversing the switch," she said. "If you can find me a dish, I will put water in it and scry to see where your friend is. Then I will aim for him and try to exchange."

Gogo Maya improvised as she went along. She knew the whole business of switching was too inaccurate for her to exchange with the boy, but confusing them with a scry would buy her time to think of a plan, and had the added advantage of showing her where the boy, Joe, was. Now that she thought about it, she *would* feel bad if the Tokoloshe had abandoned him and he had fallen into the wrong hands, especially if those hands were her village headman, Tacari's.

After a heated discussion amongst the children, two girls set off reluctantly down the road.

"They get dish," nodded the boy with the red shirt and the dirty hat. "But they say no more stories till they get back, please. Is not fair if they miss out."

"Don't rush back. I can only scry after dark," Gogo Maya called after them. She had already threatened to disappear the way she had come if anyone brought any grown-ups. The longer they took fetching the bowl, the more time her amulet would have to recharge, and the more likely it was that she would be able to switch.

Back in her shady spot beneath the mahobohobo tree once more, she flopped down on the ground, while Salih went to speak to the crocodiles. Most of the children wandered off and took up with various swimming games, but some followed her, begging for more stories about Karibu. They introduced themselves with lovely exotic names: Tendayi, Tafadzwa, Tekeramayi, Jimoh . . . and one girl, Happymore, but you could hardly tell. She wore the same khaki shorts that everyone else did. Ethan, had been dressed much more smartly. He took off his wet clothes and shoes and laid them out to dry. Even the underpants he had on smacked of rich boy and Gogo Maya noticed how awkwardly he seated himself in the dirt.

Salih came back, having established that they were indeed not too far from Karibu as the hawk flies, but that the only way in was to follow a dangerous river that ran through the mountains to the east and enter Karibu through the underground water system.

Gogo Maya pursed her lips. If this river ran into Karibu from underground, could she really send the boy that way? Goodness knew what kind of raging torrents swirled around the caves under there. It was rumored in Karibu that Sobek gods lived there. She wondered if these crocodiles were aware of that.

Amazingly, Salih assured her that the crocodiles had passed that way before and would help the boy to navigate there. She thought of mentioning the gods but decided not to spoil the plan; surely Salih knew what he was doing.

"If I cannot make an exchange, you will have to go down the river to Karibu to get your friend," Gogo Maya began.

Ethan's eyes were already as wide as saucers. "What, on my own? With those crocodiles?"

Gogo Maya gave a sharp intake of breath. She hadn't realised the boy could read Salih unless the leopard deliberately channelled thoughts straight at him. Another thing she would have to investigate. *Darn*, she realised, *to be able to do that he must have some very powerful magic of his own.* Where on earth had he got it? Well, it couldn't be helped; she and Salih would just have to watch what they said to each other while the boy was around. It would make it a little easier if Salih did not sidle up to the boy like that, she thought. Couldn't he see the boy was trying to pull away from him?

One way or another she was going to have to persuade the boy. If she could convince him to go on the journey, then it would be only a matter of time before he accepted the idea of being guided by the crocodiles.

SWITCH!

"You could take another boy with you," she said. "I am sure the crocodiles can manage two boys if you want."

Infuriatingly, the boy didn't buy it.

"We can't go down the river," he said. "I don't care what your crocodiles think, those mountains are impassable." He appealed to the boy in the red shirt, who he called Jimoh, for confirmation.

"Yes. Very, very dangerous," Jimoh, the one in the red shirt, said. "Water like washing machine for Mama Joe." He dry washed his hands to demonstrate, but added helpfully, "Don't worry, Ethan. I come with you to find Joe. Crocodile, he help us. He got very strong *mshonga*."

"Please, Missisi!" volunteered a small boy, clicking his fingers and waving his hand up in the air. "Those crocs. My dad says they are magic."

"Yes, yes," nodded a couple of the other kids. "It is known. Those crocs are magic."

It was starting to dawn on Gogo Maya that they quite possibly were. "Yes, I believe they are." Now she was getting somewhere. If she could persuade Ethan that the crocodiles were magic . . .

But Ethan still refused to be guided by crocodiles. He was so stubborn! "If you switch, and get exchanged for a rock or something instead of Joe, why can't you just give him the amulet and get him to switch back by himself?" he asked her.

"Your Joe will not know how to do it on his own," Gogo Maya explained as patiently as she could. She was not known for her patience.

"Well, why don't you switch there, fetch Joe, and switch back again with him?" said the boy.

"No, then I will have to switch back to Karibu again. That would make four switches. I'm a very old lady. It will kill me." *And bring the whole forest running to see what's going on*, she added to herself. Why wouldn't the boy just do as she wanted?

"Well, why me? Why not a grown-up?" Ethan said.

"Because you have taken the healing power of the amber,"

BEGRUDGING HELP

Gogo Maya said decisively. She hadn't wanted to tell him, but she could think of no other way to persuade the boy to do what she wanted. It had to be him. She needed to get him to Karibu where she could find out where his magic had come from, and how come he was able to read Salih so clearly. Then there was that sneaky feeling she had that his magic had somehow interfered with her own ability to read Salih's exchange with the crocodiles. Drat, now she was going to have to explain about the healing. Well, perhaps not all of it.

"Er, were you hurt? When you went down for the amulet," she said.

Ethan pulled up his leg to inspect his wound. If she looked closely, she could see two faint white rows of jagged teeth marks across his shin, and the back of his leg, from the crocodile bite. The boy with the wild hair, Tendayi, helpfully pointed them out to Gogo Maya, and several boys nodded. Yes, they agreed. It was a crocodile bite even if it looked like an old scar now.

Gogo Maya poked at the scar. "The scoundrel definitely bit you, but the power you sucked up out of the amber repaired the damage. For a while, if you don't do it too often, your body will self-repair. That's why you are the best person to make the journey." She glared at him as if daring him to argue, then muttered bitterly, "You shouldn't have touched the stone."

Ethan glanced in the direction of the crocodiles and shuddered. Then he rounded on her accusingly. "I could hardly help touching the stone. The crocodile was after me. When I saw the amulet swimming towards me I just snatched it up and tried to save myself."

"It swam towards you?" She gave a start. It was the first time she had ever heard of such a thing. Why on earth would her very own amulet be attracted to this stubborn boy? Amulets have strong attachments to their owners, and she had made this one with her own hands.

"The blowing in your mouth?" suggested Salih.

SWITCH!

Gogo Maya gaped at Salih. Could it be possible that the boy had sucked up some of her power before he even touched the stone? Enough to confuse her own amulet? "I guess that might do it," she agreed reluctantly.

She cleared her throat. "It's not that I'm blaming you, mind, it's just that you've drained all the healing power. It will take time to replenish itself." She fondled the amber lovingly. It wasn't the amulet's fault. "Were you ill or anything? It's drained a lot."

"No," Ethan said. Then he seemed to remember something. "Not ill, exactly. I have asthma."

"That would do it," she sighed, vaguely remembering asthma from her childhood. People in Karibu didn't get it. "Fixing the asthma has taken the energy. Did you touch the opal?" She was almost afraid to ask.

"I don't know, I was busy drowning at the time." Ethan's steely blue eyes held a hint of a challenge.

"Sorry, I'm just trying to gauge whether it has enough power to get me back to Karibu tonight."

His shoulder lowered a little. "So, what? Is the asthma gone for good? Or just till the, um, spell wears off?"

Gogo Maya held the amber up to her eye, examining it in the sunlight, then turned to him sternly. "I have no idea. The amber makes up its own mind. You are bloody lucky it didn't kill you."

"Could it have?" he asked. "Killed me, I mean?"

"I've seen people disintegrate before my eyes after touching someone else's amulet," she said. "For some it has been a little slower . . . But since you are not dead, I guess it must like you." She'd seen nothing of the sort, of course, but if the boy was going to Karibu, she could not have him going around looking for other people's amulets to drain.

Ethan put his hand on his chest and took a couple of deep breaths, as if he did not believe it, then sighed. "I suppose it could be true. I can hear the leopard talk." He reached out and almost touched Salih, who had settled down for a nap beside the boy, and

66

then jerked his hand away, obviously afraid of the leopard.

"What does the opal do?" he asked, a bit too eagerly for someone who had not touched the thing.

Gogo Maya gripped the amulet protectively to her chest. "I have hardly begun to understand," she said evasively. "It has no healing power. I use it to switch." Not that she was trying to finagle her way out of her responsibility for the situation or anything, but she was not about to go into the dubious mind-manipulating skills Salih had contributed to the thing, even if she understood half of them. The boy was better off not knowing.

He regarded her steadily with those flinty blue eyes. Could he sense that she was holding back? At least he looked a little less put upon, almost on the verge of agreeing to go.

Suddenly Gogo Maya felt very tired. It was about time for her mid-afternoon nap, and it had been a harrowing day so far. Perhaps she should give the boy some time to come to his own conclusion that he had to go. "Now off with you boys. I need to have a little sleep. You should go and make whatever preparations you can for a river journey."

CHAPTER 8
A BIG DECISION

Ethan leaned up against the tree trunk, flicking the blade of his knife open and shut with sullen resentment while he watched Tariro rummage through their kit in that domineering way of his. In his opinion, Tariro knew less about what to take on an expedition into the wilderness than the small girl, Ketty. She, at least, seemed to have some connection with the crocodiles. He, for one, was not fooled into believing the crocodiles had had a sudden change of their cold, reptilian hearts, and were going to guide them down the river, whatever the girl said – or the leopard, for that matter.

And that was another thing. He glared at Tariro. "Let me get this straight," he said. "You believe the crocodiles told Ketty that they would take us safely down the river without biting us, but you don't believe I can hear the leopard?"

"I don't know why that leopard has taken to you, Ethan, but I'm not going to let you use it as an excuse to take charge and order everyone about." Ethan watched as Tariro reeled in a length of rope and wound it around his crooked elbow, then considered the two crocodiles sunning themselves peacefully on the riverbank. Hitching a ride with the creatures seemed to worry Tariro no more than taking a trip into the unknown wilderness. "Look at them," he shrugged, "they don't look like they'd bite anyone."

Ethan gestured angrily at his obvious crocodile bite.

"Well, anyone else besides you," Tariro amended. "I think the croc was trying to help you. With all that farting about under the water for so long, he probably thought you were drowning. You have to stop showing off like that, Ethan."

Ethan shook his head in despair. "Tariro, we seriously can't go off into the bush to look for Joe," he said. "We should go right now and fetch my uncle while it's still daylight. He will call out the Police Reserve and they will search for Joe."

"The witch said that would be a mistake because Alan would not believe," Tariro insisted, "but don't worry, Ethan, I am sure we are not going to do anything too dangerous for you."

Ethan ignored the implication that he was a coward. Rather that than get themselves killed. "We don't even know where we are going," he said, stabbing a finger in the direction of the mountain range. "What part of impassible mountains don't you understand? If nobody goes there, we could get into all sorts of trouble – slavers, militia, wild animals. We could wander into another country and get arrested."

"Ethan, you watch too many movies," Tariro said with a long-suffering sigh. "It's just down the road and I don't think we have a choice." He reached for Ethan's backpack, and Ethan let him rummage through it. It wasn't as if he could stop Tariro. Once the boy had his mind set on a thing, it seemed, he did it.

Spotting the corner of his laptop poking out of his backpack, Ethan wondered if there was enough battery to leave a note on it for his mom and step-dad. There had been an hour or so of electricity supply the night before, and he had managed to recharge it, but his cousins had promptly used up most of it. He wished he was home with his folks now, in the air-conditioned comfort and safety of his own room. Something caught in his throat. He wished he had not come to this horrible place, and he wished he didn't have to deal with this difficult boy. He wished none of this had happened at all, that it was a week before and he was still in his house in Cape Town, playing computer games and drinking fresh orange juice.

But if he hadn't come, he would never have known he could talk to a leopard. Would the others have been able to rescue Joe without him talking to the leopard? Were they going to be able to rescue Joe even if he could talk to it? He wished Joe would pitch up soon – preferably with a more plausible explanation for his disappearance than a magic switch – and put a stop to all this.

"Oh my word!" Tariro said suddenly. Hauling a giant-sized tin of assorted chocolates and toffees out of the bottom of Ethan's backpack, he clutched it to his chest, grinning a slightly maniacal grin. "Ethan, have you been holding out on us?"

"Don't get too excited," Ethan said, wondering how Tariro could be so amped over sweets at a time like this. "I'm planning to share that with everyone tonight. You'll be lucky if you get more than one."

"What these rural kids don't know, they won't worry about," Tariro said, tearing a small hole in the corner of the inner packet and popping a chocolate-coated toffee into his mouth. "Honestly, Ethan, they have never even come across sweets like this. I can't remember the last time even I had imported chocolates."

"All the more reason why *they* should have them and not *you*, Tariro. Don't be so selfish." Ethan stood up and tried to grab the tin from the other boy, a wave of anger boiling up in him, which felt odd because he didn't even like sweets that much.

"If you take one more I'm going to smack you," he found himself saying, frowning at himself as he said it. Ethan had never threatened a person with violence before, much less smacked anyone, unless in a formal Taekwando match, and he was notoriously terrible at that. It did not give him the empowering feeling one was supposed to have when standing up to a bully, and as upset as he was, Tariro was not a good place to start.

Fortunately, it seemed to work. Tariro returned the chocolates to Ethan's backpack with a petulant shrug, rather than taking up the challenge. "We will need something to strain our drinking water through, like a hanky or something," Tariro said, changing the subject.

Ethan suddenly felt bad. He hoped Tariro didn't associate his threat with what those other boys had done to him . . . He promised himself he would try to be kinder to Tariro from now on. "I suppose we could use my Kanga," Ethan said, indicating the maroon-and-blue-striped length of cotton he had tied around his waist while he waited for his trousers to dry. He tried to relax his hands, which seemed to want to ball into fists.

"What about fire? Do you have a lighter or matches?" Tariro said through a mouth full of toffee, oblivious to Ethan's struggle for control.

"No. No lighter and no matches. You may remember I shot the matches out of the tree this morning before we came up with this stupid plan." Ethan tried to say it casually, or even jokingly, but his jaw felt tight, so it came out sounding harsh. "Besides, I've only brought dry provisions and I don't see any point in having a fire if we have nothing to cook." They would have a fire if it was the last thing they did, Ethan thought; there was no way he was going to sleep in the wild without one, but he wasn't going to tell Tariro that.

"We will be in the bush, Ethan, obviously we'll shoot something, or we could always forage for grubs and things, like they do on your Discovery Channel." His dark eyes held Ethan's in a challenge. "You're just scared, city boy."

"You know what, Tariro?" Ethan yelled. "It has nothing to do with being scared, although God knows, I am. I don't want to go down the river, or off into the mountains. I want to fetch a grown-up. And I'm not counting the old woman. If I knew the way back to the farm I would've tried to walk there hours ago – lions or no lions." The angrier he got, the less he was able to control himself. What was happening to him today? Was it a panic attack? Pins and needles prickled under the skin at the base of his scull, and his head felt hot. He reached for his asthma pump before realizing he wasn't in the slightest bit out of breath.

He went on, unable to stop himself, and beyond caring if he offended the boy. So Tariro had gone through a horrible experience, but that didn't mean he had to inflict his need for adventure on the rest of them. "I'm trying very hard to get on with you, Tariro, because you're Joe's friend, but quite honestly, I'm sick of your hunting and adventures crap. This is real life, and these people are seriously considering letting us drift down the river with no plan, chasing some fantasy story, with a couple of dangerous wild animals to guide us. The only one amongst us with an ounce of bush skill, a twelve-year-old boy!"

"Fifteen," he said. "Jimoh is fifteen. He's just small for his age, and you should be so lucky, he's a better tracker than all the grown-ups around here combined."

Tariro flopped down on a rock beside the shelter. He suddenly looked vulnerable, as if he was trying to convince himself. "Ethan, I'm as worried about going as you are. Don't think I haven't considered going back to the farmhouse and phoning my dad. He could get the army out, but it would do no good. They won't believe it. Jimoh says there are legends about his people going there before, and we have to listen to the witch. We just have to man up and do what she says. I mean, this is Joe we are talking about!"

Ethan sagged. Hearing Tariro admit that he was afraid did not make him feel very triumphant. Instead, he felt more worried than ever. He understood Tariro's need to save Joe – perhaps it was even greater than his own need at this point. But still, the anxiety in his stomach pulsed with a beat he couldn't explain. It felt almost what he imagined Tourettes must feel like, only, he didn't feel the need to swear, he felt . . .

He wasn't sure what he felt like doing, so for the first time in his life he stomped off in what looked and felt suspiciously like a sulk. Out of the corner of his eye, he noticed Salih watching from a nearby branch.

By the time the sun dipped behind the trees Ethan felt much calmer. He had paced up and down near the rapids till he caught a whiff of barbecue on the evening breeze and wandered back to the camp. A fire had been lit in the fire pit.

One small girl squatted in the dirt poking a stick into the fire, whilst two others took it in turns to rotate the duiker on its pole. None of them looked old enough to be tending a fire. *I should have done that*, he told himself with a pang if guilt, *instead of throwing a hissy fit while everyone else worked.*

"Hey, Ethan, come and look at this," Tariro called, as if there had been no altercation between them before. Ethan didn't want to speak to Tariro; he was embarrassed about his outburst, but he guessed the boy was attempting to make peace, so he wandered over.

Tafadzwa had hold of a foot pump, which he used to pump up the inner tube of a tractor tyre, beside the pool. He gripped the footplate between his bare toes and pumped the handle up and down.

"I don't know how he plans to keep that lot inflated," Tariro laughed. "It looks like they're more patch than tube."

"Can't see how we are going to stay dry on them anyway with the holes in the middle," Ethan said. Not that it mattered. If they did end up going down the river, it wouldn't be cold enough to care if they got wet or not – although he would rather not touch the water at all.

Soon, to Ethan's relief, Jimoh came over, bringing grown-ups with him.

"Greetings, I am father of Jimoh," said a kindly looking man in the same stilted English as his son. Ethan was reassured to see he looked official in a faded, but neatly ironed ranger's suit. Unfortunately, he carried a rusty iron plough disk, which meant he agreed with the concept of attempting a scry. Surprised at the man's apparent gullibility, Ethan leaped forward anyway, to help him place it on the ground.

The man smiled his thanks, holding his hat against his chest while he went through the tribal handshake with Tariro and then a straightforward handshake with Ethan. It was a fancy Australian outback-style felt hat with a leopard skin band. Ethan wondered how friendly the leopard was going to be when he saw that.

"This is grandfather of Jimoh," Jimoh's dad introduced another, much older man, whose eyes crinkled up with mischief as he shook hands. He wore much-mended khaki trousers and a smart, green shirt with the sleeves rolled up. Ethan couldn't help staring at his sandals. They were made entirely out of what looked like car tyres. Jimoh's grandfather said something in Shona that sounded as if he was glad Ethan admired his sandals. He mopped his brow with a bright green and yellow floppy cloth hat with "Tobacco Sales" printed on the side and settled it back on his shock of curly white hair.

"Please tell me we are not going to go with those crocodiles into the wilderness," Ethan blurted out to the two men, anxiously hopping from one foot to the other. "Please tell me you know how to find Joe."

Jimoh's dad gripped Ethan's shoulder and gazed into his face earnestly. "Ah, Ethan, we talk with witch. She is right. You will have to trust crocs to take you to find Joe."

Feeling his last hope of common sense slipping away, Ethan stammered, "Wh-what about my uncle? Surely we must fetch him, or the authorities."

"Ethan, Alan is very far on other side of farm with safari client," Jimoh's dad said. "It will take long time to fetch him. Then he will call police." His fingers worried at the brim of his hat. "Then police will waste many days walking through the bushes. They will not find Joe there. Those from city will not believe story for crocs or witch. Maybe they arrest her. She has no identity card. If they take her away, she cannot help us find Joe."

"What about my aunt?" Ethan said, almost bursting into tears.

"She must stay with girls. This job for men. Now come, we make raft." He turned and strode purposefully towards the pool, jamming the hat back on his head as he went, allowing no further argument.

Jimoh's grandpa instructed Tariro to lift the disk and before Ethan had time to argue with them, the two of them went off in the direction of the witch. He could not win. One way or another, he was going to end up going down the river.

Jimoh and his dad wrapped lengths of hessian around the inflated tubes, and sewed the fabric on, using a tobacco-baling needle. When they were done, they had produced very acceptable rafts for the trip. The kraal boys kept up a steady stream of begging and cajoling at Jimoh's dad in Shona.

"What are they saying?" Ethan asked Jimoh.

"They want to come with on adventure, but my dad says same as witch. It is too much work for crocs. It can only be you and Tariro and me. And that leopard who is for some reason liking you."

"The leopard?" Ethan said, taken aback. Somehow he had got the feeling the leopard and the witch were inseparable and there was no way the witch was going to attempt the river. He knew he'd feel safer if it did come with them. What was it about the leopard? As menacing as the creature was, he felt strangely drawn towards it. From time to time, he caught himself scanning the Crystal Pools area for the cat, and every time he found it, he caught it staring at him, with a sort of . . . expression.

"Well, as long as no one expects me to touch the animal," he shuddered. Although, he might, just once, to see if he could.

"Also, there is place, on journey, where these small boys will not be able to hold breath for long enough," Jimoh went on. He did not seem in the least bit shocked that the other boys wanted to go on the adventure, or worried about his own safety. Ethan felt as if he was the only one who had any sense of the danger at all.

A single drum began to beat a tattoo that sounded almost like Morse code, and Ethan could hear an answering drum in the distance.

"Is signal to come off fields now, and message to tell about witch and about duiker," Jimoh said. As people arrived, another drummer and another joined the first drummer, until eventually the drumming changed from a message to the regular rhythm of a tune.

A group of mothers wove their way up from the kraal, balancing groceries and utensils on their heads. Ethan marvelled at the front two, each of whom carried a heavy cast-iron cauldron with only a rolled up scrap of fabric and their own curly hair to cushion their heads.

The women laughed together and greeted their children, then noisily set about preparing a meal. Maize meal was poured into boiling water in one enormous cauldron and churned into a very stiff porridge. Onions and a spinach-like vegetable called rape bubbled away in the other. When the roasted duiker was ready, a grizzled old lady took charge of plopping down spoonfuls of porridge onto tin or plastic plates with a shaking hand. Small girls distributed these amongst the community, starting with Gogo Maya the witch, whose fear of grown-ups had evaporated at the friendliness of the villagers – or everyone's willingness to believe her story. It looked to Ethan as if she was the guest of honor, holding court from an old fold-up chair someone had fetched her from the kraal. She grinned happily, enjoying the fuss, and a large tin of the pungent local beer, which had bits floating in it. Ethan had literally gasped at the smell of it when Tafadzwa took it to the old woman.

Hunkering down on his haunches beside the fire with the rest of the boys, Ethan felt at a bit of a loss. He was so worried about Joe, he was not sure if he could eat; besides, there were no knives and forks. He was going to have to dip his fingers into the same bowl as everyone else. The thought made him nauseous.

"Like this," Jimoh said, squeezing into the circle beside him. He broke off a bite-sized piece of stiff porridge and rolled it into a ball, pressing a hollow in to it with his thumb. He dunked the ball into the communal gravy, filling up the hollow, and popped it into his mouth, then turned grinning to Ethan, whose stomach growled loudly. Without thinking too hard about it, Ethan did the same, sending the kraal kids into fits of applause and hilarity.

After eating, everyone shared in the work of cleaning up. Even the littlest, who could barely walk, took their plate to the water's edge beyond the pool and rubbed it clean with sand, then rinsed it and returned it to a plastic basin. A murmur of excitement ran around the camp as young and old gathered around the witch for the entertainment. Most of them had heard of scrying but no one had ever seen it done before. Mothers sat on the floor with their legs straight out in front of them, their small children clambering onto their laps, making themselves comfortable. Despite their skepticism, several men sat around on low stools, or upturned paraffin drums, enjoying beer out of mugs made from used baked bean tins with wire tied onto the sides for handles. Ethan, Jimoh and Tariro sat cross-legged right in the front, near the witch, and waited.

CHAPTER 9
SMOKE AND MIRRORS

The witch stood up and stretched, sending armfuls of ivory and seed-pod bangles jingling down her upraised arms to pool at her elbows. Ethan was sure she only did it for dramatic effect. Her creamy white dreadlocks hung in fat sausages down to her waist as she turned her face to the stars.

What she wore did not look in the least bit African to him, or witchy, for that matter. It looked more like plain black pyjamas – loose-fitting trousers with a tunic. Her tattered skirt lay drying over a nearby bush. It seemed the only purpose of the skirt was to hold the scores of pockets sewn onto the inside of it. After a good long stretch that focused everyone's attention, she fished the skirt off the bush, but instead of putting it back around her waist, she lay it out like a picnic blanket beside the sunken plough disk, and rooted around in the pockets till she came up with a pouch of tobacco and a small pipe.

"The tobacco smoke attracts the spirits to the material world," she explained to the assembled crowd. Someone handed her a burning stick from the nearby fire and she lit her pipe. Soon its rich aroma wafted into the night air. After settling herself cross-legged on her skirt and taking a couple of puffs, she blew gently on the stick to coax a flame and carefully lit the fourteen citronella candles which Joe's mother had packed in his camping gear to use as a mosquito repellent. Two for each night they were supposed to be camping. As each candle ignited, the witch planted it in a circle in the sand around the disk. The acrid smell of insecticide wafted up to mingle with the rich smell of the tobacco.

The disk, sunk to its brim in the sand, looked like a perfectly spherical puddle. They all gazed at it with bated breath as candlelight flickered and oscillated, casting a strange glimmer over the surface of the water in the dark night. Ethan wondered if the candles were cheap and faulty, or if the witch was making them burn so strangely.

The clearing grew eerily quiet, the only sounds the soft tinkling of the rapids beyond the pool and a single drum beating a slow rhythm in the background.

The witch seemed to be in no hurry as she brought her tin mug up to her mouth and took a swig. A small rivulet of beer ran down her chin. She lowered her mug, wiped her mouth with the back of a wrinkled hand and said, "I'm so sorry about all this . . ."

"Where is our boy?" interrupted a fierce-looking man Ethan had not noticed before, his patience with the slow ritual wearing thin. Eyes gleaming in the firelight, he stood at the back, leaning on a long pole, its one end sharpened into a stake. Jimoh's father glowered at the man.

The witch paused, her pipe halfway to her lips. "We had no choice in the matter. It was a life or death situation," she said indignantly.

Uncoiling himself from his warm place by the fire, the leopard padded softly over to the witch, butted his head against her hand, and then sat beside her, radiating disapproval.

The angry man was not intimidated by this display, but the other villagers shuffled back a little and watched the cat warily. Ethan felt a knot of tension grow in his stomach. Most of the villagers had relaxed around the cat once they realised it was her pet, but the animal still gave him a creepy feeling.

The witch relaxed her hand on the leopard's back and his expression softened a little. "Your boy has been pulled into Karibu, where I come from," she explained. "We were captured and feared for our lives, so we had to make a switch. Unfortunately, I believe, when we jumped into your world, your boy jumped into our world."

An angry murmur rose from some of the men as this was translated to them, and they realised that the witch herself might have somehow caused Joe to disappear. The leopard bristled with menace, but Ethan seemed to be the only one aware of it.

"Do not worry," the witch said quickly. "The boy will be quite safe. The ones who captured me have no fight with boys, only witches."

"What if they think Joe is a witch who has changed herself into a boy?" one of the mothers said, pushing her bottom lip out in an angry pout. Ethan was shocked at how easily the villagers seemed prepared to believe that Joe had traded places with the witch. Then again, he had bought her story too . . .

"Witches in Karibu cannot change shape," the witch reassured the woman.

"It was bloody irresponsible of you to take the risk," the angry man sneered at her.

"I was drawn here by those crocodiles," she snapped back at him, jabbing her pipe pointedly in the direction of Jimoh's grandpa. To Ethan's astonishment, the two crocodiles lounged like dark shadows in the firelight beside the old man, almost part of the circle of people. No one seemed to be afraid of them. Grandpa smiled at Ethan when he caught his eye.

"Then is prophecy," nodded one of the mothers with satisfaction.

"Yes. Yes. Is prophecy," the villagers murmured, poking each other on the shoulder or rocking back and forth in excited agreement.

The angry man glared around him as if he could not believe such stupidity.

Ignoring him, the witch cocked her head inquiringly at the mother, who in turn gestured towards the old man. Jimoh's grandpa patted the crocodiles on their brow ridges and came forward carrying his upturned paint tin seat, which he set by the fire opposite the witch. Ethan hoped it had been cleaned properly. It would only take one spark to set any paint residue off and blow the man up like a firework. Grandpa sat down and cast a twinkling eye over the group. After a long pause which Ethan guessed was to ensure the audience were on the edge of their seats with anticipation, he cleared his throat and told the tale of the crocodiles. Tariro translated for Ethan and the witch and, although he didn't know it, for the leopard too.

"When the first white man passed through the valley he shot and wounded a crocodile by this very pool," Grandpa said. "As was often the way of white hunters in those days, he left it there to die and went about his killing ways further along the valley. Some children found the crocodile the next day and fetched their grandfather who was a powerful sangoma." A sangoma was a witch-doctor, Tariro explained to the witch.

Grandpa paused for dramatic effect. "The sangoma patched it up and stayed with it for five days and six nights, never resting himself until the crocodile was well enough to survive on its own. By and by it swam away down river." He gazed wistfully in the direction of the rapids. The villagers gazed wistfully too, and murmured agreement, as if they had heard the story before. All except the angry man who shook his head as if he had never heard such nonsense.

The old man lowered his voice. "Nobody knew what had passed between the sangoma and the crocodile during his long vigil, but sometime later, two very large crocodiles moved to the rapids below the crystal pool, and the sangoma said they had come to repay their debt. A prophecy grew up around this tale, that the crocodiles would stay here, keeping the people of Tjalotjo kraal safe until they were able to take their revenge for the shooting." He let this idea sink in and then went on.

"At first the people at the kraal were afraid of them, but as time passed they came to enjoy a feeling of safety around the crocodiles, and an odd feeling of happiness and good health whenever they spent time swimming in the pool. The descendants of the old sangoma had a special relationship with the crocodiles and some of them were even able to communicate with them." The villagers nodded in agreement. After all, they were the very people he spoke of, and they all knew someone who knew a person who claimed to be able to talk to the crocodiles.

"About a hundred years ago," Grandpa went on after the babble of voices had died down, "a white family moved onto the land west of the valley. When they started to camp on the other side of the pools, the villagers waited for the crocodiles to take revenge for the shooting. As they got to know them better, the Tjalotjo villagers even warned the white family of the prophecy, but they persisted in camping and swimming there. Rather than wreak vengeance upon them, the crocs seemed to include the white family under their protection." The crowd shook their heads and tsk-tsked. Ethan couldn't tell if this was at the stubbornness of the white family or the failure of the crocodiles to wreak vengeance.

"From time to time sangoma come from far away and take water from the pool," Grandpa informed the witch. "We know it is because of the crocodiles."

"Yes," agreed the villagers. "We know it is the crocs."

"Will they go away now that they have fulfilled the prophecy and taken Joe?" a young man asked the witch.

"No. They did not take Joe, and my leopard would know if they were planning to wreck vengeance on anyone," the witch said firmly.

"Lucky for you," Tariro said, poking Ethan in the ribs.

"No, boy," the witch said. "Crocodiles don't notice the colour differences in humans, much like we can't tell one zebra from another."

The leopard sat up and stared intently at the crocodiles, giving off a low throbbing purr that made Ethan's scalp prickle. Then, just as suddenly, the tension in the air dissipated and the leopard stretched out once more beside Jimoh. "They have smell memories of the blood of the sangoma's descendants, and bring magic from Karibu to protect them," he told the witch, with a meaningful look at Jimoh.

Ethan looked around in astonishment to see if anyone else had noticed the leopard communicate with the crocodiles, and then shook his head. He was having enough trouble getting his mind around prophecies and switching witches without having to think about crocodiles with magic. And what was that meaningful look? Was Jimoh a descendent or was the cat amused that Jimoh stroked him?

"Can we get on with the scry thing?" Ethan said to the witch. If there was a chance that he could see where Joe was, however slim, he was anxious to find out. "Joe may be in danger if the people who were after you have him instead."

The witch fished out a pendant from between her breasts where it hung on a leather thong. Light from the glowing red crystal slowly died away as she placed it in the plough disk. Taking a flat oval piece of wood from a skirt pocket she placed it beside the plough disk. Another pocket held a small leather pouch and a tiny glass vial containing a transparent liquid. She shook a pile of dark grey crystals out of the pouch onto the wood and made a well in the middle of them.

When everyone was quiet and she had their full attention, she hovered the vial theatrically over the crystals – making sure to jingle her bracelets, Ethan noted with a smirk – before pouring the contents into the tiny volcano. The small explosion gave off a whiff of burning metal, like the smell of welding, which floated through the air to compete with the scents of the citronella candles and pipe tobacco. A wisp of purple smoke curled up eerily, then dissipated in the dark.

The villagers expelled a collective breath.

"It's just iodine and turpentine!" Ethan's disappointed mutter was cut short by a glare from the witch. He was beginning to make sense of the angry man's skepticism. If it weren't for the creepy way he could understand the leopard, Ethan would also have suspected the whole thing was just a series of tricks.

While the purple smoke distracted them all, the witch pricked her finger and allowed a drop of blood to fall in the plough disk. "I need five people who know the boy well to come and put their hands into the water," she said.

Ethan, Tariro and Jimoh crept forward and gingerly put their hands in the water. It felt warm and oily. Ethan hoped the witch's blood did not carry hepatitis or anything worse. It would be a pity if he were completely free of asthma, only to fall prey to some blood-born disease. He wondered if his body would really repair itself as she'd said, then smiled at his own gullibility. Of course his body would heal itself – that's what immunity was all about. The crocodile must have got a light grip on him coming out of the pool, that's all.

"Not right in like that," directed the witch. "Just the tips of the fingers on the edge of the disk."

Jimoh's dad leaned forward and added his hand as instructed. The angry man pushed his way forwards and grudgingly added his hand. "I do this against my better judgement," he said under his breath. "We should be calling the police."

"Now close your eyes and concentrate hard on the boy, Joe," the witch said.

She hummed in a deep bass voice while the leopard made a rumbling sound beside her. For a long time nothing happened. Then one of the women screamed and Ethan's eyes shot open. It was not quite like television, but there was a clear, slightly rippled, vision on the water surface, of a blonde boy walking out of the ocean, holding a surfboard.

"He's at the sea?" Ethan gasped, splashing water all over the place. He'd thought Karibu was just over the immediate mountain range. The nearest ocean was over a thousand kilometers away. The image disappeared as suddenly as it had appeared. The witch glared at the angry man but it was Tariro who looked embarrassed.

"Sorry, wrong boy," Tariro mumbled and then, in reply to Ethan's snarl, "What! I didn't think it was actually going to work, so I wondered what Darryl was up to . . . from school."

Some of the villagers hadn't believed it was going to happen either, Ethan noticed. They scrambled up and moved away, clicking anxiously, no longer wanting to take part in this sinister thing. Others moved forward curiously. The angry man's composure vanished, to be replaced by a slightly wild-eyed look, but he added his hand to the disk with the other four and the witch resumed her humming. Ethan squeezed his eyes shut, thinking about Joe with all his might. He willed the disk to reveal to them where Joe was.

Jimoh nudged him softly and he peered through his eyelashes. A wavy image passed over the water in the disk and settled there. The witch exhaled sharply.

"Karibu is somewhere in India?" Ethan whispered, not wanting to disturb the image a second time. India was even further away than the ocean. The boy he saw was Joe. Still in his electric blue board-shorts, short blonde hair and his bare, peeling shoulders, only he lay fast asleep in a forest, cuddled up against a tiger.

"No, he is close by," the witch said, "and he will be safe with Hajiri, but not for long. Hajiri is a kindly tiger but he is the pet of the Almohad and inevitably he will lead the boy there." Then she muttered under her breath, "Drat! This is going to get complicated."

The Almohad enslave their captives!

Ethan intercepted the warning between the leopard and the witch. Neither of them said it out loud, or even thought it. The information was just there without having to think. Like how to make your lungs inhale, or your heart pump. He wondered if they were aware he had received it. More importantly, though, he wondered if these Almohad would enslave Joe.

Peering more closely at the dish to see if Joe was tied up, Ethan caught a glimpse of dark shadows moving stealthily in the jungle behind where the tiger slept, and for a split second another image of Joe flashed into his mind. There was blood on his face! But when Ethan peered closely at his cousin it was as if he had imagined it. Joe looked perfectly peaceful sleeping against the tiger.

Glancing from Jimoh to Tariro, Ethan wondered if they had seen the blood too. Tariro shook his head and rubbed his eyes as if he could not believe them. Jimoh shook his hand in the water, trying to bring the image back, but the witch had lost focus. From the expressions on their faces, Ethan was sure none of them had seen it. A cold shiver ran through his body. Had he imagined the blood on Joe because he was spooked by the shadows? Was the tiger as safe as the witch said it was?

Suddenly he noticed the leopard, Salih, staring at him. "It is what may be," purred the cat. "Gogo has been working on her powers of seeing into the future, but so far she has proved to be terrible at it. Sometimes she flashes. It's probably inaccurate."

The witch would not allow the villagers to stay and watch her switch back to Karibu at midnight. It would be upsetting for the little ones and too many witnesses would put her off her stride, she'd said firmly.

But she had not been as firm with the camping boys. Tafadzwa, Simba, Tendayi, Tekeramayi, and many whose names

Ethan did not remember, all stood around her in bright-eyed anticipation. Giving her leopard one last hug before pushing him away, she clutched the opal, screwed up her eyes and muttered something that sounded like a curse.

There was a soft whump, and for a moment she appeared less solid in the firelight, but no matter how fiercely she contorted her face, the amulet failed to move her. She smacked her lips as if she had tasted something nasty. Ethan could taste a faint hint of tin in his own mouth, and from their disgusted expressions, it looked as if the other boys did too.

"Well, that's disturbing," Salih said.

"No energy. You've drained the lot!" the witch grumbled, glaring at the opal in her outstretched palm.

Even some of the assembled campers let out a groan and looked accusingly at Ethan for spoiling the trick. It was a huge responsibility being the one with magic, Ethan thought bitterly. He wondered if any of them would like to trade places.

"Could the opal take the power back if I hold it again?" he offered, eyeing it nervously as it fizzled and cracked like a wet firework in Gogo Maya's hand. He was loath to touch it in case it burned him, but he hoped it would take back its power. He wondered why they hadn't thought of doing that before. It wasn't his fault he'd touched it, and he wanted nothing to do with its power. At least that was what his head told him. His hand felt strangely drawn towards it.

"Don't be silly," Gogo Maya huffed, "that would be like trying to herd hornets back into their nest. If you touch it again, anything could happen."

But when Salih cocked an eyebrow at her, she gave a long-suffering sigh and handed it over to Ethan.

As soon as it touched his palm, the fizzing stopped and its glow oscillated gently.

"Oh, close your hand, you stupid boy!" Gogo Maya snapped.

As he did so, Ethan felt a wave of cool calmness pass over him, beyond anything he'd ever felt before. It only lasted an instant, and when he opened his hand to look at the opal, it lay dead and cold in his palm. "Oh no . . ." he said. "I've made it worse!"

Unexpectedly, a gleeful smile spread over the witch's face, and she stretched out her hand for the amulet. Then she hugged her skirt around herself tightly, screwed her eyes shut in concentration, muttered a curse, and disappeared with a thunderous thwack, leaving a slight vacuum in the air as she went.

"It probably just needed a kick start," said Tariro, who was the first to get his breath back. "You know, like loosening a jam jar." Immediately he laid claim to the witch's abandoned cat, putting an arm around Salih's neck and knuckling him on the forehead. "Don't worry, Puss," he said in the patronizing tone used to pet a dog. "We'll look after you."

The leopard looked like he bore the indignity bravely, but Ethan's skin crawled. He wasn't sure why, but his hands twitched with the effort of not pulling Tariro off it. Strangely, it didn't seem to have anything to do with vermin, or anxiety over Tariro getting his hands dirty. He just didn't want the boy touching the cat.

They hovered in the clearing beside the Crystal Pool for a while, in case the witch had been able to switch with Joe. It crossed Ethan's mind that if Joe did reappear, it would spoil the adventure. *No!* He shook his head. Why on earth had he thought that? He did not want an adventure. He wanted his cousin back.

Moments later, a large, motley collection of skin and bones exploded out of the darkness, yelped, rolled over and over, ricocheted off the riverbank and came to a halt before the campfire, looking slightly dazed. It stank of swamp.

"Who are you?" it said indistinctly, staggering towards the boys as they scrambled backwards to get away from it, nocking slingshots and raising machetes as they went. Ethan scanned their faces to see if anyone had heard it speak. No. Of course they hadn't. It hadn't actually spoken. Just a knowing, similar to the cool wave Salih sent through his head, but harsher, and warmer. It felt almost like a hot flush of embarrassment. His hand flew to his cheek. It even felt hot.

"Be careful what you wish for, boy," the leopard said to Ethan in a smooth, wry tone before disentangling himself from Tariro, suddenly all sleek power. "Welcome," he said to the hyena. "Do not be afraid. You appear to have been summoned to this place in error, but we will soon have you home again. Can you swim?"

"I'm Kishi," it said, sticking its chin out in a determined way. "Kishi are never afraid." Then its brain caught up with its mouth. "What do you mean 'swim'?"

"Yes, we are going to swim down this river, back to Karibu with these boys," Salih said to it, brooking no nonsense. "It is all arranged." And with that, he stalked off into the bush.

Ethan directed a sour look at the cat. Distracted by the arrival of the hyena, he had not understood what Salih meant till he remembered his errant thought about Joe not switching with the witch. The Leopard had plucked that thought right out of his head! It made him feel horrible. He hadn't really wished Joe would not switch back. He hoped his thought had not affected the outcome of the switch, like a wish or something.

He wondered if he should warn the others that the leopard could read their minds. At the very least, he would have to watch his own thoughts around the animal. Now Ethan wasn't even sure if the cat had actually seen the image of Joe beaten up in the scry earlier, or if it had read that out of his imagination.

Realizing that everyone was waiting on him for an explanation, Ethan sighed. "Another pet, according to the leopard," he said. "He'll be coming with." He gave the hyena a long despairing look. It had been a nonsensical day – what was one more talking animal.

One by one the boys relaxed the slingshots and machetes they had trained on the animal, and drifted off to bed behind him.

At first, the hyena hung about the camp, his head turning

from side to side as if looking for answers, while everyone else crammed themselves under the mosquito nets for the night. Then he went prowling up and down the riverbank, alternately exploring, and muttering "swim!" indignantly under his breath.

Ethan settled down in his sleeping bag, wondering what a Kishi was. He sensed the hyena brightening considerably as it stumbled upon the remains of the duiker they had eaten for supper.

Oh no! I can feel it, even when it isn't trying to speak. As he fell asleep, he wondered if that was going to be a good thing or a pain in the neck.

CHAPTER 10
A TURBULENT BEGINNING

When Ethan awoke dark shapes moved in the predawn light by the pool. Jimoh was busy packing things onto the inner-tube floats he had helped his dad make the day before.

"Only light things," he said softly, scratching the hyena behind the ear. It nipped gently at his hand. Ethan wondered if Jimoh was also able to hear the creature talk, or if he just had a way with animals.

The leopard, who had crept in sometime during the night to lie too close to Ethan, shot up at the disturbance, and swept past him into the bushes without a word.

Ethan switched on his headlamp and quickly scanned his body to see if the leopard had passed him any fleas. After rummaging in his backpack for a small trowel and a length of toilet paper, he carefully made his way into the bushes to dig a hole, ever watchful for snakes. He wished he knew what it was, exactly, he had done to the opal the night before, and why he'd had such an irresistible urge to hold the amulet. For that matter, why did he feel so out of sorts with Tariro when he went to pet the leopard? It was not as if he wanted to touch the animal himself. Or did he?

SWITCH!

By the time he got back, the boys were up and dismantling the shelter.

Tafadzwa tapped him on the shoulder and stood there beaming, holding out his precious slingshot for Ethan to take. It was beautifully engraved with a double-headed hornbill, its body along the shaft, and one scimitar beak pointing up each of the slingshot's forks.

"He wants you to have it for luck on your journey," Tendayi interpreted. Ethan shifted his weight from one foot to the other, swallowing a lump in his throat. It must have taken Tafadzwa days to carve the thing.

"Please tell Tafadzwa I am honoured to have his slingshot, but I'll only be borrowing it, and I'll take good care of it. When I get back I'll return it to him." There was an awkward silence. Did the boys think he wouldn't be coming back? On impulse, he unpacked his laptop and held it out to Tafadzwa. "Please will you look after this for me?" he asked. Then, turning towards Tendayi, he said, "Do you know how it works?"

"Yes, we have them in school." Tendayi turned his attention to the computer. "Not as fancy as this, but I know how it works."

"Does Tafadzwa know?"

"No," Tendayi said. "They don't have computers at the kraal school – no electricity."

"If you can find a power source, do you think you could teach Tafadzwa? Even if it's just how to play the games. There are some great movies on there too, if he wants to show the little kids."

Two large tractor tubes floated on the water nearby. Little boys tested them for comfort and springiness with the help of the hyena, who had obviously overcome his apprehension for swimming. He wriggled about on his back on the hessian hammock in the middle of a tube, his paws in the air, laughing maniacally, while the boys jumped up and down on the edges of the tube trying to dislodge him. Every now and again they would bounce in just the right place and the hyena would go flying through the air to land with a terrific splash. Then the game would start all over again. No one seemed to care that their playmate was a wild animal, or that their trampoline was tethered to the supply tubes that were spinning and bobbing around wildly, threatening to capsize and drench the equipment which had been tied onto them.

The crocodiles lounged passively beside the pool. Not that Ethan could read their faces, but they didn't look as if they were going to bite anyone. They seemed to wait patiently while Jimoh's dad attached rope harnesses to them and linked them up, first with the supply tubes, then the transport tubes, and then a few tubes with nothing on them. Ethan could not get used to the idea that the crocodiles were behaving as docile as horses, and that they were actually going to drag him and the boys down the river. He wondered if he would be able to understand them as he had the hyena the night before. Concentrating hard on the one's face, he tried to imagine what it was thinking, but he got no response. That meant the only way anyone could communicate with the creatures was if they went through Salih. Worse still, Ethan scowled, the only way anyone else could communicate with Salih appeared to be through him. Why him?

Even though it was still dark, Jimoh's father wore his outback hat. After hugging his son, he shook Tariro and Ethan by the hand and solemnly transferred the hat to Ethan's head. "You are very pale, Ethan," he said. "You will need protection from the sun."

"Thank you," Ethan said, fidgeting the hat a little forwards on his head. He found himself swallowing the lump in his throat for the second time that day. Trying to compose himself, he turned quickly and scrambled onto the tube between Tariro and Jimoh. Tariro hesitated only slightly before he made space for Ethan, then he changed his mind.

"You got the hat, I have dibs on the middle," he said, clambering over Ethan and planting his buttocks firmly in the centre of the tube. As the sun rose over the treetops, one powerful crocodile towed Salih and the hyena through a gap in the rapids and lead the flotilla downstream.

"Do you think they could go faster? Like skiing?" Tariro said, eyeing the two crocodiles that pulled them downstream. Amun and Darwishi, Salih had called them. Ethan was not that worried that he'd been unable to convince Tariro of his ability to communicate with the crocodiles via Salih, but it was a bit disconcerting that Tariro chose to see them as pack animals. He had cut himself a switch from a low-hanging branch to chivvy them along.

"I wouldn't push your luck," Ethan said. "Unless you want to lose an arm." They had drifted peacefully behind the crocodiles so far. The river, about twenty-paces wide in places, was calm, deep green and shadowy, fringed by dense forest.

Jimoh sat on the tube propped up by Ethan's backpack, pointing out wildlife as they went. "There," he said, just before a plum-coloured starling took flight, its feathers shimmering with iridescent purple where they caught the sunlight.

"Shoo!" Tariro yelled, a moment later, firing a pebble from his slingshot at an ungainly ground hornbill as it strutted along the riverbank. It was ugly, black with vivid red patches of bare skin on its face and throat. He missed it, but the bird lumbered into the air, showing off a surprisingly large expanse of wings.

"Leave bird alone," Jimoh said, giving him a black look.

"Why? It's so ugly," Tariro said. He settled back comfortably on the tube. "If I wasn't so worried about Joe, I could grow to like this lifestyle."

Both Jimoh and Ethan gave Tariro a skeptical look. "You probably wouldn't last a day without the crocodiles," Ethan said.

"Shh," Jimoh whispered, nudging both boys on the shoulder and pointing a little upstream. A python swam along the shoreline. They watched as it slithered into the lower branches of a tree, revealing a long length of strikingly patterned coils. It hid there among the leaves, so perfectly camouflaged that they would never have spotted it if they had not seen it swimming. Ethan shuddered. It was so huge, one of the boys themselves could have been a tasty snack for the creature if they had drifted below it.

Salih and the hyena kept up a heated exchange on the other tube. Ethan grew used to the feeling of the warm and cool waves of their conversation whenever they drifted close enough.

Tariro pointed out a mother warthog, with four ugly piglets, wallowing in the mud on the narrow strip of riverbank. "They're so hideous they're cute," he laughed, then loosed off another pebble from his slingshot. Their little tails stuck straight up in the air like antenna as they ran, panic stricken, for the cover of a nearby burrow. Ethan looked at Jimoh to see if he would tell Tariro to stop that.

Instead, Jimoh shrugged. "Also good for eating, if you can hit them."

Gradually the cliffs grew closer together until they found themselves floating through a narrow gorge. The water, which had seemed calm enough before, suddenly felt deeper and swifter as it pushed its way past large, smooth rocks. Ethan sat up in the tube, cocking his head towards the sound of turbulence downstream.

Rounding a bend in the river they came upon a powerful-looking vortex, beyond which the river seemed to vanish around the flank of a cliff, thundering off into the unseen distance.

The crocodiles towed the boys, Salih and the hyena into an eddy beside the cliff, to one side of the vortex, and deposited them on a narrow rock ledge.

Amun produced a low gravelly sound from his throat that was just as disconcerting as the leopard's own resounding purr, and the leopard cocked his head to one side to listen. He looked puzzled for a moment, and then rose up and padded over to the crocodile, where he looked into its eyes and listened intently while it continued to growl in a slightly higher pitch.

"Um. The leopard is finding out from the crocodile what's the safest way to pass," Ethan told the others. Jimoh's eyes widened, obviously still in awe at the idea that Ethan could communicate with the leopard, but Tariro wasn't having any of it.

"Don't be stupid, Ethan, we are just stopping for a break before going round the mountain," he said. "If these animals could talk to someone, why the hell would they choose you?"

"Suit yourself," Ethan said, turning his attention to Amun, who rested his jaw on the ledge, waiting expectantly for the leopard to convey his message.

"He says that the water over there will suck you down under," Salih said, eyeing the sinister-looking vortex whirling menacingly below the sheer cliffs. Ethan saw how you could get caught in it, and go round and round until you drowned. No wonder no one passed this way.

"Well, I could have told you that!" Tariro sneered, when Ethan interpreted.

Salih ignored him. "Then the river squeezes through a narrow gap between the cliffs and runs swiftly over the rocks to a pool below," he continued. "You cannot see the fall until you get around the corner, by which time it's too late; the current will force you over. The crocodiles will lift two of you on their backs through the vortex to look so that you can make your own judgment about how to proceed."

"How do we know the crocs won't just take two of us down the river and eat us?" Tariro said once Ethan had told him.

"There's no other way, Tariro. We cannot climb walls of cliff here to go round and if we go home this will not help Joe," Jimoh said. "If leopard for Ethan says we do this thing then we do. Ethan trusts leopard."

"Ethan, I swear, if you are making this all up so that you can be in charge, I am going to smack you," Tariro grumbled, but given the choice between riding on the back of the crocodile and waiting, he agreed to wait on the ledge. He sat beside the hyena and scratched its back nervously, working his way up its scraggy coat towards its ears while the hyena wiggled and giggled.

Ethan wasn't sure if he actually sensed the hyena's pleasure or if it was just obvious from its giggling. Either way, he wished Tariro wouldn't touch the animal; there was always the chance he might touch Ethan – or worse still, something that Ethan had to eat – without first washing his hands.

Jimoh did not look afraid to go into the vortex. He untied the floating tubes from the crocodiles, securing them to a low hanging branch, and climbed onto the back of Amun. Keeping a strong grip on the harness with one hand, he forced his hat down tighter onto his head with the other like a cowboy, and they pushed off from the ledge.

Ethan had never been this close to a crocodile apart from the biting incident. As gnarly as the creature was, it had beautiful eyes. They were a mottled mossy green, like a shady pool, with a vertical black slit. He could have sworn they crinkled into a smile as he approached Darwishi, but he couldn't help suppressing a shiver when he thought how close he had come to poking Darwishi's eyes out when he went for the amulet. The crocodiles would not have been quite so keen to help if he had succeeded. He hoped Darwishi was not just biding his time till he got him on his own before paying him back. Shifting his weight gingerly onto the animal's back, he clung on to the rope harness. The crocodile was not as bumpy as he had expected, and not slimy at all.

Darwishi struggled against the current as he swam into the vortex. At first the water tore at Ethan's legs, threatening to wash him off the crocodile, but he gripped the rope harness more tightly with his hands and flattened himself along Darwishi's back the way he had seen Jimoh do it, hooking his feet up as far out of the water as he could.

They reached a spot on the edge of the vortex, from where they had a good view of the way ahead, just in time to see Jimoh fumble for a better footing, then wash off the back of Amun and go hurtling down the rapids, Amun following close behind.

Ethan gripped Darwishi more tightly, holding his breath as he waited helplessly for the boy to surface. Eventually he caught a glimpse of Jimoh's red shirt tumbling down the rapids at a terrifying speed, his beloved hat flying off his head as he swept through a narrow gap between two rocks and came to rest about halfway down the rapids.

Ethan's sigh of relief was short lived. The water where Jimoh came to a standstill flowed over a submerged rock, endlessly tumbling back upon itself, trapping Jimoh in its grasp. Flashes of red shirt and an occasional arm waved above the foam. Searching desperately for Amun, Ethan found him, about ten meters upstream from Jimoh, but he was just as caught up as the boy, tumbling over and over as he struggled to unhitch a piece of his rope harness caught between two rocks.

Ethan was going to have to go down by himself and help Jimoh. He could not go down on Darwishi because the rest of them needed the crocodile to drag them beyond the vortex to the top of the rapids.

As Ethan was about to slide off Darwishi, Amun broke free at last and caught up with Jimoh, nudging him towards an eddy, where the boy was able to drag himself up onto Amun's back. Ethan was not sure if Jimoh was injured or just exhausted but he slumped, unmoving, across the back of Amun for the rest of the trip down.

Ethan's hands shook by the time he got back to the ledge. He was not entirely sure what to do. "The rapids are extremely dangerous and now we are down to one crocodile, and separated from Jimoh so there is no going back," he told Tariro. "Jimoh must be injured or the crocodile would surely have left him below and come back for us."

"How hard can it be?" Tariro said with the benefit of not knowing what they were in for. "We should be fine as long as we keep our feet out in front of us and fin our hands out by the side of our hips to push off from the rocks. We did this at Outward Bound Leadership Camp at school," he told Ethan pointedly.

Ethan fixed him with a baleful look and described how fast the descent was, and how Jimoh had gotten stuck in the hydraulic. "I think you and I will be able to stick to the plan and ride the rapids using the spare tubes," he said, "but the animals will not be able to hold on to a tube. They will each need help from a crocodile. One crocodile will have to make two trips–"

"The hyena will have to change," Salih interrupted. He stalked up to the hyena and stood before him expectantly, a dangerous glint in his sparkling yellow eyes.

The hyena looked up from his grooming, which consisted of sitting on his lower back with one leg pointing in the air and licking his genitals. "Errr. Don't tell them. It's a secret," he said.

"We will leave you here, in this world," Salih retaliated. He looked as if he would do it too. Ethan interpreted for Tariro, who forgot, in his shock, that he didn't believe Ethan was able to understand the conversation between the two animals.

"What the hell is he going to change into? Hyenas don't wear clothes," he said, before his eyes opened wide in disbelief. "Ethan, you are shitting me! He is not going to change into another thing!" He stared at the hyena, and moved a couple of steps closer to Ethan.

The hyena writhed in embarrassment. "Okay, I will do it, but you are not allowed to look," he grumbled.

Ethan agreed and the boys turned their backs, but Tariro peeped out of the corner of his eye. "Bloody hell!" he shrieked at the sound of a wet plop. He grabbed Ethan by the arm.

Ethan was too flabbergasted himself to do much more than stare. A young man stood where the hyena had stood. He looked a little older than the boys. In sharp contrast to the ugliness of the hyena, he was almost impossibly handsome: all sleek gymnast's muscles and pecan-nut brown skin, with perfectly symmetrical features set in a square face with high cheekbones. His hair, a glossy patchwork of auburn, black and gold, looked much like his fur had looked before, making him look still slightly hyena, as did his dark hazel eyes. The smell of swamp still clung to him like his own brand of perfume.

He picked his nose with nonchalance and inspected it, before popping it into his mouth. A bandana that looked like his own pelt dangled around his neck, but otherwise he was stark naked.

Tariro was the first to recover. He snatched up a kanga from Ethan's backpack and handed it to the youth, who accepted it with a smile showing even white teeth.

"So what? Is he human?" Ethan said quietly to Salih.

"Not quite," Salih said. "His name when he takes this shape is Fisi. But don't let the pretty face fool you – he is also a hyena. He is just as likely to attack you as befriend you."

"The leopard is joking," the hyena guy laughed, in strangely accented but surprisingly good English. It was a moment before Ethan realised the youth could still understand what the leopard said, even though he had changed. With a smug grin at Tariro, Ethan wondered if he regretted scratching the animal's back now, but Tariro hardly seemed to remember. He stared openmouthed.

When they were ready to go, they left Salih waiting on the ledge and Darwishi dragged all the tubes towards the narrow gap in the cliff. Ethan, Tariro and Fisi bobbed up and down, their backsides firmly squashed into the centres of the spare tubes with no hessian on them. While Darwishi struggled to hold everyone at the top of the rapids, Ethan untied the transport and equipment tubes and posted them one at a time through the gap, watching them as the current caught them and they hurtled over the rapids, bouncing from rock to rock on their downward journey.

Fisi settled his buttocks further down into his tube and Darwishi nudged him out of the vortex. He gave a half-giggle, half-grunt of excitement and plummeted down the rapids.

"Don't forget to try and keep your feet in front of you!" Tariro yelled after him as the river took him. There had been no time for him to get over his shock at the youth's change because of their rush to get down to Jimoh, but Ethan thought he looked quite excited at the idea of a hyena who turned into a man. At least he was willing to take instructions from the leopard now, even if they were relayed through the hyena.

Ethan watched Tariro struggle against the current to line up his own feet with a gap in the middle of the channel, and then he too surged forwards and raced through the jagged rocks, the water spraying up all around him.

Checking one last time that his hat was tied securely to his tube – he did not want to lose it like Jimoh had – Ethan pushed away from Darwishi into the cataract. He was surprised by his rush of excitement as he surged through the gap.

Bouncing straight out of the tube at the very first hurdle, he tumbled into the water. It frothed and churned around him till his lungs burned, eventually spitting him out into a dark channel. Jagged rocks and branches whipped passed him in a blur of black and green. Ethan reached up to catch an overhanging branch to slow himself down, then shrieked in agony as he was hurled with bone-shattering force against unseen debris, trapped beneath it. The force of the water passing through the trapped debris pinned him there, quickly piling up behind him, pushing him under the water. He wrestled himself up and onto the branch where he clung for a moment, his heart beating painfully in his chest.

About twenty metres downstream his tube floated in the same eddy Jimoh's had, and he decided to retrieve it if he could because it had his hat. Letting go of the branch, he surged forward, water washing over his face. Miraculously, he made it to the gap between the two rocks. Pointing his feet out in front of him, he passed through with no room to spare, threw out an arm and snatched the tube up as he went. Using all his strength, he forced the tube under his bottom and hurtled down the rest of the rapids. Six feet from the bottom his tube took flight over a small waterfall and then crashed back into the water, throwing Ethan headfirst into the deep pool below.

I did it! I actually did it! he thought as his feet touched the bottom of the pool. Oddly, he felt no aching, smarting, tenderness or anything. Nothing was sore at all. Perhaps the witch had been right about the self-healing. Or it could be excess adrenalin, a little voice at the back of his head warned him.

He turned to push himself towards the nearest shore. There, he came face to face with what he knew was one of the most aggressive creatures in the world, certainly one of the most dangerous animals in Africa.

CHAPTER 11
A VICIOUS ENCOUNTER

If Joe shut his eyes, he could imagine himself in the bush near his home. The forest smelled of moist earth, compost and wood smoke, but the resemblance ended there. Everything seemed to be oversized, as if the plants were on steroids. He squatted on his haunches, poking at the ashes of his fire with a stick. Without the protection of a shirt, he shivered in the early morning chill. The fire had gone out in the night, soon after the tiger left him.

At least the tiger *had* left him, he thought. It had been a traumatic night. For most of it he lay against the tiger for warmth – and because the cat had insisted – but he had hardly dared to breathe in case the strange animal's mood of conviviality wore thin. One swipe of its irritated paw would have broken bones, if not killed him. Eventually he had fallen into an exhausted sleep, and was only half-aware when the tiger slipped out from under him sometime before dawn, and slunk off into the forest.

I hope it's gone for good, he thought, checking the surrounding forest in case it hadn't.

A purple crested lourie rustled in the canopy far above Joe's head, its scarlet flight feathers flashing as it glided the short distance from branch to branch. His hand moved absently to the slingshot around his neck but he did not pick up a pebble. He easily could have shot it down, but he just didn't feel hungry enough to kill such a beautiful bird.

"I'll probably regret that when I'm starving later," he muttered out loud. He knew he had to size up his situation as soon as possible. First evaluate his physical condition, then take stock of his surroundings, and then make a survival plan. According to Jimoh's dad, who had been teaching him to hunt since he was little, you had to find water, then food, and then shelter. He wished Jimoh was with him now – he would know what to do – then dismissed the thought; there was no point in both of them being lost.

I suppose I'd better get on with it, he thought, pulling himself up to his feet. As long as he kept busy, he didn't have to consider just how dire his situation was. And how lonely he felt . . . At least he was in good shape. His fingers, when he held them out before him, were quite steady, and he had no injuries. The strange weakness of the night before seemed to have worn off. He knew there was no point in questioning *why* he was here; all he had to do was figure out how to get back home.

He thought he would start by looking for ants. If he could follow them he knew they would eventually lead to water. With a bit of luck he might find a stream, which in turn would lead him to a settlement. Although he shuddered to think what kind of a settlement he would find. Talking tigers and Tokoloshe! He didn't think he would ever get over it. A cursory look at the nearest trees didn't reveal even a single ant. He would have howled in frustration if he hadn't been afraid of attracting something horrible. He already felt vulnerable in his electric blue swimming shorts, hardly the most effective camouflage for a forest.

A huge cashew tree, full of fruit, stood tantalizingly on the edge of the clearing, but he'd heard they were poisonous when raw. He was not sure if that applied to the apple or the nut, but he did not dare eat either. The bent nuts poked out of the bottom of each red apple like the handle of a baby's pull toy. *And why not?* Joe thought. With all the other weirdness around him, it wouldn't surprise him if the fruit played a tune if he were to pull on one of those nuts.

Just beyond the cashew a baobab tree towered above him. Damp weather had rotted the centre, leaving a void inside, about three paces in diameter. It would make a good shelter when night fell, Joe decided, if he hadn't found a track by then. But when he stepped inside to check it, the trunk was hollow to the sky. He could see a hawk flying in lazy circles overhead.

A plantain, just beyond the baobab, reminded him of something he'd learned at school. If he could cut it down and scoop out a hollow in the centre of the stump, water should draw up from the roots. It was quite nice to think he had not wasted his time at school entirely. The tree even had fairly ripe plantains that he could eat later when he got hungry. He would start there.

Joe stopped to kick the tree in frustration. Without the aid of a knife it had taken him hours to hack away at the trunk with a sharp stone. He had a feeling that he had lost more water through sweating than the amount of water he was going to find. Not a good start. If he had known he was coming, he would have brought along some tools, a machete perhaps, or a knife at least. But it had all happened so suddenly . . . like magic. Joe shook his head. *No time to think about magic. Be practical!*

Finally he managed to push the trunk over with a resounding crack, and scooped out a shallow bowl shape in the stump with his stone. To Joe's relief, the depression started filling up with water almost immediately. Not sure if it was safe to drink without filtering, he stripped off his shorts and knelt down beside the stump, put the fabric against his lips and had just started to suck up the liquid, when the plaintive, wistful sound of a thumb piano drifted through the trees towards him.

Humans! Joe thought with sudden relief, but then just as quickly wondered if he shouldn't hide. There was no telling who they were, or how many. On the other hand, he was desperate for the water he had worked so hard for, so he sucked it up through his shorts as fast as he could.

Halfway through scrambling back into his shorts, a young girl broke into the clearing. She stared at Joe with a strange expression while he hopped up and down on one leg, mortified with embarrassment, trying to get his other leg into his shorts.

With both hands clutching the tortoise shell resonance chamber of her instrument, the girl's thumbs wound down her tune to a distracted plink . . . plink. She continued to stare at him incredulously.

"Excuse me," Joe said, trying to turn his back on her, but his toe caught in the shorts and he let go of them before they made him topple over and fall to the ground.

"Don't move a muscle," growled a low, gravelly voice as a second girl, a bit older than the first, stepped out from behind her. She held a Y-shaped sapling in front of her like a water divining rod, with one hand on each of the forks, and the stem pointing at Joe. The brindle pelt of her tunic was an exact match with the hair on her head. No ordinary hair, either. It looked more like wiry fur, in various shades of ginger, darkish brown and grey, decorated with plant fibres and bird feathers.

Lowering her sapling, she began to circle Joe, catlike, placing one bare, dark brown foot warily before the other. Amazingly, she looked like she wanted a fight. At first he couldn't take her seriously. She was a lot smaller than him for a start and he wasn't about to fight with a girl – especially when he was naked.

He wondered if the sapling she held was some sort of weapon. Smiling at her unsteadily, he was about to explain that he had found water, which they were welcome to share, when, in a vicious blur of speed, she slammed him to the ground. The two of them grappled with each other, but as small as she was, Joe was no match for her in strength, and he couldn't bring himself to hit her. Within seconds she had him on his back, his hands pinned above his head, her angry amber eyes glaring into his.

Joe didn't know what to do next. "Okay. You win," he shrugged awkwardly, trying to get up. Joe was no coward, but his shaky voice betrayed him. There was something not quite right about her. Apart from her impossible strength, close up she smelled more like an animal than a girl.

The smaller girl dropped her thumb piano and came over tentatively, to help roll him on to his side and tie his hands to the Y-shaped branch behind his back. They yanked him to his feet and he stood unsteadily.

He wanted to rewind. He wanted to say, "I didn't realise you were this serious." What he said was, "Can you at least put my pants back on?"

The vicious girl did not deign to reply. She turned on her heel and walked back into the forest the way she had come without looking back. The other one helped him put his shorts on, all the while shaking her head as if he were an idiot for taking them off in the first place, and then picked up her musical instrument and followed her friend. The haunting plinkity-plink of her piano drifted off into the forest.

Joe hovered near the clearing. They hadn't ordered him to follow them. How could they be so confident that he would? He could simply work his bonds loose and go his own way.

No matter how hard he strained, though, Joe's hands were unable to reach each other, or wiggle free. Each hand had been bound tightly with lengths of leather, from fingertip to elbow, to a fork of the sapling.

He tried easing the sapling underneath his legs, to bring his hands to the front, where he could chew through the binding, but he found they'd strung a chord between the forks to prevent him from doing that.

SWITCH!

Defeated, Joe tried to sit down on the ground and think, but he found he couldn't even do that. The stem of the sapling, which hung downwards, dug into the ground behind him, jarring his arms painfully, and toppling him onto his side. Grimacing with pain and frustration, he pulled himself to his knees but the sapling stem trailing out behind him forced Joe forwards into an awkward bow.

It dawned on Joe that he would not be able to defend or feed himself all trussed up, and the only ones around to untie him, possibly for hundreds of miles, were fast disappearing into the forest. Praying they did not mean to kill him, he stumbled in the direction of the music, as fast as the thick undergrowth would allow.

Branches scratched at his arms and chest and tore at his exposed face as he hurried after them. He stubbed his toe, and swore angrily, wishing he'd been wearing shoes when his world had turned upside down. He even looked over his shoulder from time to time, almost hoping to see the tiger.

By the time he caught up with the girls, and fell in behind them as he suspected they knew he would, the vicious one had cut herself another dowsing rod. She stripped the bark off it with her teeth and held it out in front of her, completely ignoring her prisoner. When he tried to negotiate, she slapped him so hard across the mouth he tasted blood.

The other girl at least interrupted her tune to hold the thorniest branches aside for him so that they didn't scratch him. Eventually the undergrowth became so dense she gave up on the tune. Dangling her tortoise shell finger piano at her side like a small handbag, she fell to pushing the foliage aside in a rhythmic movement. If Joe moved quickly he found he could slip in behind her before the branches switched back to slap him in the face.

As the day grew hotter, flying insects gathered around his lips and his eyes, and no matter how much he spat and shook his head, he was unable to chase them away. Eventually he felt so defeated he could have wept. Tariro would have seen this coming, he thought bitterly. Tariro would have smacked her.

Who ever said manners cost you nothing?

They wove a path through the forest in silence till the vicious girl's divining rod turned her sharply and homed in on a snake hiding in the leaf litter under a nearby tree. A gaboon viper, its colouring and markings so close to autumn leaves Joe thought even Jimoh would have missed it. This vicious girl would have too, if it weren't for the divining rod, he thought derisively.

Lifting its large triangular head, the snake gave off a series of loud warnings, its head flattening slightly with each hiss. Small horns just above its nostrils quivered in alarm. Undeterred, the vicious girl stroked it gently on its head with one point of the divining rod, whilst her other hand shot out in a blur and snatched the snake up by its neck.

For a horrible moment as she came towards him, Joe thought she meant to have the snake bite him, but instead she posted it head first into a long thin basket-weave tube she had hanging on her belt. Pulling a cord to lace the tube tightly against the body of the snake so that it couldn't move at all, she secured its tail to one end and slung it over her shoulder onto her back where the snake dangled, dead straight and upside down. Joe wondered if she had deliberately left its eyes exposed, so that it could see the ground flash past it as she walked. He wished it would slip a little in that tube, just enough to bare a fang and bite her on her backside.

About thirty paces ahead of them, the clearing ended abruptly in a precipice. Below the plateau, the forest stretched eastward and then fell away again to some sort of a rift valley miles below, with what looked like a wide river running across it, stretching endlessly to a range of mountains he could barely see on the distant horizon. His spirits sank further. Even if he could escape from the girls unbound, it would take him weeks to make his way to the river.

SWITCH!

Wisps of smoke wafted up over the edge of the plateau, bringing with them the faint whiff of humanity. Joe recognised the strong fragrance of burning acacia wood. It was the same wood the Tjalotjo villagers near his home used to mask the smell of their latrines. Any slight relief he may have felt at the familiar smell was soon banished as they made their way down the steep path to the girls' village. Vicious seemed totally oblivious to the danger the incline posed to Joe without the use of his hands, but the other girl reached down silently and steadied him from time to time so that he did not pitch forwards and fall down.

At the bottom they came up against a thick tangle of thorned acacia branches surrounding a settlement. Joe's dad built similar bomas around his safari camps to keep the lions out, but this was tinder dry, and unkempt, and at least five times the size. Access was gained via a crawl space. Both girls dropped to their hands and knees, but Joe hesitated. He couldn't very well crawl on his hands and knees without any hands.

"In," Vicious spat at him. Pushing him down onto his knees, she shoved him towards the entrance where he had to balance carefully in a crouched position, with nothing to protect him from the long sharp acacia thorns that grew in pairs all along the twisted branches. His knees scraped badly, and his face and shoulders grew scratched and bloody, but if he did not move quickly she grabbed the sapling stem that trailed in the dirt behind him and yanked it upwards, sending sharp pains up his arms. Once she pushed him so hard he fell forwards and smacked his brow on the ground, opening a cut above his eye.

When they emerged from the tunnel, the younger girl went her own way, whilst Vicious took hold of the handle of the sapling stem and marched him, roughly and bowed over, through the tumbled-down encampment.

Strikingly beautiful people, mostly women, wearing the same brindle tunics as Vicious, barely paused in their work to watch him as he passed.

A VICIOUS ENCOUNTER

Two hyenas slunk forwards from a shady spot and sniffed at him. One licked at the thin trickle of blood running down Joe's face, but he did not flinch. There seemed to be nothing threatening in its stance. The creature behaved more like a pet than a wild animal. He guessed that was what they had in place of dogs. Vicious kicked it and the hyenas slunk off to their shade like dogs do.

While Vicious hung her snake up on a hook dangling from the roof, Joe looked around her shelter. Rough tree trunk posts stood on the four corners, with supporting beams of twisted branches in between to hold up a crudely thatched roof. The walls, which were made up of a motley collection of hides, thrown over some thinner poles, only reached chest height, leaving the top half of the walls in full view of the rest of the village and open to the elements.

Vicious had hold of a vine rope, which she threaded between Joe's hands and threw over a support beam, hoisting him up; his arms stretched out behind him till he was almost doubled over. She tested it to make sure it was just tight enough that either he would have to go up on his tiptoes, or put painful pressure on his arms. Once satisfied that she had achieved the maximum point of discomfort, she tied the rope.

He yelped.

She smacked him hard across the face.

A group of women sitting in a circle stringing an assortment of beads and feathers into the baskets they wove glanced at him furtively, but looked away again at Vicious' glare. She left him, slumped forward, facing a wooden carving of a double-headed warthog in amongst the ostrich eggs and antelope horns on her dung floor. The warthog had nails bashed into its torso between its two heads that stuck up like a hedgehog. He wondered if that was her idea of an ornament or if it represented something sinister to do with witch doctor medicine. If he managed to escape from his bonds, he would hit her over the head with it, girl or no girl.

SWITCH!

In no time his arms and neck were ablaze with pain. Even his toes ached from trying to relieve the pressure on his arms. He clenched his teeth as his chin sank to his chest. Sweat and blood dribbled into his eyes, and flies hovered around, trying to get at the moisture.

A pile of pebbles, scattered near the doorway, would make good ammunition for his slingshot, but what use were they if he couldn't reach them? At least she hadn't realised his slingshot was a weapon or no doubt she would have taken it away. She probably planned to strangle him with it. Surely this could not be right. Why did no one do anything about her? Surely they should give him a chance to explain that he was just trying to find a way home? They couldn't all be bad. The other girl had been almost kind, once he was safely tied up.

A loud whoop, more a beast sound than human, caught his attention, and Joe found if he strained his head painfully upwards he could just peep over the hide wall to see people gathering in the yard. A group of musicians played thumb pianos in an open shelter on the far side of what probably passed as a village square. Their thumb pianos were not inside tortoise shells to catch the sound, like the young girl's had been, but just short planks of wood with metal tines attached.

A man carried a marimba over, made of a row of rough-looking planks arranged along a frame from smallest to biggest. The gourds attached below did not range from smallest to biggest, resulting in a random, discordant noise when he drummed on the planks. Soon, a variety or rattles, sticks, gongs and bottles joined in to produce a horrible din.

An argument broke out in the yard. Joe pushed against the floor with his toes and craned his neck as far as he could without crying out in pain. A grizzled old woman stood in the middle of the clearing, arms akimbo, her short-cropped hair flattening in her rage, like the pet hyena that stood rigidly beside her.

"You are malicious and cruel, Mesande," she growled. "He is

just a boy from one of the villages in the valley. Lost."

"He is a demon!" Vicious said in her low gravelly voice. "We found him right where my boyfriend should have been. Fisi is at least a day late, and this demon has something to do with it."

"Nonsense. Fisi has found out what a manipulative little trollop you are and has changed his mind. He's probably back with his pack by now." The old lady hawked and spat something red on the ground between their feet, before snorting. "As for this lost boy, he is no demon. You just want to vent your spite, or use him for your own dark medicine. You will not get away with it."

Two wiry-looking girls, one with a slash mark across her cheek, took up positions on either side of Vicious and glared at the old woman menacingly.

"I am not afraid of you!" the old woman added, shaking an elephant tail fly-whip at the three of them, her voice quavering slightly. Joe hoped that was from age, not fear. It would be good to have a friend in the camp. If only she wasn't the oldest and weakest one here, he thought. He didn't want to be used for medicine, dark or otherwise.

"Look at his skin, and he has hair the colour of lion grass. Where in the valley kingdoms did you ever see such a thing?" asked the girl beside Vicious.

"And he was naked when we caught him," Vicious said. "You can ask Chuki. She saw him. He must have been doing a ritual just before we came upon him."

"It is true, Gogo Nagesa," one of the musicians joined in the argument, his arms folded across his chest defensively, every bit as if he had been there when she had captured Joe. "The demon was naked, as if he had changed shape. There have been some strange happenings in the Forest. Fisi is nowhere and the witches have been searching for one of theirs too."

"Rumor and gossip," the old woman snorted angrily. "That witch is probably up to some mischief of her own. I know that Gogo Maya, it wouldn't be the first time. Maybe the boy was just taking a piss."

It was a good thing no one went in search of Chuki to confirm this story. At the sound of her low hiss, Joe turned to see her creep cautiously into the shelter where she squatted in front of him, one hand covering her mouth in a sign indicating the need for silence, the other hand holding a shard of gourd filled with what looked like stew, some twisted stalks and a rough-skinned fruit.

"Aw . . . Boy," she said softly. He could hear a slight crack in her voice.

Only then did Joe's composure break. He started to weep quietly, and wished he could hide his face in his hands. He could see she was also close to tears as she hunkered down awkwardly on the floor and tried to feed him, the gravy running down her fingers and dripping on the floor. She made no move to untie him but she did not seem to mind the mess.

"Why didn't you run when you heard my music?" she whispered.

Joe was so shocked; the food in his mouth went momentarily unchewed. "I waited for you. I did not think you would attack me. Why did you attack me?"

"That was Mesande," she said.

"You helped her tie me up."

"I had to, or she could accuse me of failing to help capture a demon."

"Untie me now, then."

"Later. If I untie you now she will know it was me. I am also a hostage here, but not like you," she whispered. "My people live far to the north. I, and the other hostages, cannot leave Malamulu village except with one such as Mesande. They will not let us escape, but they may not harm us or our people will kill their own hostages and attack this pack."

Joe took a bite of the twisted stalk she offered him. It was tough and irritating against his mouth. Bitter starbursts of flavour set his tongue tingling and his eyes narrowed as he spat. Could she be feeding him some sort of poison? No, she really was upset, and she *had* tried to help him on the track.

"Why are you helping me now then?" he said uncertainly.

"I do it to annoy Mesande," she said with a wicked grin, "because I like Fisi, the one she is planning to mate with. I play the music to warn the others that she is coming and she knows it but she dare not stop me. She is cruel. You see what she does with the snake." She ran a hand soothingly down the length of the snake's back and tut-tutted. "Poor creature, all its blood has gone to its head. I am sure she means to set it on someone. If it lives long enough."

"Well, I am not an animal," Joe said. "I expected help."

She wiped the side of his mouth with her thumb and sucked the gravy off. "And you shall have it," she said, patting his cheek kindly. "I cannot help you but my friends will come for you as soon as it is dark. I will create a diversion with the snake, and I will make sure the villagers in the yard see me in the square while my friends cut you down. You must take off the strange clothing and put on the pelt that they bring you, and then follow them. The others must think you are a shape-changing demon when they see the empty clothing." She laughed softly. "It will delay them from going out to search for you."

After she snuck out again, the time dragged by. Joe's arms ached so badly he wanted to cry. His bladder grew so tight it was painful, but he was damned if he would give Mesande the satisfaction of seeing him wet himself. The argument in the yard went back and forth, but he was too miserable to look over the wall.

Shortly after the sun went down, a long shadow detached itself from a nearby shelter and slid silently in beside Joe. A stocky young boy, clutching a rusty knife in one hand, gave Joe a nod, gripped the snake gently around its neck, unhooked its tail and slid it cautiously out of its prison, then tiptoed out into the night with it.

SWITCH!

The effect of the snake was satisfyingly electric. A piercing shriek split the air and pandemonium broke out. Villagers and hyenas scattered in all directions.

Joe felt his hands released from the beam and his knees buckled under him. He fell to the floor, writhing in agony as the muscles in his feet and his arms adjusted.

"No time!" a boy hissed, dragging him up to his feet and hacking at the ties that bound him to the divining rod with a knife, while another struggled to remove Joe's shorts and replace them with a skirt-like pelt.

With trembling hands Joe grabbed a handful of pebbles from beside the doorway and stumbled out behind the boys as they ducked into the shadows, crouching low. Joe followed his rescuers as silently as possible under the boma down to a stream that ran beside the settlement.

"Walk in the middle of the stream as long as you can to hide your scent," one of the boys said, pressing a water skin, and some dried meat into Joe's hands. "We must go back and cover your tracks."

Joe hesitated. He was still unsteady on his feet.

"The witches are that way." The other boy pointed south-west, back up the plateau, the way the girls had brought Joe.

"Thank you . . ." Joe whispered, wondering why they would be directing him towards witches, but before he could ask, the two boys had melted into the shadows.

He would worry about that later. For now, he was free, but he would not be for long if Mesande could weasel her way out of her demon lie.

Joe ran downhill beside the stream for about twenty paces to throw her off track and then waded into the water, making his way upstream as fast as he could, trying not to splash water as he ran. He could see his way quite clearly in the moonlight. Of course, it meant she would be able to see him too. Not that she needed to; she would set her hyenas on him. She could probably smell him out herself, the vicious brat. What he would have done for a can of pepper to put her off the track.

As soon as he reached the top of the plateau, he relieved himself, drank as much water as he could stomach, refilled the skin the two young boys had given him from the stream, and set off at a brisk trot, heading towards the distant mountains.

CHAPTER 12
A DUBIOUS POWER

Ethan fought the urge to run as the hippopotamus stood eyeing him on the bottom of the pool. It was barely two meters away. Its massive grey head scythed slowly from side to side almost level with his. The skin around its eyes and the sides of its face was an unexpected salmon pink and single spiky whiskers stuck out of crater-like pores all over its broad muzzle. One lone bubble escaped in slow motion from its closed nostrils, and drifted to the surface. He wasn't sure if it could open its mouth underwater without drowning, but he knew it had enormous tusk-like incisors inside that could cut a human in half. The rest of its giant barrel-shaped body was hairless, and looked nearly as big as a rhinoceros.

He'd read in his survival manual that hippopotami were extremely aggressive and were responsible for more human fatalities than elephant, rhino and buffalo combined. Any sudden noise or movement may be all that would be needed to trigger an attack. Barrelling into the water at speed had not helped his cause. The manual had told him to jump off the path and stand dead still, but there had been no advice for the eventuality of meeting one in deep water.

Rotating his hands slowly by his sides, trying to keep in the same spot under the water, Ethan struggled to remember what other advice the manual had given. It claimed that hippopotami do not swim but walk along the riverbed, and Ethan wondered if it was as simple as pushing up to the surface, out of the creature's reach. There had been nothing about how far or how fast a hippopotamus could push off from the bottom, but it definitely had mentioned that hippopotami were faster than people both on land and in the water.

Staring at the creature in horror, he knew he would have to make up his mind quickly. His lungs were already burning and he thought the hippopotamus could hold its breath for at least five minutes.

"Don't bite me," he prayed, as he slowly bent his legs in preparation to push off. An overwhelming surge of hostility swept over him from the beast as it hovered indecisively between savaging him and walking away.

It was not as if he were reading the thoughts or emotions of this creature like he could with Fisi and Salih. Anyone could have picked up the hostility from the animal's body language, but, on the other hand, he could have sworn the feeling radiating off it went deeper than that. Sulkiness immediately came to mind, and a feeling of having been cheated. If he could feel all that from the animal, Ethan wondered if it could feel anything from him. It seemed almost too much to hope for but he glared at it with all his might and thought, "Go away!"

Suddenly something else plunged into the water beside Ethan, and Darwishi swam between Ethan and the hippopotamus, drawing the hippopotamus' attention away. The hippopotamus whirled around in slow motion and bounded after the crocodile, propelling himself at considerable speed through the water by pushing his stubby little legs off the bottom of the pool in forward leaps. The animal *was* much faster than him underwater. Ethan wasted no time shooting up to the surface of the pool.

Salih floundered on top of the water. "Push me under the

waterfall, Ethan," he spluttered. Ethan could see what he meant. Partly concealed behind a waterfall near where they had landed, the rest of the group huddled together in a shallow cave-like depression in the riverbank. Ethan pushed Salih towards them, and Tariro and Fisi hauled him up beside them, where he limped to one side and fell panting to the floor.

Ethan climbed up after him, and they all turned to watch as Darwishi shot out of the far side of the pool with the hippopotamus in hot pursuit. The animal soon got bored with the chase, and lumbered back to the pool to join his pod on the far side. He lurked belligerently amongst the water hyacinth in the shallows, his ears, nose and eyes poking up above the water, letting off a series of disapproving grunts from time to time. Ethan suppressed a shudder as another hippopotamus lifted its massive mouth out of the water and yawned, showing incisors almost the size of Ethan's forearm.

"We thought you were a goner," Tariro said, palm pressed to his chest dramatically. Then, unexpectedly, he grabbed Ethan in a bear hug. "I know you can hold your breath for a long time, but you were down there well over a minute. Amun guided us all to this shelf as we landed, and we sat here watching that hippo get madder and madder till he slunk under the water. We saw him walk along the river bed and we saw you land practically on top of him, but there was nothing we could do."

Fisi gave Ethan a hug too, even though Ethan tried to ward it off, remembering that Fisi had picked his nose earlier. Fisi's hug was stiff, and wooden, as if he was trying to learn the customs of his new friends, but didn't quite understand the sentiment.

"Yo," he said in perfect imitation of the way he had heard Tariro say it, and then stood awkwardly beside Ethan. *Too close.* Ethan had to hold his breath against the smell. He hoped the hyena youth would learn the concept of personal space quickly, and personal possessions too. He was wearing Jimoh's hat. Jimoh, himself, sagged against a rock at the back of the shallow cave,

120

breathing with difficulty. He looked ashen. Salih padded over to him and prodded his stomach gently, then licked his face.

"This one is hurt, Ethan," he said. "You must send the other two away before we can help him because they must not see. Tell them I have power to heal him but I need your help."

Ethan hesitated. He wasn't sure Tariro would believe him if he said it was the leopard's idea to send Tariro out to gather up their equipment from amongst the hippopotami while he stayed safely with Jimoh. Tariro would think he was copping out of the more difficult task. When he suggested it, however, Tariro shook his head, more as if to clear it, than to argue.

"You are something else, Ethan," he grinned, obviously still not entirely happy to believe Ethan could understand Salih, despite the evidence of his own eyes when Fisi had changed. He looked worriedly at Jimoh. "Do you really think the leopard can help him?"

"He says he can," Ethan said firmly.

"Okay, me and Fisi will get our stuff together and go and find a place to camp." Ethan guessed the idea of a talking leopard was easier for Tariro to swallow than the idea that Ethan had spontaneously guessed that the hyena would change into a man. He wondered if he should remind Tariro that the leopard considered Fisi to be a potential danger, but the two of them had already sidled out from under the waterfall and were headed down the riverbank.

Ethan crouched beside Jimoh after they left, and took the boy by the hand. "What can you do?" he asked Salih.

"I was hoping this wouldn't come up." The leopard's face had an innocent expression, but Ethan sensed something else. Shiftiness, he thought. "It is you who must help Jimoh," Salih said.

"That's your plan, Salih? I can't help him. He looks hurt inside! He probably has a broken rib or something." He stared at Jimoh in astonishment. Jimoh had a broken rib! He knew it without a doubt. Just by touching Jimoh, he knew it. He let go of the boy's hand as if it had scalded him, and glared at Salih. "How am I supposed to fix this? I'm not a doctor."

Salih dropped into a low crouch beside Ethan, his tail twitching gently back and forth like a metronome.

"When I saw how quickly the crocodile bite healed, I thought you must have power of your own," he said, "but the more I see of you the more I begin to suspect the only power you have is what you sucked out of the witch." He cocked his head as if he'd had a thought, and then went on.

"It is not easy to suck the power out of a witch. I would like to know how you knew you could do that, and how you managed to shield yourself from her." He regarded Ethan for a moment with appraising eyes. Then he shook his head ruefully, and went on, "But that is for another time. If I had known, I would never have risked sending you to fetch the amulet. As it is, you have absorbed enough of her magic to heal this boy. Enough from her, and certainly enough from the amber of her amulet.

"The power is in your blood," he explained. "It makes you strong and capable of healing very quickly as the witch told you. Within reason, of course. Nothing could have saved you from a bite from that hippopotamus." He gestured towards Jimoh. "But you can also use this blood to heal others."

Ethan ran a finger under the collar of his T-shirt, and cleared his throat, but struggled to say anything. Was he going mad? He thought he believed the leopard. Why shouldn't he? His own injuries, when he reached the bottom of the rapids, were not consistent with the pounding he had taken coming down. At one point he had been sure he had cracked a couple of his own ribs, yet instead of feeling grim, he felt a mild euphoric feeling in the pit of his stomach, completely at odds with the situation he was in.

He knew replacing lost blood could help to heal a person, but mending bones? He wished Salih would stop swishing his tail like that, so that he could think.

Of course he wanted to help Jimoh, but even supposing his

blood could do it, how was he going to extract it without a syringe? How would he get it into Jimoh's veins for that matter?

He took a deep breath, puffed his cheeks up and let the air out slowly. "How?" he asked.

"Good boy," Salih said, his tail coming to a rest. "Take your special knife and make a small cut here." He indicated a small vein on the outside of Ethan's ankle. "This place will be the least noticeable. Then let it bleed." He looked around for a receptacle and his eyes came to rest on Ethan's water bottle. "Enough to fill the lid of that. Maybe twice."

Ethan backed off in shock when he realised Salih intended him to have Jimoh drink the blood.

"Are you going to stand around making up your mind while your friend dies?" Salih growled.

One look at the sweat glistening on Jimoh's forehead made up his mind. He would have to do it; and the sooner the better.

Taking his Swiss Army knife out of his pocket, he selected the sharpest little knife and held his breath while he made a small cut in his ankle. It smarted momentarily and then blood slowly trickled out of the nick. He cupped the cap beneath the vein to collect it as it oozed out thickly, all dark red and repulsive.

I must pull myself together, he told himself through gritted teeth. Now was not the time to faint at the sight of his own blood, but he could not help the familiar signs of lightheadedness and nausea creeping up on him. Struggling to stay conscious, he leaned his head over the side of the ledge and let the waterfall splash on his face.

"Ethan, why you cutting yourself?" Jimoh rasped.

"Jimoh, I know it sounds gross," Ethan said weakly, "but Salih says I must give you some blood. It will make you get better."

"I cannot take your blood! I can see it is bringing pain."

Ethan shook the water out of his hair. "Is there a religious or tribal problem?" he said. He knew there wasn't, because he had seen two of Jimoh's hunters pierce the tips of their fingers with the blade of a machete and press their wounds together. He had been appalled at the time, worrying about all the diseases they could be passing to each other. It didn't seem to matter now.

"No, Ethan. I do not want to take it because it will make you weak. You will not be able to find Joe," Jimoh said. Ethan could see he was fighting for every breath.

"Jimoh, it is not that sore, and when a person loses blood, their body makes more. In Cape Town we go and have some blood taken out every year or so. The nurse puts a needle in here," he indicated the crook of his arm, "and they suck out two tins full of blood. They store it until they need to put it into someone else who needs it." Ethan did not mention that the someone was not required to drink it. "Then they give us a cup of tea and send us home. We don't even notice the blood is missing." He gave a self-depreciating laugh. "I usually pass out then too, but it is only because I hate the sight of blood."

"I will try it then, Ethan," Jimoh said, "but if I do not get well you must go with Tariro and find Joe. Amun will try to take me back to Tjalotjo village to get help."

Ethan grinned at Jimoh. "Then you will have to get well because if I have to go by myself with Tariro, you know I am going to strangle the boy."

Ethan handed him the lid and Jimoh took a tentative sip. His face contorted into a disgusted grimace; then he looked embarrassed at this reaction.

"All of it," Ethan said sternly, handing Jimoh the water bottle to wash it down. Jimoh drank the blood in two consecutive gulps and lay quietly with his eyes shut. Ethan could tell that he was struggling not to vomit.

After the second capful, Salih said, "Stop now and see if there is any improvement before you use any more. Gogo never uses a lot." He had started to get that shifty look about him again, so Ethan glared at him expectantly till he went on.

"Ethan, it is a big responsibility carrying the magic," he

explained. "You must guard this secret with your life, or you will be destroyed for it. There are those who can persuade you to drain too much for their own ends, even your friends. You will be surprised at how quickly it is used up, and once it is gone, it is gone." He brightened considerably. "But as long as you have the power in your blood, no parasite or disease can harm you. I think you will like that."

Ethan could not help wondering if Salih was holding something back, but he explained it all as best he could to Jimoh, swearing him to secrecy. Then told him about the hyena changing.

"Is Kishi," Jimoh said with wonder, "but different. Kishi, he has nice friendly face in front to trick you. Then when he gets you into his house, he can turn around and show evil hyena face hiding under hair at the back. Maybe eat you."

"Ya, Salih said to be wary," Ethan said, "but Fisi seems okay. He seems just as nervous of us as we are of him."

Jimoh nodded. "Can you hear what I am thinking, like the leopard and the hyena?"

"No," Ethan laughed.

He thought they were over the worst when Jimoh scratched his short curly hair and said, "I want my hat back."

When Darwishi swam by to help Ethan and Jimoh off the ledge, Jimoh showed very little sign of ever having been hurt, and Ethan felt as if he was going to explode. He did not feel ill, exactly, just extremely irritable. Pins and needles swelled in waves through his hands and feet uncomfortably, almost as if he could feel his own blood pumping through his veins. He did not know whether to laugh or whimper.

Jimoh put a hand to Ethan's forehead after he'd expelled a small shriek at a particularly strong wave of pins and needles, and then, unexpectedly, checked the area between Ethan's neck and his jaw to see if his glands there were swollen, just like a doctor.

"Are you sick from taking out blood?" Jimoh whispered. "You

are not hot inside head."

"You are not ill, boy," Salih said. "Surely you realised there would be consequences for paying out the blood? That feeling is your body producing new blood to replace that which was lost. The magic-tainted blood will reject it at first. Don't move about too quickly – it will soon even out." He uncoiled from where he lay and went to balance on Darwishi's back. "Just don't bleed anytime soon," he said over his shoulder. "It gets worse every time."

"No, Jimoh, I'm okay," Ethan sighed, trying hard not to twitch while climbing onto the crocodile's back behind Salih. Because he didn't want Jimoh to feel bad, he explained to Jimoh what the leopard had told him.

By the time Darwishi dropped them near the others, it was late afternoon and Tariro and Fisi had set up camp. The river basin widened considerably for a couple of miles, creating a small valley. Fisi had taken over as camp leader in the absence of Jimoh, and had chosen a site under a shady tree at the top of a steep embankment a little way down river from the rapids.

"Oh! This is not good," Jimoh said. "The crocodiles will not be able to reach us there."

"Salih says it is a good site because the hippos can't reach it," Ethan said, trying desperately to act normal and sit still on the back of Darwishi.

Tariro came to the water's edge to help Jimoh up the embankment and backed off in surprise when he saw how well the boy had recovered. "You were probably just winded," he shrugged.

With a warning not to disturb the hippopotami, and not to wander about in their grazing area at night, Salih slunk off into the bush to hunt. Ethan hoped he *was* going hunting and did not plan to abandon them, now that they had passed the main obstacle on the way to Karibu. He needed answers from Salih.

Between moaning about their aches and pains from the rapid ride and boasting about their bravery, Tariro and the hyena youth seemed to be getting on very well.

"You should have seen me, Ethan," Tariro said, grabbing him by the hand and hauling him up the bank. "A supply tube landed right amongst a group of hippos, so I had to float in a tube nearby to distract them while Amun snuck in between them to get it. You will be particularly glad because it was the one with your sweets."

Ethan just wanted to lie down. He felt cold and shaky.

"Sweets?" Fisi said.

"The best sweets ever," Tariro said, his eyes lighting up as he rummaged among their wet salvaged things for the tin. He opened the lid and offered one to Fisi who stared at them, confused.

"Like this," Jimoh said, selecting a toffee and unwrapping it to demonstrate.

Fisi chose a sweet very carefully, removed the wrapper as he had seen Jimoh do, and popped it into his mouth. He shut his eyes and adopted a blissful expression.

"Honey," he said. "Tastes like honey." He pushed the tin towards Ethan. "You might be able to trade this for the missing boy," he said. Then he leaned forward and grabbed another handful, as if he could not help himself.

Ethan took the tin from them and climbed into his sleeping bag.

"Who stole your cell-phone?" Tariro sneered, but Jimoh berated him firmly in Shona and Tariro backed off. Ethan hoped Jimoh had not told Tariro about the blood.

Jimoh made Tariro go through the equipment with him carefully. They separated the wet stuff from the dry. He sent Fisi to dig a hole close by to bury the sweet papers and any equipment that had been bashed beyond repair.

"We will cut this up for catapult," he said, untying the hessian cover from the tube they had floated on in the morning. It had burst during its descent. The mosquito nets were soaking wet, but he assured Ethan that they would dry by nightfall in the sweltering African sun if he hung them along a branch of the tree. He behaved as if it were perfectly normal for Ethan to be huddled up in a sleeping bag against the tree trunk in the middle of a hot afternoon while everyone else worked.

Jimoh untied Ethan's hat from its tube and placed it on Ethan's head, darting a glance at his own hat resting on Fisi's head. Ethan found he was hugging himself to stop shaking. Looking over at Fisi, now enjoying his fourth sweet, he was not resentful, exactly, but he wished Fisi would give Jimoh his hat back. He should have given it back to Jimoh as soon as they returned.

Moments later, aware of movement behind him, he turned to find Fisi standing awkwardly with the hat in his hands. He shot Ethan a knowing look, plonked the hat on Jimoh's head and wandered off towards the river.

Did I do that? Ethan thought, just as a sharp pain seared through his head. Great, that was all he needed – a headache.

But the headache did not last. It was just the one sharp pain, like an ice-cream brain freeze. Had Fisi done it to him? There was definitely more than met the eye with the folk from Karibu.

Jimoh showed Tariro how to make a fire. He tied together a small bundle of dry sticks, roughly the length of his foot, and placed them on the ground on top of some dry tinder. Then he threaded a length of vine from his right hand under the bundle to his left hand. Holding the bundle of sticks down with his feet, he pumped his hands up and down alternately, rubbing the vine against the bundle till the friction caused enough heat to make the tinder smoke. By the time Fisi came up from the river with two enormous freshwater bream from Darwishi, they had a roaring fire going.

CHAPTER 13
AN UNEASY HOMECOMING

Gogo Maya was woken at dawn by a din of high-pitched whispering in the branches overhead.

"Nomatotlo," she grumbled, still half-asleep. She should have known they would find her too early in the morning, busy little bodies that they were. After her terrible night sleeping in the forest, she was in no shape to work out what they were saying. She hadn't felt this weak for years and her amulet hadn't been much help, seeing that it had been virtually drained by the boy, Ethan. Come to think of it . . . there was something not quite right about that boy. She had studied him closely at the pool and found nothing remarkable about him, so how had he known he could suck power out of her? How had he dared?

"Five more minutes," she scowled at the little information-gathering spirits, trying to rearrange her leaden limbs into a position in her bed of leaves that didn't involve sticks digging into her back. She needed a little time to put her thoughts in order.

Feeling the warmth of the rising sun on her skin, her eyes drifted shut, and she thought about the first time she had come across the Nomatotlo.

SWITCH!

She still felt a pang of sadness after all these years as she remembered her young self, bending over her dead mother in that detached sort of way of the near starving. Despite the twisted knot of hunger in her belly and her dry lips, she had not wanted to go back to the swamp for water. Even that small action had seemed like too much effort.

It was no one's fault, her mother had told her when they'd reached the derelict cottage two nights before. People went hungry everywhere. It was the depression. That had done nothing to ease the aching in Maya's chest, and no amount of crying seemed to be able to revive her mother. Sometimes, when the pain in her stomach became too bad, she'd heard high-pitched voices whispering to her from the rafters:

"Follow," they'd murmur softly.

She couldn't see them, but she could smell them. The faint scent of burned cookies wafted off them, setting her mouth watering every time they drew near.

On that day she followed the smell, and their voices, out the door and down the road towards the swamp. Not sure whether she would catch them and eat them, or if they would coax her into the water and drown her, she stumbled after them till she saw the man sitting cross-legged on the ground waiting patiently for her.

He stood up when she came, smoothing out his white robes, and advancing cautiously. One hand clutched a felt hat, decorated with an assortment of fur, feathers and seed pods, while the other hand smoothed back a shock of snow-white hair. His kindly face seemed to glow from within.

"I have come to take you home," he'd said with a radiant smile, before turning towards a peculiar doorway hovering incongruously in the clearing. It looked like a slab of glass that had turned to gel.

At first she'd been unable to focus as they stepped into the icy opening, only vaguely aware of the tightness in her lungs and the freezing air that burned her throat when she breathed. Shivering, she'd held her arms tightly across her chest and walked beside the man. Heaven was a bit cold for her taste, and she'd felt poorly dressed for the weather up there, and for meeting God. But they had not gone to heaven. Instead they'd stepped out of the opening into the warm heart of Africa. Home.

That warm, fuzzy feeling did not last long. She'd found herself plunged into a hard and primitive way of life, almost before she had got her strength back. Up at dawn to see to the animals; a pole and mud hut; no electricity; no indoor privy. Still, she could not complain – there had always been enough to eat, and there were no white folk to boss you around. Even now, Gogo Maya allowed herself a satisfied smile. Was that why she was wary of the boy, Ethan, she wondered? It had been so long since she had seen a white person. He certainly had not seemed that bossy with the others at the pool. Had she exaggerated their arrogance in her memory of them over the years, or had they changed with time?

The serene man, Tacari, had explained to her that the opening they passed through to the magic place had come about by accident. One of his ancestors, a crafty *nyanga*, had been carried off from what they now believed to be Cameroon as a slave. Once the *nyanga* recovered from her shock and the terrible boat journey to the new world, she had set about constructing a powerful amulet, with which she opened up a tear in the clearing beside the swamp, to get herself back to Africa. Unable to find Cameroon from so far away, she had been drawn towards the magic in this rift valley. She and her friends came through to the Karibu forest where they'd set up Waheri village. The little information-gathering Nomatotlo attached themselves to the villagers, and had been spying for them ever since.

"Maya . . . Maya . . . Maya," whispered the Nomatotlo. "There is work to be done." She pulled herself up with a sigh. They were not that hard to understand when they spoke directly to her, and in a language she understood.

"Okay, I am up, but I am not strong enough to do anything,"

she warned, turning towards the faint biscuity scent of them. "Where am I?"

"You are in Karibu forest. Near Malamulu settlement," they whispered.

Well, that was a bit disturbing. She did not feel up to dealing with anyone from the Kishi hyena settlement, Malamulu. Not that the Kishi people would dare to attack her, but Gogo Maya was not altogether sure *they* knew that. She liked Gogo Nagesa as much as anyone, but the old hyena woman had allowed the young ones in her pack to degenerate into a bunch of hooligans, especially that Mesande and her crowd.

It could have been worse – she was lucky she had not ended up down in the rift valley. That would have been a long walk without the powers of her amulet.

"Lewa is here," whispered the Nomatotlo, "and that new boy, Aaron. If Lewa cannot help you, Aaron can carry you back to Waheri village."

"Over my dead body," Gogo Maya bristled, wobbling to her feet and glaring into the forest. There was no way she would submit to the indignity of being carried by anybody.

"Okay, you can come out now. I can see you," she called. Not that she could, but the inexperienced Aaron could not possibly know that.

Aaron pulled away from the shadows several metres to the left of where Gogo Maya was looking. He was a dark young man, with an open expressive face and a ready smile. Well, he'd proved to be stealthy, but it didn't do to let the boy get too cocky. Besides, he had a head start. She understood he'd been a thief and a burglar in New Orleans before he'd come through Tacari's opening.

"Where's your friend?" she said.

"Can't see her myself," he said, opening his hands in a gesture of futility, giving no indication that she had been addressing the wrong spot.

Lewa emerged from the gloom of the forest, giving Gogo Maya

a little start. She had been standing less than six paces away, waiting to see if she would be noticed. There was a twinkle of mischief about the girl. With her jet-black skin and short, kinky hair she was easily camouflaged in the forest. Today she wore her hair sectioned off into squares and pulled tightly into plaits, which spiked out like exclamations all over her head. Gogo Maya could hardly believe she had failed to spot the iridescent beetle shells attached to the end of each spike. What would that girl be wearing next?

"Thank you for coming," Gogo Maya said, in a tone almost bordering on respect. She had not yet fathomed the depths of Lewa's magic, except to know that it was many times more powerful than her own. The villagers at Waheri thought she had come from Bahar Dar, across the valley, but Gogo Maya was not so sure. Lewa had appeared one day, in the magic forest, as a young child. The Kishi hyena pack from Maradzi village, ever the opportunists, had captured her and, before they had worked out that there was no one to ransom her to, Lewa had succeeded in bending the entire pack's will to her own, making their lives hell. The pack had ended up begging the witches to take her and, come to think of it, had never taken a human hostage since.

"Gogo Maya!" Lewa took Gogo Maya by the hands, her dark eyes sparkling. A wall of raw energy rushed into Gogo Maya like a tidal wave, almost taking her breath away. Her blood virtually crackled with it. Lewa didn't heal exactly; she just bombarded you with enough energy to recover by yourself. "Where have you been?" Lewa asked, as if nothing powerful had happened.

Gogo Maya struggled to appear casual against the sudden barrage of sharpened senses. "I went to put beads into the bottom of Rafiki's well to make amulets," she said, resisting the urge to rub her tingling extremities, "and some other stuff of course," she added casually, avoiding any mention of mbogo roots. Was Lewa acting all serene to impress Aaron? No, she decided. The girl genuinely dispatched her magic with as little effort as that.

SWITCH!

Lewa turned towards Aaron and explained in that teacher's voice she liked to adopt: "Gogo Maya specialises in amulets. She will make you one like mine." She lifted her black tunic, loosened the drawstring of her trousers and pulled them down slightly to reveal a string of ceramic beads around her hips. "It will protect you from the Almohad if you bump into them in the forest. They are very strong, but that is not what you have to look out for. They have developed extraordinary beauty and seductive ways to go with it. One or two Waheri witches have almost been lured into slavery by them over the years. Gogo Maya soaks her beads in the magic of the Tokoloshe well before she makes her amulets." She beamed fondly at Gogo Maya. They both knew Lewa had no need of the amulets and she only wore hers to humor Gogo Maya.

Gogo Maya relaxed slightly. "Speaking of Almohad, someone, or something to do with Morathi's clan – and probably the Almohad, themselves – has got hold of some new magic. They captured Salih and me," she added with a sniff. "They were very threatening, too. We had to do my special switch to escape, but we jumped too far – right out of Karibu. I'm afraid we sucked a boy in. He's a bit younger than you, Aaron. It has caused many complications. That is why Salih isn't with me."

She hesitated for a moment, debating whether or not to tell Lewa about the other boy, Ethan, then shrugged. The Nomatotlo would tell the girl anyway. "Well, that and the fact that another boy drained so much energy from my opal that there was not enough for us both to switch back."

Lewa gave her an incredulous stare. "Gogo, it is not like you to allow an amulet to get so low in magic . . ." Her voice trailed off and her eyes widened. Gogo Maya would not do that.

Gogo Maya nodded. "The amulet was fine. The boy had the power to drain it."

"You got Salih to stay with the boy?" Lewa asked, her frown deepening.

"Better still, I persuaded the boy to come to us. Once I showed

134

him the switched boy in a scry, he agreed to come and rescue him. We saw the other boy with that tiger, Hajiri, who lives with the Almohad. There were a couple of questionable crocodiles living at the place where we switched to. They offered to show the boy with the power the way into Karibu through some caves under the forest. They claim the Sobek are real." She shook her head. "I never would have believed it. It must be like living in a hurricane down there! Salih is coming with them to keep an eye on the boy, of course."

"Them?" Lewa asked.

"Er . . . he has friends. Two," Gogo Maya said.

The girl looked excited. Gleeful even. "Tacari is going to be so mad," she beamed, helping Gogo Maya to her feet.

"What's a Sobek?" Aaron asked, tentatively offering Gogo Maya an arm. Just to be gentlemanly, his expression told her, nothing to do with weakness. "And I thought Tacari's opening was the only entrance to Karibu."

"Sobek are gods that live under the forest. We don't know much about them but we know there is water under there because it squirts into the valley," Lewa told him.

She glanced in the direction of the branches and spoke directly at the little spirits. "The Nomatotlo can ask Rafiki the Tokoloshe to find a way down to the waterfall and look for the boys who come from beyond. Then they can see if the boy who switched with Gogo Maya is in Almoh. And they must find out who attacked her." She patted Gogo Maya kindly on the arm, and then, not finding that expressive enough, hugged her.

"Are we going to Almoh then?" Aaron said. "I am dying to go to Almoh. I am told it is breathtakingly beautiful."

"You won't think it's so beautiful if they capture you and make you stay there," Lewa said impatiently. "All that magic spent making themselves beautiful has sucked the empathy right out of them. In any case, first we have to get Gogo Maya home. She is exhausted from her ordeal."

CHAPTER 14

STOLEN GEMS

Ethan stood just outside the camp, trying to brush his teeth without spilling the carefully sprinkled salt off the brush. He rinsed his mouth with water from a tin that had been converted into a mug. Jimoh would not allow anyone to use toothpaste, saying animals could pick up the scent for miles around. Ethan felt strangely energised, despite the terrible night that he'd had recovering from the bloodletting.

Jimoh crouched over a rock hyrax that Salih had brought in the night before. He was trying to gut and skin it without dirtying his new clothes.

"I don't know, Ethan," he said with a wry smile when he felt Ethan's eye on him. He stood up and turned around, inspecting the designer combat trousers and camouflage T-shirt Ethan had given him to wear the night before. "Is too fancy for bush. Feels like uniform for school."

"Well, you're going to have to wear it now," Ethan laughed. "There's nothing left of your shorts after those rapids, and you would have had to take off your red shirt sooner or later. It was too bright for the bush."

STOLEN GEMS

Not to be outdone, Tariro had given Fisi a pair of board-shorts and a T-shirt in his blue school colours, so the two boys looked like a team as they wandered up from the hippopotamus pool, laughing and bantering in the early morning mist.

"I don't know how he puts up with the smell," Ethan joked with Jimoh, jerking his head in the direction of Fisi and Tariro.

Jimoh's eyes twinkled. "Tariro, he take hyena boy down to river this morning and give him good wash with soap." He shook his head and tsk-tsked.

"Was Fisi okay with that?" Ethan was surprised. He'd seen his cousins wash their dog once, with disastrous results. He wondered how much of the youth's hyena personality lingered. Fisi cleaned up really nicely, even with his strange hair, but he still kept scratching his groin and sniffing at things.

"Oh yes, he love this thing," Jimoh wrinkled his nose, "but now they both smell like lady."

Fisi pulled a pebble back on the inner tube bands of Ethan's slingshot, and let it fly towards them.

"Eh!" yelled Jimoh, diving to the ground besides Ethan. "Fisi, you must not shoot at your friends!" But the pebble whizzed over their heads, hitting a soft custard apple, which exploded in a mess all over Jimoh's sleeping bag.

Fisi gave them an enigmatic smile, which made Ethan wonder how sharp the youth's hearing was. Perhaps he'd heard Jimoh say he smelled like a lady.

Ethan still felt a stab of regret at the loss of the slingshot, and not least because Fisi had proved to be a much better shot than himself. It was odd how Fisi had inveigled it from him. He had woken up to find the hyena youth gazing at him and it had occurred to him what a great idea it would be to lend him the slingshot Tafadzwa had given him. Then, as Fisi wandered away with it, his feeling of generosity had faded to be replaced by a vague feeling of having been had. He'd tried to coax Fisi into giving it back as he had done with Jimoh's hat, but it hadn't worked.

Everyone except Ethan ate the rock hyrax and then broke camp. By mid-morning they floated swiftly through another narrow gorge. Sheer jagged cliffs towered above them, casting a shadow over the water, but even in the shade the heat was oppressive. Ethan lounged on the one remaining large tractor tube, which he shared with Salih and Jimoh. Tariro and Fisi drifted behind Amun on two smaller tubes. From time to time, when they thought no one was looking, one of them would haul the supply tube towards himself and pinch a sweet from the tin. Ethan couldn't decide which one was a worse influence on the other.

Tariro had picked a couple of horned cucumbers off a vine before they set out, which the two boys threw back and forth between them like rugby balls. It had taken Fisi a couple of moments to understand the concept, and a couple of smashed cucumbers, but once he caught on, he was as good a throwing buddy for Tariro as Joe had ever been.

After cutting his new designer trousers into shorts using the scissor attachment on Ethan's Swiss Army knife and stashing the discarded legs in a safe place for some undetermined use later, Jimoh nestled down into the tube and busied himself cutting the damaged tractor tube into strips to make Fisi his own slingshot. Ethan smiled at him, shaking his head. The Italian clothing designer would have a fit if he saw his precious work of art slashed in this way, but somehow it seemed the right thing to do. Ethan thought he might cut up his own pants if he could wrestle the knife away from Jimoh long enough to do it. Jimoh sure loved that knife. Not that he felt coerced in any way, as he had been by Fisi and the slingshot, but Ethan would let Jimoh keep the knife if they ever got home again. He was sure his step-dad would understand.

Ethan fanned himself with his hat, squinting into the sun. The general heat of the day seemed to be gradually expanding through his body and then, oddly, it passed. He realised that the feeling had not, in fact, been warmth, but a vague feeling of excitement. Since there was nothing exciting about his own set of circumstances, he looked at Salih, wondering if the leopard was somehow making him feel that way, but the leopard lay half-asleep beside Jimoh as if he hadn't a care in the world.

Salih's ears pricked up when he read Ethan's confusion, though. "You can feel it?" Something that might have been shock flashed across his face before he went on in a lazy drawl, "It's the crocodiles – I imagine it's because we are close to their home. When we get there I think they might change."

"Do you mean like Fisi did?"

"I'm not sure. The crocodiles are Sobek. All I know about them is what these two have told me, and of course, the legends of the forest. Not that you should believe any of those legends. With everyone wanting to scare everyone else out of the forest, half those stories are made up."

Ethan reached into the far recesses of his memories of history lessons at school but could not remember anything about Sobek beyond the fact that they were Egyptian gods with the body of a man and the head of a crocodile. The way things were going, the world had got that wrong too, he supposed, but he wondered if Amun and Darwishi would look like that if they changed.

Salih looked as if he was settling down for another doze, but Ethan wanted answers. He prodded Salih in the shoulder, and then trailed his hand in the water to clean it. "Is that why nobody from our world knows about Karibu? Have they been frightened off by the legends?"

"I suppose so." Salih did not bristle at Ethan's touch like he did when Tariro stroked him; he relaxed, arching his back as he stood up to stretch, rocking the tube in the water. "Also, the ring of mountains between the Karibu rift valley and the outside are rugged and dangerous to cross." The leopard gestured towards Jimoh. "Some people have known all along, I think, but it seems they don't want to admit it."

Jimoh was not the type to actually lie about anything, but Ethan supposed it was fairly likely Jimoh's people knew something about Karibu. They had been far too willing to accept the witch at face value.

"So how big is Karibu? The part you do know," Ethan said to change the subject.

Frowning, Salih considered that for a while. "It would take a full moon cycle for a man to journey from one end to the other and perhaps a little less than half a moon cycle to travel from side to side."

"Oh . . . So how are we going to find Joe if it is so huge?" Ethan was beginning to realise their journey was going to be a lot longer than he had imagined. Certainly longer than the week they had planned to spend at Crystal Pool. He wondered how long it would be before his family came looking for them.

"Gogo Maya has ways to find the boy wherever the tiger takes him," Salih reassured him.

"The tiger is going to hurt him, I saw it in the scry," Ethan said, remembering his cousin asleep against the tiger, and the sudden flash of his cut face.

"No, I'm sure what you saw was just Gogo Maya, worrying. Hajiri is a kindly cat." Salih put a soothing paw on Ethan's arm and considered him through half-open eyes. "I am more concerned with where he is taking the boy," he said. "The people Hajiri lives with, the Almohad, are very strange. They imagine they own everyone in Karibu and gamble and trade freely with them as if they were livestock. If they get hold of the boy it may be hard to persuade them to give him back without some sort of a trade. We need to get there quickly too. Before they persuade him he does not want to leave."

"Can't your Gogo Maya do something to get him from the tiger, or from the Almohad?" Ethan said, wondering what the Almohad could possibly offer Joe that would keep him from wanting to come home to his family.

"She would have if she had not been drained of all her power," Salih said with a meaningful sigh. "She has ways to replenish it, but the source of Gogo Maya's magic is a little . . . shall we say . . . dubious sometimes, so she will not wish to get help from the other witches. It will take time for her to build enough power to take on the Almohad." Salih stretched luxuriously and settled down once more beside Jimoh. "Don't worry, Ethan, I am impervious to their beguiling ways, and I think perhaps you are too, now that you have her power. Between us we will think of something."

Ethan was not so sure he was impervious to anything of the sort. Fisi had been able to charm his slingshot out of him. On the other hand, he was sure he had somehow made Fisi give back Jimoh's hat. There was definitely something strange going on inside himself.

"Does the power I drained from Gogo Maya have anything to do with the hippo not attacking me?" he said to Salih.

"Maybe . . ."

It did not look as if he were going to get any more information out of the leopard, so Ethan turned his attention to a fish eagle. It swooped down from its great height and plunged into the water not far from where they floated, then came up with a wriggling fish caught between its talons. Ethan took a long contemplative breath, closed his eyes and concentrated on the bird. He held his breath until a wave of giddiness washed over him.

"Drop the fish," he commanded the fish eagle. In his imagination he had a low bass voice.

"Yewk, yewk," it cried in triumph, ignoring him completely. It soared back up to its perch on a branch jutting out of the steep cliffs.

"Yep! Not really charming anything from anybody here," Ethan said out loud.

"Be careful with that power," Salih said with an amused

expression. "There are always consequences." He turned to look upriver. The distance between the cliffs grew narrower, and soon, a dark cave mouth yawned before them, wide, with a low ceiling. They drifted inexorably toward it on the powerful current.

Before Ethan had time to fumble in his backpack for his headlight, the tube they were floating on rushed down a four-foot incline and then drifted sedately down a long dark tunnel. He wished he could feel the sides of the tunnel to gauge how far or how fast they were going, but he was afraid he might touch a spider or something slimy. Once, they drifted beneath a small underground waterfall and Ethan got drenched.

Ghostly lights gradually began to play on the surface of the inky black water, and then, without warning, the entire flotilla went flying through the air. Ethan struggled to right himself before plunging feet first into an indigo pool. Swimming towards a shelf at the entrance of a small tunnel just above the water line, he belly-slid himself up and sat there scanning the water anxiously for his friends. Salih was the first to surface, followed by Jimoh and then the two other boys. Tariro came up screaming and swam towards Ethan in a panic.

"Something brushed against my leg!"

"It was probably Fisi," Ethan said, hauling Tariro up as quickly as he could before diving in to push Fisi to the ledge. If the hyena youth's spectacular belly-flop into the pool were anything to go by, Ethan guessed he would be a little worse for wear. Sure enough, he coughed and spluttered, then lay on his back, a picture of abject misery.

"Well, that was creepy!" Tariro grumbled, looking down into the gloomy depths of the water below.

Jimoh muttered something to him in Shona. "He says it felt as if the giant hand of the devil was going to come up from the bottom and pull us under," Tariro interpreted, nodding in agreement.

Ethan, too, was aware of an indefinable fear, even though there was plenty of shadowy light pouring in from the open sky. "At least it's a sinkhole and not a cave," he said, trying to cheer everyone up.

"What is sinkhole?" Jimoh asked.

"An underground cave, but with the roof fallen in," Tariro explained.

Several waterfalls cascaded into the hole from various tunnels – some large and fast flowing, some smaller, diminishing down to one that was barely a trickle. The river must have split up somewhere inside the mountain, Ethan thought. A faint smell of rotting vegetation hung in the air and, oddly, a whiff of sulphur.

"Our crocodile friends are going to drag us through that underwater tunnel connecting this pool to a lake, which is their home," Salih said, pointing at a sinister-looking dark spot several metres below the surface of the water. He did not look happy.

"Underwater?" Tariro said dubiously when Ethan explained that to him. "Look, I am not afraid or anything, but do these guys understand how long we can hold our breath before we drown? Are you sure they don't plan to take us under there and drown us anyway?"

"Tariro, is better to drown than to stay here. This place very creepy," Jimoh shuddered.

"No, Jimoh! Is better we get out of here alive and go find Joe," Tariro said.

"They understand this with the breath. They have taken a human this way before," Salih said. "I will go first to make sure it is safe. Then they can come back for you." Ethan sensed that even Salih was anxious to get away from the hole. He wondered if the leopard knew something they did not.

While they waited their turn, Jimoh gathered the equipment. He let the air out of the tubes regretfully. "We have lost foot pump by hippo pool, Ethan, but can cut up for sling."

Remembering his aunt's advice about the mosquito nets, Ethan tied them up in a bundle to take through the tunnel. He suddenly realised he hadn't worried about malaria in days – not since his aunt had asked him about the anti-malaria pills. Could the magic be protecting him from that too? He hadn't felt asthmatic either . . . Maybe this journey wasn't so bad after all.

Stashing the sweets and his penknife in the watertight compartment of his rucksack, he zipped it up tightly. He would have to remember to oil his knife later as his step-dad had shown him, whether or not it got wet.

Eventually the two crocodiles reappeared without Salih and swam up beside the ledge, indicating that they were ready for the next passengers.

Tariro and Fisi went after Salih. In the end, Tariro was more spooked by the creepiness of the sinkhole than the danger of the underwater tunnel, and couldn't wait to get going.

Having ran out of tasks to keep them occupied, Ethan and Jimoh huddled together in the disquieting sinkhole alone, chilled and wretched, listening for the sound of Amun and Darwishi's return. Ethan stared down into the water. He could not shake the dreadful feeling that something dark moved in the gloomy depths below watching every move they made.

As he watched, a shaft of sunshine grew slowly across the water and the sun moved vertically overhead. The nature of the grotto began to change. Gradually, the water lightened to azure blue. Mist thrown up by the waterfalls displayed an almost perfectly circular rainbow that looked like a Catharine Wheel in the sunlight. Hundreds of colourful little fishes darted to and fro just below the shelf.

"Look, Ethan!" Jimoh grabbed Ethan by the back of his shirt and pointed down into the depths of the water. A couple of metres below, sunlight bounced off a small pile of multicoloured crystals spilling over a narrow ledge.

"That's what's making the coloured reflections on the walls," Ethan began, then his eyes widened in disbelief. "Oh my word – they're gemstones!" He shook Jimoh excitedly. "Do you think there will be more on the bottom?" He put his face into the water and tried to see the bottom of the sinkhole. It was deep, but there were definitely colours down there.

"I am going to dive down and have a look," he said, starting to remove his trousers.

"What for we want this thing, Ethan," Jimoh said, dismissing the idea.

"Jimoh! The stones are valuable," Ethan said.

"Then he belong to someone, Ethan. Is stealing. Stones like money, they do not grow together all in one place like this. You have to dig them. Someone, he put these stones here." Jimoh rubbed the back of his neck.

"Jimoh, do you remember Salih told us we might have to trade to get Joe back? Well, this is the perfect thing," Ethan pleaded. "Even if we don't have to pay to get Joe back, we could keep them. Just think how much you can uplift your village with this stash. We could run electricity there. You could have computers, TV, build proper houses. Besides, there are piles – no one would notice if we took some."

Jimoh looked at Ethan as if he was out of his mind. "Tjalotjo happy with houses we have got, Ethan. We build ourselves, from nature." He shook his head. "Cement for city . . . TV also." Then his eyes widened. "What if stones evil, like Gogo Maya stones?"

"No! No. Jimoh. I don't think Gogo Maya's stones are evil," Ethan said. "Look at me! There is the healing and I am so strong now."

"Also reckless, Ethan, and greedy, I am noticing." Jimoh wet his lips, and then gave a nod of assent. "But you are right, maybe is only way to save Joe." He took his hat off his head and twirled it nervously in his hands before him, ready to dive.

"Not so fast, Jimoh, it's very deep." Ethan did not want Jimoh to drown, or get the bends from diving too deep. He wasn't that sure how deep they would have to go before they got decompression sickness. Ethan had seen divers on TV drop down with a weight to make the descent faster, and come up slowly, in stages, to stabilise the nitrogen buildup in their bodies caused by the pressure of all the water above them. Come to think of it, they also used scuba-diving equipment, but he was just going to have to do without. If one of them was going down, he decided, it had better be him. He was beginning to suspect that he could hold his breath for longer than usual because he had done it when facing off with the hippopotamus. He realised he had done it at the Crystal Pools too. There was no time to explain all that to Jimoh before the crocodiles returned. Feeling only slightly guilty about his subterfuge, Ethan said, "I think it is safer for me to go down because of the amulet magic." He folded Jimoh's hat under his arm and searched the ledge for a suitable rock to use as a weight.

It was too dark down there to see properly what he was doing, so he dug Jimoh's hat in under the pebbles and gathered up whatever stones lay on the floor, then floated warily upwards through the water, stopping twice and treading water as he had seen on TV. He rushed the last five metres or so because his lungs were fit to burst, but a quick check of his limbs revealed that his body was none the worse for the dive.

Amun and Darwishi lurked, waiting for him on the surface, and before Ethan could take stock of his haul, Darwishi took the hat gently in his mouth and started to tip the contents back into the pool. Jimoh spoke rapidly to him in Shona and, amazingly, he stopped.

Ethan whipped round to stare at Jimoh. "You can talk to the crocodiles? They speak Shona?"

Jimoh laughed. "Not like you and Salih, Ethan. More like . . . dog. But better. Sometime he do what I want. If he want same thing."

Ethan tried his luck. He explained to Darwishi, more slowly and elaborately than was probably necessary, "I hope you don't mind. We need the gems to get our friend back. If you want, I will put them back in the water again."

Darwishi, not all that expressive at the best of times, appeared not to care either way, but he let go of the hat. After a moment, Ethan picked it up and started to stash the gems into his pockets. A quick glimpse at the stones told him he had scooped up more than he had bargained for. "They're not just semi-precious crystals," he said with a sharp intake of breath. "They're emeralds and tanzanite! And . . ." He pocketed them more quickly, in case Darwishi changed his mind.

Climbing on to the backs of the crocodiles both boys took a deep breath in preparation for the dive through the tunnel. Ethan almost gasped for air as Darwishi dove beneath the water. A searing sensation struck his temples, as if he were passing through eucalyptus oil or concentrated mint. Then a vision of a dangerous looking dragon flashed into his head, hanging there for several terrifying moments.

It had one sharp rhinoceros horn sweeping back from the middle of its snout, one from its forehead, and an even bigger one on the top of its head. A row of horns decorated each of its brow ridges. All sloping backwards like greenish flames caught in suspended animation and petrified to look like stone. Slanted eyes stared red and angry.

Then, just as suddenly the image was gone and Ethan knew it had been sent to him by Amun or Darwishi. Was that an early warning of what the Sobek change into, or were they just trying to frighten him? And if so, why? After they'd been so friendly and helpful all the way from Crystal Pool, were him and Jimoh about to be eaten?

CHAPTER 15
THE SOURCE OF THE MAGIC

Darwishi pulled Ethan swiftly through the under water passage, and he had only become slightly worried about his next breath when the end of the tunnel lightened and he braced himself to plunge into yet another pool. He was quite taken aback when they emerged smoothly, still underwater, and burst up to the surface to find themselves in an underground cave. He took a deep breath and tried to orientate himself before staring open-mouthed at the immensity of the cavern.

Rocks, the size of houses, lay scattered along the water's edge, fallen from a hole in the massive vaulted ceiling. A shaft of sunlight beamed down through a lacy fringe of long dangling vines. Giant stalactites clung to the ceiling like petrified stone icicles. Ethan felt almost as if he had shrunk.

"Look, Ethan!" Jimoh pointed skywards. Swallows darted in and out of the brilliant shaft of sunlight, so far up, and so small, they could have been mistaken for butterflies.

An eerie light reflected off the surface of the underground river. Puddles of petrol-coloured liquid floating on the water beside him, absorbed sunlight, held it for a heartbeat, pulsing with an ethereal glow, and then released it back into the atmosphere. Ethan was strangely drawn towards it. He sliced his hand slowly through the nearest puddle, dispersing the liquid, feeling the iciness of it against his hand. He watched it ripple apart into smaller puddles and then drift together again to be reabsorbed like mercury. He snatched his hand away at the thought, hoping it wasn't poisonous like mercury. A slight smell of tinned pears wafted off it into the air.

"We must find Tariro and Fisi," Jimoh beckoned, applying pressure to Amun's left flank with his knee and Amun turned away from the sunlight towards the gloomy interior. Was Jimoh riding the crocodile like a horse now? It wouldn't surprise Ethan, but he was not about to test it himself. Darwishi would probably bite his leg off. He wondered if the crocodile was angry with him, or disappointed about the gemstones. He could tell nothing from Darwishi's stony expression.

The underground river was deep and slow flowing. It emptied into a lake in a cavern, even larger than the one before. The light from Ethan's headlamp barely penetrated its vastness, and, if anything, seemed to make the cavern behind look even darker.

Jimoh spotted the others first. They were waiting on the edge of the lake, surrounded by a number of burly-looking people carrying lit fire-torches. Thankfully, there was no sign of the frightening dragon Ethan imagined earlier.

He scrambled off Darwishi's back and waded through the shallow water towards them. Close up, the Sobek people had a powerful, muscular look about them, with dark ochre-coloured skin and viridian green eyes that flashed in the flickering torchlight. Some looked hairless or had shaved heads, and some wore pitch-black wigs that looked as if they were made out of raffia, which fell in a multitude of plaits to just below their shoulders. They wore layers of wildly patterned, colourful kangas like swimming towels, which seemed appropriate with so much water about. The men wore them tied around their waists, and the women wore them tucked up under their armpits. Single polished gems, mostly topaz or garnet, the size of pigeon eggs dangled from leather thongs strung around the men's necks. Some of the men wore deep red or blue opaque gems with a six-rayed star that reflected from their depths when they caught the light. Ethan wondered if there was any social significance or hierarchy symbolised by the gems they were wearing, or if they were just a personal choice.

A man crushed Ethan's hand in a vice-like grip, hauling him out of the water as if expecting something much heavier, and spilled him onto the bank. He rumbled something in a voice so deep Ethan could hardly make out what he was saying. His square, short face crinkled into a benign smile and he removed the shocking pink outermost Kanga from around his own waist and offered it to Ethan. The man appeared to have several layers underneath, in a kaleidoscope of patterns and colours – gaudy, even in the gloom of the cave.

"Thank you," Ethan said. He was not sure he wanted to wear the man's Kanga but Tariro already wore a similarly donated bright kanga, so he guessed that was the polite thing to do. After wrapping it securely around his waist, he wriggled out of his cargo pants underneath, then rolled them into a ball and gripped them under his arm, acutely aware of his own gems hidden in the pockets.

Pulling Ethan roughly towards himself, despite Ethan's reluctance, Tariro gave him a hug. "As usual, you two took so long, Ethan, we thought you had drowned. Not that we would miss you, but I have grown rather fond of Jimoh." He put an arm around Jimoh's neck, pulling his head down into an arm lock, spilling his sopping wet hat onto the floor, and ruffled his hair with a fist. "Fisi didn't have a great crossing," he added, cocking his head towards the back of the group of men. Ethan opened his mouth to protest. He had not taken a long time. He had hardly run out of breath. But when he looked in the direction Tariro indicated he frowned worriedly.

Fisi looked terrible. He walked over unsteadily, smoothing back his bedraggled brindle hair. The deep growl in the back of his throat adjusted itself into a hawking and spitting as he advanced.

"I ran out of air," he complained. He mimicked Tariro by hugging first Jimoh, and then Ethan, his gesture stiff, his eyes darting warily from Sobek to Sobek. Ethan wondered if Fisi had been frightened by his underwater swim or if he had a reason to be afraid of the Sobek. Could Salih have misplaced his trust? Should they all be afraid of the Sobek? He stifled a shiver when he thought of the dragon.

The crowd parted and a thickset man in a white linen kanga with shiny gold tassels, wandered forward in no particular hurry. Hanging from around his neck was a splendid gold breastplate in the shape of a stylised hawk. Its wings spread-eagled across his chest, each feather intricately carved and inlaid with jewels, each talon gripping a ruby the size of an eagle egg.

Ethan shrank back involuntarily, tightening his grip on his rolled up cargo pants. He wondered if those rubies had come from the sinkhole. Then he pulled himself together and stood beside Salih while the man inspected each one of them for a long while, his thin black crocodile pupils narrowing disconcertingly at the exact moment Ethan hoped he would not find out about the gems he'd stolen. Could it have been a coincidence? The man's eyes shifted to Tariro, who gazed back at his breastplate in stunned awe.

He glanced almost dismissively over Fisi before coming to rest on Jimoh. Such a powerful ripple of excitement and pleasure passed over the man, that Ethan stifled a small gasp and reached out a hand to grip Salih, wondering if Jimoh were in danger, but Salih looked unafraid, and Jimoh appeared not to have felt it at all.

The man turned immediately towards Ethan, as if to allay any fears. "I am Kashka," he said evenly. Ethan found, if he cocked his head just slightly, he could almost make out the words. Salih translated anyway.

Ethan stepped forward and held his hand out, bracing for another forceful, finger-crushing grip. "I am Ethan," he said, turning to introduce the others, but Salih interrupted.

"He knows that, Ethan. That is what he has been finding out since he came in. He hears every thought that passes through your head. They all do."

Oh drat, thought Ethan, trying desperately not to think of gems, or bloodletting. No wonder Fisi had been so jumpy. He wondered what the hyena youth had to hide. Kashka smiled, momentarily revealing faint traces of the green and grey markings of crocodile in the crinkles at the corners of his eyes. He didn't say anything about gems, or offer any comment on what he had read in Fisi, just motioned for everyone to follow him.

Kashka herded them to the back of the cavern where they climbed up a flight of steps into a narrow tunnel. The boys and Salih looked curiously from side to side as they passed by a row of subterranean caves, each with a fire pit in the middle and a chimney funnel leading up to the surface overhead. Hundreds of small square scraps of reflective metal hung down, catching and multiplying the sunlight as it shone down through the funnels. Cave paintings and murals decorated almost every wall.

Some caves had clay shelves running along one or two of their walls where Sobek people and a few crocodiles lounged on pallets chatting to one another or playing a complicated-looking game with sticks and stones. Kashka turned in to a cave with four small alcoves scooped out of a wall about waist height off the ground. Bedrolls, in the same colourful cottons as their Kangas, were stacked neatly in each alcove. Three walls were decorated with murals depicting scenes that looked remarkably like Tjalotjo village and Crystal Pools. A large cartoon mahobohobo tree loomed over a cartoon pool, with a set of rapids and an unmistakable baobab tree in the distance. Even the intricate map depicted beside it looked familiar.

THE SOURCE OF THE MAGIC

Ethan watched as Jimoh ran his finger over an illustration, which could easily have been himself in his hat. "Who does painting?" he asked, his eyes wide with wonder.

Kashka adjusted his voice a couple of octaves higher and spoke a little faster. "Each clan paints its own area," he said. His rich, low tone still boomed around the cavern, but was a lot easier to follow.

He motioned for the boys to take a seat on the floor after unloading their backpacks beside the remainder of their equipment, which had been stacked neatly in a corner of the cave by a Sobek.

"They get the oxide from merchant vessels on the larger rivers when they travel," Kashka continued, once they had seated themselves around him. "They go off into the world from time to time in crocodile form in pairs or in groups and when they return they paint the story of their travels for future generations."

From Salih's sharp intake of breath, Ethan got the feeling he was surprised that the Sobek came and went so freely without him and his witch friends even knowing it.

"Amun and Darwishi will add to these paintings once they have changed back into their man form. They have been studying the people at Crystal Pool," Kashka explained.

Young men and women, carrying wooden bowls piled high with fish and some sort of dried root vegetable, interrupted his narration just long enough for Ethan to whisper a warning to Tariro that Kashka and the rest of the Sobek could read his mind.

"You mean they have been hanging around Crystal Pools reading everyone's minds all this time?" Tariro gasped, his face a picture of horror. Ethan grinned. He could not tell if Tariro was more shocked at the thought of having his mind read, or if he had just discovered that the beautifully presented fish he had just bitten into was completely raw. Ethan had to admit, Tariro could be very entertaining when he wasn't vying for Joe's attention all the time – quite likeable even.

"Yes, and infusing the pool with health and well-being in

exchange," Kashka said, a little sternly, but without malice.

While Kashka explained how the magic they'd seen floating on the surface of the water was absorbed by the crocodiles and slowly released into the water at Crystal Pools for the benefit of all who swam there, in exchange for the privilege of studying them – a long standing arrangement from many years ago – Salih took the opportunity to have a private conversation with Ethan.

"I believe you have taken some stones," he said, his expression set for scolding.

Ethan tightened his grip on his rolled up cargo pants guiltily. "We took them in the hope of ransoming Joe." He swallowed and looked Salih straight in the eye. "You said yourself, we would probably have to give them something. We did offer to put them back." He was about to start emptying his pocket to return the gems to Kashka but the Sobek's hand shot out and covered Ethan's to stop him. Kashka shifted his voice an octave lower again and rumbled deeply and unintelligibly to Salih.

"Stop!" Salih flashed a warning at Ethan. "You must not show the gems to the other boys. Kashka knows why you took them. He says it is not up to him whether you keep them or not. The gems do not belong to the Sobek." Salih's pupils narrowed to thin slits and his tail swished anxiously. "He says it was very brave of you to steal them from the Mokele Mbembe. I have heard of this thing, Ethan, and it is very dangerous, even for me."

Ethan knew without asking that the Mokele Mbembe was the dragon-like creature that had flashed into his mind in the sinkhole. So that was what Darwishi had been trying to tell him.

An expression that might have been fear crossed Salih's face when Ethan remembered the thing. "Yes!" he confirmed. "Apparently, he is asleep in one of the tunnels at the moment but if he had been awake there would have been an accounting. As it is, he will go in search of his treasures when he wakes up. Kashka says, even though the treasure looks like many, Mokele Mbembe knows each stone intimately. He will be able to tell if some are missing and will be able to track them down."

Another rumbled exchange between Kashka and Salih followed. "They don't want anyone bringing strangers to this place to die in an attempt to reach the stones either," Salih continued to interpret into Ethan's head. "There is a spell on the hole. Anyone who dives down the hole for them dies with the pain."

Or they get the bends, thought Ethan, but a knot of tension was growing in his stomach. He wished he did not have to keep the gems a secret but there was no way he was giving them up. He might need them to get Joe back. On the other hand, he was having a hard enough time keeping Tariro and Fisi out of his sweets and his personal backpack. They would find the gems sooner or later and guess where they came from. He was pretty sure Fisi was able to coerce the source of the gems out of him if he wanted to.

Kashka's features relaxed into a gracious smile as he spoke to Salih. "He does not want to take them back. He says your lives may depend on them," Salih said. "Although he is unable to explain how they do it, he says the Sobek feel some events in advance. For instance, Amun and Darwishi had been expecting the witch." He looked quite perturbed at that news, and then adopted his usual expression of studied nonchalance. He arched his back and stood up. "Just be careful who you give them to because Mokele Mbembe will catch up with them. Even the Almohad do not deserve the dragon."

"What are you guys talking about?" Tariro said, evidently beginning to get irritated with the private exchange.

"Oh, sorry, Tariro," Ethan said. "The two of them are discussing a dragon. Nothing to worry about, apparently he is sleeping."

"As if!" Tariro laughed.

"Okay, they are planning our next move," Ethan said, and true to Ethan's word, Salih sat down again and explained to Kashka how Joe had exchanged places with the witch, and how Amun and Darwishi had agreed to guide the boys to Karibu to rescue him. Ethan interpreted for the boys, feeling more and more wretched as he realised that while he had been fretting and complaining about having to go and rescue Joe, worrying about his own personal safety, Jimoh's family and friends had been losing the magic the crocodiles brought to the pool.

He hadn't really believed in the magic, although he had been surprised at the contentment of the villagers with their meager lot. He wondered how powerful the infusion was, and how much it contributed to that contentment. Had the Tjalotjo villagers known, and given the magic up willingly to save Joe? He vowed to himself that if he survived the rescue attempt and got home to Cape Town, and his step-dad's millions, he would do everything in his power to help the kraal.

"Do not assume they need help, Ethan," Kashka said quietly. "Although it will take a long time to get others to the Crystal Pool, and Tjalotjo village will be vulnerable while the magic is not there, they will manage." Then he said, louder, so that everyone could hear. "As fascinated as I am with your thought patterns, there is one here who has travelled. He can help you to plan for your quest. I will take you to him."

Kashka led them up a long flight of ancient steps to a series of sinkholes closer to the surface. The afternoon sun streamed in through a hole in the ceiling only ten metres or so above their heads. Water from an artesian well gurgled and bubbled to the surface through a small fissure in the rock below and pooled at their feet before meandering away into the darkness of the passage from where they had entered. Ethan could hardly take his eyes off it, as it shimmered golden and petrol blue, and almost syrupy with magic.

Amun and Darwishi, still in crocodile form – but looking softer somehow – and five Sobek men joined the boys and Salih, who seated themselves on rocks in a crescent around Kashka.

A Sobek man with a boxer's build, seated besides Kashka, rubbed his huge sapphire pendant between thumb and forefinger reflecting on Salih and each one of the boys in turn, then rose from his rock, nimbly for one so muscle-bound, and broke a branch from a small tree that grew out of the side of the cavern where the sun shone.

He cleared his throat. "I am Nuru," he said in his deep voice. Ethan glanced at Jimoh and Tariro. They had understood the man perfectly. He'd been somewhat easier to understand than Kashka. Ethan wondered if he travelled because he could be understood more clearly, or if he had learned to articulate himself better because he travelled.

Nuru drew a large oval in the sand at their feet. "This is our lake," he explained, "and this is where you came in." He added a winding tail to one end of the oval he had drawn. "Amun has told of your quest to rescue your brother from the magic forest that lies above us." He jabbed his stick towards the ceiling.

"It will not be easy," he went on, flashing a rueful smile. "You could go back the same way you came and forget the boy, but it will be a lot harder to climb up the waterfall to the river from within the Mokele Mbembe hole than it was to fall in."

"There is no way I am going back that way!" Tariro gasped in dismay. "We had better find another way home. That was too creepy, even for me."

It was too creepy for Ethan too. He shivered at the thought of the dragon. Thank goodness he had found a quiet moment to warn Jimoh to keep the gems a secret; if they survived their journey, he wouldn't put it past Tariro to overcome his trepidation and come back for more. Even if he told Tariro Mokele Mbembe was the name of a dragon, not the name of the sinkhole, Tariro would never believe him.

Fisi's eyes narrowed to suspicious golden slits, making Ethan wonder if the youth knew more about dragons than he was letting on, but he didn't say anything.

Salih frowned. "We cannot go back the way we came," he said firmly. "We need to meet up with Gogo Maya in the forest above."

Nuru did not seem so interested in the objections of Fisi or Salih. He folded his arms across his chest and fixed the three boys with a tentative grin. "You could all stay here for a while and soak in the magic till its power gives you the ability to travel underwater to the forest," he said. "That is the shortest and safest route."

"How long would we be underwater for?" Tariro pushed a dreadlock out of his eyes, and exchanged nervous looks with Fisi, who was shaking his head.

"How long would we have to soak in the magic?" Ethan said at the same time.

Nuru looked from Tariro to Ethan with a puzzled frown. "I am not sure how you measure time, but it has taken the Sobek thousands of flood seasons to do all that we do with the magic. A small skill such as holding your breath would take about two moon cycles to perfect. Less time if you work hard at the learning." Then he turned towards Tariro and Fisi and tut-tutted at them with an indulgent grin. "You have to hold your breath many times longer than you did in the passage that leads from Mokele Mbembe to our lake."

Ethan's spirits sank. He had thought the man meant days, not months. He'd had enough of magic anyway. "Forget it!" he said, remembering the gash above his cousin's eye. "Joe could be lying in the forest bleeding to death as we speak. We need to get there as soon as possible."

"A great pity," Nuru shrugged. "We were looking forward to spending time with you. Not this one, of course." He swept a dismissive arm at Fisi, who didn't appear to care. "We already know all about him, and his people, but this one," he put a hand on Tariro's shoulder, "he has a fascinating history to read."

THE SOURCE OF THE MAGIC

Tariro pulled back, startled. "No way! I'm not sticking around here letting you guys read stuff out of my head."

The Sobek laughed, then he looked at Jimoh kindly. "This boy can tell us all about the Crystal Pools. We have been following the life stories of the folk who live there. Amun and Darwishi can tell us all about whether the beautiful one from the town has kissed the young man, Tendayi, yet and whether the old man, Ephraim, recovered from his illness, but they cannot tell what has happened to those who do not use the pool. We would like to know what happened to the young lady who moved to the city for education and the man who was bitten by the viper. We worry."

Ethan almost laughed out loud when that strange, warm emotion he had felt when Kashka first clapped eyes on Jimoh became clear. These people were fans of Jimoh. Fans! It was almost as if the Crystal Pools was a reality show for the Sobek, starring Jimoh, and the hunters, and every other kid who thought while he swam there.

"And you, boy." Ethan flushed when the man's attention fell upon him. He urgently retraced his own thoughts since he had arrived at Crystal Pools, and more disturbingly, thoughts he had had since arriving in the caves, but Nuru seemed not to come up with anything compromising. At least anything he was willing to share. "I think you have been many places you could tell us about. Darwishi says you have been thinking about caves even larger than our own."

"Son Doong," Ethan nodded, relieved that he was not going to have to explain about gems . . . and blood.

"Ethan has never been to Son Doong caves," Tariro protested. "He's seen them on the internet."

Way to go, Tariro, Ethan thought. As much as Tariro objected to having his own thoughts invaded, he obviously still wanted them to be more interesting than Ethan's. Still, it was very worrying having the Sobek tap into any of their thoughts like that. As friendly as they were, he was not sure he could trust them.

SWITCH!

"You can," Salih projected into Ethan's head. He nudged his face against Ethan's palm, shifting his body under Ethan's hand until he gave in and stroked the leopard.

Looking towards the water with the magic floating on top, Ethan realised that the urge to clean his hand after touching the leopard was not as strong as his reluctance to touch the water, but eventually washing his hands won out.

"Do you mind if I touch the water?" he asked Kashka.

"The magic is for everyone. You may have as much as you want, but it will bend itself to your will, so be careful what you wish for."

Once he had washed his hands, Ethan would have liked to find out more about the magic, but Salih brought the meeting back to order.

"Nuru, as much as we would love to stay and exchange information, there is some urgency in our quest to rescue the boys' friend," he said. "They are very fond of him, and he may be in grave danger."

"Then the only path you can take is north-east," Nuru said. "The river will take you to the waterfall in the cliffs, but there is no access to the forest from there. You will have to journey all the way down into the valley and follow the cliffs till you find a suitable path back up the escarpment." Nuru's sparkling green eyes flashed a warning as he pointed the way on his map in the sand. "That road is long and treacherous. If you survive the climb down into the valley, you will have to sneak past the Adze who live in the swamps below. Even though the magic is destabilised and lost to the wind when it tumbles down the waterfall, the evil little Adze come out at night and fly up to replenish themselves."

"What is Adze?" Jimoh said.

"They are tiny little fireflies." Fisi curled his lip back in disgust. "They can steal your soul."

"Gogo Maya calls them vampires," Salih told Ethan, who thought of explaining to Jimoh, but guessed the boy hadn't heard of vampires anyway, so there was no point in confusing him.

"Are they any smaller than a mosquito? Because we have mosquito nets," he said to Nuru instead.

"Yes, that will do," Nuru said, after Ethan explained the principle of a mosquito net. "They are only active at night. But even if you pass the Adze, you will have to go through the bush before you can find a way up into the magic forest. There are lions living there, and hyenas," he added with a meaningful look at Fisi.

Jimoh fingered his slingshot nervously, his eyes darting from Fisi, to Tariro, to Ethan. "We can do this thing! We have to go this way. Is only way to find Joe," he said.

CHAPTER 16
A RIDE ON A TIGER

After a night spent cradled in the upper branches of a baobab tree, Joe awoke stiff, his legs ablaze with pain from running, and his arms almost too sore to reach out and pluck a fruit growing less than a metre from where he lay. Ears straining for any sound of hyenas, he craned his head over the treetops, and followed the path he had taken the night before, to see if Mesande had followed him. Chuki had said "pack". Did the people of the forest roam in packs like gangs in movies? If he found other people living in the forest, would they attack him or help him?

Even from his position, elevated above the treetops, Joe had to move a few branches to get a clear view of his surroundings. The forest fell away abruptly, not far east of Mesande's village, into a deep rift valley. Dense acacia woodland filled the valley floor, with a river meandering through the middle, which flowed into a large lake. And on the far side of the lake there were definite signs of a settlement. Although it looked many days hike away, he wondered why his rescuers had directed him south-west, towards the mountains, instead of east towards the settlement. Had they really meant witches? Anything was possible. The tiger had mentioned witches, and the villagers had been prepared to believe that he was a demon, but surely that was just ignorance?

In the end, as tempted as he was to strike out towards the lake settlement, that way lay past Mesande's village. Joe rubbed a knot of tension in his neck. He did not want to risk going anywhere near Mesande's village.

His stomach rumbled. Almost groaning with fatigue and stiffness, he stretched out a hand to pluck a fruit and bashed it against the trunk of the baobab tree, the shock of the impact rippling painfully up his arm. Despite its velvety coating, the gourd-like casing was too hard to crack against the bark of the tree. Instead, he had to ease his way to the forest floor, where he managed to crack it open against a rock. Sticky powder-covered seeds spilled out onto the ground.

After sucking the tangy flesh off the seeds he lined them up on a rock and carefully broke them open with a stone to get at the soft nutty-tasting core, which he felt must be nutritious. His mother always cracked open the pips of plums and apricots to get at the goodness hidden in them. He washed them down with a swig of water from the water-skin Chuki's friends had given him the night before, and picked up two fallen fruits for later. He absentmindedly patted down his sides where his pockets should be, before he remembered that the pelt-like garment that they'd given him hadn't any. He balked at the pelt that looked just like Mesande's unkempt hair. Although the same thing hadn't looked so bad on Chuki, he felt like a savage. Was it less than a week ago that he had been wearing a smart school uniform, laughing and joking with his friends? How had everything gone so wrong?

He rubbed the backs of his hands roughly over his eyes, trying not to dwell on the idea that he had lost everyone he had ever known. He set his jaw and forced himself to concentrate on the task ahead, pretending he was not afraid. It was time to get busy again, distract himself, make a plan to get to safety and back home. "Towards the mountains it is then," he grumbled, and gripping the stalks of two baobab fruits in one hand and a hand-full of pebbles in the other, Joe strode purposefully into the forest.

The tiger came upon him when he was trying to cross a small stream.

"Oh! Look who it is! Gone all wild and native." Hajiri coiled his body tight, and then sprang across the gully. He rubbed up against Joe, almost knocking him sideways into the water. Joe dropped his pebbles, hesitantly lifting his hand to stroke the cat. Hajiri's purr rose to a loud friendly throb. Despite his trepidation at befriending the strange tiger, Joe was quite relieved to see him. Hopefully he would take care of Mesande if she caught up with them.

"It's a good thing I found you," Hajiri said. "The forest is full of angry hyenas this morning. They don't usually hunt in the magic forest because, well, it's magic, but something's got them in a lather today."

Joe tensed. "They're looking for me," he admitted in a shaky voice. He rubbed his sweating palm down Hajiri's back.

"Don't look so worried. You can come with me," Hajiri said. Then he eyed Joe suspiciously. "Why were you going this way?"

"I was looking for the witches," Joe said, a little embarrassed at his gullibility, even as he said it.

"Don't be silly!" the tiger said, shocked, "What on earth would you want with witches? Evil creatures." Then he calmed down, touching the cut above Joe's brow with claws carefully sheathed. "But look at you. You are injured. No wonder you are not thinking straight. There is a well nearby, where we can see to those cuts. Do you think you would be able to hang on if I carry you on my back?"

It wasn't that hard to stay on after a while. The tiger's gigantic leaps were remarkably smooth and controlled. As the tiger came down to land, Joe's body would become slightly airborne, but the tiger's next forward leap caught up with him, propelling them forward smoothly. Hajiri hardly seemed to notice the extra weight. Not that surprising, thought Joe, since the tiger looked roughly the weight of a small horse. It would have been an exhilarating ride if it weren't so terrifying.

Hajiri took Joe to a miniature village, nestled deep within the forest. Lala Salama, he called it with a sly smile. Joe thought it meant sleep in Swahili.

Tiny double-storey huts, thatched from floor to rooftop, with a little chimney funnel sticking out of a tuft at the top, looked like giant half-coconuts scattered haphazardly into a clearing, surrounding a central well. Each hut had a wedge cut out of the side, with a front door cut into the downstairs section and a balcony jutting out of the second floor.

As unusual as the vegetation in the forest had been, the territory surrounding Lala Salama village was incredible. Joe recognised some of the tropical fruit trees, but all had taken on bizarre properties. The usually small muroro bush, with its sugar apples, towered over the clearing whilst rows of usually huge marula trees grew in a bonsai crop, to one side of the village. Avocado pears the size of rugby balls hung pendulously from below the branches of a large tree, threatening to damage huts or knock someone out if they fell.

An ancient-looking Tokoloshe crone rocked back and forth on her chair on a balcony. "What do you want!" she grouched before being whisked inside with a hand clapped over her mouth.

"Just ignore them," Hajiri said. "They become so annoying if you encourage them. Now see if you can work out how this well contraption works and get us some water."

"Where are the rest of them?" Joe said, chewing on the inside of his lip. He didn't want to set the tiger off, but he hoped these Tokoloshe were the ones he had met the day before. They had at least looked safe and friendly.

"Oh, they are hiding in the forest," Hajiri said. "They are afraid of us. As well they should be, because their magic does not work on me." He lowered his head and lapped at the little bucket of water Joe had drawn from the well. An old Tokoloshe man slipped out of the shadow of his hut and beckoned to Joe.

"Get away from the tiger," he mouthed. "It is very dangerous." A couple of wisened old heads poked out from behind huts and trees and nodded in agreement. Joe couldn't see how he was to get away from the cat, even if he wanted to. And he wasn't all that sure he wanted to. After all, the tiger had rescued him, in a way, and he seemed friendly enough.

Suddenly, Hajiri pounced in a vicious blur of orange speed, dispelling that theory. The well bucket went flying as he landed in front of the little Tokoloshe, his face a hairsbreadth from that of the petrified little man. He unsheathed a claw, longer than one of Joe's fingers, and flicked the old Tokoloshe with it, sending him tumbling into a deep-red gooseberry bush. "Go away, tiresome creature, and let us drink," he said in a mild voice, completely at odds with his tense body.

Joe picked up the bucket shakily, torn between irritating the tiger further, and drawing himself a drink from the well. The Tokoloshe melted into the shadows. The old one hid in the bush where he had landed. Joe hoped he wasn't hurt. He drew more water from the well and drank as fast as he could, splashing some over his scratched face. The water had a greasy film on top and felt a little sticky, but it was a relief to be able to clean out his cuts. Once again Joe smelled a strong smell of pears.

"Not like that, dear boy," the tiger said, crouching beside Joe. "You have to put the magic on the wounds." Tapping his claw impatiently against the bucket, he scanned the area for anyone still brave enough to show their face. "You!" he said, eyeing the old lady, back in her chair on the balcony, "Fetch me a cloth."

"Fetch your own cl . . ." she squealed as she disappeared into the recesses of her house, but soon a soft cloth came flying off the balcony and landed at Joe's feet.

"Come along, let's go and find some food," the tiger said after

A RIDE ON A TIGER

Joe had wiped the dried blood from his face. "As tempted as I am, we can't eat these creatures, their magic gives me indigestion."

Joe mounted his unlikely companion again, nervously gripping Hajiri's fur behind his shoulder blades, and with giant leaps they disappeared back into the forest. He wondered if the Tokoloshe would have been able to get him to the settlement on the other side of the lake if he had been brave enough to leave the tiger. Hajiri must have been joking about eating the Tokoloshe. Surely.

The second settlement they found was on the bank of a river, flowing quietly and gently out of the bottom of a low plateau.

"This is Kapichi village," the tiger explained. "The magic flows underground from those mountains in the south, past the well at Lala Salama village and comes out at this river. If you look closely, you will see the Tokoloshe have built up the area underneath the water so that it flows smoothly, rather than falling in a waterfall. Apparently the magic loses strength if it is shaken."

The tiger made for the center of the village. The huts, scattered untidily all over a clearing, were similar to the ones in Lala Salama, but the occupants were not so cowering. Some sort of a commotion broke out around the corner at the news of their arrival, and Tokoloshe scattered in all directions. Several came running towards them.

Not all the Tokoloshe here had spiky hair and dark brown skins. Some of them looked almost rubbery and soft. One had turned so light and glassy Joe could hardly see him. They wheeled in mild panic at the sight of the tiger and ran back the way they had come, squealing more in mirth than fright, as if they were children, up to no good.

"Not as hostile as the last lot, but every bit as stupid," Hajiri commented. He followed them around a large prickly pear cactus and found the source of their excitement. A pile of raw honey, still attached to the honeycombs, lay dribbling off a rock table outside one of the huts. The entire hive of bees seemed to have come with it. Several Tokoloshe jostled each other for handfuls of the honeycomb, swatting bees from it and stuffing it into their mouths.

Joe slid off Hajiri's back as the tiger sat down quietly to watch. One by one the little Tokoloshe became aware of the tiger and tried to look innocent as they stuffed a last bit of honey into their mouths.

"We found it!" one said guiltily, spitting bees as he spoke.

"Just sitting there in a tree," agreed another with a ruddy face covered in bee stings. He was turning invisible right before their eyes. *That's probably why they aren't as afraid as the last lot*, thought Joe. *If they become invisible, the tiger can't catch them.*

"We're not going to take your honey," Hajiri said with a winning smile. "Tigers don't eat sweets, but perhaps you could spare a bit for my friend. I don't think he has eaten for a while." All eyes turned to Joe as if the little creatures had noticed him for the first time. One grabbed a handful of honeycomb and offered it timidly, and then withdrew his hand in panic when Joe reached out to take it. The honeycomb dropped on the ground between them where it broke into pieces. Joe picked up a piece with a polite smile to put the little guy at ease, dusted a few bees and a bit of sand off it and popped it in his mouth. It was like no honey he had ever tasted. He couldn't quite put his finger on it but it had hints of almond and vanilla, and again, that faint smell of pears.

"That won't fill the tummy of a growing boy!" A larger, female Tokoloshe kicked the dust around her bare feet in disgust, scattering the honeycomb. She plunked a huge green prickly pear down on the stone table and jabbed a pointed stick into the top of it. Then, taking great care to avoid the thorns, with the precision of one performing delicate surgery, she cut off both ends of the fruit, made an incision in the fleshy peel from end to end, peeled it aside and plucked out the orange fruit.

"There." She handed it to Joe, and then stood back, folding her arms across her chest with satisfaction.

"Thank you," he said, glancing towards the tiger for assent.

"Go ahead, dear boy. Tigers don't eat fruit either," Hajiri drawled. Joe took a bite out of the cactus fruit. It was difficult to get his mouth around it but it tasted cool on his tongue and absolutely mouthwatering, a bit like watermelon.

"Delicious," he nodded and grinned his approval, at which the Tokoloshe woman spun on her heal and stomped off as if she had other important matters to attend to.

Hajiri lounged about in the shade of a mango tree while the Tokoloshe brought them water and Joe finished his prickly pear.

As friendly as Hajiri was with the Kapichi villagers, Joe noticed that some of the Tokoloshe were wary of the tiger. He could see it in the way they looked at each other, and the way they skittered around, just out of his reach. He may not be in the habit of eating them but one or two were definitely scared of him. He wondered what the tiger did eat. He hoped it was not eventually going to be "dear boy".

He wondered what Jimoh and Tariro were up to, and of course Ethan. Was his family looking for him yet? Would they ever be able to find him in this strange place? He somehow doubted it. His last swallow bubbled up his throat again, prickling the back of his tongue. He pressed his lips together tightly. Now was not the time to dwell on home; he needed to have his wits about him if he was going to survive.

Joe and Hajiri emerged from the forest about half a kilometre away from the edge of the escarpment where the tiger sat down abruptly, spilling Joe off his back.

"Home," he said with satisfaction, walking towards the cliff tops. Joe followed. All he could see was endless cliff tops stretching in both directions and a valley hundreds of metres below. Assuming the tiger had some sort of cave hidden in the cliff face, Joe hoped it was not too difficult to climb down to. As they got close enough to see a little way over the crest of the cliff, Joe spotted a spire, poking up above the escarpment. He rushed forwards and peered over the edge. What he saw nearly took his breath away.

People! A whole city lay hidden beneath the cliffs, in the shape of half a rugby stadium, but ten times as big, and without a roof. Square, flat-roofed buildings that reminded him of Morocco had been built or possibly carved into the cliff face. Below him Joe could see people in flowing robes tending vegetables and fruit trees on some of the roof tops, or hanging brightly coloured garments on wash-lines. Others sat in courtyards, open to the sky, shaded by exotic-looking trees. Thin spires towered above the city on either side.

"Lookout towers," Hajiri said, following Joe's gaze. "They house the spyglasses used to see what is happening on the other side of the river." Joe peered into the distant valley below. It felt like being in a documentary, filmed from an airplane. A herd of zebra grazed just below the city, ambling slowly between flat-topped trees. They started at some sudden movement, and turned as one, like a shoal of fish, plunging into the thicker cover of dense msasa woodland. He thought he could see a herd of brown antelope closer to the river, but they were too far away to tell for sure. There was definitely a settlement on the eastern bank of the lake, although Joe was glad he had not struck out in that direction. He would never have come upon this city.

The river they had followed from Kapichi village flowed into a square reservoir at the top of the city, where it split off into smaller streams that meandered gently in a zigzag pattern to the bottom of the city. There it pooled in another square reservoir before plummeting into the valley below.

The smell of roasting meat and freshly baked bread wafted up from the houses below him. Joe's stomach rumbled. They may not eat creatures from the forest but they were getting meat from somewhere; probably the valley below.

"Let's go and find Galal," Hajiri said, padding softly down the central stairs. He nodded at a group of men as they passed, each wearing a turban with a face covering that left only their eyes exposed, and long flowing cotton robes in muted shades of cinnamon, turquoise and yellow. They nodded back, their dark almond shaped eyes crinkling at the corners; then they melted gracefully away into the shade of a building.

A young girl rushed up to meet Hajiri. As she ran, the slits up the sides of her emerald green silk tunic opened up to reveal flowing baggy white trousers underneath. She stopped in front of the tiger, put her hands together in front of her chest in a spire and bowed low. Her thick, wavy, waist-length hair fell forwards across her face.

"Hello, Hajiri," she smiled, giving Hajiri's face a hug. Then she turned towards Joe and held out her hands to him. Metallic gold embroidered peacocks winked at him from around her cuffs.

"Have you brought this one for me? I am sorely in need of a friend," she said to Hajiri, taking both Joe's hands in hers and holding on to them. She seemed to be searching him for a weapon or something, the way she looked him over, but she didn't even notice his slingshot.

Now that he was amongst people, feeling less scared, Joe was sure Hajiri was as tame as he had come to believe. The tiger seemed to be quite well liked in the city.

"No," Hajiri said. "I will keep the boy for myself, but you are welcome to socialise with him."

The girl looked a little taken aback. "Then so be it," she said with a puzzled smile, then let go of Joe's hands, steepling her hands once more and bowing low to him. "Welcome, I am Nandi, second daughter of Galal, friend of Hajiri, and therefore, I suppose, friend of yours." She fell in beside them as they went in search of her father.

When they passed a massive hall, Hajiri peered in. The walls were lined with shelves carrying hundreds of leather bound books that smelled dusty and ancient. A group of men and a woman lounged around with their feet up on a table at the far end listening to the ranting of an intense young man who paced up and down before them until he spotted Hajiri.

"Hajiri!" he cried, with a delighted smile that Joe noticed did not quite reach his eyes. "You have come! I feared you had left us. What is this you bring before us?" He strode over to the doorway; his robes flying out behind him were more intricately embroidered than Nandi's. The group of marimba players, who had been playing quietly in the corner, stopped in mid-note to stare at Joe.

This time Hajiri looked taken aback. "He is my human," he said in a slightly condescending voice, as if Joe were some sort of pet. "I found him in the forest. He made me a fire and everything. He is very important – the captain of the rugby team, he tells me. He calls himself Joe."

The man barely looked at Joe, before rounding on Hajiri. "Hajiri, you know that the next one belongs to me," he said, his arms folded across his chest, daring Hajiri to object. Thin parallel slash marks across his cheek that appeared to Joe a little like a cat scratch, looked suddenly lighter against his flushed face.

"He is not a captive, Kitoko. He came with me voluntarily, and I am keeping him," Hajiri said in a reasonable tone. Then he wheeled around and stalked off down the passage as if that was the last word on the matter. Joe shrugged helplessly, his palms turned up in front of him in a gesture of futility, and took off after Hajiri. Nandi ran to catch up with them, followed closely by Kitoko, and a dozen or so of his friends from the library, their richly decorated robes billowing out behind them as they went.

Galal, when they found him, was in a corner of a large crowded chamber of theatrical splendor. Intricate, jewel-encrusted mosaics and beautifully carved wooden latticework decorated the walls. Persian carpets of all shapes and sizes lay spread on the floor. More marimba players struck a quiet tune, accompanied by a kettledrum and, of all things, a man blowing into a kudu horn. Galal lounged on a divan in the cool shadows with a group of men, sipping coffee and puffing at the ancient ivory mouthpiece of a water pipe. An exquisitely carved mancala board lay between them with about thirty holes for the stones. Joe remembered Ethan loved to play the game because he always won, but he insisted that it was called bao.

The moment he entered the room Joe could feel every eye on him. Their gaze, whilst not exactly menacing, made his skin crawl just for a moment before an oddly tranquil feeling put him at ease. Too tranquil, he realised suddenly. A thought tried to formulate in his mind – a hint of danger, perhaps? – but he couldn't quite pin it down.

Several people, both men and women, in dazzlingly bejewelled, long flowing robes and tunics came forwards, each bowing with the steepled hands, before patting or hugging the tiger. Galal stroked his short, well-kept beard with one hand and weighed his playing stones in the other. He watched Joe through half-closed green eyes that flashed in sharp contrast with his dark skin, and the matt black robes and turban that he wore.

After bowing somewhat awkwardly as he had seen Nandi do, Joe came to attention before the man's inspection. *Pick me*, he thought absurdly, puffing himself up like any six-year-old being chosen for his first rugby match. Again, that hint of danger fought to infiltrate his thoughts, but drifted away before he got a grip on it.

Galal eased himself off the bench, rising to his full six-foot-three, and strolled over to Joe who stood as still as his shaking knees would let him, while the man slowly prowled around him. Eventually Galal reached out and hefted Joe's slingshot in his hand.

"What kind of a jewel is this?" he said, giving himself a mild scare when he let it go and it bounced on its rubber strips before settling back on Joe's chest.

"Er. It's a catty . . . a slingshot," Joe said, nervously reaching for the right description.

"Needs gemstones," Galal said.

"Um, it's not a jewel, sir, it's a weapon," Joe said, wiping the sweat off his top lip with the back of his hand. On some level he realised it was not a good thing to volunteer the information that he carried a weapon or even to speak at all but, with those green eyes on him, the truth just slipped out.

"Show me," Galal gave Joe a good-natured pat on the back that somehow felt a hairsbreadth away from turning violent.

"What, in here?" Joe said, looking about him. He could not see anything in the room that would make a suitable target.

A lithe, elfin-looking lady in a blood red tunic over black pyjama trousers peeled away from the group of people who had followed Kitoko from the library and strolled over to a fruit bowl. Selecting a grapefruit, she strode over to an archway, open to the view of the valley below and held it out to the side of her. She nodded her head once, her pixie-cut hairstyle springing back into perfect place as she waited for Joe to shoot.

"Go on then," she said, flashing a wicked grin.

Joe patted his pelt, where his pockets should be. "I . . . I need a pebble."

Galal handed him an emerald playing stone.

Joe took the stone with shaking fingers and nocked it into the little leather holder of his slingshot. He pulled the rubber back, but not too far. He wondered if Galal would be angrier if his priceless playing stone went sailing down to the valley below, or if Joe accidentally hit the girl. He shut his eyes and prayed to Jimoh for the boy's accuracy. Then he aimed and let the pebble fly.

It hit her in the rib cage; in that especially sensitive area right under her armpit.

CHAPTER 17
SOME HYPERACTIVE HELP

Fifteen crocodiles glided across the glassy surface of the lake. Breezes did not reach the interior of the cavern. As the sun rose outside, it streamed through funnels in the ceiling, glinting off the myriad of tiny bits of glass and tin dangling from the ceiling, and casting a kaleidoscope of light reflections on the water.

Ethan lay on his stomach across the back of one of them. Socially, it was a lot more awkward than riding a horse. What do you say to an intelligent stranger who is giving you a piggyback across a lake, Ethan wondered? He would have preferred to ride on Darwishi. He was used to that. But, apparently, Amun and Darwishi had begun their transformation and would be sequestered for several days in a special cave. There had been no shortage of volunteers among the Sobek to transport the boys and Salih to the waterfall exit, though, so he felt sure they did not mind. Several Sobek crocodiles, with Sobek men on their backs, had joined them just for the ride.

Nuru, himself, rode upon the back of a friend to make sure they passed safely, and to try and persuade the boys to make a return trip someday to spend more time with the Sobek. His crocodile swam beside Tariro. The three of them discussed Tariro's dad's political campaign tactics. Nuru posed a question, and the two Sobek read the answers right out of Tariro's head.

"Fascinating," Nuru nodded, his eyebrows almost disappearing into the hairline of his wig.

Tariro shifted uncomfortably on his mount and tried to deflect the Sobek's attention towards Ethan. "Ethan's step-dad is a dot.com millionaire," he said. "You should ask him what that is all about."

Ethan ignored them. If he was honest with himself, he was quite enjoying watching Tariro squirm; he had learned a thing or two about political tactics himself in the last half-hour.

Trailing his hand in the magic on top of the water, Ethan could just make out the shapes of it shifting and changing and reshaping itself into its marble pattern by the light of his headlamp. He wondered what he would draw from the magic, given enough time. Not that he needed any more magical upheavals, but he wondered if he was absorbing enough of it to turn into something else, and what he would want to turn into. Would it hurt? Fisi had not seemed to suffer any great discomfort when he changed.

"It takes generations of living with the magic before you can change," Salih told him. He lounged across the back of a crocodile swimming beside Ethan, looking unusually relaxed for a cat floating on top of the water.

"Oh, I don't really want to," Ethan said, jerking his hand out of the water.

"Don't look so guilty, boy, you can have as much magic as you want. There is plenty to go round, and as you heard, what isn't used is lost over the waterfall. The boy, Tariro, has drunk up enough to satisfy an elephant, and he has filled his water bottle with even more." Salih rapped his unsheathed claws lightly on the hard hide of his crocodile ride and shook his head with an amused sigh. "The silly boy wants to become an osprey and fly. It won't happen, of course." Salih sheathed his claws and leaned over to pat Ethan's hand. "Don't worry, he will not become as powerful as you. You have the witch's power, which is condensed, and the magic he carries with him will become destabilised just as soon as he shakes the bottle."

Ethan wasn't at all bothered if Tariro filled himself up with magic. He could take enough to *become* an elephant for all he cared, just as long as the boy didn't do anything stupid, or read Ethan's mind like the Sobek did and find out about the gems.

"I'm more worried about Jimoh," he said to Salih. "He hasn't said much since Kashka told us there would be no magic at Crystal Pools for a while. I know he would sacrifice anything to save Joe but I think he's worried about his family."

"Ethan, we have a difficult and dangerous journey ahead," Salih said. "Jimoh will have to focus on staying alive himself, before he can turn his mind to helping his village. The Sobek have been bringing magic to the Crystal Pools for generations. Anyone who has been swimming there will have a bit of power. Jimoh, more than most, because he has taken your blood." The leopard looked as if he had a sudden idea. "You could make him less worried if you want, but you would have to project into his mind. It would be . . . rude, and intrusive, and it would not be without some consequence to yourself."

Ethan shook his head. Why did the leopard always have to make things so complicated? "I could just tell him not to worry, without being rude," he sighed. "It wouldn't stop him worrying though."

"Or I could show you how to compel him with the magic. He wouldn't be any the wiser," Salih said.

Ethan was shocked – he wasn't about to go hypnotising his friend without consulting him, even if he could.

On the other hand, it would be nice to see Jimoh relax, and they really needed their best ranger to have his wits about him if they were heading into lion country. Besides, so far Salih had not been very instructive about what Ethan could do with the power. Perhaps now was a good time to learn.

"Okay . . ."

"Close your eyes and imagine a drop of water. Imagine you could shape it into a crystal form," Salih said.

"Like a snowflake?"

"Don't know it. Does it reflect light?" Salih asked.

"I suppose it does, it's a frozen drop of water," Ethan said.

"Ah yes, like hail. Yes, that will do. Now imagine many, suspended in the air around you." He waited until he was satisfied Ethan had imagined enough snowflakes. "Now, infuse each particle with reassuring thoughts, and gently push them towards Jimoh. With a bit of luck, as the thoughts bounce off each facet of the crystals they will split and multiply, bouncing off other crystals, much like mirror reflections, until there is an explosion of good will. Jimoh will be unable to resist."

More like a nuclear explosion, Ethan thought worriedly, but he stared intently at Jimoh and tried. He thought reassuring thoughts about the world beyond the Crystal Pools: computers and the internet; computer games; shopping malls, with wonderful gadget shops . . . air conditioning. Then he imagined all these wonderful things of the snowflakes whirling around his head, and he nudged them gently towards Jimoh.

Suddenly Jimoh looked up at him, a puzzled grin spread across his face.

"Did you get my message?" Ethan said.

The boy shook his head, more confused than ever, and then he lounged back against his crocodile and whistled a low complicated tune. He looked happier, at least. Perhaps the exercise had been a success.

Salih laughed. "He can't hear your actual thoughts, only the sentiment. Which is just as well. I don't think Jimoh has a use for any of those strange things."

Ethan did not respond because suddenly his senses started to tingle with the schizophrenic confusion in his brain pattern he'd had when he lost his temper with Tariro back at Crystal Pools. But this time something cold flowed into his head with it, and a chilling pain, worse than any brain freeze he'd ever experienced, lanced through him. It washed away as suddenly as it had come; seeping down his central nervous system and out of his body, leaving a foul metallic taste on his tongue, with a hint of the taste of snow.

Salih waited patiently for the pain to pass. "As I said, not without cost."

Ethan put his hands up to his head and took a ragged breath, then slumped forwards against his crocodile, who, oddly, seemed to shake a little as he pulled through the water, with a definite grin on his face. Ethan glowered at the other smiling crocodiles. He wouldn't be doing *that* again in a hurry.

The low murmur of rushing water grew into a roar.

Early morning sunlight filtered into the tunnel entrance. It was wider here, and the ceiling had grown so low they had to flatten across their crocodiles' backs to avoid bumping their heads. The crocodiles discharged their passengers on a narrow path running beside the river and then slipped slowly back into the water one by one, oozing sadness and reluctance to part with their new friends. Nuru was the last. He reminded Jimoh several times to look out for a vine rope, hidden on the north side of the waterfall. It would assist them in their climb. Then, with a last invitation to visit in happier times, he slipped quietly away on the back of his friend.

Ethan crawled along the path, on his hands and knees, to the entrance of the tunnel, which opened out onto a ledge beside the waterfall. Pressing his stomach hard against the ledge, he looked over the edge of the precipice down into the rift valley. His heart pounded at the exhilarating feeling of being up in the air, and then lurched as a terrible wave of vertigo swept over him.

Jimoh crawled up beside him and flashed an unsteady smile.

Even Tariro looked alarmed as his eyes followed the waterfall's precipitous plunge down the vertical cliff into the valley far below.

"How the hell are we supposed to climb down that?" Tariro grumbled, settling down beside Jimoh.

The early morning sun bathed the nearby cliffs in an eerie pink glow, as if they were made of marble. On closer inspection Ethan realised they *were* marble. He wondered if it had something to do with the magic.

The valley spread out before them like a miniature topographical map. The river pooled below the waterfall before disappearing into a sizable swamp. Small rivulets emerged from the far side of the swamp, joining together again to continue their course eastwards where they met up with a wide river running from south to north across the valley.

"Eh, eh, eh!" Jimoh breathed in wonder, pointing out the thousands of flamingos gathered in the mud flats where the two rivers met.

In the far reaches of the south, a multi-tiered waterfall, almost obscured from view by its own spray, emptied itself into the river. Ethan shaded his eyes as he followed its path. It snaked its way through the middle of the wilderness, emptying into a vast lake, and then meandered northwards, finally lost to sight.

A green mosaic of crop fields clung to the eastern banks of the lake, dotted here and there with the early morning cooking fires of small settlements. Vast plains of game country spread away behind them to the distant mountains.

Jimoh bounced and pointed so excitedly beside him, Ethan had to remind himself that the boy had probably never experienced an aerial view above the bush.

"See there, Ethan," he whispered, squinting into the distance. "Elephant. There, between big rocks and river." He pointed towards a rocky outcrop and Ethan traced a line from it towards the river. A herd of forty or fifty elephants, mostly still under cover of thick msasa woodland, ambled towards the water.

SOME HYPERACTIVE HELP

"My people too," Fisi said. "You may not see them because of their ability to melt into their surroundings. But there they are, tracking those impala."

"Well, are they people or hyena?" Ethan was unable to see them, and he was not sure he would be able to recognise an impala from this distance.

"Hyena," Fisi said, sitting up and scratching his groin, dangerously close to the edge of the ledge. He seemed to hold no fear of being sucked over the precipice. "We hunt in the wilderness below in hyena form, and we live in the forests above in our man form," he explained.

Suddenly the herd of impala broke out from the cover of the undergrowth as tiny as ants, and Ethan saw several hyenas giving chase but even from this distance he couldn't bear to watch them go in for the kill.

A scuffling noise coming from the cliff face above him made him jump and stagger awkwardly to his feet, the blood draining from his face. He fumbled to open a blade on his pocketknife.

Jimoh and Tariro both rose swiftly and stepped back, towards the precipice, nocking their slingshots. The air shimmered, and abruptly smelled dank. With a soft whoop sound, Fisi changed back into a hyena. Emitting a low growl, he stalked towards Ethan, whose heart skipped a beat before he realised Fisi's eyes were fixed, not on him, but on a hole in the cliffs above his head.

Salih sat, perfectly composed, watching expectantly for something to drop out of the hole. Presently, a small hairy bushman-like man squeezed out, landing on his feet with a grunt of triumph.

"Aah!" he jumped back in fright at the sight of the crouching hyena, fumbling desperately to remove a quiver full of arrows from his back, almost garroting himself on the string of his bow, which hung diagonally across his chest. Managing to separate the two, he dropped the bow at his feet and shakily balanced the quiver on his head, sending a shower of arrows skidding across the floor. Ethan realised he was trying to make himself look more imposing.

"*Sheet*!" Jimoh swore, hopping up and down on one foot. An arrow had bounced off the floor grazing his ankle.

Another small creature dropped out of the tunnel, almost bowling over the first, followed by another and another, until there were a pile of them scrambling to their feet, dusting off their strange twisted animal hide skirts and straightening their head gear.

"What are you doing?" one said, staring in astonishment at the first one, now standing sheepishly with a quiver on his head for no reason. A quick glance at Tariro confirmed to Ethan that the other boys could understand the little man. Fisi, having taken advantage of the confusion to change back into a young man, leaned innocently against the wall of the cave, an embarrassed grin on his face.

"Hyena!" muttered the first one, pointing at Fisi with one hand, easing the quiver over his shoulder to settle in its place on his back with his other hand. He drew himself up to his full height of about two feet, and made a surreptitious attempt to shift his headband from around his neck, where it had slipped, to his head, taking care not to prick himself on its hedgehog spines.

"Riiight," the second one said, unconvinced. He scratched absently at an old wound that ran from his bare nipple to his belly button.

"Tokoloshe," Jimoh breathed in awe. He quietly replaced the slingshot around his neck so that it looked once again like a necklace, and returned the pebble to his pocket moving towards Fisi.

"What's a Tokoloshe?" Ethan said, a little unnerved by Jimoh's anxiety.

"Mythological creature," Tariro whispered. He rubbed his eyes and stared at the ugly little creatures. "They're supposed to have a penis so long they wear it slung over one shoulder or tied around their waists."

Fisi let out a whooping hyena giggle. Not only was there no evidence of any penises, but these Tokoloshe didn't look that scary to Ethan; if anything, they looked disorganised. Most of them carried primitive-looking bows slung over one shoulder and bark quivers full of arrows over the other, that didn't look big enough to inflict much damage unless they were poisonous.

Salih smiled a wry smile and said in tones of molasses, "Boys, meet your new guides."

"Nomatotlo sent us," the leader said to Salih. He appeared to have no trouble understanding the leopard. After introducing himself to the boys as Rufiki, he gathered up a few of his clan and they arranged themselves sitting cross-legged, in a semicircle on the floor in front of the leopard. Salih was trying to hold their attention long enough to find out what was happening in the magic world above the cliffs by swishing the tip of his tail back and forth hypnotically. It was not working. Their eyes darted distractedly between the cat and the river. Ethan sat beside Salih watching the rest of the Tokoloshe splash about in the river above the waterfall, worried one of them would be swept over the edge.

"They have the attention span of a gnat," Tariro grumbled irritably. One had been explaining to Tariro that the pelts that hung from the thong around his waist were those of the giant golden mole, and that the assortment of seed pods and rodent sculls intertwined with them were hunting trophies, when, without warning, he was overcome with the urge to swim. He had sprung up, mid-sentence and hurtled into the water, followed by most of the rest of them.

A whiff of catnip floated up off the Tokoloshe. It was so strong when you got near some of them; it smarted in Ethan's nostrils. He shuddered to think what effect it was having on Salih. Jimoh lay fast asleep, propped up against the wall of the cave. The Tokoloshe arrows, whilst not poisonous, were tipped with a powerful sleeping draft. According to Fisi, they preferred to capture their prey and hold them for ransom, rather than actually killing them. Since they wouldn't eat any of the creatures in the magic forest, for fear of overdosing on two lots of accumulated magic, this turned out to be more agreeable to all concerned.

It was Fisi who marshalled their attention in the end. He dug the tin of sweets out of Tariro's backpack and, with an apologetic look at Tariro, banged it loudly.

"Damn!" Tariro muttered, obviously reluctant to give up his power over the tin. He had guarded the treasure so possessively since the hippopotamus pools, eking out a daily ration of one sweet each. The Tokoloshe erupted out of the water and swarmed all over Fisi almost immediately upon opening the tin.

"It's as if they can smell the chocolate," Tariro wailed.

"Tariro, I think you are right." Ethan drew in a sharp breath at the sight of one Tokoloshe who was beginning to shimmer and shake in a disturbing way. The long hair on his back seemed to thicken and started to bounce as he moved about.

"That's it!" Salih exclaimed. "Stop them eating the sweets!" He jumped into the fray, hauling Rafiki and a couple of others away from Fisi. Some Tokoloshe backed away of their own accord once they saw some of their friends shimmer and shake and become almost translucent.

"Someone has been feeding Morathi's tribe sugar," Salih panted. He tried to round up a handful of unaffected Tokoloshe into a corner of the cave. "I think it is reacting with the magic to make them hyperactive. And stronger!" he added, struggling against them.

"Like they weren't hyperactive before!" Ethan tried to pull one back and then jerked his hand away with a yelp when the creature bit him on the arm.

"I haven't got any stronger," Fisi puffed, trying to pry the tin away from little fingers.

"More!" a Tokoloshe shouted, climbing up the back of Fisi and perching on his shoulders.

SOME HYPERACTIVE HELP

"More! More!" others took up the cry.

"No!" Fisi growled, snatching the tin away. The lid flew off, showering the cave floor with the remaining sweets.

"So much for that," Tariro sighed after Ethan had explained Salih's theory of the sugar to him. He flopped down on the cave floor between Ethan and the still-sleeping Jimoh. The sweets had all been eaten and the resulting chaos had died down. Ethan noticed that Fisi had managed to rescue one or two sweets for himself, and then smiled as the hyena youth handed one to Tariro. Rafiki, who hadn't got any, shot him a resentful glare.

"What?" the hyena said to him. "They're not making me go crazy."

"Who knows how the sugar is affecting you Fisi," Salih laughed. "Perhaps it is turning you more pleasant in your ways."

Most of the Tokoloshe had had to take a nap after all the excitement and were lying flat on their backs snoring. One cuddled a rat scull close to his chest.

Salih quickly became more serious. "It was good to observe our Tokoloshe friends because now I know what was making Morathi's clan so crazy as to attack Maya Gogo," he said. "We don't have much time for this lot to sleep it off. We have to climb down the escarpment before sundown when the Adze come out, otherwise we have to spend a night here."

"What if it doesn't wear off?" Rafiki said. He was one of only two Tokoloshe remaining unaffected by the sugary treats.

"I've seen it wear off Morathi's men," Salih said. "Now try and sit still long enough to report on the boy Joe."

"Ah!" Rafiki said, suddenly remembering his mission. "We were sent to guide these boys down the escarpment and up again by another path to go and rescue a boy from the Almohad. We know where the vine is hidden. We use this route from time to time."

"And are you sure the boy we seek is with the Almohad and not with one of the packs?" Salih asked, eyeing Fisi.

SWITCH!

"Ah . . . the boy is definitely with Galal," Rafiki said. "We found him in the forest, but then Hajiri came and captured him, then Grandma Wanyika said they came together to Lala Salama village to fetch water. She said the tiger must have beaten him. There was dried blood all over his face."

Ethan exchanged a worried look with Salih. Was it just that Salih did not want to believe Hajiri was bad because he was a cat?

"Also," Rafiki pointed at the thickset Tokoloshe with the chest scar, now fast asleep on his back, "Jelani has met with his relative, the spy, from Kapichi. He says that Jabibi heard from his friend, Ali, that a guy called Ziwa saw the boy enter Almoh city with the tiger at sundown last night." He shuddered at the thought of the tiger, and then remembered something else, "Um! You had better hurry up if you want to rescue him, Ziwa said the Almohad are planning a game of Jendayi." He said it in an ominous voice, nodding with satisfaction at Salih's sharp intake of breath.

"How many days have we got till the full moon?" breathed the leopard in alarm.

"Not many," Fisi giggled nervously.

"What's Jendayi?" Ethan asked, his throat suddenly dry with fear at Salih's alarm.

"It's a really stupid and dangerous game the Almohad play sometimes, around the time of the full moon," Fisi said. "We usually stay hidden in the upper forest till it is all over. We don't go hunting for days afterwards. Everyone gets upset."

"Well, we cannot waste a night here then. You had better wake your men and hurry up," Salih sighed, prodding a nearby Tokoloshe with his paw. "If they make the boy play, he may be in greater danger than we thought."

At a signal from Fisi that they were moving out, Tariro shouldered his bundle and followed the leopard.

"You don't think Joe would play this game, do you?" Tariro said over his shoulder to Fisi. "Joe wouldn't do anything stupid."

SOME HYPERACTIVE HELP

"You do not know the Almohad, Tariro. If they get bored enough they can persuade anyone to do anything," Fisi said, "except maybe a witch."

Ethan hovered momentarily beside Jimoh, not quite sure what to do. Fisi shrugged as if it was no problem. He hauled the sleeping boy up into a fireman's lift as if he weighed nothing and bound him to the end of the vine that lay coiled on the north side of the waterfall, as promised.

With the help of the sugar-strengthened Tokoloshe it only took an hour or so to lower the sleeping boy to the valley below, with a small group of Tokoloshe clinging on to him as he went, to guard him till the others could catch up. They lowered Salih in the same way, although Ethan was sure the leopard could have managed the steep path more easily than he could. After pulling the vines up and re-coiling them the way they had found them so that nobody from the valley below would gain access to the waterfall, Fisi, Tariro and Ethan eased themselves onto the path leading down to the valley floor, their backs pressed flat against the cliff wall, a string of strong but sleepy Tokoloshe in their wake.

"Don't look down," Fisi advised, a moment too late. Ethan almost succumbed to the pull of the sheer drop to the valley floor way down below. Soon his muscles strained and ached as they continued their climb. All thoughts of Jendayi were put aside while he kept one eye open for snakes or venomous insects. He shivered violently. As invincible as he felt with the magic, he did not like to imagine the result of a couple of thousand years of magic exposure on a tarantula or a snake.

CHAPTER 18
A HIT AND MISS STRATEGY

Everyone was tired, dirty and very hungry by the time they staggered off the last boulder into the valley below.

"That was a nightmare!" Ethan said, knuckling the base of his back and flopping down under a msasa tree beside Jimoh, who'd been awake for a while. "You should have seen us. Even Tariro came dangerously close to falling off the cliff a couple of times."

Tariro shook his head and clicked his tongue, "Those Tokoloshe are incredibly strong," he told Jimoh. "Also more stubborn and independent than my grandpa. They pick the steepest and most dangerous path down, and then fight anyone who suggests a more sensible route."

Ethan grinned. It would have gone easier on Tariro if he had not tried to boss around the Tokoloshe as if they were his younger brothers, but he nodded in agreement. He also suspected his guide of deliberately taking the more difficult paths. "I wonder if that is the way they always behave, or if they are still under the influence of the chocolates. Speaking of influences," he said, turning to Jimoh, "are you feeling better after your sleep?"

Jimoh stretched and yawned. "Yes, Ethan, but very hungry

now. What was in arrow?"

After Ethan and Tariro had caught Jimoh up on all they'd learned about the Tokoloshe while he slept, Jimoh said, "We must do as Tokoloshe do. We must find something to eat before sun goes down and Adze come."

Rafiki and his gang had spread out in the nearby bushes in search of snacks. They picked small sections of bark off the trees and ate the grubs wriggling underneath. Ethan tried, but as hungry as he was, could not bring himself to eat them.

"Ethan, you must eat this thing, you fussy boy. There is no time to cook something," Jimoh said. He popped a brightly coloured mopane worm, the size of a finger, into his mouth and smacked his lips.

"Yes, Ethan, you fussy boy," Tariro echoed with a smirk. He popped a mopane worm into his own mouth, stifling a gag reflex behind his hand.

"Suit yourselves," Ethan laughed, "I am going to go and set up camp." Apart from the disgusting meal, he was acutely aware that they were tramping around the bush where wild animals may be lurking and he had an urge to have his back to the safety of a tree trunk.

Setting up camp only took a couple of minutes. After hanging the four mosquito nets from the lower branches of the msasa tree, as they had done at the hippopotamus pool, and putting their backpacks underneath, Ethan flopped down on the ground, and waited for everyone to come back from their foraging. He tried to ignore his grumbling stomach. Finding himself entirely alone for the first time, he longed to take a peek at the gemstones, but did not want to risk them being seen if Tariro or the Tokoloshe came back suddenly. Instead, he took out his small Swiss Army knife and a tiny vial of machine oil and rubbed the blades with a corner of the mosquito net. Once he had done that, he looked for the bigger knife amongst Jimoh's things, to oil it, but was unable to find it. Jimoh must be wearing it he guessed. He would have to explain to the boy that the knife needed oiling from time to time, he thought, but then shrugged; Jimoh knew as much about equipment as he did, more, probably, since he came from a farm. It felt odd to think that he had grown closer to the boy in one short trip than he was with any of his friends at home. Tariro too, he admitted grudgingly to himself. His uncle Alan had been right; the boy kind of grew on a person. Yet he still knew very little about either of them. Following Jimoh's practical example Ethan turned the scissors attachment of the knife on his trousers and cut them into shorts. They were much more comfortable afterwards.

Eventually, at sunset, Tariro, Jimoh and the Tokoloshe drifted back and crawled in under the nets for protection. With an approving glance at Ethan's handiwork, Jimoh slipped Ethan a handful of marula berries.

"Here, Ethan," he said. "I feel sorry for you. This I think you can eat."

Ethan guessed Jimoh had picked them up off the floor. Some of the little yellow fruit had started to ferment, but he was so hungry he ate them anyway, stopping only to inspect them for maggots.

The Tokoloshe laughed when they saw the fermented fruit, and told a story of baboons falling over drunkenly after eating them. Then nothing would do but that they should find the tree and gather some to see if the fruit could make them fall over.

Jimoh pointed out the marula tree through a gap in the trees, then scanned the nearby scrub and pointed. "I see Salih in tree over there, but where is Fisi."

It still gave Ethan a little bit of a chill, the way Salih disappeared and then you found him right nearby, slung over the branch of a tree, and he had been there all along.

"I have been meaning to speak to you guys about Fisi," Tariro said. "I am not a hundred per cent sure we can trust him. You see how quickly he changed shape and went on the attack at the top of the waterfall. I am beginning to wonder if there isn't any truth in what the leopard told you at the whirlpool, about him being just as likely to turn on us."

"Tariro, you were getting on so well with him," Ethan said. "I thought you liked him." The hyena youth was also beginning to grow on Ethan, despite his dubious personal hygiene, but Tariro was probably right; it was a bit odd the way he had run off as soon as they reached the bottom of the escarpment.

"I do like him," Tariro said. "He's fun in a shallow kind of way, but have you noticed how we all seem to give in to him." His tone was suddenly sombre as he regarded Ethan with a calculating expression. "By the way, heads up on getting Jimoh's hat back, I kept meaning to tell Fisi to give it back but sort of got distracted every time I wanted to. No. Not even distracted. I would go to say it, and then the idea would just slide right off into the ether, like he was deflecting it in some way."

"Maybe Tariro is right," Jimoh said, rubbing his leg where the arrow had hit him. "But Fisi also big help today with getting down cliff and with luggage. I am liking him."

"I kind of like him too," Tariro said, "but I am worried that Fisi is up to something."

Intense negotiations interrupted them from beneath one of the other mosquito nets. A Tokoloshe crept out from under the net, tugged anxiously at the few wisps of hair sprouting around the base of his head, and then, apparently making up his mind, dashed towards the marula tree. Quietness and stealth clearly not a priority, he was accompanied by the loud jangle of the assorted bits of tin and seedpods dangling from his waist, and equally loud cheers from his buddies. He shimmied up the tree and started throwing fruit down towards the others.

More Tokoloshe ducked out from under the other nets, made a wild dash for the marula tree, collected the fruit and bolted back towards the safety of their nets.

Suddenly, lights erupted out of a nearby bush and streaked after the scrambling Tokoloshe.

SWITCH!

"Oh! No! The little guy in the tree!" Ethan yelped. But when he looked for the Tokoloshe he seemed to have melted against the bark and disappeared from sight.

"Legend say the Tokoloshe go invisible when he is scared," Jimoh said.

"Not quite invisible, but they are most adept at camouflage," Salih said. "You won't be able to see him unless he moves."

Ethan whipped around to find the leopard had snuck inside the net behind them at the first sign of the Adze. He wondered if Salih was afraid of them, or just being protective.

It took over an hour for the little man to leopard-crawl back to the safety of the nets once the lights had wandered off into the jungle in search of easier prey, but a loud whoop went up when he made it. Eventually everyone settled down to sleep, except an old Tokoloshe who volunteered to keep en eye out in case they came back.

Salih curled up against Ethan's back. He found the closeness of the leopard quite comforting. After several days without bathing, he realised the leopard was no dirtier than himself. Being dirty had turned out not to be as terrible as Ethan had imagined it would be. He hardly thought about it any more. Another thing he no longer bothered to do was search himself regularly for fleas. Perhaps he did not have enough fur for them to cling to because Salih's fleas made no attempt to transfer to him.

An occasional pinprick of light hovered nearby, but the Adze seemed to understand that they would not be able to pass through the nets, so eventually Ethan dosed off.

He twitched angrily in his dream; his path to the wonderful thing was blocked by a thick rope net. His frustration at not having the strength to break through was just escalating into rage when he heard Tariro calling out to him. His eyes flew open and he froze. Salih was no longer beside him.

Barely a foot away from his face, Adze were trying to rip a hole in the mosquito net. His own anger had been so real, Ethan wondered if he had read their minds.

They scattered at his sharp intake of breath, and then drifted back tentatively, trailing phosphorescent light off the ends of their wild, long-flowing hair. Ethan's hand crept carefully to his forehead. He flicked on his head lamp and peered intently into one's miniscule face, which looked unearthly, but would have been quite beautiful if it were not pinched into such a hateful, benevolent scowl.

"Ethan! Thank God you're awake," Tariro whispered. "I've been trying to reach into your head like Salih does, but I don't think I've drunk enough magic. I didn't want to wake everyone up and have a panic on our hands. I think I can hear these little creatures in my head. Their thoughts woke me up. If I concentrate very hard I can still hear them."

"You can hear them buzzing," Ethan said, realising that that was probably what he had heard.

"No. No, I can hear them thinking. One minute they were all angry, searching for a big enough hole in the net, and the next they were terrified. Something startled them."

"That was me feeling terrified," Ethan said.

"No, it was definitely them!" Tariro said. "I can't read your mind. After drinking the magic, I already tried . . . Okay, maybe it was you! Do it again."

Ethan studied the tiny creatures. They had elegant, sylph-like bodies covered with a scrap of a velvety petal in different colours. Their wings beat so rapidly he could not make out the shape of them. They look more like fairies than vampires, he thought, except for the sharp pointed teeth. Not that they looked big enough to bite anyone. He'd had such faith in the mosquito nets. Perhaps he had not taken the Adze seriously enough. He wished he had found out more about them from Salih, and what to do in case they broke through the net.

"Hurry up, Ethan, I can hear them planning another surge forwards!" Tariro said, and Ethan cocked his head to one side.

SWITCH!

Tariro was right. If you listened really hard you could hear them. Not their voices, exactly. Their voices were pitched too high, but he could hear a miniscule general roar and then they surged towards the net for another attack.

"Salih showed me a trick to get into their heads that might manipulate them," he whispered to Tariro. "Do you think I would scare them if I imagine the net to be red hot?"

"Don't give them any ideas!" Tariro said. "We don't want them setting the net alight with their glow."

"I don't think they can," Ethan said. "If they are anything like fireflies their glow comes from some sort of bioluminescence. It's not actually flammable."

"For goodness sake, they are vampires, Ethan. This is not exactly the real world, in case you haven't noticed. Who knows what they are capable of? Think a scary movie at them or something," Tariro said.

What could scare such a thing? Ethan wondered.

"Bats!" Tariro urged. "Bats are fast and eat insects, that should scare them."

Ethan imagined the snowflake particles whirling around his head. He searched his brain for an image of bats. He had seen a documentary once of bats boiling out of a cave, their call so disturbing that they had to contract their own middle-ear muscles when emitting it to avoid deafening themselves. He tried to match up bat images with snow particles. He could almost hear the boom as the snow particles fragmented and each bat doubled and then became four, then eight, then sixty-four, then four-thousand-and-something, then hundreds of thousands of bats exploded outwards, concentrating their sonar on the Adze as they searched for them.

He opened his eyes. The Adze glared back at him, unmoved. They carried on working at tearing a hole in the net as the bat tornado passed them by.

The Tokoloshe all lay wide-awake now, stiff with fear. Only

their eyes were darting to and fro as they followed the bats in ever increasing circles before they disappeared into the forest.

Ethan flinched as millions of burning hot arrows, the thickness of a hair, shot through his head. Was that a mind attack from the Adze, he wondered, or just another of Salih's consequences?

"They're not real!" he decided. "It's only a sensation."

"Of course they're bloody real," Tariro shouted, obviously assuming Ethan meant the Adze. "And what ever you did, they don't seem to care." He pressed his fingers to his temples in exasperation. "Are you sure you're doing it right?"

"I sent them bats! Just like you said. They don't seem to be afraid of them," Ethan panted. Fortunately, his pain passed as quickly as it had come.

"Hey! You know before, when they scattered like that? It was actually you who was scared. What if you project your own fear on them? What about thinking about something that scares you?" Tariro said.

"They scare me! . . . Okay, I'll show them themselves." He gathered the snowflakes in his imagination. Turned each into a shard of glass, converted the glass into a mirror and pushed away from himself with all his might, watching the imaginary glass fragment and multiply as it flowed out around him.

Ethan sensed rather than saw his mistake as the first few Adze forced their way through cuts in the net. He'd thought the scaring was a manipulation of their imagination. Shockingly, several of the shards of glass had materialised into something more tangible.

Pain lanced through him, and he staggered back, clutching his head with both hands. If he didn't hit on a solution soon, the pain in his head alone would kill him, he thought, watching in horror as they came drifting towards him. What was going to repel them?

"Repel!" he yelled. "Insect repellant!" He twisted around to face them once more. Weak now, and queasy, he desperately tried to rally his imagination. Snowflakes. Whirl. Fragment. He hurled out imaginary particles of pyrethrum and watched them multiply. The acrid stench of the insecticide swept outwards in a slow oily whirlpool, causing even Tariro to stagger back holding his nose.

The nearest Adze writhed, baring its sharp, pointy little teeth at him and fell to the ground. Followed by another, and another.

"At least they're backing off," he gasped as overwhelming pain burned into his head. His vision a kaleidoscope of white lights, Ethan wavered and sat down abruptly, putting his head between his legs. It passed. Not as quickly as the other two headaches had, but as completely as if he had imagined it.

Everyone coughed and spluttered around him, and when he looked up he saw a group of Adze staggering towards him on foot. They stopped at the edge of the net, where Jimoh had carefully laid out their unconscious comrades. Each one heaved a limp Adze over their shoulders and stumbled off into the forest, emitting an occasional shower of sparks, leaving nothing behind but the fading stench of the insecticide.

"Are you okay? You look very pale." Tariro hunkered down in front of Ethan. "That was pretty crafty. Pretty vile too." He said, "Who would have thought you could fish such a horrible smell out of thin air. Man, I cannot wait to sharpen my magic skills. When I get strong enough, will you teach me to do that?"

"I don't know how I did it. I seem to just make it up as I go along," Ethan said, hoping to divert Tariro. He felt quite nauseous. Somehow, being able to hypnotise someone into believing they were under attack seemed a lot less sinister than being able to call up something real out of thin air, no matter how tiny. He was going to have words with that leopard when he got back.

CHAPTER 19
A HORRIBLE SHOCK

"I didn't mean to hurt her," Joe said shakily. "I just didn't know what else to do."

Long moments passed while the young lady stood silhouetted against the backdrop of the valley, glaring at him. Her hand moved towards her wound as if she couldn't quite believe it, and lifted her tunic. A single drop of blood travelled down her side. A deathly chill swept over the vast hall as the Almohad stood silently waiting for . . . something.

She moved so fast, Joe had no time to react. One minute she was standing in the archway clutching her side, and the next she was behind him. She grabbed his wrist and twisted it cruelly up behind his back, bringing a gasp from him.

"Missed!" she hissed into his ear, her voice heavy with the promise of lethal consequences, her warm breath on the back of his neck sending a chill up Joe's spine.

Hajiri reacted almost as swiftly, his huge face looming up in front of Joe. His yellow irises turned to dark ochre, making them even more startling and terrifying, as he glared menacingly past Joe's face at the lady. "Drop . . . my . . . boy!" he growled through clenched teeth. All trace of his charming, convivial persona vanished.

"Make me!"

Hajiri's eyebrow lifted just a hint. "Praxades," he purred in a low dangerous voice. "I will not be drawn in to your psychotic game. You asked for it."

"I want retribution," Praxades said, looking over at Galal.

"Oh, it was not that bad, you hardly felt it," Galal said dismissively. "You can lop off a finger."

He's only trying to scare me, Joe thought, glancing anxiously at Galal's face to gauge if he was serious, but Galal accepted his emerald bao stone from a girl who had retrieved it from the floor and turned back to his game, wiggling his fingers in a dismissive gesture to indicate he was not to be disturbed.

Joe shot a baffled look at Hajiri. What he saw in the tiger's face confirmed that despite Galal's disinterest, they were in fact about to cut off one of his fingers. Instead of standing his ground against Praxades, the tiger nodded once to the girl, Nandi, then turned and stalked out of the room, stiff with suppressed rage.

Praxades jerked Joe's twisted arm further up his back and marched him out of the room, across a courtyard and into a small chamber with a number of horrible looking knives and plier-like tools hanging from the walls. A torture room. Joe could not believe his eyes. The young man from the library, Kitoko, trailed in behind her. He held Joe from behind while Praxades placed Joe's right hand on a wooden block.

No, my bowling hand! he thought in panic.

"Don't move," Praxades said, gleefully tucking three fingers under his palm, leaving his middle finger awkwardly exposed. Joe gritted his teeth and tried not to panic, but instead he was overcome by a bewildering welter of emotions. Nothing in his short life had prepared him for such a virulent bout of spite, or casual willingness to cause pain. How had he gone so quickly from normal everyday life to this destructive madness? His three uncondemned fingers started to creep out from under his shaking palm of their own accord and Joe struggled to hold them in place. Good grief, he thought, what if she missed, and took off his whole hand? He froze, trying to ignore the *woosh-woosh* of his heartbeat roaring in his ears as he waited for the blinding pain to shoot through him, desperately hoping he would not give her the satisfaction of hearing him scream.

Nandi's green outfit pushed its way in between two of the youths from the library. Her velvet brown eyes stared intently into Joe's. An intoxicating glow wrapped around him, and Joe felt himself losing his sense of time and place, and even the will to brace himself.

The blade swung down.

"Bugger!" Praxades cursed, her black eyes glaring suspiciously around the room before she bent down to pick up her bloody prize from the floor and stormed out.

Kitoko let go of Joe and ran out after her, followed by his entourage from the library.

Joe stood as if in a dream. He wasn't sure if it was the shock, but he felt strangely detached from the incident. It hadn't hurt nearly as much as he'd thought it would. Nandi watched him with solemn eyes, an expression of frantic concentration on her face, till the last person had followed Kitoko out of the room. As she broke eye contact with him, excruciating pain shot up Joe's arm. He gripped the block for support, his breath coming in shuddering gasps. She ran forwards to catch Joe as he slumped to the ground.

Some time afterwards he lay on his back, his eyes squeezed shut. He'd tried to lift his hand to look at it, and pain such as he had never known shot up his arm. He flinched as someone touched him on the shoulder.

"It's not that bad. She only got the tip of your finger," Nandi said, as if that were some great victory. She leaned over him and placed her small hands on either side of Joe's face, turning it towards herself. "Now open up, I can only reduce the pain if I can see into your eyes."

Her face swam momentarily in front of Joe, but his pain subsided to a dull throb the moment he looked into her eyes. Quite a lot of time must have passed, he realised, because she had changed into black pyjamas, and wore her long unruly hair pulled back tightly into a plait that hung down her back.

Joe coloured as he glanced down at himself. He was clean. His dirty hyena pelt had been removed and he was wearing some sort of white linen pyjamas. He grimaced as a wave of pain threatened to overcome him again.

Nandi pulled his face back to face hers. "You have to keep eye contact, or it will hurt. Don't worry, the healer removed your clothing and put the kurta on you. She has gone to fetch some herbs for the pain so that I don't have to keep looking at you like this."

Nandi climbed up on top of him and sat on his chest, gazing steadily into his eyes, but went on speaking in a conversational tone. "Don't be too angry with Praxades. She has been here since birth so she does not understand how painful pain is. Most of them don't. It's just a word to the Almohad. She doesn't make trouble out of malice . . . just out of bored frustration."

"She should be caged!" Joe grumbled. "What kind of people are you?"

"Praxie is so focused on learning the magic of the beauty that she forgets to apply herself to the magic of the coaxing," Nandi explained, as if that made it okay. "I haven't spent much time becoming beautiful. I'm working on becoming a healer. I am going to be a *great* healer one day."

Joe was about to argue, because she was in fact prettier than Praxades, but the healer returned just then, and Joe was even more embarrassed than he had been when he thought Nandi had undressed him. Out of the corner of his eye he saw that she was not much older than Nandi, and breathtakingly beautiful. He wished she had not seen him like this.

He drank the bitter concoction she gave him and she said jokingly, "You can safely tear your eyes away from Nandi now."

Closing his eyes for a moment did not bring back the pain, so Joe tried gently to detach Nandi's hand from his face with his good hand. But she seemed reluctant to let go.

"He's such a funny colour," Nandi said to the healer.

Joe was amazed at how quickly he felt better, but that was no reason for her to take advantage of him. "Excuse me, I am right here, and I am not a funny colour. Lots of people are this colour where I come from, even if most of them look like you," he said, taking a proper look at her. She had mocha brown skin, like Jimoh's family, but as unruly as her hair was, it was not as kinky. More like the silky stigmas from the ends of a leaf of corn, except jet-black.

"I want him!" Nandi said, leaping off his chest onto the floor. "I am going to ask Daddy for him." With that, she spun on her heels and rushed out of the room.

"What is she talking about? Wants me? Is she the captain of some sort of team?" Something told him this had nothing to do with gangs or teams.

"What do you mean team?" the healer said. "Do you mean 'tribe'? There are no tribes here. The tribes live beyond the river." She pointed over the balcony to the silvery lake across the valley.

If they had no concept for team, and she did not belong to a tribe that she wanted Joe to join, what could she possibly want him for? She couldn't possibly want to marry him or anything, he told himself. Or could she? They were both years too young. But he had heard of such things happening in India and other places, and with a dad like Galal, they could probably make him do it too.

"What does she want me for?" Joe said, scrubbing his fingers through his hair with his good hand.

"She wants you to be her bondsman," the healer said, as if that had been obvious.

SWITCH!

"I can't be her bondsman, or anything else, for that matter!" Joe yelped. A bondsman sounded suspiciously like a glorified servant. "I have to get home before my folks go down to the pools and find me missing . . . Or there is going to be hell to pay!"

"Young man, you will do whatever Galal decides, and like it," the healer said with an exasperated sigh. Then she shrugged, "Well, it would be better than being given to Kitoko."

"What do you mean, 'given'!" Joe said, realizing with a sudden chill what the elusive thought had been. "They still have slavery here?"

Joe stumbled after Nandi towards the grand hall. He couldn't remember the way but he had no trouble following Kitoko's raised voice.

"No!" Kitoko shouted. "I want him. She cannot have him!" Joe could almost imagine the spoiled brat stomping his foot.

"I don't see why you should have him, Kitoko!" Nandi shouted back at him. "You have had the last three captives, and hardly anyone ever comes across the river these days!"

"Those boys were unsuitable, Nandi," he spat contemptuously. "They tried to escape. I cannot be forever monitoring my minions. They must do as they are told and be patient until I see fit to release them."

"That's exactly what I am talking about! You fail to release them, even if they have given you good service. And you deliberately withhold from them the ways of the magic, so they are never ready. You treat them so badly, they would rather risk the hunting, or even the witches, than stay with you."

Joe heard Kitoko shift to a more wheedling tone. "No, those ones were cowards! This one is better. He hardly flinched when we cut his finger off."

Joe pushed his back into the wall, cradling his injured hand in his other hand, a knot of dread growing in his stomach. He should run right now and get it over with, he told himself. If he could reach the stream above the city he could follow it back to the Tokoloshe. He licked his lips. It was no good; he had a strong feeling from all this talk of hunting that he couldn't outrun the Almohad. His injured hand would most certainly hold him back. He glared at it. It didn't hurt now but he had no idea how long the painkilling potion would last. And if they caught him, they would probably cut something else off! What on earth had the tiger been thinking of? Things had obviously not panned out the way Hajiri thought they would, but the stupid cat must have had some inkling. These people were lunatics – if they chopped fingers off as minor punishment, what did they do when they were really angry?

Nandi, the only one who seemed at least partially sane to Joe, started to say something but stopped suddenly. Ears straining towards the door, Joe heard the sound of people shushing others to be quiet. With a horrifying compulsion to look inside, Joe crept forwards and carefully poked his head around the door.

"Ah! Just the boy!" Galal had risen from his divan beside the bao board. The way he strode towards Joe, it was as if he had felt him just outside the door. Putting a comradely arm around Joe's shoulder, he drew him into the room.

"What to do . . . what to do?" he said as if choosing between sugar or honey in his tea. "Nandi wants so badly to have you, but alas, she is too young to be training an attendant, and Kitoko wants to have you but he has misused his last three attendants." He shook his head and tut-tutted at Kitoko, but Galal did not look too distressed about it.

"What to do?" he said again. "Do I give you to Nandi? She is, after all, my favorite." His eyes crinkled indulgently at the young girl. "Or do I give you to Kitoko? He is, after all, my heir."

Joe didn't know what to say. Was the man actually asking him? If he had to choose it would obviously be Nandi, but either way it amounted to captivity. He felt himself getting angry with the girl. People here were just not normal. She should have warned him. She should have helped him get away, not jumped on the bandwagon. And where was Hajiri when he really needed him?

"Bao," suggested a barrel-chested man with a shock of wavy hair.

"Bao . . . Bao," nodded several others.

"Well, bao it is then," Galal agreed, losing interest just as suddenly as he had when he had made the decision to have Joe's finger chopped off. He went back to his own extravagantly carved game, and his pipe in the corner. His opponent and the group of spectators around his game had hardly moved a hair.

Nandi came over to Joe and took him by the hand. "Don't worry," she said, "I am particularly good at bao."

"You're gambling for me now?" Joe pulled his hand away. "I don't want to belong to you. I don't want to belong to anyone. I have to get home to my family."

Nandi sat down on a low divan, motioning Joe to sit beside her. He watched in stunned silence as Kitoko and his friends arranged a low table on a carpet in the middle of the room and found seating cushions.

"Joe," Nandi said earnestly, "I thought you understood. You can't go home. I don't know how you got here but there is no way out of Karibu, and someone has to teach you the ways of the magic."

"I don't want the magic. I will go to the people across the river and try to find a way out," Joe said. He refused to believe there was no way out; he refused to believe he would never see home again.

Nandi's eyes opened wide. "Don't even say that!" she whispered. "Even the tribes-people who come from there are never allowed to go back once they have seen the magic. They would bring others. Worse still, they would go back with the magic and upset the balance in the kingdoms." She looked at him imploringly. "Joe, I am sure I can make you happy here. Even though I am younger than Kitoko, I already know so much more than him. If you work hard and learn fast I will release you from bondage even sooner than you think."

It did not look like much of a goal to Joe. The magic seemed to focus on making folk beautiful and strong, and strangely beguiling, but what was the point of being all that if you were stuck in this one city all your life, with no family and no contact with the outside world? His eyes shot from Nandi to Kitoko and back.

"Those are the choices I have? Being somebody's slave until it suits them to release me and then being stuck here anyway? People where I come from are never held captive unless they commit a crime. I can never be happy here. Not belonging to Kitoko and not belonging to you. What kind of people are you?"

Nandi scowled at him. "Do you want me to fight for you or not?"

Joe turned his back on Nandi, as much to avoid breaking down in front of the girl, as to hide his bitterness. He missed his family already, in a way that he did not miss them when he was at boarding school. At least then he had known he would be coming back. What if Nandi was telling the truth and there was no way out of here? What if . . .? If he were stuck here, it would be a hundred times better to be stuck with Nandi than with Kitoko. He closed his eyes and nodded.

"There!" she said, suddenly all smiles. "I am sure you will be happy with me. Now don't despair, I can win this game."

She left him to go and play bao, and Joe slumped dejectedly on the divan. No one stopped him – he did not have a master or mistress yet. He looked at his finger. It was strange how it seemed to be healing so fast. At least Nandi appeared to be winning. She had a much larger pile of ivory beads in her home trench. He closed his eyes for a moment.

Joe woke with a gasp as Kitoko yanked him up into a sitting position using the slingshot around his neck. For a long moment

SWITCH!

Kitoko stared reproachfully into his startled eyes, his face inches from Joe's, while Joe struggled to breathe. Then he yanked the slingshot from around Joe's neck.

"I'll have that," he said. "We don't want any more accidents around here."

Joe froze. Kitoko must have won him after all.

"And that's enough lying around for you," Kitoko said, kicking Joe to chivy him along. "Come on, get up, you lazy boy, and come with me. And keep up. I am only going to go through the rules once."

Joe shot up off the divan to follow Kitoko, and promptly sat down again as the blood rushed suddenly to his head.

"He must have cheated!" Nandi wailed. She helped Joe up and dragged him down the passage as Kitoko disappeared around a corner, followed by his entourage. "Hurry up, Joe," she said. "You have to do exactly what Kitoko says, or he will have you beaten . . . Or worse." She stopped as he winced in pain from the kick in his ribs. "Don't worry, Joe. Just keep your head down and try to blend in. He should get bored with you quite quickly. And I will try to stay close by so that Kitoko does not get out of hand."

"And I will expect you to carry my arrows . . ." Kitoko said, bumping into a couple of his entourage as he backtracked around the corner to see where Joe had got to. "You haven't heard a word I said? Have you?" Then he rounded on Nandi. "And you! push off! He is my boy now. And you can go and find his clothes while you're at it. I won't have him running around in a proper Kurta till the little savage has earned it!"

So much for blending in, Joe thought, as he followed Kitoko's litany of rules down the passage.

CHAPTER 20
LIONS!

The sun beat down on them as they trudged, single file, across a section of open bush-veld, following the cliffs north in search of the trail Fisi had said lead up the escarpment. Jimoh had made them start out before dawn, to ensure they reached the safety and shade of the woodland before the worst of the heat. Not that Ethan felt in the slightest bit hot. If anything, it was as if something was shielding him from the heat of the sun, or else his body was repairing itself as he went. Apart from the blinding headache, which had gone as suddenly as it had appeared, and a slightly bitter tingling on the sides of his tongue, he felt no effect from his chasing off of the Adze either.

Tariro, on the other hand, sagged visibly as he trudged ahead of Ethan. Sweat trickled down his face, his shoulders stooped, and he kept putting his hand up to shield the back of his neck which his dreadlocks did not quite cover. Lifting Jimoh's dad's hat off his own head Ethan quietly placed it on the boy in front of him.

"Ethan, I can't take your hat." Tariro turned around, placing it firmly back on Ethan's head. "With your white skin you will probably get sunstroke. That's if we haven't already all died of hunger and dehydration before we get to the spring." Tariro looked at the remaining magic water in his bottle. "This bloody stuff better be working! It isn't exactly thirst quenching."

"No, Tariro, Ethan is right about hat," Jimoh smiled patiently from behind. "Ethan can make hat with kanga." He lifted the hat off Ethan's head, swiped good-naturedly at a swarm of midges circling his head, trying to get to the moisture in his eyes, and placed the hat on Tariro's head. "Leopard told Ethan magic from amulet will protect him from getting sick from sun."

"Okay, well I will take the hat for now," said Tariro, "but only until my own magic kicks in."

That was another strange thing since being at Sobek Lake, Ethan thought; the midges, who seemed to cluster around everyone else, avoided him. They flew towards him, but changed direction at the last minute.

"Look, not long now," Jimoh said, pointing across the vlei at a copse of trees. "Rafiki say spring is in those trees."

The Tokoloshe had shown no discomfort at all at the blistering heat and the long trek. They were as exuberant and inquisitive as a bunch of five year olds at a theme park – dashing out on side trips to overturn rocks or investigate an anthill, and then running back shrieking and flicking their hands as the venom from ant bites trickled up their arms.

The spring, when they reached it, was already occupied.

"Rafiki say, baboons no problem but we will have to wait for sable to move away," Jimoh said, leopard crawling up beside Ethan. "I know there is no problem if we are disturbing this beast but Tokoloshe are alarmed for those horns."

"I am alarmed that they are pissing in our drinking water," Tariro joked, but it was the first time either of the boys had ever seen a live sable and they were happy to sit back in the shade and watch them. Sweeping, metre-long, sabre-like horns arched over their black backs, with raised bangle-like bumps along the length of them. The antelope were also struggling with midges, constantly twitching their shaggy manes and swishing their tails in the heat. After twenty minutes or so they moved off quietly.

A baboon, who had been sitting on an elevated rock like the king of the water, barked his defiance at their retreating backs as if he had ordered them off. Ethan caught a glimpse of his sharp molars, easily as lethal as Salih's, and wondered at the wisdom of the Tokoloshe's choice of what represented danger and what did not.

The Tokoloshe were all business after the antelope left. They lay flat on their stomachs beside the water and drank deeply, cupping the water up into their mouths, while the king baboon glowered at them from his rock. The rest of his troupe went about their business, picking fleas off each other and lounging about, completely ignoring his posturing.

From amongst the assorted dangly things tied around their waists, each Tokoloshe produced a small calabash with a gum stopper, which they filled with water. While Jimoh strained water through Ethan's kanga to fill his water bottle, Ethan commandeered Jimoh and Tariro's hats and strung a curtain of pods around the brim of each to shoo away the midges. He had seen a similar thing done in a documentary about the Australian bush. Within minutes several Tokoloshes had fashioned themselves hats from broad leaves with pods dangling from their rims.

"Fast little learners," Tariro said.

Salih came back with two baby warthogs, sending the troupe of baboons scattering into the bushes, but they soon crept back and took up their previous positions. Salih seemed as wary of them as they were of him.

"As weak as I am with hunger, I don't think I will be able to eat those ugly little things with all their warty bumps and bristly hairs," Ethan said.

"You are going to starve," Jimoh said, exasperated. He rallied together some Tokoloshe to collect dry twigs and helped them start a fire. He pulled his Swiss Army knife out of his pocket to a chorus of *oohs* and *aahs* from his little friends and they set about skinning the piglets and cutting them into narrow strips, which they threaded onto sticks to suspend above the fire.

"I have a plan," Jelani the Tokoloshe said, sidling up to Ethan and wiggling his bushy eyebrows up and down suggestively, almost spilling his new leafy hat on the ground. He chose a small calabash from his skirt and waved it in front of Ethan's face.

"Sleeping poison," he said with relish. "The witch makes it for our arrows." Before Ethan had finished wondering what the little man planned to do with the sleeping potion, Jelani had dashed into the spring with it. He poured the contents of the calabash out in a circle around himself and then started to gently agitate it into the water with his hands. Several more Tokoloshe jumped into the water after him excitedly. They had obviously done this before. After a few seconds, finger-sized fish floated to the surface to be collected by the Tokoloshe.

"What a brilliant idea!" exclaimed Ethan, wading in to help.

"Not so fast," Salih laughed, "that one is already looking sleepy." Sure enough, one Tokoloshe slipped quietly under the water. Tariro had also noticed and, being the closest, dashed in and hauled him out, laying him gently in the shade to sleep it off.

They threaded the fish through their gills onto skewers and roasted them over the fire.

At a signal from Rafiki, Jelani lifted the sleeping Tokoloshe over his shoulder and everyone followed him into the bush, much to the relief of the fractious baboon, who barked his truculence as they went.

Rafiki lead them to a small cave he knew of. One moment they were hacking away at the dense undergrowth and the next they were in a clearing up against the cliffs and there it was. It was too early to break for camp but the opportunity of a ready-made shelter was too good to miss.

LIONS!

Dark clouds built from the direction of the lake and a steady breeze smelled like rain. The Tokoloshe assured them that a tropical storm, if it broke, would be short. With a bit of luck it would pass even before the sun went down. Ethan wasn't that tired but preferred to rest in the cave while the Tokoloshe took the other boys hunting. They were dying to exchange hunting techniques with Jimoh, and Tariro wanted to test his skills with his slingshot.

Alone in the cave with Salih, Ethan carefully unpacked his backpack. Jimoh had suggested they pare down their equipment for the trek up the escarpment, and Ethan was glad for the opportunity to take stock of his equipment in private. He laid out his knives and his pocket full of gems on a kanga. Casting his eyes over the gems, he was shocked at how many he actually had, and the quality of them. He was no expert, but it seemed that there were millions of dollars worth of diamonds, rubies and emeralds, ranging from pea-size to grape-size. There were several sapphires there and something that looked like his mother's Tanzanite ring, but he couldn't be sure.

"Do you think we have enough here to pay a ransom for Joe?" he said to Salih.

"The Almohad are particularly fond of jewels. It may be enough, but they are just as likely to snatch the jewels and all of you too. They are not renowned for their sense of fair play. It might be better to persuade the witches from Waheri village to extract Joe."

"But what if we go all the way to the witches and then we don't get to Joe in time?" Ethan said. Even though he agreed that they needed food and a storm was coming, he was very worried about wasting the afternoon.

"Gogo will meet us on the way," Salih said. "Now put the stones away. No one must know about them," he added hastily. Three Tokoloshe were coming up the path with wood for a fire. Ethan divided the gems up into two equal piles, stuffed them into his cargo pants pockets, and closed the zippers.

Ethan was starting to be able to tell the funny little guys apart. These were Akin, Dembi and Manu. Dembi was still getting over the effects of the sugar, even though everyone else had stopped ages ago. Ethan suspected he had a secret stash of toffees hiding amongst the things in his skirt. He stopped what he was doing, gave a tremendous shudder, flashed almost transparent for a moment and then settled down with a contented sigh.

"Chocolate!" he uttered with relish. He seemed to be just as enamoured with the word as the actual sweet.

Akin and Manu exchanged a mischievous wink, their little black eyes twinkling as they hunkered down opposite each other to start the fire. Ethan noticed they were preparing to do this with a bowstring and a stick.

"Here, let me show you," he smiled, scooting between them. There was just enough sunlight for him to show them how to start it by directing the rays of the sun onto the dry tinder through the magnifying-glass attachment on his knife. He would show them that Jimoh was not the only one with a trick up his sleeve.

Salih padded over to sit beside the Tokoloshe. He cocked his head to one side and watched as a wisp of smoke emerged from the tinder and curled towards the sky. Ethan cautiously cupped the wad of tinder in his hands and blew gently on it till a small flame appeared. Careful not to burn his hands, he quickly transferred it to a spot near the entrance of the cave where the Tokoloshe had placed three stones and the firewood, in readiness for the fire. He built a neat pile of small sticks on it, careful to leave gaps for oxygen to get sucked in by the heat. He turned back to the three Tokoloshe.

"There you go," he said, proudly pointing out his first-ever fire. But they had shifted their attention to tickling Salih. The leopard lay on his back, wriggling from side to side and grinning while three sets of hands scratched all over his underbelly. His hind leg jerked spasmodically in the air. Ethan gave a wry shrug and continued to add slightly bigger branches to his fire. Not long ago the lack of validation for his efforts would have irked him almost as much as having to make his own fire. But there was a sense of affirmation within himself that he had never felt before. This journey had made him aware of just how capable he was; he no longer needed his dad to say, "Well done, Ethan!" Well, at least not as much as he had before . . .

The storm, when it broke, was torrential. A flash of lightning lit the clearing like a strobe light, making the surrounding trees dance momentarily before disappearing behind a solid wall of water. Ethan had hardly begun to worry if Jimoh and Tariro had found shelter from it, when the storm passed almost as suddenly as it had begun.

A huge black cloud hovering over the clearing in front of the cave turned out to be flying ants by the millions. Akin, Dembi and Manu rushed out and caught as many as they could, using Ethan's kanga. They might as well have conserved their energy because soon the ants homed in on the light of the fire and the cave was full of them, their bodies making strange clicking sounds as they crawled about. Akin and Dembi scooped them up by the handful and de-winged them while Manu threw hands full of the insects' plump juicy backsides into a shield and fried them in their own fat over the fire. On closer inspection Ethan saw the shield was none other than the sweet tin lid, bashed into a concave shape. Overcome with hunger, he tried one and then another and another. The idea of it turned out to be much worse than actually eating them. They tasted like squishy buttered popcorn.

He was glad to be relatively well fed by the time the others returned. They were saturated but proudly carrying a porcupine strung up on a pole. Ethan wasn't sure he would be able to eat it with that little wet face hanging down all cute.

"Don't touch it!" Jimoh said when Ethan went to pluck out a quill. "Spikes can still stick you, even when animal is dead. Then stick there like hook for fish. Cannot take out without tearing your flesh."

"Ouch!" Ethan said, testing Jimoh's theory with his thumb against a quill. Microscopic barbs scored a graze across his skin, making it bleed. He put his thumb in his mouth and sucked it, then folded it into his fist to hide the small wound, and the fact that it had started to close already.

"You just don't learn," Tariro laughed. He lifted Jimoh's dad's hat and flicked the rainwater off it before settling it back on his head, then handed Ethan the water bottle he'd borrowed from him because he'd forgotten his own at the spring. "You should have seen Jimoh!" he said. "Just before the rain came, he had the beast cornered outside its burrow. It stuck out its tail quills and spines, and started grunting and rattling them and stamping its back feet." He stamped his own feet in imitation and then lunged towards Jimoh who ducked out of the way. "Then suddenly it ran at him sideways like that! So fast. Eh! Ethan. Don't be fooled by those stumpy little feet. It was as quick as lightening, but not as quick as Jimoh. He stabbed it with his stick. Did you know they do not shoot their quills?" He lowered his voice to a whisper. "The Tokoloshe were kind of cowardly though. They scattered and ran."

"Tariro, you know how they have a sleeping potion on their arrows? I am not convinced they are cowardly – I think they just have a problem actually killing things," Ethan whispered back.

The porcupine was delicious. Jelani took charge of the plucking and skinning, carefully polishing the microscopic barbs off the ends of the quills and distributing them amongst the tribe to use as decoration. Once the rodent had been staked and roasted it looked almost like supermarket meat, so Ethan ate it.

Jimoh built an A-frame structure with a pole across it, to hang their nets on in case the Adze came back. He and Tariro set it up near the entrance of the cave, away from the smoke of the fire, and everyone took shelter under the nets as soon as it grew dark.

For a long time, Ethan struggled to get comfortable on his

LIONS!

back on the hard rock floor. He couldn't sleep on either side without gemstones digging into him and if he lay on his back, the buckle of his headlamp dug into his head. He had been wearing it on his head since the incident with the Adze. "I made the fire all by myself," he boasted, but there was no one awake to be impressed.

A piercing scream woke Ethan out of a deep sleep, followed immediately by a blow to the head. Dazed, he struggled to sit up, but seemed to be pinned down by something. It's only the mosquito net, collapsed on top of us, he realised with some relief. He reached for his headlamp, but it must have been knocked off his head.

Everyone else was awake and stumbling about in the dark yelling by the time he'd disentangled himself and staggered to his feet. He found his headlamp dangling around his neck and switched it on with shaking fingers to see what Tariro was screaming about.

Momentarily distracted by the bright halogen beam, a lion, barely ten metres away, let go of Tariro's leg and dropped into a crouch beside him, ears flattening against his head as he snarled at the source of the light.

"*Voetsek!*" yelled Jimoh, shooting the animal on his nose. He nocked a second stone into his slingshot, ready for the next shot.

The animal flinched, but stood his ground, his nose wrinkling back into a snarl so loud and angry, Ethan could almost feel the ground vibrate beneath his feet. It sent ripples through the dark ochre fringe around the beast's cheeks. The lion bent his enormous head down to pick Tariro up once more but then flinched and shook out his thick black and tan mane. By the light of the headlamp Ethan could see several of the Tokoloshes' little sleeping arrows sticking out of the short hairs of the cat's upper belly, where his mane ended.

Jimoh's second pebble hit the lion right between the eyes. He reared sideways, backing away from Tariro a little and another volley of arrows found a target where his mane covered his shoulders.

"The arrows are not strong enough to pass through his hair," Jimoh gasped. "I have no more stones to shoot! Look! Ethan! More are coming."

Ethan peered through the darkness. Sure enough, dark shadows moved in the forest beyond the clearing, just outside the beam of his headlamp.

Oh, man! The only thing he could think of vaguely resembling slingshot ammunition was Joe's ransom. They were going to have to use the gems if Jimoh was going to keep the lions off Tariro. Ethan hesitated for only a moment before withdrawing them from his pockets, and handing them to Jimoh. He would worry about how to rescue Joe later. Right now, they had to save Tariro!

Almost immediately, the lion yelped and backed off further, bringing one giant paw up to its face.

"I got him in eye!" Jimoh yelled excitedly, and kept up a steady stream of priceless shots, but it was no use. The lion stood his ground, snarling. Two females slunk forward and hunkered down on either side of the giant male, emitting a low rumble, their heads lowered, eyes fixed on Ethan's headlamp.

A group of Tokoloshe dashed forwards, waving their arms in the air, shouting. Rafiki beat a stick against the sweet tin lid, but did not get too close. Akin got hit by a stray arrow from behind and stumbled sleepily back into the cave. Ethan wished the sleeping draught would affect the lions that fast but instead a lioness inched slowly towards Tariro.

"The one on the left!" Ethan yelled to Jimoh just before the boy smacked her on the nose with a diamond. She backed off, snarling angrily, but turned straight around and advanced once more on Tariro, who lay writhing and screaming on the ground.

"Tariro! Try and get up!" Ethan shouted but he didn't think Tariro even heard him.

LIONS!

Rafiki, Jelani and Manu edged forward to within a metre of grabbing Tariro when a cry went up.

"Adze!"

Everyone scattered. Rafiki, Jelani and Manu dashed back to the cave empty handed. They struggled to pick up the fallen nets, to scramble back underneath them, while the forest filled with the high-pitched battle cry and the iridescent glow of the little vampires advancing.

Ethan ran towards Tariro, panicked now, beyond any thought for his own safety. If the lions did not get Tariro, the Adze certainly would. No amount of stone throwing would protect the boy from them. Jimoh, who jumped forward almost at the same time as Ethan, grabbed the sweet tin lid and stood over Tariro, banging on it and waving his arms in the air in an attempt to look frightening.

"*Voetsek*!" he screamed at them again, whirling around as something struck him from behind. Some of the Tokoloshe shouted advice and encouragement from behind the safety of the nets, and some lifted the net for short bursts of throwing things in the general direction of the lions. Dembi shrugged sheepishly at Jimoh, then hefted another rat scull from hand to hand in preparation for another shot at the lions.

Ethan also waved his arms about, but it was more like swatting at the Adze who slowly circled his head. It was difficult to keep track of them, and the lions at the same time. The lion and both lionesses crouched low in front of him with their ears flattened against their heads, the black tips of their tails flicking back and forth. Ethan noticed out of the corner of his eye, just beyond the beam of his torchlight, more dark shapes slinking in the shadows. He swayed, more frightened than he had ever been in his life.

If the Adze took his soul, he wondered, would they leave any of himself behind? Would he be him, or them? Would his body just walk around without a soul? Would it have the sense to avoid being mauled by the lions? And eaten! Urine trickled down his leg.

He tried to think of crystals, icicles, anything that would reflect, but nothing came. It was no use. One way or another, they were going to die.

An Adze flew so close to Ethan, it brushed against his hair. Without meaning to, probably because they grew tired, Ethan's jerking arms slowed down, but they did not stop. They continued to wave in a strange pattern, as if someone else was controlling them. Mentally squaring his shoulders, Ethan slowly regained control of himself. He almost forgot about the lions as his arms wove the pattern above his head. Such a lot of adrenalin pumped through his body, he felt as if he would explode, until, amazingly, he did.

A powerful wave of air shot out of Ethan, as fast and as unstoppable as a giant sneeze. He could almost see it as it washed outwards like a mini-nuclear explosion. Jimoh staggered back from it. It sent ripples through the dark mane of the lion, who looked for a split second as if he would bolt. The Adze were like illuminated dandelions, scattered to the wind. The jungle grew quiet. Or were his ears blocked?

"Oh my . . ." Ethan said, as he closed his eyes and slumped onto the ground. He could almost feel the lions drag Tariro and Jimoh away from beside him, but he was too drained and paralysed by fear at the enormity of what he had done to move.

Then suddenly he was swept off his feet by someone who smelled as bad as Fisi. His eyes shot open. It was Fisi! The young man threw Ethan over his shoulder, and carried him back into the cave, depositing him in a heap beside the other two boys.

"We were tracking you when we heard the noise. I had gone to fetch those hyenas we saw from the waterfall," Fisi explained, indicating a pack of seven hyenas who sat panting by the fire. A dirty young girl in a skin skirt was propped up between two of them, fast asleep. The rest wore the same skirt-like garment as a bandana around their necks. It looked very much like their own hyena pelts. Ethan shuddered. Yussy! Were they wearing their dead comrades or something? The Tokoloshe pushed themselves as far back against the cave wall as they could go, eyeing the hyenas nervously.

"What were you doing, Ethan? You cannot just stand in front of a lion with your eyes closed like that. The thing will eat you. And what the hell happened to those Adze?" Fisi added. "They were tracking you too. We could not pass through them to chase off the lion and then suddenly they were scattering everywhere, screaming. They took off."

"Um, that was me," Salih said, dropping into a crouch beside Fisi. "I chased them."

Ethan whipped around to confront the leopard. He knew whatever had happened had come from himself. He could still remember the sharp after-pain in his head. Ears wickedly cocked, Salih shook his head almost imperceptibly, reminding Ethan that he did not trust the hyena youth. Perhaps Salih and Tariro were right. There was something a bit furtive about the hyena, even if he had come back and saved their lives. He'd caught Fisi staring at him in a contemplative way once or twice after the incident with Jimoh's hat. The hyena already suspected Ethan of some sort of mind manipulation. He would have to remember to warn Tariro not to tell the hyenas about the night he chased the Adze.

"You are lucky I got back in time," Salih said smoothly.

Jimoh got up from fussing over Tariro and tugged at Ethan's T-shirt sleeve. "Come, Ethan, Tariro not so good," he said with an imploring look on his face. "He has fainted now. He has big bite and lots of scratches."

"Yes! See what you can do for the boy, Ethan," Salih said, his meaning clear. Which was all very well, but apart from the cave full of witnesses, Ethan was not looking forward to the awful feeling afterwards. He wished the cat would make up his mind. One minute he was warning Ethan not to give blood too often, and the next he was telling him to give it.

Salih seemed to have the witnesses covered, though. "Well done for chasing off the lionesses," he said to Fisi's pack, "but the danger has not passed. The lion has fallen asleep from the effects of the Tokoloshe arrows at last, but it is too close. Could I impose upon you to help move the beast to a further location?"

"I know just the place to leave him," Fisi said. Ethan wondered if he knew what was going on, and was being tactful. He signalled for his hyenas and six of them got up and followed him into the night, leaving the seventh to look after the sleeping girl.

The Tokoloshe trailed out after them, carrying scraps of leather rope in a very professional way, as if they had done this before. They whispered and elbowed each other, but did not look like they were going to let a couple of hyenas ruin the opportunity of handling a sleeping lion.

"Why don't they just kill it?" Ethan mumbled half to himself.

"No, Ethan. Is not good to kill lion. He only protecting his area," Jimoh explained. "We are ones who should not be here. Also, if we kill him next leader of pack will kill all young from this lion. Upset balance." He took his Swiss Army knife out of his pocket and handed it to Ethan.

"What if the girl by the fire and the other hyena see?" Ethan said.

"No. She get hit by arrow for Tokoloshe. That is why she change. She will sleep a long time now. Other one is not looking," Jimoh said.

"I am afraid to give him blood, Jimoh. If he knows about the blood he might tell someone else and I might end up getting drained for it. Salih said I could also use spit." Ethan took off his T-shirt and spat on it, and then groaned. Tariro had two large puncture wounds where the lion's teeth had gripped his calf and several deep scratches on his ankle. He could see spit wasn't going to be any use even before he wiped the T-shirt along the worst of the scratches. All it did was relieve Tariro's pain enough for him to wake up and scream.

LIONS!

"Ethan!" Jimoh said, his hands on his hips in exasperation, "This is boy you have just faced lion for. Are you going to let him die now?" Then he glanced furtively towards the remaining hyena, but she continued to lie with her back towards them, licking the sleeping girl.

Jimoh grinned as if the idea came to him out of nowhere. "Maybe we cut him little bit with sleeping arrow?" he said. "Then he will not wake up and scream and also maybe not know about blood."

CHAPTER 21

AN IRRESPONSIBLE OWNER

Joe woke at sunrise. He had slept on the bare marble floor at the foot of Kitoko's sleeping pallet. Kitoko could have given him a pallet of his own – Joe could see a pile of them against the back wall of the room. There was a massive ornately carved chest holding plenty of linen, too, but Kitoko wouldn't let Joe touch it. Kitoko said if he chose that Joe sleep on the floor without a blanket, Joe had to do it.

Joe wondered at the heir's spectacular room. It was at least thirty paces long and twenty paces wide. Huge tapestries, depicting hunting scenes, hung down from the six-metre high ceilings to the floor on three sides. The fourth side opened onto a vast balcony overlooking the rift valley. Kitoko had a bird's eye view of the wildlife activity in the jungle between the escarpment and the river, and beyond. Joe looked yearningly at the countryside beyond. He could imagine sailboats drifting up or down the river in the far distance. He wished he could be over there. No, he corrected himself, he wished he could be snug in his own bedroom at home.

At the thought of Kitoko sleeping, dead to the world in

sumptuous comfort, Joe's hands coiled into fists. He realised with wonder that his finger hardly hurt at all. He removed the bandage, marvelling at how quickly the wound was healing, when he felt a soft nudge and jumped, his hand flying to his throat. But it was only Hajiri.

"Quiet, boy," the tiger whispered. He cocked his head to indicate Kitoko. "He's a heavy sleeper, and there's not much danger of him rising before noon, but we don't want to wake him up until we've shown you around and explained a little about how everything works. I did not expect to be brushed aside for the revolting youth yesterday. You can be assured, there will be a reckoning, but in the meantime, come, we will do our best to prepare you to make things easier with him."

Joe wondered who Hajiri meant by "we" until he saw Nandi waiting for them around the corner. She was still in her pyjamas.

"I thought you would never wake up," she said, grabbing Joe by the hand and dragging him down the passage. "Come on! If we hurry, you will have just enough time to bath and have something to eat. Once Kitoko wakes up, we will not be able to interfere with his wishes."

After handing him a loofah and a towel, Nandi lead Joe down some steps, where she split off from him and Hajiri to go to the ladies' baths, and Hajiri took him to the men's. "Come to the kitchen when you are done," she called after them.

The bath was a swimming pool carved out of the rocks, and at this time of the morning Joe and the tiger were the only ones there. Joe was a bit taken aback when Hajiri jumped in, sending the water cascading down the outlet.

"Come on in, exposure to the water will help the healing," he told Joe.

Puddles of a sticky, oily substance floated on the surface of the water, smelling like strawberry, or watermelon, but Joe washed himself in it anyway.

Afterwards, Hajiri led him into the bustling kitchen where

they found Nandi, already sitting at a communal table on the far side of an immense cooking range, eating something out of a bowl. The aroma of baking bread wafted up from several ovens to mingle with the smells of exotic spices and a wood fire that burned in a compartment beside the ovens.

Joe felt self-conscious as he slipped onto the bench opposite Nandi. He wished he could have hung on to the pyjama-like kurta the healer had given him. Now that he was clean, the hyena pelt felt dirty and awkward. Nandi, dressed in a richly embroidered tunic over lustrous silky pantaloons, looking every bit a princess, did not seem to care what he wore. She pushed a bowl towards him; it smelled like curry. Strange choice for breakfast, Joe thought, but he was worried that Kitoko would come in at any moment and take even that away from him, so he tucked in, stopping from time to time to fan his good hand in front of his mouth to dissipate some of the heat.

Hajiri hunkered down on the mosaic floor besides them, and tore chunks out of a small antelope he had grasped between his enormous paws. Several people interrupted their chores to give the tiger a scratch behind the ears on their way past.

"Where do all the servants come from?" Joe asked Nandi between mouthfuls.

"From across the river," she said.

"I thought you didn't allow people over from the other side of the river."

Nandi looked a little guiltily at Hajiri, who cleaned his face with a paw and then licked it.

"Oh, they allow people to cross over if they dare, dear boy, it's the going back that they are a bit fuzzy over. Now, these people," he swept a paw around the room. "These people are all carefully chosen captives. The Almoha have raiding parties that go over the river and blend in with the locals. They find suitable candidates to do all the things the Almohad don't want to do themselves."

Hajiri clucked at the look of shock on Joe's face. "Now don't take on so, dear boy, they are lucky to be here. They live in abject poverty over there, and appalling squalor. The scouts only choose people who are unlikely to be missed."

Joe stared around the room. "I suppose they don't look unhappy . . ." He guessed there was no point in escaping, only to go back to a horrible place, but he knew he could never get used to this life – he promised himself he would strive to get home until the day he died.

"You see those two over there?" Nandi pointed at a couple tasting dishes behind what looked like a spice shop counter. "They keep everyone happy."

"Over the last two millennia or so the Almohad have developed their ability to persuade people to do what they want," Hajiri explained. "Their other trick is to convince people that they are happy to oblige."

Joe glanced over at the couple. Both wore simple cotton tunics over comfortable baggy black trousers, and both were radiantly beautiful. The man was tall and muscular. He had dark skin with very thick long hair, worn in a ponytail hanging down his back. The woman was willowy and doe-like. She reached up and pulled a bottle from the shelf behind her, twisting the top off as she turned. Her eyes fell on Joe, staring at her from across the room. They were the most beguiling eyes he had ever seen – soft, and deep brown, almost violet. Her lids lowered languorously and Joe relaxed, his vow to get home already forgotten. He rose to go over to her because he just knew she would be so happy if he did . . .

Hajiri directed a low rumble at her, and, after a moment of disorientation, Joe sat down with a jolt. What had just happened? She flashed him a wicked grin, her perfect teeth contrasting with her velvety bronze skin, and turned her attention back to her work.

"That was weird . . ." Joe shook his head to clear it. He felt a slightly desolate feeling at the loss of the woman's approval. "Can you all do that?"

"Well, she has been practising for nearly fifty years," Nandi said.

Joe was shocked. He was no expert but she barely looked thirty.

"Okay, this is how it works," Nandi explained. "The magic in the water makes us strong and healthy, and we live for much longer than the people in the valley kingdoms, but some of us also study it really hard to get it to give us what we want–"

Nandi stopped speaking, eyes widening suddenly. The next thing Joe knew he lay sprawled on his back on the kitchen floor clutching his head.

Praxades' face swam in front of his eyes. "Up, boy." Her laugh was vicious. "I want a pear from the cliff garden for my breakfast. Kitoko says you can get it for me."

Joe was sure he was staring at his boiled and polished finger bone swaying hypnotically back and forth in front of his face. She was wearing it on a leather thong around her neck!

"I will have it carved once it has dried out enough," she boasted, seeing his eye on it.

His jaw clenched with fury at the sight of it hanging there, but before he had time to react Kitoko grabbed him by the ear from behind and dragged him to his feet.

"Come on, you can't sit around here all morning chatting to your friends," he sneered. "Things to do . . ." He turned on his heel and strode out of the kitchen.

Joe was shocked to discover a sort of eagerness within himself to do what Kitoko commanded. He shook his head. No, he was sure he just felt that way because Nandi had suggested he might, but he ran after the heir anyway, followed by Praxades, and the colourful entourage, who had been hovering at the door.

Sweat stung where it ran into Joe's eyes. He wished he could wipe it away. He wished he had on a pair of track shoes to provide a little more friction between his bare feet and the rock face. The pear Praxades wanted was in a tree overhanging the cliffs. It had seemed like a great idea to climb up the bare face of the rock for it when Kitoko had told him to. His thoughts had been full of the excitement of the challenge as long as the heir had been close by, but the mesmerising influence of the youth had gotten weaker and weaker the further up Joe climbed. He wasn't sure if it was the distance between himself and his new owner, or if the stupid youth was simply losing interest. Now he was urgently aware that he hung from a rock face hundreds of metres above the rift valley, and one false move would see him plummeting down the cliffs.

He backtracked a step, but the taunts yelled up at him by Kitoko's friends waiting below, left him in no doubt that they would enjoy flinging him the rest of the way down the cliff if he did not complete his task.

"Oh. Let me try!" Praxades said, in a long-suffering tone, as if the broken spellbinding link were Joe's fault. A look of fierce concentration passed over her face and Joe screwed his eyes shut. He recited the six-times table over and over in a desperate bid to repel the girl's thoughts. Without a shadow of a doubt, he knew that if he let her interfere with his thoughts he would fall to his death.

"No, I am sick of this," Kitoko said, kicking the dirt at his feet with a multi-bejewelled moccasin. "Let's go and get something to eat, Praxie."

"We *are* getting something to eat!" Praxades glared at him. "I want to eat the pear."

Joe didn't look down to see her expression, but a deathly hush told him she had overstepped the mark. Out of the corner of his eye he saw Kitoko turn on his heel and march indoors. Praxades followed close behind.

"Kitoko . . . Kitoko . . . I was just saying . . ." her voice drifted back towards Joe.

"Best not to look down, boy," a skinny boy in a purple kurta with gold trim called up to him. He was the smallest of Kitoko's entourage. "Just hug the rock and look up towards your right hand. You will see a small depression in the rock. Put all your weight on your feet and move your right hand into that depression. That's it. Now pull yourself up by your hands, there is a good foothold near your left foot. Don't look down – feel for it. One step at a time. If you look closely, you will see a path has been cut in the rock face." He laughed. "Don't think you are the first to attempt this."

"Thank you," Joe said. "Won't you get into trouble for helping me?"

The boy contemplated that for a moment. "No, I am not important enough to be missed. Besides, the heir has not yet eaten. Getting a pear to impress his girlfriend would have lost its charm at the first sign of a hunger pang in his own body. He will be a while yet. He likes to send the dishes back until they suit his taste. You can catch your breath once you reach that small tree growing out of the crack."

If I ever reach it, Joe thought bitterly, but he resumed his climb up the rock. His finger throbbed. The wound had broken open and the blood mingled with his sweat to make his hands slippery where he gripped the rock. And the rock was getting uncomfortably warm in the sun. His arms and legs grew weaker by the minute. His foot slipped as he put his weight on it and his heart lurched in dismay. A stone bounced down the cliff face and disappeared into the valley below.

Joe jerked and almost let go of the rock face as something brushed his cheek.

"Grab the rope!" shouted the boy. To Joe's enormous relief he felt a length of thick hemp rope against his back. He snatched it, clinging tightly to it. Whoever had hold of the rope did not haul him directly up the cliff face, but left him dangling. Joe wondered, for a moment, if he was supposed to climb the rope or if this was a new game of torture, before he realised he was being eased towards the pear tree.

"That's it!" an amused voice drawled from above the cliff. "You still have to get the bitch's pear. You don't think they will let you get away with it, do you? Grab us a couple while you are down there."

"Thank you!" Joe panted as three pairs of hands reached down to help him up onto the cliff. He pulled the handle of the woven sling bag over his head, dropped it between himself and the friendliest of the three young men and held out his hand. "Joe," he said.

The man glanced down at Joe's bloody hand and then crushed it firmly with his own. "You are welcome, boy." The man glanced at his two companions. "But this does not make us friends. So don't expect any more help and not a word to anyone about this. We just wanted the pears." He reached into the bag and pulled out three pears. "One for the Heir, one for my stupid brother, Jwahir, down there, and one for you," he chuckled, not unkindly, before squeezing through a gap between two stones and disappearing into a fissure in the cliff face after his friends.

Joe sunk to his knees. He had no idea where the fissure lead but he wanted a rest before he felt up to following them. He wondered if he could pretend to have fallen to his death and just quietly slip away into the forest.

"Don't eat the pear," Jwahir said when he had made his way up to where Joe rested. He flopped down beside him. "They will smell it on your breath."

"You did it!" Praxades squealed when Joe and Jwahir walked towards them in the kitchen. "My pear. Give me my pear."

Kitoko looked quite surprised that Joe had made it at all. "No, I want it," he said. He took it out of Joe's hand. Praxades looked crestfallen but did not seem ready to push her luck.

Joe couldn't see what was so great about a pear. "Um, I've got another," he ventured.

"You can give that to me too," Kitoko said, staring intently at Joe. An erratic current tried to soak into Joe's head. A pulse of dominance all mixed up with wild bursts of power. It felt to Joe as if Kitoko was trying to manipulate him but was getting the signal all mixed up with his own feelings instead of enforcing his wishes.

Ha! Still a novice, Joe thought with a smirk, remembering the overpowering urge he had felt to obey the lady in the kitchen.

"Two?" Praxades stared at the other pear with open longing.

"The boy climbed for me, Praxie! Me!" Kitoko's face contorted oddly, still trying to convey the correct message into Joe's head. Eventually it came. Joe felt a strange tightness in his temples, before a wondrous sense of achievement swept over him and he found himself basking in Kitoko's approval. For just a moment, a contrary idea hovered on the edge of his conscious, but he dismissed it. He was just so happy; if he'd been a dog he would have wagged his tail. He even felt bad for thinking mocking thoughts about Kitoko . . .

"Three," Jwahir said, breaking Kitoko's concentration and his tenuous link to Joe's thoughts. "Your bondsman is still a bit tongue-tied, but even he knows how fond you are of Praxie. He brought three. Two for you because you are the most important, and one for Praxie because he is sorry for hitting her yesterday."

Joe recoiled from the mind bending and shot Jwahir a grateful look, avoiding Kitoko's eyes in case he started up again, but either Kitoko was mollified, or his mind-bending talents were exhausted for the day, because he stared at Joe blankly and held out his hand for the other pear. Praxie absently caressed the finger bone that hung around her neck as she stretched out her hand for the third pear.

Either Jwahir was a very good diplomat, or he knew Kitoko well, because Kitoko lost interest in his competition with Praxie and abruptly dismissed his entourage so that he and his girlfriend could enjoy their precious pears in peace. He gave Joe permission to go off and gloat to his previous attendants that the climb was, in fact, possible.

Joe had no intention of gloating but went in search of his predecessors to get some insight into what he was facing as Kitoko's attendant. "Thank you for helping me," he said to the boy that fell in beside him, before looking up to see it was not Jwahir.

"Damn, I knew Jwahir had helped!" the boy said. "Don't worry, I will not tell. Did Jwahir eat one of the fruit?"

"No – he said Kitoko would be able to smell it on us."

"Wise move."

"What is it about the pears?"

"Wouldn't you like to know?" the youth said enigmatically, peeling off down another path. He stopped and turned, pointing to the north side of the city. "The prisoners are through there."

They were kept in cages like at a zoo. Most cages consisted of a barred enclosure with a room at the back to provide shade and shelter. An elephant, chained by her back leg to a tree stump in the clearing in front of the cages, swayed disconsolately, swinging her trunk back and forth. Joe wondered how they could possibly have got her up the cliffs. And how they could ignore the fact that she was so stressed? A large enclosure in the middle held a pack of five hyenas. Quite a few people were kept in cages amongst the animals, some in single enclosures and some in groups. Joe's face went hot when he saw the human captives. Jungle gyms, in every shape and size, decorated the fronts of their enclosures, exactly like a monkey park. It was even more shocking to see some of the humans using the apparatus.

The three he was looking for were playing a game of bao in the sand in the shade of a lucky bean tree. They were in a large pen with some other young men. The occupants ranged from the deepest black man to a mocha-coloured boy – who looked as if he might be Indian from his dead straight, thick hair – and everything in-between. No two looked as if they came from the same place. They appeared to be wearing whatever they were captured in, because one was neatly dressed in a white kurta whilst another wore nothing but a loin cloth, and yet another wore what looked like full war regalia – leopard skin cloak and all.

"What do you want boy?" said a thickset young man with rich scar adornment across his forehead and cheeks. He had on a length of red and black cotton, held up at the shoulder by a lethal-looking copper pin. He scooped a handful of scarlet and black lucky-beans out of one of the little bao wells scooped out of the dirt and played his hand.

"I came to see the men who have been . . . er . . . working for Kitoko," Joe said.

"Well, you've found them," the young man snorted, his wide nostrils flaring, "but nobody works for that boy, they slave. Now pull up a rock over there if you want and don't wrinkle your nose like that. It's not our fault we stink. They hardly give us enough water to drink, never mind wash. They filter the magic out first, the bastards, so that we don't get stronger and escape."

"Or smarter!" laughed a rangy young boy in a white kurta, which looked spotless, despite the shortage of water.

"Ah Jumoko, it wouldn't take much to be smarter than Kitoko." A man got up and leaned against the bars of the enclosure, to stare appraisingly at Joe. He wore chamois trousers and a black vest, partially open in front, showing the taut muscles of a hard worker or a soldier, but his wide, generous mouth split into a grin, which hinted at a joke.

"Here, boy," he said. "Fetch us some water from the spring."

Filling the wooden bucket at the stream behind the shelters, it occurred to Joe that it would be fairly easy to redirect the stream to flow right through the cages, if he could get his hands on a hoe or something, and sneak back here. He'd look in to it when he had a better idea of his situation; he was pretty sure he would lose another finger if he were caught. For now, he brought the bucket back and passed a drinking gourd back and forth between the bars until each prisoner had drunk greedily.

"What is it you want to know?" the man in the black vest said, wiping the water from his lips with the back of his hand. He called himself Iniko.

"Why don't you try to escape?" Joe looked across the rift valley. They could see right over the river to the settlements beyond.

"Are you out of your mind?" Jumoko, the boy in the white kurta said. "That is what they want us to do. They like to hunt us down in the valley."

"They look all rich and lazy but you will be surprised at how strong and agile they are when they put their minds to it," explained a man in baggy black trousers and a sleeveless shirt that did not quite cover the scars striped across the back of his shoulders.

"But to keep you here like animals!" Joe said.

"Ha! Some of the animals here are not animals." The one with the face scars laughed bitterly. "You see that pack of hyenas? I have seen at least two of them change shape when they first came. They cannot do it anymore. The Almohad withhold the magic from them too."

"It is not a bad life," Scar Face's bao opponent sighed. He was in full war regalia, right down to the cat-tail skirt and seed pods strapped in rows to his calves, that jangled every time he moved. "We escaped here in the first place. Where I lived, across the river, is even worse than here. A terrible old man, King Ulujimi, runs the kingdom. He tends to fly into rages at any excuse. I was about to have my eyes put out for looking at his granddaughter. Not that she was anything to look at. And not that I was looking . . . But I cannot go back." Joe was flabbergasted. It sounded like these people were living in the dark ages.

Iniko, the soldierly man in the black vest, smiled warmly at the youth and said, "You did well to escape, Kimoni. If you were blinded, you would have been a burden to your family." But Kimoni's shoulders slumped. Whether he had done well or not in escaping, Joe could see he wasn't happy with the outcome.

SWITCH!

"I will go back, eventually," Iniko told Joe. "I have no fear of being hunted between Almoh and my homeland, but first I must gather enough magic to challenge chief Boblengula, who rules my people in the north."

He went on to explain how the evil tyrant had a death grip on his country, rewarding his own incompetent family and friends with high positions, which they would then exploit for further enrichment while the rest of the people starved. Even if people did well, Iniko told Joe, they chose to hide their wealth and live like paupers, rather than give it over to the ruling family. Everyone else just gave up, not wanting to expend the effort of building anything or even repairing what they had, because it was sure to be conviscated.

Jumoko, the one with the spotless kurta, had a similar story to tell about feudalism and corruption. "I thought I might find a gap in the valley to escape to the outside world," he said. "I had heard there may be a pass through the mountains to the south-west. The Almohad caught me in their hunting grounds so I said I was trying to come here. I heard they sometimes take servants from across the river. They gave me to Kitoko instead."

The boy called Jabari shook his head sadly at Joe. "I was the last to serve Kitoko," he said. "He is just going to make you do more and more dangerous things till you have an accident. I ran away when they told me I would have to do Kitoko's initiation for him."

"Initiation . . .?" Joe asked.

"Yes, this year it is Jendayi," Iniko said. "It's a game they play with the lions down in the valley, to keep the lions fit, you know. Otherwise they get fat and lazy with all those animals to pick off and nowhere to go."

"Er, what exactly do they do with the lions?" Joe had been initiated before. It had involved eating a vile toothpaste concoction and running a gauntlet of senior boys flicking you with wet towels in the locker rooms. But lions?

"They chase them with the buffalo," the man with the scarred face said in a flat voice.

Joe stared at him. "How do they get the buffalo to chase a lion?"

Jabari looked around at his friends guiltily, as if it were somehow his fault that Joe was in this position. "They climb on the backs of the buffalo and guide them."

"What? They get on the buffalo? Are the buffalo tame?"

Iniko sighed. "Yes, they all get on a buffalo, and no, they are not tame. And I'm not going to lie to you, people have died. You will have to run away before you are next." The look in his eyes said he did not think much of Joe's chances either way.

CHAPTER 22
A NEW COMPLICATION

Waheri, the witches' village nestled amongst the mountains to the west, was separated from the magic forest by a narrow range of hills with a series of confusing maze-like tunnels running through them. Gogo Maya had a panoramic view of the village from her cottage verandah, situated a little way up the hillside.

Not everybody chose the witching, she mused, as she watched the smoke of an early cooking fire curl up, twisting itself around the thick, oily fumes of whatever potions the witches and wizards were concocting down below. A lot of the villagers chose instead to farm their little patch, watering their crops from the fresh water streams that ran off the western mountains. Well, some of them used a little help from the magic, but they had to go east, into the forest to get it, and not all had the stomach for it.

Lewa drained the last bit of herb tea from her cup and stood silhouetted against Gogo Maya's own breakfast fire. Leaning as far over the rickety verandah balustrade as she could, she rinsed her cup in a waterfall that tinkled besides Gogo Maya's cottage. Gogo Maya raised an eyebrow.

"What?" Lewa said. "It's just a bit of herb tea. Honestly, if the stream ran past my house into the village I would do *all* my washing up in it. Not to mention adding a few surprises of my own."

Gogo Maya eyed the girl warily. She wondered if she'd thought that up herself or if she suspected Gogo Maya put stuff in the village drinking water. Well, she only put in herbs that were good for folk, to chivvy them along, and then only once a week. And the occasional sleeping draught, but only when she needed to be absolutely sure they would sleep through her more interesting experiments.

The angry yowls of a cat drifted up towards them, followed by the stomach turning fecal odour of someone extracting ambergris from a civet cat.

"You should have a word when we get back," Lewa said to Gogo Maya, sniffing the air and wrinkling her nose. "I am sure there is something synthetic that Mawulol could use, if he would only ask Tacari to bring it through the tear."

"No point," Gogo Maya said. "That man is as stubborn as his badger. He has been making his perfumes that way since long before you were born. He won't see any reason to stop now, besides, he would never ask Tacari." Her ears pricked at a faint whispering sound and she sniffed the air, nodding when she caught the comforting slightly burned smell of Nomatotlo. "Shh!" she said. "They're here."

Gogo Maya searched the underside of the thatch of her verandah and the plethora of decorated cattle horns, bead covered calabashes and etched ostrich eggs that hung there, turning gently in the breeze. It was no good. You never actually saw the Nomatotlo. The soft, whistling sound that came from the thatch, although unintelligible at first, soon settled into one or two tongue-clicking voices.

"Maya, we come from Kapichi village and the news is not good," they whispered. "The entity you seek – the entity that threatened you – lurks at Almoh City, and we believe it is some sort of soul that jumps . . . called a jumper."

"How many troubles can I bear?" Gogo Maya moaned in disbelief at this new complication, even though she had half-expected it. "Couldn't the stupid thing lurk around Morathi's village till we've rescued the boy? " She couldn't let a jumper – *whatever that was* – get in her way now. She'd heard from the first group of Nomatotlo that Joe had arrived at Almoh with the tiger, but he looked somewhat banged up. She was sure the tiger had not injured the boy, but the cat was obviously out of his depth. She had hoped to rescue the boy before they had to decide what to do about the jumper.

"Well, what does it jump on? And why did it want to attack us?" she said impatiently, addressing a set of masks decorated with bird feathers and plant fibres that hung over her cottage door – that was where she suspected the Nomatotlo hid.

"Wise Tokoloshe said it is a soul that jumps into a new body when it is tired of its old body. It can do this simply by touching the host body."

"What happens to the soul currently occupying that body?" Lewa said grimly. She did not speak towards the masks, but chose instead to gaze out over the village.

"It dies," the Nomatotlo intoned in unison. They were not the most sympathetic of creatures, having spent so much of their energy on achieving accuracy.

"Whose body is it wearing at Almoh then?" Gogo Maya said to the masks.

"We were unable to winkle this information out of the Tokoloshe, or why they attacked you," the Nomatotlo whispered. "They are either too terrified to tell, or they have forgotten. One of them thinks the thing is after Galal."

"Oh, good grief! This jumper must be able to make the Tokoloshe forget." Gogo Maya said. "Even Morathi's crowd can't be that stupid on their own." She tried to remember the voice from the forest. The Tokoloshe had been pretty terrified of it until it left, and then they had been their usual rapscallion selves. She wouldn't admit this to anyone else, but she'd been a little unnerved by the voice herself.

"It occurs to me that the Almoh are in as much danger as the boy," Lewa said. "I have never come across a jumper before, but I think I can handle one, as long as I know who it is," she added, less doubtfully.

"Not our problem . . ." Gogo Maya frowned. She had no idea how to ward off a jumper, but she was sure she could work it out. She was damned if she was going to let Lewa take over, even if the young girl was more powerful than her. Lewa would only complicate things with weather and things bursting into flames, or push the entity through into another world causing even more complications. Besides, Gogo Maya was the one who had been attacked, she was the grown-up, and she did not want to abandon her carefully laid plans.

She'd spent days making amulets to protect the group who would go with her to Almoh to rescue the boy. Her stash of ceramic beads was busy soaking up the magic in the well at Lala Salama village, to be added to the amulets at the last minute. True, she was worried they would not be strong enough or that some of Rafiki's Tokoloshe may have disturbed them, but that was no reason to defer to the girl.

"I wish we could speak to Tacari," Lewa cajoled, turning towards Gogo Maya. Her eyes had an excited intensity to them.

"You're finding this thrilling, aren't you?" Gogo Maya grumbled. Lewa had been wishing pointedly that they could speak to Tacari from the beginning. He may be able to help, but he would be so furious with Gogo Maya when he found out what she was up to, and he may refuse in any case.

"Perhaps he knows something about jumpers," Lewa said in mock horror that Gogo Maya would think she was enjoying Gogo Maya's discomfort. "He might be able to shed some light on the powers of your boy, Ethan, too. Nomatotlo told me yesterday, the boy held three lions at bay while they waited for Fisi and the Kishi to pitch up. Perhaps the boy has more power than you think."

Lewa leaned back in her chair with an impish grin. "And that's another thing Tacari is going to be angry about," she said. "The hyena! At least the boy, Joe, was a mistake."

Gogo Maya eyed Lewa, shifting uneasily. The twinkle in the girl's eye told her she was joking, but she wondered if she could really trust her. "Drat, of all the luck, couldn't I have changed places with something simple like a squirrel or a rock?"

At last, Aaron strolled out of his hut down in the village as if he had no particular destination in mind. He patted old Gogo Hasina's vulture, before making his way up the path towards Gogo Maya's cottage.

"Good!" Gogo Maya said to Lewa. "The boy is very sneaky, but you must remember to warn him not to touch other people's familiars. Are you quite sure you wouldn't rather leave him behind? This adventure is becoming more dangerous by the minute."

"And risk having him tell the whole of Waheri village as soon as we have left? Not likely," Lewa snorted.

Gogo Maya thought that was just as well. She knew it was too late to back out now. Aaron had been sucking up to her for days in an effort to persuade her to take him with on her rescue. He had fed her piglets, milked her goats, even tilled her small maize patch further down in the valley. He would be mortified if she didn't let him come. Oh well, she sighed, he was Lewa's responsibility anyway.

Gogo Maya tapped her pipe out against her boot and stood up. "I don't suppose there's any point in putting it off then," she said, hefting her sack of amulets on her back and turning towards the path to meet Aaron. She would have to remember not to let anyone snoop in her bag. She'd packed her last remaining mbogo root in there. She was going to need it now if she was going to construct a powerful enough ward against the jumper.

A NEW COMPLICATION

The three of them stole quietly out of Waheri village towards the tunnels that led through the hill to the magic forest. Gogo Maya was sure old Gogo Inaya could see them go, as clairvoyant as she was, but she was also a close-mouthed old bat, and slow. She wouldn't raise the alarm till they were well on their way.

Slipping inside the maze tunnel, Gogo Maya was careful to place her feet exactly where Lewa had placed hers. Her eyes were not what they used to be, and there was no point in setting off the miniscule traps hidden along the path.

Originally intended to keep the forest animals out, a delicate creeper had been planted there, which bore extremely fragile, spiny-faceted bag-like flowers, the size of a pea, that gave off a puff of vapour if you popped them, that created a wooly sort of confusion in your mind. Strangers approaching from the forest, who did not know where to step, would find themselves turned around and facing the way they had come. Gogo Maya would have gathered some of the flowers up if she thought they would confuse the jumper, and if it were possible to gather them up without causing a fair bit of confusion to herself. *Drat*, she thought as she plodded along behind Lewa, *I hope I am going to be able to construct a strong enough amulet to repel that jumper.*

CHAPTER 23
THE JUMPER'S PLANS

Drogba had watched keenly as the boy climbed the cliff face to retrieve the powerful pears. Apparently there was a trick to it. He'd only ever seen one youngster survive the climb and when he had wondered out loud why anyone would take such a risk, had been told about the potent magic-enhancing properties of the fruit. It was good that Joe was capable of making the climb because Drogba needed to accelerate the boy's transformation if his plan was to work.

Although he would go back to his original plan of taking Galal if things did not work out, Drogba was more resolved than ever that he should take the boy's body. He felt a pang of regret because the boy was charming, but he would die anyway at the hands of the insufferably reckless heir. It was only a matter of time. The Almohad, who apparently set great store by such things, were already fascinated by the boy's exotic looks and with his natural ability. If Drogba combined that with his own centuries of experience he would be able to do wonders in the Kingdoms of Karibu.

The problems with the slaves, and the troubles across the river had been going on for decades. Drogba felt sure they could hold out just a little longer . . . Just until he could appropriate the boy, and set himself up. Yes . . . He hoped the boy would survive Kitoko just a little longer. Just long enough for Drogba to manoeuver himself into position.

CHAPTER 24
A HOSTAGE SITUATION

Ethan hugged his knees to his chest where he sat at the back of the cave. Tariro was well on his way to recovery but he wondered if things could possibly get worse. He had taken off his wet trousers and wrapped a kanga around his waist, but there was no way of washing himself; he had run out of waterless hand sanitiser days ago. The only thing more embarrassing than having wet himself was that Jimoh had noticed, and offered him his spare set of trousers back. He hadn't taken them. He kicked listlessly at his bloodied T-shirt lying on the floor. A wave of nausea passed over him, leaving him faint and on the verge of tears. He wondered how much of that was due to the shock of the lion attack and how much to his blood settling, as Salih liked to call it.

Clutching the remaining five gems tightly in his fist, he felt a further stab of panic as he wondered if they would be enough to ransom Joe. That was always supposing he could get the gems to Almoh before the Mokele Mbembe came looking for them . . . For a moment, before Jimoh had dozed off again beside Tariro, he had been on the verge of blurting out his worries about losing the rest of the gems but stopped himself when he realised that would only make Jimoh feel guilty, and there had been no choice about using them against the lions. Perhaps they could look around and try to salvage some more in the morning, he thought, as he rolled himself up in a ball besides Salih. He closed his eyes and tried to get some sleep before morning.

But sleep wouldn't come. Instead, predatory feelings drifted into his mind, more vivid than a dream. His eyes flew open in astonishment, breaking the thread, and he stared at the shadows from the fire flickering across the ceiling of the cave. The Tokoloshe snuffled and grunted in their sleep around the fire. They had all returned brimming with excitement, after stashing the lion in a safe place, but not before plaiting its mane and giving it a general tidy-up, according to Manu, who had added a small scrap of plaited lion mane to his skirt.

Salih lay purring softly beside Ethan's head and he wondered if he hadn't somehow picked up on the leopard's dream. He closed his eyes again and deliberately let his awareness spread out, the way Salih had taught him, to see if he *could* tap into the leopard's dream.

He felt himself moving outside the cave, but he was loping rather than slinking, eyes fixed intently on the brindled form of the sister in front of him. He realised, with some discomfort, that he was intruding on Fisi's mind. Alert to every nuance of scent and sound as he stalked along the path running parallel to the river, he was surprised to sense that he was not in control of the hunt. Instead, he followed the sister's coolly efficient progress through the bush. Other dark shadows loped effortlessly on either side of him. Ethan was aware of a feeling, not a thought, exactly, just a general knowing, that the success of the hunt was especially important to Fisi because he wanted to ingratiate himself to Ethan. Suddenly, with a grunt of triumph, the sister streaked across an open patch of ground, sailed over a low boulder and launched herself onto the back of a young sable antelope.

"No!" Ethan shouted. "Not the one from the spring – I know

that one." He felt Fisi's body falter for only a heartbeat before it went in for the kill. Had the hyena felt Ethan prying in his mind? And why was it so important to the hyena that he curry favour with Ethan? Was he trying to lure him into something?

Tariro awoke with Ethan's shout and groaned.

Panting from the exertion of the hunt – or was it the excitement? – Ethan tried to focus on Tariro. Jimoh already lay next to Tariro, quietly consoling the boy in Shona.

Despite the early hour, woken by the noise, several of the Tokoloshe got up and began to build a fire. Ethan wondered if he had merely dozed off for a bit, and dreamt of being in Fisi's hunt.

He rose to go over to the fire but as soon as he moved he felt his face flush unnaturally, and sat down with a thump, putting his head between his knees. His hands and feet pulsed with something worse than hot pins and needles. It was like the feeling he got sometimes when he struck a nerve in his elbow. He felt agitated, to the point of screaming.

Salih raised his head and examined Ethan, his golden eyes thin slits of anxiety. "Are you well, Ethan?"

"You mean apart from wanting to explode, thinking I'm a shady hyena and worrying myself sick about the gemstones?" Ethan asked grumpily.

Salih took a long, contemplative breath. "You must sleep, Ethan. You have drawn blood for your friend. Too much blood, too soon. There is a fine balance with the magic. If you don't rest you will be unable to repair yourself."

"I can't sleep. If I shut my eyes I think I am Fisi," Ethan said, surrendering himself to the urge to scratch all over. "Yussy, do you have any idea how much vermin that guy carries in his fur?"

Salih smiled. "You do not have vermin, Ethan. Your magic repels them because you think of them all the time and avoid them. What you are feeling now is your blood stabilising, just as before. It will get worse every time you do it." He regarded Ethan sternly, as if there had been any choice. "Beware. If you do it too often, this feeling may not go away."

"You told me to do it! And speaking of magic," Ethan said, still rocking back and forth on his bottom in agitation, "what the hell was that earlier with the lions? It was nothing like splitting crystals and exploding them outwards to multiply and stuff. I don't even know where I got it from."

"That would be because it came from me," the leopard said. He looked to Ethan almost as if he was a little contrite. "In an emergency I can channel my magic through you."

Ethan's eyes narrowed. "You mean without my consent?"

"Regretfully, yes."

"And how will I be paying for that, may I ask?" Ethan groaned. With blinding headaches every time he tried to manipulate anyone's thoughts – not that there had been any choice in that matter either – and unbearable agitation every time he bled, he shuddered to think what horrible side effects Salih's magic would have on him.

"It is a bit of a gift," Salih said with a wicked glint in his eye. "The more I channel through you, the more you will be able to move through people's thoughts, and of course, the more you will be bound to me."

"I don't bloody want to move through people's thoughts, Salih," Ethan said, thinking about the distressing hunt Fisi was just in and feeling even more worried about the hyena's shifty feelings. He scratched wildly in his agitation. "Why didn't you channel your emergency magic through Jimoh, or through Tariro in the first place? If he'd been able to get up off the floor it would have spared the rest of us a lot of trouble."

"You kissed the witch, Ethan. I can only channel through you." Salih stretched luxuriously in front of the flickering fire, and purred contentedly, signalling that that was that.

Ethan did not want to be bound in any way to the leopard either. He wondered if Salih was imprinting his creepy witchy familiarness on *him* now, instead of the witch. What was he supposed to do with the leopard once they rescued Joe and went home? He supposed he could swing it with his parents, they were indulgent that way, but sooner or later the law in Cape Town would require the animal to be put on a leash. *Good luck with that,* he thought, and then a more troubling thought crept in: What if the leopard wouldn't let him leave? It was probably best not to ask.

Salih laughed. "You are the only one *present* to whom I am attached."

Well, that was exactly what the leopard would say if he planned to stop him from leaving, thought Ethan, before he tried not to think about anything at all. Then he smiled ruefully at Salih, who stared blankly at him as if he had no interest at all in Ethan's thoughts.

"Okay, I will try to go back to sleep, but wake me up at first light," Ethan said. "I have to go and find those gems. We shot them at the lions. They're scattered all over the bush. I don't know how we are going to get Joe back without them."

"Wait!" Salih said, sitting bolt upright. "What did the Sobek, Kashka, say to you about the gems?"

"He said they would save Joe's life."

"No. He said they might save lives. And they did! I don't think Kashka meant for the gems to reach Almoh. As fond as the Almohad are of gems, they would have gone looking for the source. Kashka would have had nothing to give you that resembled ammunition for your slingshots, but I think he knew you would meet the lions. Apparently the Sobek are talented that way. Amun and Darwishi had been expecting Gogo Maya at the Crystal Pool. Perhaps it is best if you leave the stones here, the ones in your pocket too. Mokele Mbembe will come looking for them." Salih flopped down to the ground once more and went back to sleep. Typical cat, Ethan thought, patting the gems through his pocket. There may be only a few left, but it was the only leverage he had; he was not quite ready to give them up.

Besides, what was the likelihood of there really being a dragon? Quite high, he admitted to himself with a worried glance at the entrance of the cave before closing his eyes and trying to get some sleep himself.

"You are something else, Ethan," Tariro beamed at him in the morning, showing barely any sign of his ordeal from the night before. "How did you chase the lions? Did you think at them?"

Remembering the dreadful agitation of the night before, Ethan couldn't help giving his head one last vigorous scratch. He was beginning to wonder if he had picked up lice. He was glad to see Tariro up and about though.

"No. Jimoh and the Tokoloshe kept them at bay till Fisi came. He chased them while I was scaring away the Adze. With my awesome fear power."

"Fisi came?" Tariro said.

"Yes, they are hunting now. Will be back soon," Jimoh said. He seemed to be collecting himself a bunch of interesting treasures. So far he had a row of baby warthog teeth on a length of twine around his neck and several interesting tails hanging over his trousers from a leather chord tied around his waist. He was trading dangly things with the Tokoloshe, Ethan realised. Several of them now wore roughly carved slingshots around their necks.

"I thought I was going to die. Literally," Tariro said, and then he cocked his head to one side and regarded Ethan seriously. "Did you piss on me?"

Jimoh threw back his head and laughed. "He could not miss you. He was standing on top of you to stop lion. Very scary job."

"That's just crazy." Tariro pulled the back of his T-shirt around to the front and sniffed it, wrinkling his nose, but he didn't take it off. "Who knew you had it in you . . . I don't know what happened after that. I think I passed out. My foot was really sore." He drew up his foot to inspect his wounds for the umpteenth time, and showed his leg to Ethan. "It's just like your croc bite at crystal pools, Ethan. The lion bite has almost healed up from the magic I drank at the Sobek Lake. Will you teach me to scare things away too?" He yawned. "Funny, I slept really well. Do you think one of the Tokoloshe shot me?"

Ethan was on the verge of telling Tariro about the blood he had fed him. He couldn't have the boy going around thinking he was invincible because he had drunk the magic. Knowing Tariro, he was bound to take unnecessary risks, but Jimoh gave him a warning look and then said, "Yes, Tariro, Tokoloshe shoot you by mistake. Don't feel bad. One sister for Fisi also fall asleep when she get shot. She is fine now. Gone hunting."

Ethan's eyes widened in astonishment as he watched Fisi heft the sable off his shoulders and heave it up over the ledge as if it were no heavier than a sack of potatoes. He'd suspected the hyena youth was stronger than he'd been letting on, but a whole sable? Well, a sable calf, but still! Fisi said they would carry it up the escarpment to share with the pack. There was no danger of having to share it with Ethan – it would be like eating his own pet, after he'd watched it while it was alive, drinking at the spring in the valley.

Not that Ethan had ever had a pet. He'd always been loath to touch any kind of an animal, much less feed one. Their food was always so gross to prepare, and generally smelled repulsive. Salih was probably the closest thing he'd ever had to a pet. Ethan was starting to enjoy giving the leopard a good scratch behind the ears every now and again. The cat seemed happy to allow Ethan to stroke him, and tended to lean up against him at every opportunity, yet as time went by, he seemed less and less tolerant of being handled by Tariro, and even Jimoh.

"What are you smirking about?" Fisi said, bending to make a stirrup of his hands to boost Ethan up onto the ledge beside the dead antelope, and then leaping nimbly up the side of the embankment to rest beside him.

"I was just thinking what it would be like to have a leopard as a pet."

Fisi's mouth hung open. "I wouldn't let Salih hear you say that!" His eyes darted nervously to the trail up ahead to make sure Salih was out of earshot, but he needn't have worried. Everyone else was a long way ahead of them. Ethan could see Jimoh and three Tokoloshe inching their way up the secret pathway like spider monkeys. The rest had already disappeared around a crag in the cliff.

Ethan had dropped behind to help Fisi with his load. It was the least he could do after the hyena had saved his life the night before. Also, he had to admit to himself, he wanted to try and slip in to Fisi's thoughts, but only to work out what the hyena's intentions were. Not that Fisi needed any help. Apparently he hauled game up the escarpment all the time, without any help from the sisters. It was the way.

"I did not think you would return after you disappeared at the bottom of the waterfall," Ethan said as they rested on the ledge, getting their breath back.

"I went to find this pack. To see if they would help guide you through the lion territory." Fisi dangled his legs over the precipitous drop on the other side of Ethan, sending a few loose pebbles cascading down the cliff. Not for the first time, Ethan wondered at the young man's complete lack of any feeling of vertigo.

"This pack? Are they not your pack?" The hyenas had changed to their human shape for the climb up the escarpment. They had all turned out to be girls and women, but at least one bore a close resemblance to Fisi.

"No, they are the pack that we saw from the top of the waterfall, but I knew who they were. I have hunted with them before."

"Well, why did you come back?" Ethan said. "And for that matter, why did the sisters come to help us if it was so dangerous?

They don't even know us."

Fisi hesitated, fidgeting with a tail hanging from his pelt skirt, trying to find the best way to say what he wanted to say. "We could not lose you, Ethan," he said at last. "You have the power, and I think you are not afraid. There is something you can help us with. Something we never thought we could do."

Oh no, thought Ethan, payback. "I am having enough trouble just staying alive and I have my work cut out for me trying to get my cousin back."

He shifted uneasily at Fisi's woebegone expression. Surely he owed it to the pack to do whatever he could, even if it sounded dangerous. Could Salih have been wrong about whether they could trust Fisi? Because all the hyena had done so far was help them. "What is it you think I can do?" he said

Fisi began in a low, soft voice. "I was with a girl, Tabita, from this pack but she was captured by the Almohad. It is our hope that you will find her and release her while you are there to fetch the boy, Joe."

"Why haven't you rescued her yourself?" Ethan said. He had rather hoped Fisi would be the one helping him to rescue Joe.

"If we go into Almoh in our human form they mess with our minds, confuse us and capture us. If we go in hyena form they can't really manipulate our thoughts, but our natural human cunning is dulled and they can easily trick us. If they can trap us there, they withhold the magic until we are no longer able to reshape." He looked a little embarrassed. "Even if we successfully rescue her without harming any of them they will hunt for another Kishi hostage."

"That's not very nice for the other Kishi," Ethan said, although that was all very well for him to say, he realised. He would not leave Joe there to stop the Almohad going after someone else.

"I need this one more than any other," Fisi said.

"Why don't they just capture all of you?"

A HOSTAGE SITUATION

"They don't need all of us. They just need a few hostages to ensure that they are never attacked in the forest. They are much stronger than us but a pack of hyenas would be able to overcome one Almohad or a pair. If they are harmed in the forest, they will execute a hostage."

"Can't they make some sort of a treaty? A promise, instead of keeping hostages?"

"Not all Kishi are friendly. Some are positively sneaky. You never know which ones will turn. The Almohad see us as a group who will all behave the same way. We don't blame them. Even we can't guarantee cooperation amongst the packs. That's why we keep hostages of our own."

"You keep hostages?"

"Well, yes, otherwise we have no leverage ourselves, in case of an attack. But we don't keep them for ever like the Almohad do, unless they want to stay with their host pack." Fisi stretched his arms out in front of him, his palms upwards in a gesture of futility. "The Almohad imprison them and then just sort of forget about them."

Ethan moaned under his breath. "Anyway, I don't know how you expect me to help. I don't even know how we are going to rescue Joe."

"You have the power of the witch, Ethan," Fisi said. "Tariro told me you kissed a witch. Not many have the courage to do that." He whistled in disbelief, then picked up a stone and idly tossed it down the cliff face, following its progress all the way to the bottom. "A boy from my pack kissed a witch once and he drew power from her. He drove the whole pack crazy with it until he used it all up. They had been friends before – him and the witch – when they were children. Then the other witches took her away. They bumped into each other in the forest many years later, and she kissed him. After that he could make us do things we didn't want to. Like you made me give Jimoh his hat."

"It's not only about kissing witches, Fisi," Ethan told him

firmly. "You made me give you my slingshot."

"No, I was just looking very pitifully at you for the thing, like Jimoh does for the knife. You give up things too easily. You would not have given it to me if you really needed it." Fisi hefted the slingshot in his hand as if he were going to give it back, but changed his mind. "No, this is different. This is more like bending someone to your will, so that they can't help but do the thing."

"I tried to make a fish eagle drop his fish," Ethan volunteered. "He just ignored me. So did the Adze the first few times."

"I know nothing about what frightens a fish eagle, but the Adze are not easily frightened. What did you threaten them with?"

"Well, bats, to start with. The Adze looked a bit like insects. Bats eat insects."

Fisi guffawed. "Adze are not afraid of bats, or lions for that matter. I will tell you what my pack brother used to do. Look, you can try it out on me if you want. Take your knife and cut your finger, and while you are feeling the pain, think hard about how you would like me to feel the pain."

Ethan opened the knife and sat poised to prick his finger. He concentrated hard on Fisi, and how much he would like Fisi's finger to hurt. He thought he felt a warm crawling sensation ripple over his skin, but that could easily have been the rocky ledge, grown hot in the midday sun. Resisting the urge to scratch, Ethan pressed the knife into the soft pad of his finger, wincing as a thin trickle of blood oozed out.

Fisi shook his head in exasperation. "Such a small cut! Ethan, you are much too soft. That hardly hurt at all, but you see how you can do it if you try," he said, holding his finger up for Ethan's inspection. Ethan watched with wonder as a tiny drop of blood beaded on Fisi's index finger. "Will you at least think about helping?"

Ethan nodded. Of course he would do his best. Fisi had saved their lives. Without thinking, he placed his own bleeding finger against Fisi's as he had seen Jimoh's friends do. Fisi's face split in a delighted grin. Too late Ethan wondered what kind of a deal he had struck with the hyena youth. Well, he would worry about that when the time came. First he had to rescue Joe . . .

As creepy as this new skill was, it seemed like a useful skill to have. He wasn't sure if he could summon enough evil intent to use it, or the courage to injure himself badly enough to have any effect on anyone else, but he would ask Salih.

"Why didn't Salih tell me all this?" he wondered out loud, eyeing Fisi, suddenly wary.

"The leopard is a wily cat. He must have a devious reason of his own," Fisi said gleefully.

With renewed energy, Fisi hefted the calf over his shoulders and started to work his way up the path. "Come on," he said, "we have to catch up with the others."

Ethan waited a moment before following Fisi. He was starting to wonder just who he could trust on this journey.

CHAPTER 25
A CUNNING PLAN

The forest gave way abruptly into a strange vineyard leading into a miniature village. Akin and Manu immediately fished around amongst the broad, domed leaves of the vines with their doily-like edges, to get at the purple, sausage-shaped fruit underneath.

"You try," Manu said, extending one gelatinous-looking opaque fruit cautiously towards Ethan, careful not to burst it. It looked fragile, and when Manu bit into his own fruit with obvious relish, a sticky mess of purple splattered down his belly like a popped water balloon.

Ethan took a careful bite out of the end of his, and his face almost caved in on itself, the fruit was so tart. "Man, how can the Tokoloshe possibly eat this stuff?"

"It's what they drink!" Fisi laughed. "It is the fruit they use to make their ceremonial wine. They have ceremonies nearly every night."

To Ethan, if he could ignore the fact that they were more sour than lemons, they did taste vaguely of grapes.

The tiny thatched houses in Lala Salama village were too small for him and the boys to fit inside, Ethan realised with a groan. He had been looking forward to a good night's sleep in a proper shelter and something other than peculiar fruit to eat. At least the food situation seemed hopeful. As they entered the village, the savoury smell of stew hit his nostrils, making Ethan's mouth water.

Rafiki had sent most of his men on ahead to alert Lala Salama to their coming, and although all the Kishi with the exception of Fisi and one of the sisters, Shenzie, had branched off to Maradzi, their own village, they had sent a hind-quarter of their sable on with Rafiki's men to Lala Salama to prepare a feast. It looked to Ethan as if every table in the village had been dragged outside into the central square, where they groaned under the weight of all sorts of strange and exotic fruits. Root-like tubes with soft down on their skins were piled up next to a jumble of twisted stalks that may or may not have been dried mushrooms.

A pruny old Tokoloshe woman stood beside a well in the center of the village square. Apart from the usual animal pelt skirt, she had on the same hedgehog headband as Rafiki's, which held her clay-orange hair up in a style that made her head look like a sucked mango pip.

"Water," she grinned toothlessly, handing Tariro a furry looking gourd-like shell full of water from the well. Tariro took the water eagerly and gulped down a few swallows before spitting it out in a projectile spray, much to the hilarity of the assembled Tokoloshe.

"It tastes bitter!" he exclaimed, trying to rub the taste off his tongue with the back of his hand.

"Container taste funny, Tariro," Jimoh explained. "Is only shell for baobab fruit."

Other Tokoloshe women came forward with calabashes and helped the travellers with water from the well, which they drank warily at first, in case there was another joke forthcoming, but also because oily magic floated on the top. Ethan guessed it must have come via the underground stream Nuru the Sobek had thought they would travel down if they'd had enough time to learn to use the magic.

"Don't mind Grandma," Rafiki said to Tariro. "She likes her little joke. She says Gogo Maya is on her way and will be here before the sun goes down. But you must all eat now. She says she has seen the cousin, Joe, with that bossy tiger that the Almohad keep as a pet. She thinks the tiger may have beaten the boy up. He was so scratched. She would have given Hajiri a piece of her mind if Grandpa had let her."

Ethan was on his second plate of the sable stew he had vowed not to eat when Salih's ears pricked up and he slunk off into the forest to return a short while later with Gogo Maya and two teenagers. Gogo Maya was looking much better than the last time he had seen her, if a little distracted. She barely greeted them before hurrying to the well and hauling up a hemp rope with a sack full of small round ceramic beads attached.

She looked somewhat relieved, but she turned on the Tokoloshe with a stern look and said, "Okay! Who's been at my beads?"

A woman stepped forward without hesitation, her eyes fixed bashfully on her hairy foot as she twisted it in the dirt in embarrassment. She withdrew a handful of ceramic beads from a small leather bag hanging from her squirrel tail skirt, and handed them to Gogo Maya.

Unexpectedly, Gogo Maya's face split into a wide grin, and she patted the woman on the head, withdrawing her hand just as suddenly, as if she had been pricked by a pin, and sucking on her palm. Encouraged, a small group of Tokoloshe men and women clamoured to give up their stash, bouncing up and down to be next. They reminded Ethan of small children pushing their way to the front of the line at a tuck-shop.

"Right," Gogo Maya said indulgently. "How long did you leave them in the well?"

"Long time. Long time," the Tokoloshe assured her as they

lead her towards the buffet.

One of her companions, a dark-skinned youth who looked a couple of years older than Ethan, stepped forward without waiting for an introduction from Gogo Maya, and put a hand out to Tariro who had been the first to jump up to meet them. He looked a bit like a genie in his cotton trousers and long, sleeveless vest with intricate designs sewn down the front. A Kurdish turban covered his head, with flywhisk threads hanging down.

"Hi, I'm Aaron," he said in an American accent, "and this is Lewa."

Ethan could see Tariro do a double-take. Tariro liked to adopt an American accent himself when he wanted to act cool, but it was nowhere near as good as this boy's. He seemed at a bit of a loss for words. He turned to greet Lewa.

She looked almost as surprised as Tariro but she was staring at Ethan. She appeared to be absentmindedly counting the assortment of brass tubes, bird feathers, ceramic beads and seed pods that hung from a leather thong tied around her waist while she reached her other hand out and curled a lock of Ethan's hair around her finger.

"Gold!" she said in wonder. "Aaron told me this was possible but I thought he was teasing." She had a lovely singsong voice and spoke English with a West African accent, similar to but not the same as Gogo Maya's. "You must let me braid it for you."

Ethan frowned and pulled away from her. As dirty as he felt after all those days in the bush, he wasn't quite ready to have some stranger's fingers touching his hair.

"Er . . . I don't think so!" he said. "I think I will leave my hair as it is." Come to think about it, he couldn't believe she just put her hands in his dirty hair. She was as bad as his cousins. Were girls the same everywhere?

Her own short kinky hair was pulled untidily into many plaits that radiated like antenna around her head. He guessed it would be hard to braid your own hair, but still, that was no reason to let

259

her loose on his.

Aaron laughed and removed his loosely woven turban to reveal hair that was parted into a design of intricately shaped sections along his scalp, the end of each short twist decorated with a plain white cowry shell.

"You might as well give up," he said. "She gets around to everyone she likes in the end – whether you want it or not." With his wide mouth set in an easy smile, and his brown eyes gentle in expression, he could have been Jimoh's big brother.

Jimoh, who'd removed his hat and was twisting the brim around in his hands, quickly put it on his head again at the mention of braiding. Not that his hair was long enough, but you could see he was not taking any chances. With a quiet signal to Rafiki and his Tokoloshe companions, he went off in search of a shady spot. He'd promised to teach them how to wind his strips of salvaged inner tubing onto forked saplings to make slingshots for the rest of them.

"Okay, but this is last one!" His voice drifted back as he tore a strip off the bottom of the Kanga he had got from the Sobek for yet another Tokoloshe child who wanted to wear the same as him. Ethan noticed as he went that Jimoh's kanga was getting shorter and shorter as the day wore on, and the collection of strange dangly paraphernalia he had attached to the hemp rope around his waist was growing.

Gogo Maya and Salih settled down to trade stories about their return trips to Karibu, joined by the Tokoloshe grandma and a group of gnarly village elders, each with a decorated drinking horn full of fearsomely sour wine. Tariro sat and ate another bowl of food with Aaron and Lewa, fascinated to discover that Aaron actually was from America and wasn't just putting on the accent.

"He just loves the attention," Ethan said, to no one in particular, and then jumped when Fisi responded.

"She is the witch I told you about," Fisi said. "You should warn Tariro not to kiss her. It could only cause trouble."

A CUNNING PLAN

Ethan noticed that Fisi and Shenzie had hung back, almost avoiding the witches. Unable to imagine Tariro kissing Gogo Maya, even if she drowned again, Ethan shook his head, and then realised the hyena youth was talking about Lewa.

She did not look much like a witch to him but he said, "Jeez, if I warn him he will be all the more determined to do it. He already thinks he has the healing power from drinking the water at Sobek Lake." He was surprised to find himself just a little put out that Tariro had monopolised Aaron and Lewa. Especially Lewa. *He had bloody better not kiss her*, he thought.

"Here is what we have to do," Gogo Maya said later, once everyone had eaten and they'd gathered round the well for the plan. "We will approach the city from the north, because that is the side where the menagerie is." She drew a map in the sand with a stick, giving Ethan a long-suffering sigh that said she could have done without the added complication of rescuing hyenas. But he held fast. He had promised Fisi. They had exchanged blood over it.

"We will have to release the prisoners without being seen," Gogo Maya went on. "This should not be difficult. I understand the Almohad are too lazy to guard their prisoners well. Then Fisi and Shenzie must strike out for the safety of the nearest Kishi village, which is Mudziku village, if I remember correctly. The rest of us will look for Galal in his reception rooms."

She handed around amulets made out of scraps of carved wood, broken ostrich shell, unidentifiable tassels and copper plates. Ethan noticed she had added the ceramic beads from the well to them. "These will protect you from the Almohad's beguiling ways," she said.

Gogo Maya eyed Fisi for a moment before handing him an amulet. "You, I had to think about," she said. "Don't you go letting that Mesande get hold of this. I know you are involved with her in some way, Gogo Nagesa told me. I don't trust that girl as far as I can kick her."

Fisi's lips parted in shock at Gogo Maya's vehemence, but he was not as shocked as Shenzie. She backed away from him, clutching her amulet to her chest. "You!" she gasped "You and Mesande! She is the one who lead Tabita into the trap."

Ethan watched as Fisi's expression went from one who had just won a gold medal at the thought of owning an amulet at last, to one who has just been disqualified.

"Figures," Gogo Maya said with a shrug. "Oh, don't get so upset, Shenzie, the boy would have had no way of knowing. You have been tricked by Mesande yourself, if I remember correctly. Now you two wear the amulets around your waists. We don't want you strangling yourselves if you change." She went on in a matter-of-fact voice, seemingly oblivious to the hornet's nest she had kicked between Fisi and Shenzie. "Everyone else can wear them around their necks if they want, but beware, the Almohad might be able to slip them over your heads. Do not get too near any of them."

Bending forwards towards Grandma Wanyika, Gogo Maya handed her a pungent smelling dried root from her bag. "The Tokoloshe can come with if they want," she said. "Bring plenty of arrows – Grandma Wanyika will make the potion. Now be careful with that, Grandma. It is what's left over from my last mbogo root. If our plan goes badly, we will rely on you to put everyone to sleep."

A ripple of excitement ran through the assembled Tokoloshe in anticipation of this rare treat, but Jimoh looked worriedly at the amulet around his waist. "Gogo, what about amulet for Tokoloshe?"

Lewa laughed. "The Almohad would never touch the mind of a Tokoloshe. They believe the Tokoloshe can turn the beguiling back on them. It is a myth, of course, but they believe it."

"I started that rumour," Grandma Wanyika chortled, elbowing Ethan in the ribs. She seemed to have taken to him. She'd squeezed between him and Jimoh despite the fact that there had been no space. This close up, Ethan could have sworn he heard faint whispering sounds coming from the vermin in her hair.

"I believe they used to capture Tokoloshe but they caused too much mischief," Lewa said, shaking a finger fondly at Grandma Wanyika.

"The rest of you will pretend to be witches," Gogo Maya said, getting back to the plan. "They will believe it too, once they fail to beguile you. They are unnaturally afraid of witches. They think we can suck up their souls and send them to the other place. Some of us have the power to confuse them."

"They're afraid we'll turn them ugly," Lewa put in. "We can't really do it. They've had centuries of practice at making themselves beautiful, after all, but we can make some of them think they're ugly."

"Jimoh and Tariro will go immediately towards Joe and put this amulet on him to shield him from the beguiling," Gogo Maya went on, handing another amulet to Jimoh. "I don't think we will have any problem persuading them to part with your friend, once he stops responding to their nonsense, but we also have to find the jumper who started this problem or no one will be safe in the forest."

"What's a jumper?" asked Tariro, with a worldly-wise expression on his face that irritated Ethan. He noticed that Tariro had managed to manoeuver himself between Aaron and Lewa.

"Some kind of a body-snatcher," Aaron said.

"What is body-snatcher?" Jimoh asked.

"It is a soul that can steal someone's body just by touching it," Lewa explained, fiddling with the copper snake bangle on her upper arm and smiling at Tariro with her radiant smile.

"Will the amulets protect us from it?" Tariro said.

"Yes!" Gogo Maya said, with all the authority in the world.

"We don't know," Lewa said at the same time. She shot Gogo Maya a warning glance which did nothing to reinforce Ethan's confidence in Gogo Maya's judgement. "But it is the best we can do. Salih and me, and possibly you, Ethan, can read the Almohad thought patterns, but the jumper is in some way shielded. Gogo Maya could not read him when he attacked her in the forest."

"I think I can hear the Almohad too," interrupted Tariro. "I think I heard Fisi before, on the cliff."

"Not unless you kissed a witch," Fisi said grimly. Shanzie had stopped glowering at him. Perhaps her own mistakes with the dreaded Mesande had been enough to give her some perspective on Fisi's, but he didn't look ready to forgive himself anytime soon.

"Ethan kissed a witch!" Aaron gasped.

"He kissed Gogo Maya," Tariro said, and laughed, glancing at Lewa, knowing when he was on to a good thing.

"Eew!" Aaron shuddered.

"Moving on . . . Moving on," Ethan grimaced.

Gogo Maya took a large gulp of her sour wine and doubled over in a coughing fit. "We've made an amulet for Galal," she went on, once she'd got her breath back. Ethan was grateful for the change of subject. The amulet was similar to the ones she had given the rest of them, except for what looked like fibres from the funky smelling root woven into it. "It is very powerful, but we only had time and enough mbogo root to make one. We think the jumper is planning to take Galal's body so that he can rule the Almohad. Lewa thinks he is biding his time and studying the leader's ways, so that no one will notice when he takes over." She nodded at Lewa. "We have to reach Galal and convince him to wear it without alerting the jumper. Now if only we had something to attract Galal . . ." Ethan was sure he saw her peer at him from behind her braids before looking up at the sky.

Jimoh poked Ethan in the ribs from the other side of Grandma Wanyika. "You must give Gogo Maya stones to put on amulet to give leader for gift," he said.

Without hesitation Ethan drew the five gems out of his pocket, even though he was pretty sure Gogo Maya had set him up. Salih must have told her about them, he thought. But he would be glad to be rid of them. He was tired of looking over his shoulder all the time for the Mokele Mbembe. Salih was right – if he offered them as ransom, the Almohad would probably just keep the gems and Joe. If this insane plan did not work, the Almohad might just keep all of them.

Tariro's eyes grew wide at the sight of the enormous sapphire, violet and burgundy gems resting on Ethan's palm. "Jeez, Ethan, where the hell did you get those?"

"Er . . . The Sobek gave them to me," Ethan said. "Well, they didn't make me put them back again," he whispered to Jimoh at the boy's sharp intake of breath at the whopping lie.

"Perfect!" Gogo Maya exclaimed, accepting the gems and neatly dodging any further questions from Tariro. "Almohad love jewels, and Galal is particularly greedy for them."

"There will be consequences," Salih muttered under his breath.

"Well, we can let Galal deal with that," Gogo Maya harrumphed. "We are, after all, saving his life."

"You two," she indicated Lewa and Ethan, "will try to find the gap in the thought pattern."

"How?" Ethan said, worried.

"Everyone thinks all the time, Ethan," Lewa explained. "Our presence will make them anxious, so they will think even harder. Just look at each person for a moment till you feel his or her pattern in your mind, then move on to the next. If there is a complete absence of thought, that will probably be the jumper. I will sweep the left hand side of the room and you can sweep the right. We will meet in the middle, which will be wherever Galal stands." She pointed at Tariro, Jimoh and Aaron. "You three will pretend to do the same to make them think you are all witches."

Ethan thought it was a terrible plan. He was not so sure Gogo Maya had as much confidence in her amulets as she implied. Even if the amulets worked. If the Almohad were so strong, what was stopping any of them from physically grabbing Tariro and Jimoh before they managed to get the amulet onto Joe, and simply holding onto them as captives? What was to stop them from grabbing himself, for that matter? It was all very well for Gogo Maya; at least she looked like a witch with her hooked nose and her general oldness. What if he failed to find the Almohad thought patterns? He could find Fisi and Shenzie easily enough now, and the Tokoloshe, but they were very excitable and projected very loudly.

"What if Galal doesn't believe us?" he said to Gogo Maya. "And what's to stop the jumper from jumping the guy next to him as soon as we identify him? We wouldn't be any the wiser."

"No," Aaron said. "We thought about that. We'll know at once because the body he leaves will slump to the ground, dead."

"Dead!" breathed Jimoh, his eyes widening in distress.

"Well, it's dead already, see. Whoever had the body before would have already left it when the jumper jumped in," Aaron explained kindly to Jimoh, but Jimoh didn't look any happier. Ethan suspected he hadn't been worrying about the left over body but the newly jumped one.

"So we don't let anyone touch us!" Tariro said, self-importantly, muscling in on the plan. Ethan noticed he glanced at Lewa for approval as he said it

Ethan was woken the next morning by the sound of Tariro shrieking, as he shot up off the floor batting frantically at his arm. What now? he thought, sitting up and switching on his headlamp to check the floor around him. He hadn't tried anything with the magic for a while, so he wondered why his head felt strangely tight.

"Did something bite you, Tariro?" Jimoh said, sitting up, startled.

The sound of Tokoloshe children giggling calmed Tariro down. Someone had braided things into his hair while he slept, and then carefully placed his head on top of his arm so as to cut off the blood supply to his hand, and then aligned his hand against his face. His own numb fingers brushing against his face like a dead hand had frightened Tariro when he awoke.

"You would be laughing on the other side of your face if you had a mirror," he said to Ethan, with a big grin, flexing his fingers to get the blood flowing back into them.

Ethan's hand shot up to his own head. It had been divided into sections and felt all knobby with beads and bits of pipe. He even felt a couple of feathers.

"Lewa," Aaron said when he saw them. "She likes you guys."

Ethan's stomach lurched just a little bit. This strangely captivating girl liked *him*? He supposed she liked Tariro too, but everyone liked Tariro; it was all that boisterous athleticism. In any case, Aaron probably just meant in a friendly way.

As uncomfortable as the braids were, there was no time to untangle them before they struck camp and moved off towards Almoh. Well, theoretically, there had been time but someone had to see to the water bottles, and then Grandma Wanyika had firmly latched herself onto Ethan with a list of preparation chores a mile long.

Tariro hadn't had time to remove his either. He had been too busy helping Lewa. He twirled a plait of leather with an iridescent green feather on the end, as he walked beside Ethan and Salih on the way to Almoh. "I don't know what you are so worried about, it's not as if they can really hurt us," he reassured Ethan. "I mean, it hurts when it happens, but we can both heal ourselves. I am sure Jimoh could too, if he tried. He didn't drink quite as much magic as I did at the caves, but I'm sure he drank enough to heal himself."

Ethan looked despairingly at Salih. "We have to tell him about the blood before he risks getting himself hurt," he thought at the leopard.

Salih stopped walking and looked from Tariro to Ethan and

back again. "He won't want to experience the initial pain," he said into Ethan's head.

"Hey, I caught that!" Tariro protested. "Well, almost. What did the leopard say?"

Before Ethan could think of something to mislead Tariro, Shenzie and Fisi came up behind them. Shenzie was trying to console Fisi.

"It was my fault," Fisi wailed. "Damn, I knew there was something off about that Mesande. She was just too sweet."

CHAPTER 26
A FAVOUR REPAID

It took two days to reach Almoh travelling at Grandma Wanyika's frustratingly slow pace. Eventually, in his anxiety to hurry up and get to Joe, Ethan took her up on his shoulders. She was not that heavy, but he wished she would not keep fiddling with, and adding things to, his hair.

With a gang of compulsive gatherers to forage for them they did not go hungry either, but the closer things grew to the underground stream carrying the magic, the more distorted they were. After burning his mouth on a strange flattened vegetable with wavy tendrils, and almost eating a disk-like fruit with turned out to be poisonous to humans, Grandma Wanyika took to sorting through the offerings, from her perch on top of his shoulders, before she let Ethan eat anything.

He felt hungry for protein but the Tokoloshe were saving their arrows for their assault on the Almohad, and did not want to kill, or eat, any creature of the forest, just in case it sucked up their magic as it went to the other world. This was just as well, Lewa explained to him: Creatures who used the magic eating other creatures who used the magic could have some very unfortunate consequences.

They shimmied down on hands and knees when they approached the edge of the cliffs. Jimoh said they should not outline themselves against the skyline in case they were spotted from below. The shining silver thread of the river winked here and there amongst the dense woodland in the valley far below. Ethan spotted an enormous herd of wildebeest surging across an open stretch of grassland towards a crossing place at a bend in the river. They looked like rats following the pied piper.

The most amazing thing was the city of Almoh. Ethan had imagined a sprawling Zulu-type metropolis on top of the cliffs overlooking the valley. Instead, the city was not visible at all from above. It looked as if a giant mechanical shovel had taken a bite out of the cliffs and carved a rainbow city there.

On the north side of the bowl lay a series of outdoor dyeing vats, scooped out of the ground like a giant bao board, filled with every imaginable shade of red and yellow, and every colour in between. People poked lengths of fabric into them and hung them out to dry on a wall. The buildings themselves were no less colourful. Terra cotta buildings with cream or green around the windows, sat beside turquoise buildings trimmed with deep reds, and oranges.

Gogo Maya pointed out the menagerie beyond. It held an elephant, and an open pen with a number of hyenas that lounged under a shady tree. People leaned up against the jungle gym in the monkey enclosure.

"Well, that's going to delay us," Ethan complained to Fisi, pointing them out. "They're probably on their tea break."

"No, those are the human captives," explained Fisi.

Jimoh gasped. "I never think about this thing till I see people in pen next to animals. Do you think is same unhappiness for goats and pigs at home?"

"Don't be silly," Gogo Maya said. "Without the magic to mess with their heads, a goat is a goat and a pig does not think much

270

about anything except being fed."

The Tokoloshe ran about in their excitement, looking for a path, but Jimoh was the first to spot the trail leading down towards the menagerie beside a small waterfall. The group set off too noisily down the path. The Tokoloshe were never stealthy with all their dangly bits, and Ethan was having trouble being quiet himself until Aaron tore his head covering in half and helped Ethan wrap one half around his head.

"Thank you," he said. "I was beginning to feel like a wind chime."

Gogo Maya and Grandma Wanyika needed a lot of help with the steep parts, but Grandma redeemed herself by casting a stern eye over her raffish tribe and putting a finger to her pursed lips, achieving a semblance of quiet while Fisi and Shenzie snuck around the side of the menagerie to release the captives.

They came back with a pack of five hyenas, a badger, and a baboon. Two eagles took to the air and made for the valley below. Fisi said he had untied the elephant, but he looked worried.

"The humans will not come. Nor would the crocodile," he said. "I think you must go and speak to them Gogo Maya. They say what's the point! It is worse for them at their homes and the Almohad will hunt them if they escape and probably kill them before they can cross the river. The crocodile says he is there on purpose. He says we should take the pack and run while the Almohad are distracted by the game in the valley below. That is why there are no guards near the menagerie."

"Probably just as well," Gogo Maya said. "We don't want to start off on the wrong foot with them finding out we just released all their captives. You and Shenzie go to the nearest Kishi village, and take the badger and the baboon with. We'll sort them out later. Find an easier path up to the forest for your four-footed to use. We will sneak back up the cliff and come down the central stairs as if we just arrived."

She turned to head back up the trail, but Fisi hovered, looking uncomfortable. "Well, spit it out boy!" Gogo Maya snapped. "Don't worry, if you don't hear from us in the next day or two, you can come and rescue us. You have the amulet."

"I want to come with you," he said. "They say the white boy is down in the valley playing in the game of initiation."

"Can we hurry up then?" Ethan snapped.

Gogo Maya and Lewa exchanged a worried look. Aaron took in a sharp breath and shook his head; even Grandma and her gang looked agitated.

Lewa looked sternly at Fisi. "Don't you think you had better go with Tabita and make your peace?"

He grimaced and said, "It is better if she has some time to cool down. She is very angry. Besides, I promised Ethan."

Ethan could not remember a specific promise, unless Fisi was referring to the time when they joined bloodied fingers, but a glowering look from the hyena, Tabita, told him that following Gogo Maya was probably the lesser of the two evils for Fisi.

"Either way, can we hurry up?" Ethan said again. "I am more worried than ever if my cousin might be down in the valley."

CHAPTER 27
A DANGEROUS GAME

"You want me to do what!" shrieked Joe in a panic. Even when the captives had told him, he hadn't quite believed it.

"Get on the buffalo," Nandi said in a matter-of-fact voice. "Come on, you don't want to end up in the menagerie. You will never move forward there." She dropped down onto a ledge just below the lip of the small plateau and reached up to give Joe a hand.

"Well, let me see," he said, his face contorted into a picture of patience and congeniality. "Safely penned up with the possibility of escape? Or a buffalo horn up my butt in the next half-hour?"

"Come on, Joe. It won't be that bad."

"Easy for you to say. You have the strength of two men," he grumbled. Joe was already quite exhausted by the trek down the escarpment into the jungle below. Nandi, on the other hand, showed no sign of fatigue at all.

"Probably more, if you are talking about the ones across the river," she said. "That's why I am going to get you through this. I need you, Joe, even if you do belong to Kitoko. This is the first time I have ever had a proper friend."

SWITCH!

Joe peered over the ledge into the ravine. It was about eight metres wide and not very deep. The end of it disappeared around a bend.

A tall man landed softly on the ledge beside Nandi. He ran one hand shyly over his shaved head, adjusted his bow over his shoulder and extended the other hand towards Joe.

"Elymu," he said with a grin, and then turned to help another man down onto the ledge. It was the first time Joe had seen an overweight person in this world. A beefy man, with a deep scar running from his eyebrow into his hairline, landed somewhat heavily, grunted and turned towards Joe inquiringly.

"Joe," he introduced himself. Joe noticed, unlike Elymu, who was bare-footed like Joe and Nandi, this man wore moccasins with tin beads on every tassel that jingled when he walked.

"Faraji," the man said and, noticing Joe's eyes on his moccasins, shrugged, flashing a self-depreciating smile as if it could not be helped. "My lucky shoes," he added. He turned to help the next one down, but she didn't need his help. Like Nandi, she was incredibly agile. She jumped from the top of the plateau to the ledge in one fluid move like a gymnast, landing on both feet, perfectly balanced.

"This is Nyala," Faraji said, not at all put out that she didn't want his help. She nodded at Joe and turned her attention to the ravine. In sharp contrast to the bright, multi-coloured, richly embroidered clothes of the city, both Nandi and Nyala wore loose-fitting chamois trousers and unadorned skimpy vests that looked as if they were made out of felt. Nyala also had on one thick, smooth ivory bracelet on each arm, accentuating her biceps; she looked as lethal as a leopard.

"I have seen Azikiwe," she said in a clipped accent. "He has found the herd and is driving them towards us. It will not be long. I will partner Thandiwe. He is delayed as he is bringing Nyak and Phomelo."

A DANGEROUS GAME

"Azikiwe is going to ease the buffalo through the pass," Nandi whispered to Joe. "They come this way anyway to get water, but he is good at persuading them to come through when he wants them to."

"Does he herd them like cattle?" Joe asked, clutching at the concept that the buffalo might at least be partially domesticated.

"No, he makes them feel thirsty," Faraji said.

"Okay, now listen carefully," Nandi said. "When the buffalo pass under this ledge they will be tightly packed so they won't be able to throw you. We have to ease onto their backs. We don't want to spook them with any sudden moves. By the time they reach the end of the passage you have to slip carefully down to their necks and hold onto the horns. You can't ride on their backs because they keep their heads low, so you would slip off the front of them. Watch the people in front of you."

"Elymu, Nyala and I will get on the bigger buffalos," Faraji said. "Those are the ones with the solid boss across their heads where the horns meet. They are the most likely to turn and face the lions."

Joe could hardly imagine Faraji as one of the ones who would face off with a lion, but he couldn't see how a smaller buffalo could hold up the weight of the big man on its neck.

Nyala's friend, Thandiwe, climbed down onto the ledge, followed by two very nervous-looking young men wearing black trousers and tunics, with leopard skin headbands and ties around their upper arms. They had on moccasins like Faraji, but thankfully without jingly beads.

Thandiwe was the youngest apart from Nandi and Joe. He looked fit to burst with excitement and energy. He made straight for Nyala and chatted to her in a strange language, nervously tying his dreadlocks into a ponytail with a strip of leather.

"It's his first time," Faraji said. He put his arms around Nyak and Phomelo, bringing their close cropped heads together in a bear hug, and said in a conniving whisper, "You two, and Joe and

Nandi must choose young females because they are the most likely to run."

"And the most likely to be chased," Elymu grinned.

Joe's heart skipped a beat when he saw the first buffaloes moving towards them through the scrub.

"I'm not doing it!" he whispered fiercely to Nandi.

"She is doing the best she can for you boy," Faraji whispered behind Joe. "If you don't do it they'll put you in the pen with the other cowards, and don't think you will ever escape from there. They will hunt you down if you try to leave. A boy could get himself killed."

Much like a boy could get himself killed riding a buffalo, Joe thought bitterly. He wondered if they had any idea what it was like to attempt these harebrained schemes relying on nothing but normal strength.

Faraji swung himself onto a branch overhanging the ravine and held a pull-up position for a moment, then eased himself gently onto an enormous buffalo's neck. The beast shook his head from side to side, adjusted to the weight of the man, and walked on. Elymu slipped dexterously onto his animal straight from the ledge, followed by Nyala and Thandiwe. Phomelo and Nyak chose the animals directly behind.

"Wait a moment," Nandi said, putting her hand on Joe's chest to stay him. For a moment he thought it was all a big joke and they were not going to go through with it. Relief flooded through his veins, but then she said, "We don't want to bunch up. Look there. If Nyala or Thandiwe's animals kick out, Nyak and Phomelo might get thrown."

Joe watched the four riders flatten against their beast's necks, ease their way forward to grab hold of the horns, and then pull themselves into a sitting position behind the ears. They looked a bit like Harley Davidson riders, if you could ignore the buffaloes.

Joe and Nandi gripped the overhanging branch, holding the same pull-up position Faraji had. They had chosen their mounts,

A DANGEROUS GAME

Joe's just slightly ahead of Nandi's. Joe's biceps burned so badly by the time their mounts moved into position underneath them, it was almost a relief to ease down on to the young buffalo cow. Unfortunately, he wasn't quite accurate, landing too far back towards the tail. He shimmied forwards, scraping his bare thighs on the rough skin of the buffalo who sidestepped and rolled her eyeballs backwards in fright, but finding herself hemmed in by the herd, she soon settled. At last Joe sat behind her ears with a firm grip on her horns as he had seen the others do.

As soon as the beasts were released from the confines of the ravine, Nandi's buffalo bucked and shook her head from side to side, almost throwing her. Joe's cow tried to dislodge him by running forwards a short way, then turning and running beneath a low branch. Buffalo are not as stupid as they look, he realised. He flattened his body against her neck and hoped he wouldn't be scraped off.

The whole herd was jumpy and anxious. Joe could see Elymu, Faraji and Nyala out in front, leading the herd to the left. He looked behind him for Nandi but instead saw Nyak, whose buffalo went careening down the right flank of the herd, eventually managing to dislodge her passenger. Nyak rolled off to the side and ran for the nearest tree. His buffalo gave chase but she did not reach him before he had climbed quite a way up. Joe envied the man. He wondered if he could do the same, but realised that his chances were very slim in the middle of the herd with the bulk of the angry-looking animals behind him.

Suddenly the herd veered off to the right and started to run in earnest. Bouncing wildly, Joe twisted from side to side making a frantic search for Nandi. Instead he saw lions giving chase – at least two females, and, unusually, a large black-maned male. The lions were gaining on Phomelo till his buffalo reeled and moved deftly back into the safety of the herd.

Then, to Joe's astonishment, Nyala, followed by Elymu and Faraji, coaxed their buffaloes out of the front of the herd and wheeled around to confront the cats. The herd ran on for twenty paces or so and then slowed down and circled, milling around anxiously. Joe craned his neck to see what was happening but his buffalo cow was facing the wrong way. Acutely aware that one false move could get him killed, he gently applied pressure to the cow's left horn. She shook her head, stomped and came to rest almost facing the action.

Joe watched in awe as the three Almohad slid off their buffalos, two of which ran off, presumably happy to be out of the fray, but Faraji's buffalo stood his ground. Faraji placed both his hands on the beast's boss and pushed him till he backed off a short distance. Joe hoped Faraji planned to watch his back because the buffalo stood there glowering at Faraji as if he owed him money. Joe was starting to get some measure of the power of the magic. It just should not be possible for a two-hundred-pound man to shift a five-hundred-pound buffalo like that. He would not have believed it if he had not seen it with his own eyes. Then he shrugged to himself, remembering that he believed a tiger talked to him. After that, he could believe anything.

The lions were hesitant, as if the change of rules had thrown them off their game. They backed off a bit, the large male crouching low, his ears flattened against his head, his tail jerking up and down. Joe counted four lionesses in the grass on the male's right flank and at least one on his left. He wondered where they had come from. Had the Almohad lead the buffaloes past the lion's habitual resting place hoping they would be there, or were they able to manipulate the cats to be in the place where they wanted them just for this game?

Nyala stood to the side. She held her bow, arrow nocked, ready for an emergency. The two men stalked forward. Each carried a curved dagger in his left hand and a pole with a sharp point in his right. Nandi had told Joe that they would lean the back of the stake into the ground and see if the lions charged right onto the point. He hadn't believed that either. He caught a movement in his peripheral vision and gasped. Nyala and Elymu's buffalos had circled round to join Faraji's one and were beginning to stalk the Almohad. Now the hunters were also the hunted.

The three buffalos moved forward in unison, their heads held low. With their outstretched horns covering most of their bodies, and their solid bosses rendering their sculls impenetrable, Joe saw that Nyala's only hope was a straight shot through the eye. Even if she was that accurate, she would only save one of them – Nyala, Elyamu or herself. Instead, she called out, shifted her weapon onto her shoulder and stood perfectly still facing side on to the charge. The two men followed suit. The three Almohad held their ground until the buffalo were almost upon them and then wheeled around suddenly, ducking out of the way, like bull fighters, leaving the buffalo charging headlong into the pride of lions.

"Don't move!" Nandi yelled, easing her buffalo in next to Joe's. "You may yet come out of this alive." She clambered up behind him, climbed over him with the agility of a monkey and settled herself on his buffalo's neck in front of him. "Hang on to me," she said, taking control of the horns and gently easing the buffalo towards the edge of the herd, where she slid off, keeping a controlling grip on one horn while Joe jumped shakily to the ground.

"Let's go and find Nyak," she said. "Just back away very slowly while they are preoccupied with the lions."

Joe was still shaking uncontrollably when they found Nyak. Phomelo and Thandiwe were trying to coax him out of the tree, Phomelo whooping and yelling excitedly, Thandiwe a little more earnestly.

"It's okay, Nyak, just come down now."

Nyak scanned the bushes nearby worriedly. "No!" he said. "You come up here. She is still nearby. I know she is. I can feel her."

A nearby bush rustled, sending Phomelo up the tree after his friend, but Thandiwe and Nandi stood their ground. Joe stood frozen in fear.

A short, middle-aged man crawled out of the thicket. He wore a lion's head as a headdress, with the rest of the lion's skin hanging down his back.

"Azikiwe!" Thandiwe cried, shaking the man by the hand. "That was the best game ever."

"Young man, it is not over until all the players are accounted for," Azikiwe chided him, giving his ponytail a playful yank and looking around for the others.

"No, they are fine," Thandiwe said. "You should have seen them. Those buffalo went right past them and into the lions. I saw them climbing up a rock to watch. Eish! That Nyala can dance – Faraji too. Nerves of steel, that man. He let the buffalo touch him before he danced away! I hope they were watching properly from the city."

Suddenly his eyes went wide with fright. For a split second Joe assumed it was part of the man's narrative but Phomelo screamed and Joe, Nandi and Azikiwe spun round to face a large buffalo cow in full charge. She was heading straight for Joe, her neck outstretched, presenting her boss and her outstretched horns. Before Joe had time to think, Thandiwe and Azikiwe crouched down in front of him, imbedding their pointed stakes in the ground before them, pointed towards the underbelly of the beast.

CHAPTER 28
A SURPRISING REVELATION

Gogo Maya led her companions through the lavish gardens, and past the dying vats, in a noisy procession. Even padding softly on tiptoes the Tokoloshe could not be quiet. Ethan watched in dismay as several of them, finding the colours of the dye too irresistible, poked fingers, whole arms, and in one case, a whole body, into the vats, appearing to be delighted with the results. None of the Almohad workers remained this late in the day, except an old man who doffed his hat at them as they passed, even though it was quite obvious they had no business being there.

"Erm . . . could you direct us to the throne room?" Gogo Maya asked him. He pointed in the general direction of a large central structure with graceful arches and a lofty dome, extravagantly decorated in a variety of mosaic tile patterns in earthy shades of red, orange and yellow, and accented in blue.

The reception room, when they burst into it, was as quiet and as empty as the streets had been.

They interrupted two men at a game of bao.

"Everyone's on the balcony," one said somewhat sulkily at the interruption.

SWITCH!

"Well, would you be kind enough to take us there! Or would you rather we wait here?" Grandma Wanyika said, wiggling her eyebrows meaningfully at her unruly clan, some of whom had begun to look at things with their hands.

One young Tokoloshe sat admiring the glinting metallic luster of a finely hammered silver and stained glass lantern, by tossing it from hand to hand. One, bright orange from the dying vats, started to unravel the gold thread from an elaborately woven wall hanging to see how it had been put together. Yet another stuffed his cheeks to bursting with ripe dates he found in a bowl, just there for the taking. Half-chewed pieces of date escaped from his mouth to splatter onto the intricately patterned, priceless looking silk carpet.

The old man beamed at Grandma superciliously. "I'll take you," he moaned.

"You can't fool me. I knew he was a servant," Grandma chuckled to Ethan as they followed the man down a passage, through a shady tiled courtyard with a fountain playing in the middle, and down another passage. "He must be one of those who has almost gained enough strength to be accepted by the Almohad, judging by his superior air, but he will still be responsible for cleaning up the mess when my boys are done exploring."

They stopped in front of a gigantic, finely sculpted door that fit snugly into a scalloped, horseshoe shaped arch in the wall. The muffled sounds of a party drifted through the heavy wood.

Their guide threw the doors open dramatically to reveal a large room, at least thirty paces by twenty, with an open balcony overlooking the valley below. A row of drummers, straddling large, skin-covered drums along one wall, beat a frantic tattoo with their hands, while women in leopard skin skirts moved rhythmically, in a sinuous line, shaking bead encrusted rattles and gyrating their hips in time to the beat – all completely ignored by a group of lavishly robed spectators out on the balcony, jostling for turns at seven ancient looking telescopes set up to face the valley below.

"The wicked witches!" announced the guide in a voice, loud enough to be heard above the noise.

The room went gradually quiet as more and more occupants became aware of the visitors. One man, blowing a kudu horn trumpet with wild enthusiasm, was the last to realise, but eventually even he turned to stare.

"There's nothing wicked about us," Gogo Maya growled at the reluctant guide, and then smiled her most charming smile to the assembled Almohad, in line with not being wicked.

A strikingly handsome man in a bright turquoise robe and a bejewelled ochre headdress, with half-closed, bored-looking eyes, strolled towards them. "Ah . . . Gogo . . . Gogo . . ." he said, snapping his fingers, her name on the tip of his tongue.

"Yeees, Galal," she prompted him, but she did not give him any clue as to her name.

Ethan saw Lewa immediately start to search for the thought patterns of the assembled Almohad, who were, presumably, the robed ones. He groaned; at least twenty of them were on the right side of Galal, meaning he had to process them all. Only five were on Lewa's side. And what about the entertainment and the rest of the people, he wondered? The jumper could just as easily be one of them. They were all on his side of the room. He glanced over at Tariro and Jimoh. Both gazed intently at the Almohad, pretending to read everybody's minds. Jimoh, at least, was pretending. Tariro was alternately glaring at them and shaking his head, muttering, "Nothing! Nothing! Not a bloody thing! Damn, I really expected something by now."

"I'm not getting anything either." Ethan told him.

Fisi gripped Ethan firmly by the shoulders from behind and hissed into his ear. "It will come once you start, Ethan, just start."

Ethan took a deep breath and slowed his thoughts down. He

tentatively studied a woman in a flowing, deep red dress, elaborately embroidered in yellow, green and silver, standing on the extreme right.

"What is this now? Just when we were getting to the best part of the game," she was thinking.

"Oh, no! Witches! I wonder if they can . . .?" thought the woman next to her, just as colourfully dressed, her face turning expressionless suddenly.

"It's true! They don't seem to be affected at all," thought the man standing on the other side of her, his face screwed up in concentration. Ethan guessed he was trying to make Gogo Maya or Grandma Wanyika do something they didn't want to, an impossible task even without a protective amulet.

"Nice looking," a sultry looking woman said out loud, bringing Ethan up short. She was looking at Fisi with a predatory glint in her eye. Fisi glared back at her.

"I am still getting no thought patterns, Ethan," Tarriro said worriedly. "Is anyone thinking about the game below? Surely if Joe or anyone has been hurt, one of the Almohad will think about that."

"No, Tariro, they are pretty much thinking about themselves," Ethan said ruefully. Tariro looked so frustrated at not being able to tap into the magic that Ethan felt really sorry for him.

"Keep scanning, Ethan," Salih said, sensing his distraction.

Ethan passed over the pet tiger and started on the entertainers. Surprisingly, after reading a couple of them, it appeared that they performed because they wanted to. He wondered if they had been coerced into believing that, or if they were Almohad who liked dancing and showing off.

He stopped at the last man in his group. An intense youth with a disdainful look on his face, standing where Galal had stood moments before. *"These are not witches!"* the man was thinking. *"That one is as pale as my slave!"* His hand hovered above an ornately carved sword hilt, which he wore strapped to his belt.

A SURPRISING REVELATION

"Oh no, Salih, no one said there would be weapons!" Ethan whispered, moving closer to the leopard.

Galal gave up trying to recall Gogo Maya's name. "Welcome," he drawled in tones of carefully studied boredom.

"We brought you a small house gift," Lewa said, stepping out from behind Tariro, who seemed to have given up on his attempts to read the Almohads' minds and had joined Aaron in protecting her instead. Lewa offered the amulet to Galal. "Well, it's more of a jewel, actually," she said. "We have heard of your fondness for jewels. Plus, you already have everything for the home." She gestured pointedly at the richly decorated balcony, and then motioned to put the amulet over his head. "May I?"

Galal glanced from the fearsome scowl on Tariro's face to the sparkling jewel as if he wasn't sure what to make of either, but then bowed his head towards Lewa, his green eyes glinting at the sight of the gems.

Ethan exhaled softly. Fortunately the man was not quite ready to take the risk that Tariro might be a powerful witch, which was just as well because Ethan could see that Tariro was not bluffing. He really was prepared to put himself at risk for Lewa because he thought he could heal himself.

"It's a trick!" shrieked an angry young lady, almost knocking Tariro over in her rush to snatch the amulet from Lewa. Even her hair looked furious as it swung forwards across her face before snapping back into its carefully bobbed style. Her intense black eyes glared accusingly at Lewa. "They want to control you with it," she said to Galal.

Lewa danced away from her and slipped it over Galal's still bowed head. Ethan hitched his breath again as Lewa gripped Galal's reluctant face firmly between her hands and turned his ear towards her to whisper into it.

The Almohad froze in startled confusion. Among the general gasps of indignation, Ethan picked up that no one ever touched Galal, and here was this slip of a girl ensnaring him and pulling him towards her against his will.

But Galal did not rip Lewa's head off as some of the Almohad expected. Instead he lifted his own head abruptly, stared at Gogo Maya and said, "Really? Here?"

Gogo Maya nodded.

"I have heard of this thing," he said, his eyes darting around the room wildly. "Who?"

It must be the dark-eyed girl, Ethan decided, or why would she have tried to snatch the amulet? Besides, she looked ready for another attack.

"It's the girl!" Tariro made a grab for her, obviously coming to the same conclusion.

Galal backed away from the girl as if she had scalded him. The petulant youth with the sword struck like lightning. One moment he was standing behind Galal and the next he had his sword at Tariro's throat. Ethan went cold. The youth pressed his sword against Tariro's larynx for less than a heartbeat before collapsing to the floor, writhing in agony, his sword clanging to the floor.

What the hell's the matter with him? Ethan thought but immediately realised that he, himself, was the cause of the young man's problem. He could not help himself. A strong current of sticky gel-like air seemed to ripple outwards from him, and he could almost see it soak into the writhing youth. He glanced at Salih to see if the leopard was channelling some new power through him, but Salih looked as startled as everyone else. Ethan realised with a sense of wonder that he was doing it on his own. Some deep instinct had made him jump to Tariro's defence.

And what was it the youth had been thinking just before Lewa gave Galal the amulet? *That one is as pale as my slave.* The full impact of that thought hit Ethan. Who else in this strange world looked like him? With a cold certainty he knew that this young man was thinking about Joe and his mood turned hateful.

He had no idea where he got the idea from, but he watched those sticky tendrils of his search out the specialised, threadlike, nerve endings in every part of the youth's body. Then he unleashed a cascade of neurotransmitters up the youth's spine to his cerebral cortex, where he could properly appreciate a crushing type of pain sensation. Ethan smiled with satisfaction. He wasn't really harming the youth, he told himself. It wasn't real pain, only the impression of pain...

Suddenly, he almost lost his breath as the painful sensation doubled back upon himself and he realised he did not know how to let go.

All along the walls, there had been an unsheathing of weapons, from jewelled daggers, to ornately carved axes. Even the kudu horn became a weapon of sorts when swivelled in the musician's hand. The dark-eyed girl stood with her hands on her hips, glaring at Ethan, but even she was afraid to touch him. He was vaguely aware of Salih nudging him, but his head buzzed so badly he couldn't hear what the leopard was saying till cool hands swung his face around and he found himself staring into Jimoh's dark, worried eyes.

"No, Ethan, is not good to hurt somebody," the boy said quietly.

Abruptly, the man on the floor lay still and Ethan gave a jerk, shuddering with the power that still pulsed around him.

Tariro scrambled up and stood shielding Lewa, his hand gripping his throat, his face a picture of stunned awe. "Yussy, Ethan, how the hell did you do that?" he croaked.

"Well, not that evil, anyway," Gogo Maya said, with a satisfied grin at Ethan and then glared pointedly at the unsheathed weapons.

The angry black-eyed girl rushed to help the man on the floor.

"Don't you dare touch him, Praxades!" Galal bellowed. He stepped forward to protect the youth, and then appeared to have second thoughts because he stepped back from the snivelling youth just as smartly, staring wildly around the room.

Some of Galal's people, sensing his confusion, already had

mutinous thoughts. Ethan caught several vague snippets of plans involving new leaders. But most seemed irritated with the girl. *What has Praxades done now?* they were wondering.

When he looked at her closely, the girl, Praxades, looked pretty stricken herself. Ethan shook his head. *She has no idea what's going on either,* he realised.

"I knew you could do it!" Lewa grinned at Ethan, and he tried unsuccessfully to hide a triumphant smile.

"I didn't," Gogo Maya added sternly. "You'd better not do it again."

Most of the Almohad backed off in shock, swivelling their faces backwards and forwards between Galal, Gogo Maya and Grandma Wanyika for direction. A few braver ones stood glowering at Ethan.

"What the hell is going on?" Praxades advanced on him. "What did you do to Kitoko?"

Salih stepped in front of Ethan protectively. Gogo Maya smiled at the girl as if she were demented, took her firmly by the hand and lead her to a divan while Lewa helped the youth, Kitoko, to his feet.

"Don't be a big baby," Lewa said to Kitoko. "It was just a bit of pain. You will be fine in a minute."

Kitoko slumped down beside the tiger, putting his hand on its back for support. Ethan noticed the tiger pulled away slightly. Was that revulsion he saw on its face? Or was it intelligent enough to wonder if Kitoko was about to jump it. Some of the Almohad grinned at the young man's discomfort. *Not very nice people,* thought Ethan.

"I'm sorry," he said to Kitoko, actually feeling quite guilty now that he had let go of the strange power. "Overcome with anxiety for my friend."

"Speaking of which," Fisi said in a cold, threatening tone, "he has another friend here that he may be suffering a pang of anxiety over. A young man. Same fair skin and golden hair. I can't see him here. Is he perhaps busy doing something . . . irresponsible . . . in the valley below?"

Completely forgetting their part in the mission, which was to guard one Almohad each, and shoot him with a sleeping draught if he turned out to be the jumper, the Tokoloshe rushed over to the balcony to look for Joe. Some had the sense to look through the ancient-looking telescopes abandoned by the Almohad, but most just leaned precariously over the balcony for a better view into the jungle below.

"First things first," Galal blurted out. He had a tight grip on his amulet, and he glanced anxiously over his shoulder at the man, Kitoko. He cleared his throat and addressed his people. "The witch tells me we have been harbouring a jumper."

The Almohad moved apart suddenly as if their companions had become electrically charged.

"What's a jumper?" a pretty woman in a cerise robe said.

"Your worst nightmare," Gogo Maya said in a low, dramatic voice with just the right mixture of doom and authority. As the self-proclaimed expert on all things jumper, she went on to explain. Ethan could tell from some of the older Almohad that she wasn't getting it all right, but even the ones who had heard of jumpers radiated confusion. There had been no sudden deaths to mark the arrival of a jumper. One starkly beautiful lady, with shiny mahogany hair down to her waist, even did a mental count of all the servants, but shook her head. Everyone had known each other for years. Could the jumper have been here that long? she thought. Could it be amongst the captives?

"Oh for God's sake, stop snivelling!" the tiger snapped suddenly, pushing Kitoko, the swordsman, aside.

"That voice!" Gogo Maya gasped. "The jumper is the tiger!"

"Gogo! I see him! I see the boy! There has been an accident!" Akin, the Tokoloshe, yelled from the edge of the balcony. He pulled the looking glass off its mount and stumbled over to Gogo Maya with it.

CHAPTER 29
A PERFECTLY VALID REASON

"Joe!" Tariro gasped. He looked imploringly at Lewa, but she shooed him away.

"Go!" she said, "we will take care of this."

As Tariro barrelled his way out of the balcony room by a side door Ethan tried to slip out after him, hoping Lewa knew what she was doing with the jumper. He needed to help Joe, and he had to tell Tariro about the blood before he got himself into any more trouble. Several of the Almohad had taken advantage of the confusion and bolted outside before him.

"No, Ethan! Stay!" Salih called into Ethan's head. "You are the only one who can do this. You have Gogo Maya's power. She is too weak. Lewa is powerful but her talents lie elsewhere. Do not let her down. You will need her to get home."

Fisi vacillated for a moment and then said, "Well, I am going. I don't think I can do anything here, and I suspect Tariro will get himself into trouble with the Almohad even if they can't beguile him."

"We will fetch Joe," Jimoh said. "You try to help Gogo Maya with strange powers of the head, Ethan." Then he slipped out behind Fisi.

The Tokoloshe, Ethan was relieved to see, had cornered the tiger. Led by Grandma Wanyika, they surrounded the cat, arrows nocked. He hoped they would remember how little effect their sleeping potion had had on the lions. The tiger's fur would probably be even harder to penetrate.

"You!" Grandma Wanyika rounded furiously on the tiger. "I have been meaning to have a talk with you!" She kicked him in the foot.

"Er . . . don't touch the tiger, Grandma," Lewa said. "Don't forget he can jump you if you touch him."

"Don't be foolish!" she shot over her shoulder, and then fixed her little raisin eyes firmly on the cat. "Why would he want to jump into this tired old body? Too bloody painful for a start, what with the corns and the gout!"

"I'm only trying to help, dear lady," said the tiger in a reasonable voice, laced with just a hint of menace ready to bubble to the surface without warning. "I would be a much better leader than Galal, if only I had his body. Look at the man. He can hardly pull himself away from his bao game long enough to attend to his own family, let alone the kingdom."

Grandma Wanyika's expression softened. Ethan guessed she liked being called "dear lady".

"His heir is obsessed with risk taking," the tiger went on, stopping momentarily to stab an unsheathed claw in the direction of Kitoko for emphasis, "but does not have the courage to participate himself, choosing instead to witness an endless stream of hapless attendants risk their lives in increasingly impossible tasks. And why not," he went on disdainfully. "No one stops the revolting youth, for fear of upsetting Galal." He came to rest before Galal, and spoke through gritted teeth. "Whose daughter is running amok in the valley as we speak, playing the deadly game this bone-headed youth set up."

Judging by Galal's sharp intake of breath, and sudden

movement towards the door, he had not known that his own daughter was involved. "Nandi!" he gasped.

"And as for the rest of you!" the tiger said, contemptuously swiping Galal back towards the others with one giant paw, and glowering at the remaining Almohad. "You sit here in your comfortable towers overlooking the decedents of the people who built them. You know how terrible it is down there. You have the strength and the means to make a difference, but you don't. You are supposed to be the keepers of the kingdoms. When last did any of you go across the river and see what is going on?"

"I go shopping there all the time," Praxades said, pushing out her lower lip. Ethan stared at her in wonder. He had never met anyone with so little sense of self-preservation in his life. She just did not know when to shut up.

"Coercing market vendors to give you their goods for nothing is not shopping, Praxades," the tiger growled.

"The kingdoms are not our problem!" Galal said. "If they choose to follow that mad king Ulujimi . . ." His eyes shot back and forth between the tiger and the doorway.

"And speaking of irresponsible!" Gogo Maya interrupted him to round on the tiger. "You tried to get Morathi's gang to get rid of me! And who knows what else you had those stupid Tokoloshe do for you." She turned towards Grandma Wanyika. "No offense, Grandma," she added.

"Oh, none taken, dearie." Grandma Wanyika eyed her tribe ruefully. "One or two of my own clan are a bit stupid."

Galal sank down on a divan and put his head in his hands, anxiety for his daughter finally getting the better of him, but not quite enough for him to make a dash for the door. He seemed prepared to leave the problem of the tiger to the old women to sort out.

Ethan did not know what he was supposed to do. They hadn't discussed their plan beyond identifying the jumper. He had assumed they would capture it. It was beginning to dawn on him that they'd been planning to kill it. Unfortunately, the tiger seemed to have a point.

"The tiger kills!" Salih said into Ethan's head.

"The tiger has a point," Ethan hissed back at Salih.

"But Galal can change," Salih said.

The tiger paced back and forth along the balcony, not exactly angry but still three metres of pent up danger, with canines longer than Ethan's fingers. He stopped in front of Galal. "I'd have been prepared to put up with your indolence, even Kitoko's spite till the strange boy, Joe, had grown into a man," he said, "but under the influence of Kitoko he would never have lasted that long."

"He was planning to jump Joe at some point!" Ethan blurted out, feeling a lot less tolerant suddenly.

The tiger turned his menacing attention on him. Ethan's eyes searched wildly for Lewa. Hunting the jumper was all very well till you caught him, he thought. What on earth could he do? Lewa had her eyes screwed shut in concentration, probably trying to deflect the tiger's focus, but she wasn't getting anywhere. The tiger continued to advance on Ethan whose stomach lurched as he realised it was going to be up to him. Screwing his own eyes shut, Ethan searched frantically for an idea. He searched for the tiger's nerve endings, hoping to channel the impression of pain as he had done to Kitoko, but his knowledge of tiger anatomy was non-existent compared with his knowledge of the human nervous system. He had studied that in school.

What if he stabbed himself and projected the pain onto the tiger as he had done with Fisi? Tariro had been right. It would hurt at first but he could heal himself afterwards. Unfortunately, the swordsman had picked up his sword, and there was nothing else sharp enough nearby. Ethan reached desperately for some sort of pain memory to project at the cat. A scorpion bite!

Ethan peeped out of the slits of his eyes at the tiger who was sitting down in front of him, drumming his four-inch claws on the marble floor, waiting politely for Ethan to be done.

SWITCH!

Ethan dug deeper. He searched out every flea, louse and intestinal parasite he could find living on the cat. There was a tapeworm. He knew it. *Feel the pain,* he projected desperately at the vermin. Go mad. Bite him.

It seemed to make no difference.

Then, amazingly, the tiger began to twitch and scratch. Ethan was getting through!

But the tiger laughed. "Okay, you got me there, boy, that hurts. Oof . . . especially the thing in the stomach. Gives new meaning to the words 'gut wrenching', but you can stop now. There is nothing that you or the silly girl can do to destroy me. And I have no wish to occupy your body, any more than I wish to occupy the pain ridden old crone or any of her irritating clan."

Grandma Wanyika puffed herself up and shook her stick at him indignantly. "I'll have you know . . ."

"Who could do with a bit of watching themselves, I might add." The tiger turned and glared right back at her. "At least one has fallen off the balcony, and several have wandered off. Probably plundering the palace as we speak." He stalked over to the Almohad.

"Since my carefully laid plan hinged on taking over Galal without alerting his people, there is no longer any point in having him. I guess my work here is done. You people can go back to your selfish, irresponsible ways. So, I'll be off then." He stalked towards the edge of the balcony.

"Is that it?" Praxades shrieked, hands on hips. She turned on Ethan. "Are you going to let him get away? What about the killing? He will surely have to kill someone when his tiger body expires. And what if he comes back as something else? We won't know him."

All true, Ethan guessed, but as the tiger had just said, there was nothing he could do about it. Someone really needed to gag that girl.

The tiger leaped back into the room, all sleek, writhing

muscles. He pressed his face up to Praxades' and said in a low growl, "What I do is no worse than having people kill themselves for your entertainment, Praxades."

She pushed away from him frantically, but still with a truculent set to her mouth.

"Yes, I could jump you any time I want, young lady, and not a thing you could do about it. I have a good mind to stay, just to keep you on your toes," said the tiger.

"And by the way, Kitoko." He rounded on Kitoko, who made an ineffectual grab for his sword. "Those captives you are holding – if I don't see them cross the river in, let's say . . . three days, I'll be back."

He turned to go again, this time dipping his head towards Grandma Wanyika. "Grandma, it has been a pleasure," he purred. "Hold less ceremonial parties. It will ease the gout."

"Gogo . . . humble apologies," he said to Gogo Maya. "A bit heavy handed in the forest, there. Nothing personal, you understand. Bigger picture and all that." Gogo Maya gave him a withering look.

"Young witch." He turned towards Lewa and smiled. "Don't be disappointed. As impressive as your array of tricks is, there is nothing . . . nothing at all . . . I had been around thousands of years before you were even born. Do you think I would be thwarted by a slip of a girl?"

He paused in front of Ethan and patted him gently on the head. "Young man, go and help your friend. And do something about that hair!" He snatched his paw away suddenly as if something had bitten him.

Ethan turned towards a soft *whump-whump* sound descending out of the sky. The lower clouds twisted and boiled as if something passed through them and then it came hurtling towards the balcony. The tiger almost collided with a creature, the size of an elephant, which came in to land awkwardly, crushing the stone balcony railing as it went.

SWITCH!

"Evening," the tiger said to it with the arrogance of the all powerful, and, without breaking his stride, slunk off the balcony onto a ledge to make his way down the escarpment into the valley below.

The ugliest dragon imaginable scrabbled for footing on the edge of the balcony as awkward as a grounded albatross. He looked nothing like the sinuous snake like dragon with the flame-shaped, petrified stone horns, and the scalloped medieval-knight-like scales of Darwishi or Amun's imagination. He had a plump, grey, leathery-looking body like a rhinoceros, a longish neck and a face more like a warthog than a dragon, with one huge tooth poking out of the middle of his mouth, and a blob on the end of his long tail, that flailed wildly from side to side as he tried to regain his balance.

"Consequences!" Salih hissed in a flat voice.

Everyone else stood, frozen in terror.

CHAPTER 30
TOUGH DECISIONS

"Quickly!" Azikiwe said. "You and you, put your hands like this!" He made a stirrup of his hands to demonstrate. "Now you and you!" He nodded at Elymu and Faraji. They lifted Nandi's limp body and set off at an incredible pace through the bush. Joe ran after as fast as he could, but he could not keep up.

"She stepped in front of me!" he groaned. The buffalo cow had tossed her in the air, slicing her thigh open from knee to groin. That much he had seen before they had whisked her away.

He knew he should be on the lookout for stray buffalo – even that same buffalo – or angry lions, but he didn't care. He ran blindly after the bearers till he reached the city. They were at the top of the steps by the time he reached the bottom, and they appeared to have put her down. A large crowd gathered around her. He hoped one of them was the healer. He sat down on the step for a moment, his head swimming with shock and fatigue.

One young man peeled away from the crowd and ran down the stairs towards him. He was one of the darker ones, with rat's tails of paraphernalia hanging from his hair and the board-shorts Joe had left behind at the vicious girl's village. A man, who looked like a relative of that vicious Mesande, came down behind him.

"Oh, no! They've found me, even here!" Joe groaned. Then he saw Jimoh . . . unmistakably Jimoh. Same hat, same walk. But improbably dressed in a skirt of brightly coloured material covered over with animal tails. He had camouflage fatigues poking out from underneath. Joe's relief at finding his friend was gone in a flash, as the boy did not come towards him, even though he had clearly seen Joe. Instead, he ran away, further up the stairs. Joe felt like crying. Had he imagined it? Had they captured Jimoh too, and he was just following orders?

But then, amazingly, as the other two young men came closer, he recognised the one in the board-shorts as Tariro.

"What the hell are you wearing?" Tariro laughed, launching himself at Joe and holding him tightly. "We thought we were too late!"

Joe disengaged himself to look down at the hyena pelt he still wore and then back up at Tariro's appalling hairstyle. "You don't look so normal yourself!" he said.

Catching the eye of the young man behind Tariro who looked like Mesande, Joe backed away.

"It's okay, this is Fisi," Tariro said, putting an arm around the young man's shoulder. "He came to help rescue you. Although the whole thing has gone to pot . . . the jumper turned out to be the tiger. Ethan's in there now, with some witches, trying to sort it all out. But I have to say, man, the kid is out of his depth this time!"

"I have to get to Nandi, Tariro, she is badly hurt," Joe said, starting up the steps. "And wasn't that Jimoh I saw? What's with him? He looked me right in the eye and ran off."

"Oh, don't mind Jimoh, he has gone to fetch Ethan for the injured girl. He seems to think Ethan can fix that too." He stared incredulously at Joe. "Man, thank goodness you are alive. Have I got a story for you!"

"What do you mean the jumper is the tiger?" Joe said, running up the steps. "What's a jumper? And how the hell did you guys get here anyway?"

Even the exuberant Tokoloshe stood frozen in terror, staring at the dark shape glowering at everyone from the balcony. Ethan's eyes darted from Gogo Maya to Lewa and back again. The dumfounded expression on both their faces did not instill him with confidence that anyone was likely to leave the balcony alive. He wondered if they would all be burned to a crisp.

Jimoh appeared suddenly. He did not even look to see what had happened to the tiger. "Ethan, you have to come!" he said, and then stopped dead at the sight of the dragon.

"It's the Mokele Mbembe," Ethan said in a hoarse whisper. "He has come for his gemstones!"

The dragon did not move. Jimoh looked at it, then looked at Galal, who had shrunk back ever so slightly behind Gogo Maya. "There is no time for this, Ethan! Go! Go down the stairs. A girl needs you!" he said.

Ethan felt a moment's relief. Jimoh had said a girl, so it was not Joe, but it was someone! He would have to help. He edged slowly towards the door, hoping the dragon would be sufficiently distracted by Jimoh. The dragon eyed him threateningly . . . He stopped.

"Ah, *sheet*!" Jimoh strode up to Galal. "Dragon wants jewels," he said to the man, putting his hand out for them. Every Almohad in the room fumbled to remove their jewellery, except Galal, who clutched his protective amulet closer. "Give!" Jimoh shouted at him. "There is not time. Girl is hurt. I need Ethan!" Galal proffered the amulet reluctantly. Jimoh snatched it from him and ran towards the beast balancing precariously on the edge of the balcony.

Mokele Mbembe opened his eyes as wide as anyone else in the room, almost overbalancing as he scrambled to lift one leg and stretch it out for the amulet. Jimoh draped the string of jewels over the proffered talon, bowing low as he did so. Ethan could not believe his eyes. Approaching the creature was amazing in itself, but only Jimoh would have the presence of mind to be polite. Then, before anyone had time to think, Jimoh doffed his hat and grabbed Ethan by the hand, dragging him out of the room.

At the sight of the girl's wound, Ethan's stomach lurched. It was much worse than either Jimoh's or Tariro's wounds had been. She had a gash right down her thigh that did not look as if he could close it up even with the magic in his blood. Luckily she had passed out. He took his knife out anyway, and knelt beside her on the steps. Even if he did not have the strength to heal her, surely whatever he could give was better than nothing.

Before he cut himself Salih slunk in beside him. "No! You cannot do it here, Ethan," he said, and then was interrupted by Gogo Maya, who muscled her way in from behind, and took charge of the situation. With the help of Grandma Wanyika and her Tokoloshe, who had their sleeping arrows at the ready, Gogo Maya directed the girl to be transported to a quiet room.

Galal, having escaped from the hovering dragon once he'd given up his jewels, looked genuinely concerned for the girl, Nandi. Rather than stand in Gogo Maya's way, he deferred to the healing power of the witch. Not that she had any power at all, Ethan realised. If anyone was going to help the girl, it was going to have to be him.

Gogo Maya should not have given him time to think about it. The more he thought about it now the more queasy his stomach felt and the more he worried that the Almohad might turn on him if he did not succeed. They might not be able to beguile him as they had done Joe because of the amulet he wore, but a simple whack to the head would put paid to that defense.

At first they'd been unable to pry Joe off the girl once he'd caught up with her, but Rafiki dealt with the problem by deftly stabbing Joe in the leg with a sleeping arrow, and a group of Tokoloshe carted him off, all efficiency once they had a proper job to do. Joe looked to Ethan in almost as bad shape as the girl.

"Don't worry, Ethan," Jelani told him in his gravelly voice. "We will guard cousin Joe." He took the spare amulet from Jimoh and slipped it around Joe's neck as they went.

"You don't have to do this, Ethan," Gogo Maya told him once they had laid the girl out on a pallet. Her brow drew down in concentration and her jaw tightened. "It is not as if they didn't have it coming to them, and it is not your problem." She glanced anxiously at the door. "We will wait till Lewa has chased the dragon. She can help this girl."

Jimoh took Nandi's wrist gently and felt for a pulse. Ethan wondered who on earth could have taught the boy to do that and if he knew what he was doing, but Jimoh turned pleading eyes towards him. He knew exactly how bad it was.

"Blood is very weak, Ethan," he said. "Is going to die."

"It is a terrible risk, Ethan," Gogo Maya protested, but not very enthusiastically. "Salih says it will be the third time in too few days. You can't do it again so soon. You risk losing everything."

"Maybe Galal deserves this, but not the girl," Grandma Wanyika clucked sadly.

Ethan took a firm hold of himself. It was not as if he were being asked to donate a kidney. "What exactly am I risking?" he asked.

"Everything!" Gogo Maya said. "The power to heal, the power to make those around you feel all schizophrenic the way you do. The power to talk to Salih . . .!" She made it sound as if that was the worst loss of all. It would be kind of distressing, he realised. He could hardly imagine what it would be like, not hearing Salih in his head anymore, and he would probably get his asthma back, but if he did not help this girl soon it would be too late for her.

"Is very brave girl, Ethan," Jimoh whispered. He brushed a hair back from her forehead. Tears leaked from the corners of his eyes. "Almohad say she jump in front of buffalo to save Joe."

That, and a glance at the stricken look on the face of the

Almohad healer made up Ethan's mind. The Almohad obviously weren't all bad.

"Will I die?" he said to Gogo Maya.

She regarded him solemnly from under her frown, "You might... If you lose too much blood."

"Okay, then I am counting on you to find the balance between giving her enough blood to recover and taking out less than it takes to kill me," Ethan said, wincing as he made a small incision on the inside of his wrist and allowed his blood to trickle slowly into the scrap of gourd Grandma Wanyika held under his hand.

Ethan wiped the back of his other hand across his forehead, fighting desperately not to faint at the sight. Well, he had always wanted to be a hero and this was the sort of thing heroes were supposed to do. He wondered where Tariro, the proper hero, had got to. He was probably gallantly protecting Lewa while he, Ethan, quietly bled to death. Well, not death, exactly . . . only, he wished he were not so afraid.

CHAPTER 31
ALL SORTED OUT

Joe woke up on a comfortable pallet under a cool awning on the balcony overlooking the valley. His head felt a bit fuzzy, but he was alive. He could not believe he had fallen asleep just when Nandi needed him. Asleep of all things!

"Nandi!" he cried, trying to leap up in his sudden panic, but his head spun and he flopped down again. Jimoh's smiling face hovered above him.

"'Sokay, Joe. Tokoloshe, by mistake, he cut you with spear for sleeping," he said. "The girl, Nandi, she is okay also. The witches, they fix her. Buffalo tear will only leave small mark." He gestured towards a pallet, about six metres to Joe's right, where a young girl in black pyjamas and a surprised-looking hairstyle sat patting Nandi's arm and talking to the sleeping girl in a low voice. The beautiful healer kneeled on the other side of Nandi's pallet, staring at Nandi with an expression Joe could only describe as awe.

Laughter broke out around a patient to the left of him, whom he realised, without much surprise, was Ethan. Ethan always went to pieces in an emergency, Joe grimaced. Then he noticed the leopard lying on the pallet, cuddled up beside his cousin.

"Take the animal away from Ethan," he groaned, protectively. What was it with that boy? Any cat within a hundred yards would automatically home in on Ethan. They must sense that he hates them, Joe supposed. Well, technically, Ethan hated the vermin that live on them, but he avoided them nevertheless.

"'Sokay, Joe, Ethan he like leopard," Jimoh told him, and when Joe propped his head up on his elbow, he saw that Ethan was actually stroking the leopard weakly, with a silly, self-depreciating smile on his face. He looked more than a little disheveled, but perhaps that was because of the flotsam and jetsam he had in his hair.

Tariro sat on a low stool, chatting excitedly with Ethan, which was a surprise in itself since he had not taken to Joe's cousin. He still wore just as much rubbish dangling from his hair as Ethan did. With Ethan so picky, and Tariro so fastidious with his dreadlocks, Joe wondered what on earth could have sparked off a competition between those two for the stupidest hair.

"You should have been there, Ethan," Tariro said, and laughed. Laughed! It was a friendly laugh, not the usual derisive snort Tariro reserved for Ethan. "We went back to fetch Aaron and Lewa, and all those Almohad were standing around acting nervous," Tariro said. "The dragon just sat there looking at them. He never said a word. They kept coming forwards with more and more jewels, thinking that's what he wanted, and then suddenly the dragon took off, ignoring the pile of jewels in front of him. Jimoh says he probably only wanted his own jewels back. He thinks the dragon may just have been resting before flying home again."

"The most hilarious part was the Almohad trying to sort their jewels out afterwards," a boy with an American accent chuckled. "All that scrabbling and lying about who owned what." Joe could not see the boy's face. Like Tariro, he had his back to Joe. He wondered who the boy was and where he had come from. Or how they had all got here in the first place.

304

ALL SORTED OUT

A wisened old Tokoloshe crone came onto the balcony, followed by some of her unmanageable crew, who all fussed around Ethan. Joe recognised the one he had seen the first day in the forest, and the one with the scar on his chest. The crone jumped up on Ethan's pallet, squeezing between him and the leopard, and poked him in the ribs till he sat up with a groan. Joe grinned. The old Tokoloshe started to feed Ethan with something so pungent, Joe could smell it from where he lay. Well, that's what you got for putting on all that hypochondriac charm, he thought. Amazingly, Ethan ate it without complaining. Ethan! The pickiest eater alive! Even more amazingly, he tried to tug the leopard towards himself. The leopard stood up, stepped daintily over Ethan, and settled on the pallet on the other side of him, seeming to show the utmost caution not to disturb him. Neither Tariro nor the American boy seemed to find this odd. Joe wondered if the Almohad had beguiled the lot of them.

Apparently not. "It is all sorted out," the American boy said. "Gogo Maya is negotiating with Galal to take most of the captives back to Waheri village, so that they do not take the magic into the kingdoms. We don't know what Tacari will say, but she says it is about time she came clean with Tacari anyway. He is the leader of Waheri village, a very powerful magician. Even more powerful than Lewa, I think."

At the mention of her name, the girl with the surprised hair stood up and went over to Ethan. Sitting cross-legged beside his pallet, chin in her hand, she spoke to Ethan in an admiring voice. "It was a very big risk you took, Ethan, but it is just as well," she said. "Galal seems to have been shocked out of his stupor at the thought of losing his daughter. If she had died he may have given up and gone back to his lazy bao-playing addiction and left the city on its path to ruin." Joe wondered what risk Ethan had taken. It was not like him to take risks.

"One of the captives, a man called Iniko, is going to stay and take over the neglected education of Kitoko," the girl went on. "A bit awkward, bearing in mind the treatment the man received at Kitoko's own hand, but he does not look like a man who would carry a grudge."

Joe stifled a smile. That Kitoko was in for a surprise, a few others too. Iniko was the man from the menagerie, intent on taking magic across to his home and overthrowing the king of his own kingdom.

"Fisi said to give you this," the girl said, handing Ethan a slingshot that Joe could have sworn had Tafadzwa's trademark hornbills carved on it, and his cousin clutched it to his chest as if it were the latest cell-phone.

"Is Fisi okay?" Ethan asked anxiously.

"He has gone to make his peace with Tabita and her pack, and to persuade the Kishi to stop taking hostages. But it is for sure that Mesande is in for a surprise sometime soon," the girl laughed.

"Mesande?" Joe groaned; he would have to warn them about Mesande.

Ethan reached out a slightly shaky hand and put it on Tariro's shoulder. "I'm sorry about tricking you . . . You know . . . about drinking the blood," he said weakly, "I should have told you."

"Yeah . . . Jimoh told me . . . you sneaky little weasel – I could have got myself killed busting heroics all over the place." Tariro tut-tutted. Tut-tutted! They *must* have been beguiled, Joe thought, it was not like Tariro to tolerate a trick. And was that blood they mentioned? He was almost as shocked to find out what a dark little brute Ethan was underneath that angelic exterior.

Nandi woke up and groaned. "Joe?"

"I'm here," he said, pulling himself up and staggering, still a bit groggily, to her pallet. As much pain as she must have been in, she managed to smile at him bravely.

She took a deep, sad breath. "I will not let them do that to you again," she said. "It is a stupid game. I will make Daddy send you to the witches. You will be safe there."

ALL SORTED OUT

"Joe's friends have come to fetch him," the beautiful healer said, patting Nandi on the arm. "Although I am surprised they can recognise him. He has become a lot more handsome since last I saw him."

"He was always handsome!" Nandi said, sitting up weakly and eyeing him through half-closed eyes. Then she hugged him.

"Hello, I am right here!" he said, suddenly all self-conscious. "Besides, get off, you should be resting. That was a very bad injury you took."

Nandi laughed at him. "Witch magic, you silly boy. I am as good as new," she said, although she lay back against the pillows gingerly. "Somewhere there is a witch lying, twitching, trying to recover from the healing. I know how these things work. They will never tell you which one did the healing though, or how." Then she hugged him again, fiercely. "I am going to miss you, Joe," she whispered into his ear and when she pulled away her eyes shone with unshed tears.

CHAPTER 32
WELL, THAT'S THAT THEN, OR IS IT?

Gogo Maya sat on her verandah overlooking the village, her pipe in one hand and a mug of Grandma Wanyika's sour wine in the other. Luckily Lewa did not want to share the wine, even though she had offered. The girl was probably too young for wine anyway.

"Aaron's going to miss them," Lewa sighed, following Gogo Maya's gaze down into the village where Aaron sat cross-legged on a mound beside Salih, shooting pebbles at a row of calabash targets with the slingshot Jimoh had made him. The young man's heart was not in it. He missed more targets than he hit.

"And Salih," Gogo Maya said. The cat looked almost as depressed. It was funny how that made her feel just slightly uncomfortable. Salih had really taken to the boy, Ethan. She had not been certain if the two of them could still communicate after that last bloodletting, and Salih would not tell her. Even though Lewa had been in time to prop the boy up with her energy while he completed the healing on the Almohad girl, he had given up a lot of blood by the time she got there, so Gogo Maya was not sure how much of the power he was able to cling on to. At first she'd suspected he had very little, but he had politely declined her offer of a healing amulet to take home with him, saying there were proper doctors where he lived and he had no need for it. Gogo Maya was convinced it was because he still held plenty of the power.

However much he had, no amount of persuasion would make the boy kiss her – or give her CPR as he liked to call it – so she was unable to take it back. She'd even tried pretending to be in the throes of a heart attack as the handsome boy, Tariro, had suggested. In the end, Tariro had taken the amulet for the other boy, Jimoh, who he said did not have good access to these proper doctors.

"Thank you for covering for me with Tacari," Gogo Maya said after a long companionable silence. Well, a long silence, anyway. One in which Gogo Maya wrestled with her conscience about thanking the girl. "And for sending the boys back safely."

Lewa had shown her how to make a tear in the fabric of the world by pushing the four boys through to the pool where they'd come from. At least she hoped that was where the young witch had sent them; she only had Lewa's word for it. The tear had been nothing like Tacari's, where you step into a gel-like doorway and walk out the other end. The boys had gathered together with all their things and Lewa had pushed them somewhere. Just like that. They were there the one minute and gone the next, like a pricked bubble. It was a one-way push, Lewa had explained, so thankfully they had gone without switching places with anything unpleasant or awkward to explain. Gogo Maya wondered how long it would take her to build up enough magic to test the trick on Salih, or Aaron perhaps.

Gogo Maya was very pleased with Lewa even though she had had to share the secret of the mgobo roots with the girl in exchange for the secret of the tear. But with two of them refining the magic through the root, and with Salih's power, who knew what they may be able to concoct? Two heads were definitely better than one, she decided. She hadn't even known that with the power from her opal she could do that thing with the nerve endings till the boy had explained it to her. Not that she would like to cause that much pain, exactly, but you never knew.

"I hope that boy Tariro passes the healing amulet on to Jimoh so that his village will have something to fall back on without the Sobek there," she said to Lewa conversationally.

"Now why would he withhold the amulet from his friend?" Lewa said.

"Because he is a wily boy, and he is too eager to dabble in the magic for his own good."

"Oh, well, in that case he doesn't need the amulet," Lewa said with a knowing smile, "because I kissed him."

Gogo Maya, who had just swallowed a mouthful of wine, wheezed violently, and stared wide-eyed at Lewa. "So you chose the handsome one then, did you? It won't do you any good. They won't be back."

Lewa arched an eyebrow at Gogo and said, "No, I think I like the other one actually, there was something about him . . . but the handsome one chose me. He was very persistent. I'm not sure if he liked me or if he was after the magic." She grinned wickedly. "He sure was desperate for that magic . . . and so envious of the other one, I thought, why not let him have it? He was a good kisser. And you said yourself, we won't be seeing them again."

Gogo Maya wasn't sure if she was more shocked at Lewa's cavalier treatment of the boys or her casual attitude towards passing on the magic, but she supposed the girl was right; whatever mischief the boy planned to get up to was beyond their control anyway, so she settled down in her chair with a contented sigh to enjoy the faint whiff of burned cookies that wafted overhead as the Nomatotlo settled in to the thatch for the night.

End of book one.

Thank you so much for reading Switch! I hope you found it entertaining. If you did, please consider leaving a short review on Amazon.

For interesting snippets about Africa and fantasy, find me on my website at: www.karen-prince.com

To browse through lists of other young adult books in the genre of your choice visit: www.books4youngadults.com